D1012252

It took about twenty-five minutes to get all the prisoners out of the car and formed up into orderly ranks. Then, just as the sergeant was about to give the signal to move out, one of the prisoners' suits ruptured. Someone ran to him with a pressure patch, but it was too late. Blood was already boiling from the exposed skin of his face and hands and splashing on the inside of the transparent suit. The victim fell forward onto his face. He twitched a number of times, and then it was over, apart from a plume of blood that fountained from the punctured left leg of his suit.

By Mick Farren
Published by Ballantine Books:

THE ARMAGEDDON CRAZY

THE LAST STAND OF THE DNA COWBOYS

THE LONG ORBIT

MARS—THE RED PLANET

THEIR MASTER'S WAR

MARS— THE RED PLANET

Mick Farren

A Del Rey Book
BALLANTINE BOOKS · NEW YORK

A Del Rey Book
Published by Ballantine Books

Copyright © 1990 by Mick Farren

All rights reserved under International and Pan-American Copyright Conventions. Published in the United States of America by
Ballantine Books, a division of Random House, Inc., New York,
and simultaneously in Canada by Random House of Canada Limited, Toronto.

Library of Congress Catalog Card Number: 89-91894

ISBN 0-345-35809-0

Manufactured in the United States of America

First Edition: March 1990

Cover Art by David Schleinkofer

ONE

North air lock, Vostok Settlement—May 17 Compensated Earth Calendar (CEC)—21:47 Mars Standard Time (MST).

HIS MIND WAS IN THE WILD PLACE, AND THE ENTITY WAS forcing him on, feeding his anger and locking him to the mission. His breath was loud inside the suit. It was an elderly Russian-built Zil, the kind worn by the contract workers in the Soviet settlements. The joints were stiff, and the faceplate tended to fog each time he exhaled. The exhaust valve left a plume of condensation as he trudged across the uneven ground between the air lock and the visitors' vehicle park where he had left the surface tractor. Overhead, the starfields blazed, unwinking, unobscured by the thin Martian atmosphere. Although the night sky was spectacular, he did not look up. When he was in the wild place, the stars made him feel small and isolated, more than he could stand. He rounded the corner of the dirt embankment that protected the mainly underground installation, and the lights of the north entrance were in front of him, a dozen glaring sunfloods surrounding the big, five-meter circular port. He felt safer with man-made light. Each time his faceplate fogged, the curve of the Plexiglas split the light into psychedelic rainbows at the edge of his vision.

The air lock was deserted, nobody coming or going. During the day there was always a crowd waiting for the cycle to com-

1

plete itself. The human colonists might boast about their conquest of the red planet, but when the Martian night closed in,
they still huddled under the protection of their domes and bur-
rows. A green light on the top of the air lock indicated that it
was ready to cycle. He pressed the admission stud. The light
changed to green. The air in the lock was being pumped out. It
took about a minute before the triple-leafed iris rotated to the
open position. He stepped inside.

The iris closed behind him, but the lock did not fill. Before
it would allow him through the second door and into the settlement, it expected him to produce some sort of official pass or
identification that would define both his legal and financial status.
If there was any irregularity, a man who was already locked in
an air lock without atmosphere was very easy to arrest. He was
ready for that. He had forged the pass himself. It identified him
as an Irish contract worker called Liam Flynn, a free-lance frost
rat working a claim stake exclusively for the People's Resource
Authority.

He fed the magstrip into the flashing slot. He was very pleased
with the work he had done, quite confident that it would not
only get him past the Russian entry control computer but also
backdata it, creating the illusion that Liam Flynn had been coming in and out of the Vostok Settlement on a regular basis for
the past three months and even planting wholly fictitious records
of his payments from the PRA and his purchases from COM-
ERCH. There was no way he would appear as a significant
statistic. As far as the computer was concerned, he was suddenly
just one more dirt crawler with no history and most probably
very little future. It was comparatively easy to fool a Soviet
computer; the Soviet security was so overbearing that it could
actually be made to be self-defeating in the hands of an expert.
The KGB was so paranoid that it would never let its bright young
people brainstorm loopholes, paradoxes, and all the rest of the
techniques by which a seemingly ironclad protection program
could be beaten. Their systems became inflexible monoliths that
could ultimately be compromised.

The slot stopped flashing, and the magstrip was returned.
Even though everything was in order, the air still did not pump
in. The outer iris opened again, and a second vacuum-suited

figure stepped inside, a longrange mineral prospector with a patterned dust poncho thrown over his worn polymer armor and a chrome eagle-head crest bonded to the crown of his helmet. The longrangers had a flamboyance all their own. The newcomer raised his right gauntlet in a curt salute and then turned, took his own magstrip from an exterior pouch, and fed it into the slot that was once again flashing. The man who claimed to be Liam Flynn was sweating inside his suit. The newcomer was clearly harmless, but when the entity was with him, the anxiety and the constantly urging demon voice would not stop until the task was completed.

Air was filling the lock, and frost briefly formed on the cold outer surface of his suit. The other man shook a cascade of ice crystals from his poncho. They sparkled like rubies in the red light of the air lock, or at least that was the way it seemed to the man who claimed to be Liam Flynn. In the wild place, there was always a greatly heightened awareness. The sounds of the settlement came with the increasing air pressure. The light in the air lock changed to green. The cycle was complete. The inner iris was rotating, and the longranger was unsealing his helmet. The man who claimed to be Liam Flynn fumbled with his own seals to give the other man time to go on ahead. He did not want to risk showing his face more than was absolutely necessary. The fumbling was by no means all subterfuge. The man who claimed to be Liam Flynn had started to shake. He forced down the anxiety. He had to maintain control.

Beyond the inner door of the lock, escalators ran down to the main inhabited areas of Vostok, the oldest and largest of the Martian settlements. Built at the original designated landing site, just south of the equator, Vostok sat between the ridges to the northwest of Arsia Mons's great volcanic cone. Its central core had been constructed around the seven cargo modules from the first settlement expedition. Over the years its inhabitants had burrowed out and down into the rocky Martian soil. More recently, a surface trim of tinted Plexiglas and slab-sided polymer concrete had been added, along with the low hydroponic domes, the communications tower, and the functionalist bulk of the brand-new science complex. Beyond the ridge stood the twin cooling towers of the fusion reactor.

The man who claimed to be Liam Flynn was uninterested in the newer, more prestigious sections of Vostok. His destination was the older part of the settlement, the tunnel and gallery complex that housed the contract workers and catered in a typically minimal way to their basic recreational needs. It was there that he would find his victim.

The longranger stepped out of the lock without a backward glance, and the man who claimed to be Liam Flynn removed his own helmet and gloves and followed. He rode down the escalator, his knuckles white as he gripped the handrail. There were times when he wanted to cry out against the entity, to rage at his inability to hold it all together. His mind was being stratified and ultimately fragmented by the multiple identities. On the surface there was Liam Flynn, the Irish prospector, and all the other aliases he assumed when he went to the wild. Beneath them was the angular structure that was the true personality of John Whipple Greig, attempting to retain the illusion of sanity with the kind of special precision, deviousness, and control that was unique to individuals who constantly hid from themselves. It was the same precision, deviousness, and control that had brought him to Mars in the first place—that and the promise of an Earthback bonus generous enough to put his life in the luxury bracket. John Whipple Greig, civilian adviser to the USMC CySec team at Fort Haigh. Nobody at Fort Haigh had the slightest idea that he made those trips to the wild place. To them he was a topgrader, a heavyweight system specialist who could write his own ticket. Behind his back the marines had a very distasteful name for him and the other CAs with whom he worked. They called them ratfuckers.

Beneath his true consciousness there was the underswell. It swirled around the roots of the structure that was the mind of John Whipple Greig like an angry, black polluted sea. The underswell was where the control ended and where the entity dwelled. It seethed and curled and twisted until all of him squirmed like a toad. The underswell was why he endured these tasks. He went and sought the victim because otherwise the underswell would have overwhelmed him and smashed down his carefully constructed personality. It would have thrown him into the wild place forever. It was only after the task was com-

pleted, only after the victim was still, that the underswell became calm. Of course, at that crucial moment of completion,
John Whipple Greig always absented himself, so he never saw
and never knew exactly what had happened.

His first stop at the bottom of the escalator was at a line of
suit lockers that looked like narrow coffins. He stripped off the
bulky pressure suit, stowed it in an empty locker, and secured
it. Under the suit, he was wearing a dark blue coverall with the
red and silver badge of a contracted construction worker and a
small DDR flag on the shoulder. Along with the coverall he
wore a pair of cheap canvas inshoes and a cloth helmet liner
made from the same blue material. In the galleries of Vostok
there would be dozens who looked exactly like him; he wouldn't
draw a second glance.

From the moment the suit was in the locker, he was no longer
Liam Flynn. There was a second magstrip in the breast pocket
of the suit that would identify him as Rudi Baum, a construction
worker from the DDR in his second year of a three-year contract. The double cover was probably unnecessary, a needless
piece of track covering, but John Whipple Greig was nothing if
not careful.

His destination was the Golodkin Gallery, a grim steel tunnel
lined with some poorly stocked stores and a few bleak cafés that
was the closest Vostok came to bright lights and good times for
its bottom-echelon workers. In fact, the lights were dim and
yellow, and the vodka had an oily, industrial taste.

Greig had never before ventured into Soviet territory. He had
found his previous victims in the wide-open recreation areas of
the American dome and the tunnel towns of Burroughs and
Bradbury. The illicit hours he had put in on the base computers,
learning the intricacies of Vostok's layout, had not in any way
prepared Greig for its gloomy reality. After the slick sterility of
the marine base and the rip-roaring, neon laissez-faire atmosphere of Bradbury and Burroughs, it was like something out of
the worst depths of the twentieth century. He felt as if he were
walking through the bowels of some crumbling smokestack me-
tropolis. The air smelled rank and metallic and reverberated
with the constant bass rumble of buried machinery. The steel
walls of the tunnels he passed through on the way to Golodkin

were crusted with rust and deposits of other oxides that had
seeped through from the Martian subsoil. Openings where panels had been ripped out and never replaced revealed makeshift
repairs that were heavy on epoxy blocking and duct tape and
festoons of dirty patch cables. Water dripped and steam leaked
from poorly welded pipe joints, and three-quarters of the radiation detectors that were mounted along the tunnel walls at regular intervals appeared to have ceased to function years earlier.
Somewhere along the line some kind of algae must have been
let loose on the internal ecosystem to coat the polymer surfaces
with a thin film of green-brown slime.

Greig turned into a narrow corridor of dorm cubicles identified in faded paint as KA19-38. If his information was correct,
the corridor would bring him out onto a catwalk above Golodkin, where a fire escape would take him down to the main gallery. His information held up, but as he stepped out onto the
catwalk, a trio of militiamen in pale blue military uniforms, light
machine guns slung under their arms, sauntered slowly down
the length of the gallery. They were eyed coldly by a group of
construction workers who were lounging outside one of the cafés, passing around a bottle. There was little affection between
the Soviet police and the contract workers, the majority of whom
came from the client republics and had arrived on Mars either
fleeing poverty and pollution or out of a simple but pressing
need to disappear.

Greig stepped back into the shadows, momentarily grateful
for the low-yield cathode panels that threw the settlement into
such a depressing state of gloom. A movie image of Jack the
Ripper stalking the fog-shrouded back streets of Victorian Lon-
don crept briefly into his mind, but what was still left of John
Whipple Greig instantly suppressed it.

Greig did not move out again until the three militiamen had
been gone for a full two minutes. Even then he descended the
steel mesh steps with extreme caution. Just as he reached the
gallery itself, the doors of the Aquarium Café, across the way
from him, slid briefly open. Greig froze as light and noise spilled
out into the gunmetal night of the gallery. A loudly cursing
drunk was hurled out onto the underground street. The drunk

hit the steel plates, sprawling and still cursing. He half sat up, shaking an angry fist at the closing doors.

"You bastards! I should never have come to this goddamned planet in the first place!"

He groaned and fell back. With a second groan, he turned over onto his side and slowly curled into a fetal position.

The Aquarium Café. The sign and the shark logo were crudely painted—no lights, no razzle. He might have assumed that the place was derelict had it not been for the flash of life from the doorway as the drunk had been ejected. The inside had looked bright and warm, at least in comparison to the gray of the gallery. If his information wasn't out of date, this place was his objective. According to marine files, it was the center of Vostok's small, illegal, but generally tolerated market for prostitution. As Greig's memory fed back what he had learned, he could feel the entity's ugly, impatient anticipation. It was as though he were the computer and the entity was running him. It started him toward the café's sliding door. His heart was pounding like a drum beating against his ribs, and there was unbearable pressure at his temples. He skirted the sleeping drunk and approached the door. His vision had taken on the peculiar tunnel quality that always came as the completion drew near.

There was an access toggle on the right side of the door, but it could not be activated until he fed in the Rudi Baum magstrip. The KGB liked to have a record of who went anywhere. Greig fed in the strip. Like the Liam Flynn ID, this one would also backdata itself, showing Baum to have been a regular customer at the Aquarium Café. After a few seconds the strip came back. Apparently, all was well.

He twisted the toggle. The door slid open, and Greig stepped inside. There were maybe two dozen people in the place. A few turned and looked at him as he came in, but none of them showed any particular interest once they had seen the blue coverall. Most of the men were wearing variations of the same drab uniforms. Only the colors changed, defining job status, occupation, and skills. There was also a handful of individualists: a pair of bopniks in porkpie hats and wraparound shades; a vortecist with a cowboy tie; three tribals, probably from Nigeria, in multicolored robes; a skinhead wearing monkey boots and ankle swingers; and a nihilist with oily ringlets and blue granny glasses. There were also the women, homespun playmates advertising an age-old, primal come-on—undoubtedly contract workers themselves, there to pick up the extra ruble after shift.

A slowboat must have sailed into orbit with a huge overconsignment of rolls of blackgloss rubber. Most of the working girls in the Aquarium had a quantity of the material molded to their bodies, and all of their homemade erotic costumes employed items that had left Earth destined for very different purposes. One girl had fashioned an entire outfit from lightweight titanium lockchain.

The Aquarium Café was really nothing more than a cramped metal box, with a thick complex of pipework running across the ceiling, that had been layered with a thin veneer of tawdriness. Porn sims flickered on one wall, while against another, a holodancer on a small raised dais did a slow, clumsy nudecooch in front of the dully erotic abstracts of a foolfeel.

Greig walked nervously toward the nearest seat at the bar. It was okay to be nervous. Rudi Baum would be nervous. He was a nervous foreign construction worker who wanted sex. Be what you pretend, he told himself. He sat down on a battered plastic stool.

The bartender was a big Finn with wide flat cheekbones and a thinning crew cut. He was holding the nozzle of a chrome pressure snake as though it were a six-gun. "Haven't seen you before, have I, sport?"

Greig shook his head. "No . . ."

The bartender did not appear to care. "You want vodka, vodka, or vodka?"

"You have no beer?" Greig's Russian was not good, but that did not matter. Rudi Baum's Russian might also be poor.

The bartender laughed and shook his head. "*Na defitsit*. When did you last see beer?" *Na defitsit* was a universal term on Mars. Even the Americans used it. When a commodity ran out in the colony and then failed to show up on any of the supply ships from Earth, it became *na defitsit*—"on deficit." "You want a bottle or a glass?"

Greig's throat was suddenly dry, and his voice sounded strangled. "Glass."

He passed over his magstrip and accepted a vodka in a thick and not too clean glass. The bartender looked at him as if he were some kind of weakling. A real drinking man would have taken the bottle. The bartender returned the strip, placing it in a puddle of spilled spirit, seemingly by accident, then moved away, back to a conversation with a knot of cronies. Greig sipped the vodka and grimaced. The data had not exaggerated. The vodka was really awful.

He slowly looked around the room. His eyes homed in on the woman in the titanium chains. She had to be the one. She had long legs and small breasts, the body of a dancer. Her hair was cut in a blond bob, and her features were elfin: large eyes and a small button nose. She was the one. He could feel the warmth of her, the damp inner heat. It was the warmth that drew the entity. Mars was a cold place, and it had been there for a very long time. The chains that hung from her body swung and quietly jingled as she moved. Bit by bit their motion revealed almost every part of her. He imagined her on her back with the chains bunched up around her shoulders. The legs would be spread, and the softmoist would be radiating its dangerous heat. She would also have the expression, the knowing, unreachable, unreadable expression. It was that expression which had started it all. He had a sudden flash-splash vision of blood, the blood of the last one and the one before. The red outpouring of the heat. No! He refused to think about that. His hand shook, and some of the vodka spilled. Calm! No one had noticed, but if he didn't become calm, someone certainly would.

There was a problem. The woman in the chains was talking to an ice rigger in a red coverall, and it seemed as though they were on their way to some sort of transaction. If that was the case, they would soon be leaving together. Could he wait until they were through? Was there any guarantee that she would even come back again? Another prostitute was homing in on him. She had glossy red lips, slick black rubber across her hips and breasts, and straight black hair that was parted in the middle, and she walked with an elaborate sway.

"You look kind of nervous, sweetheart. It can't be the first time you did this, can it?"

Greig shook his head. The dryness was back. Control. "No, but I . . . it's been a while."

She smiled. Her teeth were uneven, and her eyelids were caked with mascara. "You want to buy me a drink?"

She was wearing a cheap perfume that failed to cover a lingering scent of industrial solvent. Would she do instead of the one with the chains? She didn't have the same heat. There was something already dead about her. The entity did not want her. It had to be the woman in the titanium chains. He bought a vodka for the prostitute with the black hair and red lips. This time the bartender did not put his magstrip in a puddle. He must have redeemed a measure of his masculinity. Later, they would all know about his masculinity.

The prostitute downed the vodka in one gulp. "Perhaps you're always nervous around women. Is that it, darling? Just a bit scared of us girls?"

Greig quickly swallowed the rest of his drink. "I'm not nervous. It's just been a long day."

"It's always a long day on Mars."

Greig was getting tired of the conversation, but there was no way he could get rid of the woman without attracting attention. A man could not come into a place like that and just shun the women. Maybe he should have stuck to the strip at Bradbury. It was so totally anonymous. He half smiled at the woman. "That's the truth."

Like the bartender, the woman did not seem to care. He was just another sucker to be worked. She was leaning close to him. Her half-exposed breasts were pushed forward. "If you wanted, we could go somewhere and I could make you feel relaxed."

"How relaxed?"

Why couldn't she be the one? It would be so much simpler, except that the entity still didn't want her.

She was actually pressing against him. "I could make you real relaxed."

Over her shoulder, he saw that the girl in the chains and the man in the red coveralls were preparing to leave. Greig quickly stood up. "I'm sorry. This is all a mistake. I just came in here for a drink. I've got to go."

The prostitute glared at him. "Well, fuck you, faggot."

The bartender looked in his direction and said something to his cronies. Greig did not catch the remark, but he knew that the resulting laughter was directed at him. He hurried from the bar and the sleazy sex displays and waited in the shadows for the other two to come out. The roaring had already started in his ears, and the pain in his head was blinding him. He did not think he could hold on much longer.

The pair took their time in coming. When they finally came through the door arm in arm, the girl was wearing the blue coveralls of a construction worker. Wondering if she still had the chains on under her coveralls, Greig followed at a safe distance. A smattering of people were moving up and down the gallery, and the couple did not notice the solitary figure dogging their footsteps. It became a little more risky when they turned off into a smaller side corridor, but his luck held and they still did not look back. After a series of corners and angles, the rigger and the girl turned into a dorm corridor, SJ7-19. Greig chanced getting close enough to see which cubicle they went into. It turned out to be SJ12. He found a dark service recess from which he could watch the door of the cubicle, eased back into it, and squatted down.

The rigger did not waste any time. He was back out of the cubicle inside of twenty-five minutes, zipping up his coverall and slicking back his hair with a small pocket comb. The moment the man was out of the corridor, Greig stood up. The mind of John Whipple Greig was little more than a guiding reflex. He patted the sheathed ribbon knife in the concealed pocket and then pulled out the small aerosol of stun gas, hid it in his right palm, and took a deep breath. This was it. He walked up to SJ12 and, after a moment's hesitation, rapped softly on the door. "Is that you, Jimmy? Did you forget something?" It was the first time he had heard her voice. It sounded irritated.

The words came easily to him. The dryness was gone. "It's not Jimmy. My name is Rudi."

"What do you want?"

"I was in the café, the Aquarium, you know. I saw you, and when you didn't come back, they told me I could find you here."

"Who told you?" The girl sounded suspicious.

"The bartender, the Finn."

"The Finn told you to come here?"

"That's right."

There was a pause.

"Listen . . . ah . . . Rudi, I'm kind of tired, you know what I mean? There are plenty of other girls back at the café, okay?"

"I really took a liking to you."

"Yeah, but I'm not for sale right now."

"I have a lot of money. I just picked up a bonus. I've also got a bottle of scotch, real scotch from the Americans."

Her voice softened. "You're a persuasive little fucker, aren't you, Rudi?"

The door slid back. She was standing there against a soft red light, still wearing the chains, except that they were all tangled and bunched up so that she was naked from the waist down. Her thighs were white and muscular. One hand was planted on a tilted hip, and her smile was resigned.

"So how're you doing, Rudi? You better come on in."

The sex smell in the room temporarily blanketed all the other odors of the settlement. His hand came up. The gesture was perfectly natural, just as though he were going to stroke her cheek; then, at the last minute, the aerosol went off. She did not make a sound, just looked puzzled. As she fell, he caught her with one hand, simultaneously hitting the door stud with the other. It was an easy move in the low Martian gravity.

He took his time arranging her body. When he was finally satisfied, he took out the ribbon knife. For a moment he held it almost reverently in his two hands. The sound of his breath seemed to fill the whole room. The background sound had all but faded away. He was alone in his own world with the woman helpless in front of him. His power was absolute. Taking the utmost care, he slipped the knife from the black plastic sheath and thumbed on the power. An LED glowed, and the microlite blade hummed softly. He bent over the inert, spread-eagled woman. It was at that point that the mind of John Whipple Greig made its escape. It would not return until it was needed to handle the exit from the air lock.

Shuttlecraft Hank Williams *on approach to Burroughs Interplanetary—May 18 CEC—05:07 MST.*

"You know something, Vern? I often think it's a crying shame that there were no Martians. If there had been, we could have bought the place for beads, infected them with syph, and turned them into houseboys, just like we did back home."

Vern grimaced. "I wouldn't speak too soon on the subject of Martians, old buddy. There are some times, out there in the back, when I get this low-down feeling . . ."

Vern's partner snorted. "You been getting low-down feelings again, Vern?"

Vern ignored his partner. "I get this low-down feeling that one of these days we're going to hit on them. They're only cold-sleeping out there. One day we're going to rehydrate something deeply H. G. Wells. Kiss your ass good-bye when that happens."

Lech Hammond hated noisy old hands. The two in the seats in front of him were typical of the loudmouth breed of Martian cowboys, the kind who roamed the dust plains with airbrush paint jobs on their pressure suits and coon tails hanging from the antennae. They were the same two worlds over, sounding off in a situation that had all the first-timers scared shitless. Going down the well to the Martian surface, almost everyone was a first-timer. Few came back for another tour. That was what made the pair in front of him so ludicrous. They were going back for a second bout with Mars. By all accounts they had to be crazy to work there.

Unwittingly, Vern and his partner had done Hammond a favor. They had provided him with his first Marsend brush with the phenomenon that had set him en route for the red planet in the first place: the longing for aliens. Ever since people had first spotted Mars in the night sky, they had expected Martians, and they had been damned disappointed when none had materialized. Even now they still hoped. One day a prospector or survey team would crest a ridge, and there they would be—the pyramids, the ruins, or the lost tribe. That was how it had always been on Earth, and according to parochial human logic, that was the way it had to be on Mars. Pioneers everywhere were prone to tell tall tales and mythologize, and, in the face of a whole empty planet to fantasize about, the condition tended to run rampant.

They had all come in together on the *Dejah Thoris*, a Eurospace high thruster that could make it from orbit to orbit in six months and change. More than five of those were spent in cold-sleep, but there had still been three weeks when there had been nothing for the passengers to do except work out in the gym, play poker in the lounge, or get drunk in the bar. Hammond had spent a lot of time reading and watching videos in his cubicle, avoiding the others. By far the majority of his fellow travelers were some variety of misfit. Not that Hammond could legitimately pass judgment, he realized. The one thing he had in common with most of the other passengers was that he was on his way to Mars because he had run out of road on Earth. Maybe one just had to be desperate to work on Mars.

In Hammond's case, he was being sent to Mars because he was simply too good. He had become too well known to do his job. Lech Hammond, the news commando, the star of 22C-Fox's Global News, simtraned into thirty-two languages in over five hundred markets. He had made his reputation by being the man who could go where other news crews could not, but that very reputation had eventually proved to be his downfall. His face had become too-well known. He was recognized everywhere, and whenever he was on assignment, crowds gathered. Far from going where other news crews feared to tread, he found that he was unable to go anywhere at all. Fame had completely neutralized his effectiveness. The Tokyo office had started to mutter about giving him a talk show until he had done the prima donna and chewed a lot of executive carpet. His mother had not raised him to make small talk with soap stars promoting their shows. In the end he had made the suggestion himself. Why didn't he ship out to Mars? Ostensibly he would be making a series of reports on life in the Martian settlements, but there would also be the covert objective of finding out what it was that the Soviets had found there. Rumors had been going around that the Soviets had stumbled across something significant, maybe even something alien. When questioned about it, Moscow had erected a stone wall that was massive even by their standards.

The shuttle captain cut in on the PA. "Compared with dropping from Earth orbit, the descent to Mars is a milk run. There's no dense atmosphere, and the gravity is a little over a third of what you're used to. So just sit back and enjoy the flight."

As predicted, the drop was smooth and painless, and the passengers treated the crew to a round of applause as the wheels touched. After six months in space there was something close to euphoric about the feel of solid ground. The euphoria faded a little, however, during the two hours of intensive customs and medical inspection. By the end of it Hammond was more than ready for a drink, and it was a relief to see Dan Worthing, the local bureau chief, waiting at the other end of the arrivals tunnel.

The two men embraced warmly. Hammond held Worthing at arm's length and inspected him. "So there really is life on Mars."

Worthing grinned wryly. "Yeah, well, I wouldn't get too excited. It can be real slow at times, although I guess there are enough bored blondes to keep you occupied for a while. Did you bring any drugs?"

"Huh?"

"Nah, you're too paranoid to bring even a bag of 88s through Martian customs. What about good scotch? New videos? Data cones? Didn't you bring anything?"

"What do you think I am, Trader Vic?"

Worthing put a fatherly hand on Hammond's shoulder. "There's one thing that you've got to get straight right now, dear boy. This is the ultimate boonie. It's the back of beyond and then some. Do you know what you have to pay for a pint of Guiness out here?"

Dan Worthing and Lech Hammond went way back. Hammond had first met the blandly cynical Englishman on a particularly bad night in Havana during the Demarkation Crisis. Worthing had been a junior stringer for AU, and Hammond had been free-lancing for Teldek. Over the years the employers had changed, but the life-style had remained the same. Together they had dodged bullets during the Pakistani Civil War and outwitted Volker's Three Section goons during the collapse of the Cape

Republic. Now they were both on Mars, vassals of the 22C-Fox monolith.

"So what's the word from the old planet?"

Hammond grimaced. "Mainly shitty. If economic collapse don't get us, the greenhouse will. I figure it's pretty much all over, bar the propaganda."

"Just so long as the supply ships keep coming."

"I wouldn't even count on that if the chickens really come home to roost."

Worthing shrugged. "So if they want to mess with us, we team up with the moonies and go nuke the shit out of our mother planet."

Hammond laughed. "Always a good answer. Where are we going?"

"I figured we'd ride the monorail into the settlement and take a look around. That's if you're not too tired."

Hammond shook his head. "I'm not tired. Hell, I've been asleep for five months. What about my luggage?"

"It'll take them an hour or so to break down the cargo pods. It'll be delivered to your temporary quarters."

"Where am I staying?"

"At the Burroughs Hilton, until we find you something more permanent."

They started walking toward the monorail station. Hammond put too much effort into his first step and bounced farther forward than he had intended. He landed awkwardly, embarrassed by his own clumsiness.

Worthing watched with amusement. "This is Mars, old boy. Don't overexert."

As they rode in from the spaceport, Hammond had his first ground-level view of the Martian landscape. The sun was coming up, and it looked so much smaller than it did from Earth. The sky was a clear washed-out pink, and there were stars still visible above the horizon opposite the sunrise. The mountains in the distance cast long black shadows across the rocky, red ocher desert. Hammond realized that he had a way to go before he really came to grips with the fact that he was on another planet. In the sealed comfort of the monorail it was hard to accept the fact that beyond the window it was bitterly cold and virtually airless.

"And there's really nothing alive out there?"

"Not a damn thing so far, although we keep on looking."

"So what's all this about the Russians?"

Worthing glanced around at the other passengers. "Let's save it for somewhere a little less public."

"I thought it was the big rumor."

"No point in adding fuel."

Unlike Vostok, there was a great deal of Burroughs above ground. Except for the fact that the triple spires of the central complex soared in a way that would have been impossible in Earth gravity, they might well have been transported from Dallas or downtown Los Angeles. Their mirrored surfaces flashed in the morning sun. The central complex was a comparatively recent construction, just a little less than two years old. There had been a need to build high to give the maximum range to UHF and microwave transmissions as the Martian settlements had spread out from the original equatorial landing sites, but a consortium of NASA and MarCo had gone all out and, abandoning all concepts of cost-effectiveness, had put up the gleaming development with no excuse except the time-honored one of outdoing the Russians. Burroughs also sprawled more than Vostok did. For a mile or more around the central settlement there was a clutter of storage containers, fuel tanks, power lines, and no fewer than five separate domes. The spidery structures of ice wells marked where shafts had been driven down into the permafrost. Through it all, the dead straight single track of the giant bullet train ran off to the horizon.

Worthing filled in the details. "This little train we're riding is just a baby compared with the bullet. Imagine two big commercial airlines, say DC40s, laid end to end, riding on a superconducting frictionless rail. It can make over seven hundred kph on the flat. Better than flying."

Leaving the monorail at the station in the central complex, Hammond immediately found himself in a gleaming wonderland of stainless steel and curtain glass. He gazed around in genuine awe. "This is kind of slick for a struggling colony."

Worthing grunted. "Like we needed our own Disneyland."

"You don't like it?"

"I don't like the waste of money and resources. You won't like it either, once you see how wild and woolly the rest of the town is. All we needed was an effective communication mast. Nobody asked for a luxury hotel or corporate office suites or restaurants that I can't afford to go in more than once a year even on my salary. It's the great Martian pork barrel."

"So why didn't you file a story on it?"

Worthing shook his head sadly. "You really have been a hot item for too long, dear boy. You've become insulated from reality. You no longer even notice pond scum ethics. I filed four stories. Mashimo killed all of them. Our Tokyo masters are too tightly wedged in bed with the men of MarCo."

Hammond exhaled wearily. "I guess I have been too close to it for too long."

"That's one thing about Mars. It gives you a hell of a perspective. It takes a while for it to really sink in just how far away from home you are. It takes fifteen minutes for a radio signal to get back to Earth, but that's just a number. I've seen big macho men actually crack up when the true meaning of the distance caught up with them."

Walking with the easy bouncing gait that was the most comfortable way to move in Mars gravity, Hammond and Worthing left the uncomfortable splendor of the central complex and joined a line waiting for an elevator.

"Times Square next stop."

"Times Square?"

"Big circular gallery. It used to be hub of the settlement until they built the complex. Now it's our very own red-light district."

Hammond grinned. "And that's where you spend your time?"

"That's where I do my drinking."

Times Square was much closer to what Hammond had expected Mars to be. The moment they left the elevator, they had to step out of the way of a trio of blind-drunk prospectors dressed up in totally unsuitable pump pants and mirror ripple jackets.

"They probably bought those suits the moment they came in from the cold, then burned their old work suits. You've got to realize, these guys are out in the back for months on end. When they get to a settlement, the only thing they want to do is get drunk and get laid. Drunk and laid are our major growth industries. That's what frontier towns are for.''

Hammond looked around. It was not unlike being in a giant circular hangar. Despite the garish paint and the mass of illuminated signs, there was a definite raw functionality to the place. It was still possible to see the interior configurations of the giant cargo containers that had been used as the basis for all the later construction and the joints where they had been torched together to form the original core of the settlement.

"It's kind of basic.''

"If you wanted frills, you should never have come to Mars.''

"I always wanted to visit Dodge City.''

A group of five longrangers in cowboy hats and beaded vests stumbled out of a place called the Joy Joynt. They were clinging to each other for support.

Hammond glanced at Worthing. "Are we going in there?''

Worthing shook his head and pointed to the somewhat grisly neon image of a severed head. "I usually drink in the Alfredo Garcia. It's not as rowdy as some of the other places.''

Hammond raised an eyebrow. "The Alfredo Garcia?''

"A good place to lose your head.''

There had once been an attempt to make the Alfredo Garcia into a slick twentieth-century-style bebop lounge, but style had fought a long losing battle with the depredations of drunken contract workers. The plastic upholstery of the booths and the bar stools had been slashed, scuffed, burned with cigars and cigarettes, and rudimentarily repaired with gaffer tape. In more recent times there had been an attempt at art behind the bar, a piece of primal crunch that was all bent chrome tubing, chunks of raw polymer goop, and twisted aluminum I-beams, liberally splashed with blue and silver paint.

Worthing steered Hammond to a booth. Fex Oyeah whined out of the sound system, and the bar itself was occupied by a hunched line of figures that seemed to take their drinking too seriously to waste time with small talk. A poker game was in progress at the circular central table, while over against the far wall a fat man in a cutoff pressure suit was totally absorbed in playing a flashing lexilux machine.

"Most of the customers at the old Alfredo are the permanent residents of Burroughs. It's not really lively enough for the ice cowboys and the longrangers. There's no girls dancing in cages, and we never get more than a handful of hookers in here."

A cocktail waitress came over. She moved with a bizarre version of the regular Martian low-grav walk, teetering on absurdly high heels. Her brief red vinyl uniform was straight out of "The Jetsons." There were little wings on the heels of her shoes. She treated Worthing to the kind of familiar grin that was reserved for regular customers.

"So hey, Danny, what's new?"

Worthing shrugged. "Not much, Charlene."

"Who's your friend?"

"He's just in from Earth. Big-time hotshot TV reporter."

Charlene looked at Hammond with considerably more interest. "What's your name? Maybe I heard of you."

Hammond held out a hand. "Hammond. Lech Hammond."

Charlene had a firm grip. "I seen you. You used to be on CBS, when there was a CBS, right?"

Hammond smiled and nodded. "That's right." In fact, he was less than happy. He had hoped to be a little more anonymous on Mars.

"So what's your pleasure, Mr. Hammond?"

"Scotch on the rocks."

Charlene and Worthing exchanged amused glances.

"We do have some brown stuff they call scotch, but I wouldn't recommend it," she told him. "It tastes like coolant fluid, and that's probably how it started life. We haven't had a bottle of good scotch in this place in over a month. No bourbon, either, for that matter. Whiskey, at the moment, is what the Russians call *na defitsit.*"

"So what do you recommend?"

"The vodka's always good."

Worthing sighed. "A man of taste can get mighty tired of vodka. How's the beer holding up?"

"There's a couple of cases of Sol left, but after they've gone, we're down to generic."

"And that tastes like metallic piss. Give me a cold Sol and a vodka straight." He jerked a thumb at Hammond. "He'll have the same."

As Charlene went off to get their drinks, Hammond eased back in his seat. He was starting to realize that Mars might be a good deal more rough and ready than he had imagined. The propaganda that reached Earth painted an altogether too rosy picture.

"You always have these supply problems?" he asked.

Worthing nodded ruefully. "A constant fact of life. There's really no way around it. The vital stuff comes in the way you did, on the high thrusters. The little luxuries of life, like toothpaste and branded booze, are loaded on the slowboats. Those sail-driven monsters can take anything up to two years, orbit to orbit. With travel times like that, it's bloody near impossible to predict what we're going to be needing. Particularly as no one thought the colony was going to grow at the rate it has. An added problem is that, now and again, one simply doesn't show up."

Hammond glanced around the bar. "So how do all these people manage to spend their time drinking all day?"

Worthing shrugged. "Some are shift workers, and others are just hangouts."

"Hangouts?"

"Contract workers who've completed their tours but haven't gone back. A lot get scared that Earth gravity's going to kill them."

"Is that possible?"

"Sure. If you don't keep up the exercise and calcium blocking all the time, you can just cave in under the strain when you get back." He jabbed a finger at Hammond. "You want to watch out for that yourself."

"And what about you? You going to be okay?"

"Sure. I take care of myself."

Worthing was avoiding Hammond's eyes. He did not look as though he got any exercise at all. His sallow complexion and limp hair and the purple shadows under his eyes were those of the habitual slob.

Once Charlene had delivered the drinks and the men were alone again, Hammond decided that it was time to get down to business. "So what's the inside track on this Russian thing? Do they really have something?"

Worthing downed his vodka. "Nobody really knows for sure. They're sure acting as though they do. You've never seen such a security screen."

"Tell me exactly what happened."

Worthing sucked on his beer and regarded Hammond bleakly. "You must have seen the reports."

"Sure I saw the reports, but I want to hear it from you. Reports tend to miss the odd crucial detail."

Worthing took a deep breath. "Okay, have it your way. It must have been, what—seven and a half months ago? There was this Soviet-Cuban survey team way out in the back close to Olympus Mons."

"Cubans?"

"Hell, yes, there are Cubans all over Mars. The Russians have brought in thousands of them. They do a lot of their long-range prospecting and, of course, most of the hydroponic work."

Hammond nodded. "So there was this survey team . . ."

"Well, you have to realize that up on the orbiters, they monitor just about everything that's broadcast. Normally they only pick up the more powerful transmissions. Small stuff like suit radios get lost in the background babble. If this team hadn't been so far out, nobody would have heard them. As it was, they came through crystal clear. The guy who's riding point lets out a yell that he's seen something."

"What exactly did he say?"

"Nothing concrete. Just that he's seen something up ahead and he's going to take a closer look. The nearer he gets, the more excited he becomes. He doesn't describe exactly what he's looking at, just jabbers on in Spanish like this is the big one."

"The big one?"

"The smart money says it was some sign of life."

"You think that?"

Worthing slowly shook his head. "No, I don't."

"So?"

"My theory, which ain't worth more than anyone else's, is that it was some kind of artifact. Alien but probably not Martian. If I'm right, the odds are that it's very, very old."

"How do you figure that?"

"The way I look at it, life on Mars just isn't happening. All the time we've been here, we haven't found as much as a bug. I think it's highly unlikely that we're going to suddenly stumble across some isolated life-form. Life-forms need an organized ecology, and Mars simply doesn't have it. On the other hand, though, Mars had been around for a hell of a long time, and there's plenty to suggest that, once upon a time, it may have been a lot more hospitable than it is now. It's quite possible that somewhere along the line it may have been visited by something from somewhere else."

"That's awfully close to UFO talk."

Worthing sighed. "Hammond, there's one thing that you need to realize. You're on Mars now, and things are different. UFO talk is just one example. Out here we take UFO talk a little more seriously. Guys come in from the Asteroids and the Jupiter moons all the time claiming that they've seen or felt something."

"Isn't that just capsule fever?"

Worthing grimaced. "Probably, but we're out here on another planet, and what's to say that we're the only ones?"

Hammond was silent for almost a minute. He knew that he badly needed the crash course in Marspsych that Worthing was feeding him, but he still resented it. He hated feeling like a rookie. "So what happens after this Cuban on point hollers out that he's seen something?"

Worthing half smiled as though in amusement at the human capacity to panic. "All hell broke loose, particularly in Vostok. The Russians laid every screamer they had on the transmission and completely jammed the frequency. And that was only the start of it."

"What happened next?"

"They scrambled a flight of MiG 90s."

"Military jump rockets? Just because of a wild radio call?"

"Full code red. God knows how much fuel they burned."

Hammond thought about that. "Could the Russians have had an inkling that there might have been something out there? Could they actually have been looking for it?"

"Anything's possible, although if they'd been expecting

something important, they'd have never included the Cubans in the party. Relations are barely cordial.''

"There's a problem?''

"Basically it's just that weird Hispanics and maudlin Slavs don't get along in a confined space, whatever their ideology. There's also friction because the Cubans are old, nineties-style laissez-faire commies, and an increasing number of the Russians, particularly the KGB boys, are straight out of the novostroika school, the new hard-liners.''

Hammond nodded. "Yeah, I guess that could make for friction. Back on Earth things have been getting pretty unhinged in the Soviet Union. What's the situation right now?''

"There isn't too much beyond speculation and rumor. The Russians have set up a base out by Olympus Mons that's locked up tighter than a drum. In fact, it's so secret that it's not even officially supposed to exist. Needless to say, every spy device on the planet is pointed at it, but if anything's leaked through, I haven't heard about it.''

"How are the marines taking it?''

"They're watching and waiting and getting damned frustrated.''

"Do we have an in there?''

Worthing conspiratorily tapped the side of his nose with his index finger. "My spies are everywhere.''

"I'm glad to hear it.''

"In this case, it's actually spy, singular. There's this civilian specialist called Greig attached to the CySec team at Fort Haigh. He owes me a couple of favors.''

Hammond's eyes narrowed. "Favors?''

Worthing had always shown a tendency to run it close to the wind. "We at Global are in something of a weird position. Since we're westerners but working for a Tokyo-based corporation, we're in a unique position to act as a discreet channel for information between the Americans and the Japanese up on the Sumi-Hyundai orbiter. Stuff that can't be made public—propositions, leaks, proposals, suggestions, bits of blackmail. You know the form.''

Hammond sighed. "Indeed I do.''

Even on the new frontier some business was absolutely as

usual. The media were always dragged in to lend a hand with the dark side of diplomacy.

"What's this Greig all about?"

"He's a weird one. Real withdrawn and a bit too tightly wrapped for my taste. I guess he'd have to be in his job. As far as I can tell, he's running their computer ratfuck section—designer viruses and high-level hacking. I've acted as a go-between a couple of times between him and his opposite number on Sumi. I figure if anything breaks, he'll tip us the wink."

"What's the chances of us being able to get inside this base?"

"The one on Olympus Mons?"

"Right."

"A snowball's in hell." Worthing's beeper went off. "Excuse me. I've got to call in." He stood up and walked to the pay phone beside the bar.

Hammond ordered another drink from Charlene. He felt a little light-headed and wondered what effect the low Martian gravity had on the metabolics of getting drunk.

When Worthing returned, he looked very pleased with himself. "The Russians have had their first hooker murder."

Hammond was mystified. "Huh?"

Worthing sat down. "Oh, yeah, you wouldn't have heard. You'd have been in coldsleep when the others happened. We have our very own Jack the Ripper. Four hookers have been carved so far. Previously it was confined to the U.S. settlements—one was killed here, three more in Bradbury. Now there's been one in Vostok, and the Russians can stop sounding so fucking smug about the decadence of capitalism."

"This is all real fascinating, but what does it have to do with what we were talking about?"

Worthing beamed. "Don't you see? It gives us a perfect excuse to get inside Vostok. While we're supposedly covering the slaying, we can also see if we can ferret anything out about what's going on up on Olympus Mons."

Militia headquarters, Vostok Settlement—May 18 CEC—
10:34 MST.

"The Germans have a word for it. *Lustmord*, the joy of killing."

"Pointlessly academic."

Chief Investigator Irina Orlov wished she were back in bed
with Yuri, safe and warm and enclosed, not forced to think
about dead prostitutes and deal with these three KGB men who
were filling up her small cramped office. The trio officially had
no reason to be there—a sex crime had nothing to do with planetary security and was strictly under the jurisdiction of the militia. The trouble was that the KGB liked sex crimes, and they
had even gone to the trouble of working out a rationale by which
they could horn in on the case. They reasoned that since the
Americans had already had three prostitute murders, there was
a definite possibility that the killer was from outside Vostok. If
a serial killer could slip in and out of settlement security, the
KGB wanted to know about it.

"Obviously, the first thing to do is to have a thorough cleanup
of Golodkin, round up the whores and see if six months in
Vorkuta or working on the rail line will cool their ardor. Ship
out all the rest of the trash along with them, the pimps and the
nihilists, all the hooligan element."

Irina regarded Melikov coldly. "Is that the best you can come
up with? A prostitute is murdered, and you want to round up
the rest of the girls?"

The Cubans called them the Three Stooges. Like their Hol-
lywood namesakes, they were brutal and stupid, but there was
nothing particularly humorous about them. Major Fydor Melikov and his two sidekicks, Captains Leo Turchin and Andre
Strugatsky, had arrived on Mars some eight months earlier, re-
placing the much more liberal Bulgakov, with whom she had
coexisted quite well for three years. The winds of change that
were blowing through Moscow were reaching all the way out to
the red planet. Melikov, Turchin, and Strugatsky were all prod-
ucts of novostroika, the final sweeping away of the Gorbachev
legacy, and *yedino-obrazie*—"uniformity"—with its concentration on discipline and the suppression of individualism. Those

bastards no longer apologized for Stalin; they openly admired him, calling him the ''iron man'' right out in public. Irina Orlov had seen the rise of the new grim breed of totalitarians and their constant attacks on what they saw as the frivolity and weakness of the 1990s and 2000s. They had busted up pressure concerts and beaten nihilists and shaved their heads. Now they virtually ran the KGB and were barely being held at arm's length by an increasingly weakened Central Committee. When she had volunteered for Mars duty, she had thought she was leaving all that behind her. She should have known better.

''Do you really think that shipping our poor bloody local hookers out to Vorkuta would solve anything? It's hardly going to stop the killer, is it?''

Vorkuta was the small settlement up by the north pole. Officially it was just a research station, but Melikov had turned it into a penal colony. Criminals and political undesirables were sent there or assigned to hard labor on the half-constructed rail line that was being driven across the desolation of Amazonis to link Vostok with the settlement at Pushkin.

''If nothing else, rounding up the prostitutes would deny him any more victims,'' the KGB major replied.

''You really think so?''

''You are far too tolerant of the vice that flourishes in our midst, Chief Investigator Orlov.''

''I'm merely pragmatic, Major Melikov. I am responsible for civil law and order in this settlement. This is a frontier post full of hardworking men and women of all nationalities. They spend months on end out in the freezing desert, and when they come here, they get drunk and horny. The vice, as you call it, is a vital safety valve.''

''Vice is vice, Chief Investigator.''

''And horny miners are horny miners. Deprive them of sex and booze, and they're quite likely to tear this place apart.''

''The answer is discipline, not turning a blind eye to crime.''

For men who had made a political philosophy out of the need for uniformity, the three KGB men were hardly uniform. Melikov was a short, florid individual with thinning red hair. He chain-smoked Zimbabwe Marlboros in a black plastic holder and habitually dropped ash down the front of his brown leather car coat. Turchin fancied himself as the intellectual Stooge. He was tall and thin and anemically pale. It was Turchin who regularly figured out the legalistic rationalizations for Melikov's excesses. Strugatsky was the muscle, a bullet-shaped brute with pale pig eyes, a shaved head, and the hands of a torturer.

For long minutes Irina and Melikov stood glaring at each other, neither willing to be the first to break eye contact. Detective Boris Suvorova, Irina's personal assistant, stuck his head around the door.

"I . . ." His voice faltered as he took in the situation. " . . . think I'll come back later."

His arrival interrupted the standoff between Irina and Melikov. The major gestured to his two henchmen. "We're getting no cooperation here. I suggest that we review the crime scene. It's possible that the militia may have missed something." He turned back to Irina. "Will you accompany us, Chief Investigator?"

Irina shook her head. "No thank you, Major. I've already been there."

In fact, she had been there at seven-fifteen in the morning, a bare hour after other shift workers had discovered the woman dead when they had gone to wake her. The woman's cubicle had been a bloody mess, and if Irina had bothered with breakfast, she might well have lost it after five minutes in the small room. It was not the blood that had bothered her; she had seen blood before. It was the unfortunate girl's body. It had been systematically mutilated, as if the killer had been performing some sort of ritual.

Melikov paused in the doorway. "You know, Chief Investigator, you should really make an attempt to modify your attitudes. The world is becoming less and less kindly disposed to nonconformity."

After the KGB had left, Irina sat very still at her desk.

"Sick bastard."

She was not sure whom she was talking about—the killer or Major Melikov. She knew that the killer would be close to impossible to find unless he struck again and made some kind of mistake. If he was the same one who had murdered the other women, it was quite likely that he had returned safely to the

American settlements, where he was effectively beyond her reach. She also had no illusions about Melikov. She could try treating his threats as too absurd to be taken seriously, but unfortunately, Melikov was deadly serious, and if the Politburo tilted any farther toward the hard-liners, he and his kind would have a completely free hand—and she might well find herself on the long trek to Vorkuta, or worse.

Irina took a deep breath. The only way to shake off the grim feeling of foreboding was to bury herself in her work. She hit the intercom. "Boris, get in here."

Boris was in her office in an instant. "Have they gone?"

"For the moment, thank God."

As far as Irina could tell—and she and Boris had worked together for four years—her assistant was totally loyal. If she had to sum up Boris in one word, it would be "solid." Boris could be relied on. He packed his calcium, and he worked out. He was on the settlement track team and played a handy game of chess. His sandy hair was always neatly trimmed, and with his clean, square jaw and blue eyes, he would have qualified as the model for a heroic worker statue or mural. At the moment, however, he looked less than heroic. There were dark circles under his eyes, and he had the air of a man who felt harried.

Irina waved him to the chair that had just been vacated by Melikov. "So what do we have so far?"

Boris referred to an old-fashioned spiral-bound notebook. Over the past few months they had been forced more and more often to resort to pencil and paper, as the out-of-date militia computers had become increasingly unreliable. Irina suspected that the KGB might be blocking their requisitions for replacement hardware, if not actually sabotaging the existing system, but she had no real proof.

"The woman was a construction worker called Vera Zasulich, originally from Volgograd, Labor Number 122-6551-47693. She had three months to go on her contract, but by all accounts she was in no shape to go back to Earth. Her work record was only minimally satisfactory; she drank heavily and was frequently late on shift. She had racked up a bunch of demerits, and it was unlikely that she would have been able to re-up her contract.

She was regularly engaged in part-time prostitution, always working out of the Aquarium, and there was a suspicion a while ago that she might have been involved in amphetamine dealing. She was in the typical bind. Earth gravity would have crushed her bones, but in three months she'd have no legal status in this settlement. I'm guessing that she figured her only hope was to slip away to Burroughs or Bradbury and become a full-time free-enterprise whore. There was a stash of U.S. currency hidden in her mattress."

"So she was a girl with a common dilemma."

"So it would seem."

Irina sighed. "Well, at least that's been solved for her."

"You're cold this morning."

Irina scowled. "You get that way. Particularly after a visit from Melikov. What about the man she left the bar with?"

"Kostia picked him up. We've got him in a holding cell. I entered him as a drunk anonymous."

"So our friends at the KGB don't know about him?"

"Not yet."

"Let's try and keep it that way for as long as possible. If only for his continued good health. Who is he?"

"He's a pro ice rigger on a one-week leave, a top-grade technician. A Scotsman, James Ewart. He learned his trade on the North Sea oil fields, but when they began to give out, he shipped out for Mars."

"Why's a Scot working for us and not the Americans?"

"Apparently, according to his record, we offered him a better deal. It was back in the days when we were hard up for specialists. Also, he's a communist from way back."

"Have you talked to him?"

"Only briefly. He claims that he did his thing and left. She was fine when he last saw her."

Irina raised an eyebrow. "And what was his thing?"

"Regular around the world. Nothing weird, or so he claims."

"Do you believe him?"

Boris nodded. "I think he's on the level."

Irina thought about it. "I'll talk to him later. Keep him under wraps for as long as you can."

Boris closed his notebook. "Is that all? I'd like to get back to tracking down and interviewing everyone who was in the bar."

"How's that going?"

"We've traced most of them, but they're not much help. About the only one that might provide a lead is this girl who claims that there was a stranger taking an interest in Zasulich who left around the same time as she and Ewart."

"You have a make on him?"

"According to the sales record in the bar, he's an East German called Rudi Baum, another construction worker. I've yet to dig up his records."

"So do it."

Boris nodded. "It's my next job."

The outside communicator shrilled and flashed. Irina indicated that Boris should pick up. He listened for a few seconds and then covered the mouthpiece with his hand.

"It's the federal marshal from Burroughs. He wants to talk to you."

"Lon Casey?"

"In person."

"He probably wants to come and take a look at our murder."

"Will you let him?"

Irina smiled. "Sure. If he or one of his deputies comes over here, they'll undoubtedly bring the representatives of the free press with them. The media spotlight may stop Melikov and his goons from doing anything too ludicrous."

She held out her hand for the handset. Boris handed it to her, and she settled it comfortably against her ear.

"Hi, Lon, it's Irina. It's been a while."

TWO

"**H**AVE YOU NOTICED THAT THERE ARE NO DEROGATORY
names for the Russians? I mean, okay, Ivan, ruskies, and what
have you, but nothing really nasty like frog or hun or kike. Think
about it. We had half a century of cold war and more than
enough fallings out before and since, but we've never come up
with a dirty name for the other side. You think someone isn't
taking this seriously?"

"Maybe the Germans have a name for them."

"Maybe they do. I never asked."

"Go on with your research, Worthing."

Five men were stretched out on contour couches in the darkened bubble of the observation car. Beyond the double-layered
Plexiglas the drab landscape of the northern fringe of the Araxes
desert rushed by at over five hundred kph. The bright dot of
the moon Phobos was visible against the starfields, close to the
horizon. Beneath them the single rail hummed, supporting the
giant train on the frictionless, superconductor-produced mag-
netic field.

The five men had the observation car completely to themselves, and the drinking had started even before the Red October
had pulled out of the Burroughs station. Only twenty other pas-

sengers, if that many, were on the train. There had been a time when the Red October had run daily, packed with both freight and passengers. Since the growth of the *yedino-obrazie* movement and the resulting deterioration in relations between the U.S. and the USSR the traffic had been considerably reduced. The Red October now ran only twice a week, and although the freight holds still tended to be fairly full, there were precious few passengers. In strictly economic terms the Soviets would have been better off closing the route and concentrating their resources on the new line they were building out to Pushkin, but the line between Vostok and Burroughs, the first Martian railroad, had been the Soviet Union's most prestigious project, and they would not give it up without a considerable fight.

Of the five-man party, Marshal Lon Casey and Deputy Ray Chavez made up the nonmedia contingent, on their way to Vostok to check in person on the possibility that the prostitute murder there was somehow linked to the killings in Burroughs and Bradbury. Hammond and Worthing were along for the ride, ostensibly to cover the murder but, at the same time and as Worthing had suggested, intending to use the story as a chance to sniff around in the Soviet settlement.

Casey was big and grizzled. He was in his early forties, and his hair was starting to thin. His slow, laconic way of moving and talking would not have been out of place in the American old west or, at the very least, in an old western movie. Chavez was originally from Miami, of Cuban descent. He was fast and sharp and had been brought along to assist in the event of a Cuban connection. Worthing had some doubts about the wisdom of that plan. Florida Cubans had a somewhat ambivalent attitude to their cousins in the old country.

The fifth member of the party was the cameraman whom Worthing had hired for the assignment. His name was Rat Barstow, and Hammond had a few doubts about him. Hammond had worked with Rathbone Barstow back on Earth. The man specialized in combat and civil unrest, and he went at it with the kind of reckless self-destruction that made for great camera images but a short career. Somehow Barstow had come through unscathed—he seemed to be possessed of unnatural luck. Hammond suspected that now and again that luck got a little help

and that he did the odd covert job, using his media credentials
for cover, for the CIA, Mossad, or one of the other intelligence
biggies, or else for one or both of the protagonists in the occasional local dispute. Hammond knew that sort of thing went on
all the time, and he had even had a few offers himself. He had
always shunned them. He considered that kind of activity too
compromising, although he also had to admit that at the time he
had turned the offers down, he had been pulling in a hell of a
lot more money than a free-lance camcorder jock. That made it
a lot easier to maintain his pristine principles. Still, it was not
the moral issue that bothered Hammond so much as Barstow
himself and his damn-the-torpedoes attitude. On this assignment they would be in an enclosed settlement, serious KGB turf.
It was a job that called for a certain delicacy, and there was no
way Rat Barstow could be described as delicate.

Worthing, although obviously three parts drunk, never stopped
being the investigative journalist. He peered blearily at Casey.
"So what's the story, Marshal? You figure this Vostok killing is
tied in with the others?"

Casey took his time answering. "It's starting to look like it,"
he said finally. "The militia in Vostok faxed me some pictures
of the body. The stab wounds were of a very similar pattern."

"So we really do have a Martian Ripper?"

Casey looked at him a little bleakly. "I hope to hell you don't
start throwing around names like that. Weirdos of this type start
to believe their own publicity."

Hammond raised an inquiring eyebrow. "Are we going to see
these pictures?"

Casey shook his head. "Nope."

"Why not?"

Casey looked at Hammond as though he had expected better
of him. "You know why not. Details known only to the killer,
the danger of a copycat—there are a whole list of reasons. Right
at the top is my prejudice against tittilating the public with this
sort of thing. I don't mind you coming along on this jaunt, but
the moment you step out of line, I'll dump you."

Barstow had his camcorder out of its stedi rig on the table
beside him. There was a length of tape covering the function
LEDs so that the casual observer could not tell when he was

recording. His right hand rested lightly on the camera. It all looked perfectly innocent until the turret lens slowly swiveled to take in Casey.

The marshal did not miss the surreptitious movement. He pointed angrily at Barstow. "And you can cut that shit out. The only time you tape me is when I know all about it and you have my full consent. Got it?"

Barstow took his hand off the camera. "Okay, okay. I got it."

Chavez leaned forward. His voice was soft and dangerously lazy. "Don't try that shit around the KGB, Barstow. If they catch you, they'll feed you your camera the hard way."

There was a long, awkward silence in the observation car.

Worthing glared at Barstow. "You're a fucking idiot."

Barstow sighed. "Yeah, right. Ten four."

Hammond leaned back in his seat and stared at the stars. Now he was even less happy about Barstow. They were dependent on the goodwill of Marshal Casey, and already the cameraman had started stretching it. He sat up, poured himself a drink, and tried to smooth things over. "So what time do we get to Vostok?"

Worthing yawned. "Around three."

"Standard or local?"

"Standard. Who wants to mess with local? It's just a lot of pointless arithmetic."

A slow smile spread over Casey's weather-beaten face. "You might as well go on drinking. You can't miss the stop. This train doesn't go anywhere else."

Hammond got the impression that with that smile Casey was letting them know that he was not holding him or Worthing responsible for Barstow's gaffe. Chavez produced a bottle of homemade rum that was a welcome relief from the vodka. Hammond realized that even though he had been on the planet for less than a day, already he was getting used to the bad Martian booze.

The Red October continued to speed through the night. The conversation lapsed, and Worthing appeared to be asleep. Casey read, and Chavez went on drinking slowly. Barstow tried to start a flirtation with the Russian cabin attendant, but she gave him a professional brush-off. Hammond stared out of the observation dome. He had never seen any place so dead and desolate. In the most barren deserts of Earth, where not even cactus, scrub, or yucca plants could be seen, there was always the comforting knowledge that some life lurked, if only reptiles or insects. On Mars there was nothing except relentless dust and rock and whatever humans had brought there with them. He was suddenly very much aware of how amazingly abundant Earth was and also how far away it was. Almost like a little kid, he yearned to go home again to breathable air and real gravity and sounds instead of the silence of a near vacuum. He was not sure how he was going to handle months of this place. He supposed the Moon was even worse, but he had never been to the Moon.

At one point he thought he saw lights way out in the desolation. The train was moving so fast that it was hard to focus, and he wasn't sure that his eyes weren't starting to play tricks on him. He began to wonder what the people who worked and lived out in those deserts and mountains were really like. He had already realized that Worthing, Casey, and Chavez were not strictly typical of the men and women who had come to Mars. By far the majority roamed those dead boondocks, mapping and surveying, in search of minerals or the precious permafrost that was the red planet's only source of water. Hammond had seen all the tapes, looked at the photographs, and read the articles. He had done his homework, but he still could not feel his way into the hearts and minds of the people who spent months out there, living on canned air and freeze-dried food, people for whom a ruptured air line or a malfunctioning vehicle could mean a horrible and lonely death. The frontiers of Earth had been known to drive men mad; the terrain here was a hundred times more alien. Maybe that explained the serial killer: the Martian night, with its bright sky and twin moons, had finally flipped him out.

Casey noticed Hammond staring out the window and pushed the bottle toward him. "You have to take it real slow on Mars. Take it in slow bites and chew each one real careful. It's all too easy to choke on Mars, and once you choke, watch out, because Mars will get you if it can."

"You sound like you don't much like the place."

Casey did not reply immediately. Finally he said, "I've been here five years, and more and more I wonder if we've got any business being here at all."

"You believe that?"

"Yeah . . ." Casey suddenly grinned. "But I don't go around shouting about it."

Hammond carefully examined the marshal. Casey definitely seemed to be a man he could trust. He took a chance and decided to bring up the matter of the supposed discovery the Soviets had made on the slopes of Olympus Mons.

Once again Casey weighed his thoughts before responding. "I've heard the rumors just like everyone else, but that's about it. I don't have any kind of inside information, if that's what you're looking for. I will give you a piece of advice, however. Don't go around asking questions like that once we're inside Vostok or you'll find that your welcome will be a very short one. In any matter that can be even loosely construed as espionage, the KGB's word is law. And the KGB is getting more and more rabid." Casey poured himself another tot of rum and went back to his book.

Hammond dozed for a while, a shallow uneasy sleep filled with disturbing dreams: horizons that tilted at weird angles and caused him to roll and fall helplessly; dust storms that cut him off and left him choking, struggling to breathe, and unable to walk. When Worthing shook him gently, he came awake with relief.

"It takes a few days to get used to sleeping in Mars gravity," the Englishman told him.

Hammond rubbed his eyes and blinked away the dreams. "Yeah . . . right."

"You want to see Vostok?"

"We're almost there?"

"Sure are."

Worthing pointed ahead down the line. Hammond could see no sign of the city itself, but sheets of purple-tinged lightning played in the sky.

"That's static in the air leakage above the settlement," Worthing explained. "Most of Vostok's under the ground, so there isn't too much to see until we're up close, but that's it."

The Red October was noticeably decelerating. The first real

sign of human habitation came when the rail line passed the Vostok spaceport. Floodlights illuminated a half dozen ghostly white shuttlecraft, emblazoned with bold red stars, that were parked on the taxi aprons or upright on their blast pads, readied for takeoff. Five angular shapes were swathed in camouflaged dustcovers and guarded by armed figures in pressure suits. They had to be MiG 90s, the rocket interceptors that were custom-designed for Martian operation.

Hammond turned in his seat, watching them pass. "Back in the USSR?"

Worthing shrugged. "Kinda, but don't forget that it's still Mars."

Hammond continued to peer into the darkness. "I don't think that I'm about to."

From ground level there was nothing particularly impressive about the Soviet settlement. All that Hammond could make out in the dark was a collection of boxlike buildings, a low dome, and a number of communication spires with glowing red marker lights.

"This is the biggest installation on the planet? It doesn't look like much."

Worthing nodded. "Like I said, most of it's underground."

The train ran down a slight incline and entered a tunnel. For about a minute they moved through total darkness, and then they emerged into what could only be described as a giant subway station, a place of steel pillars, functionalist statues, and baroque mirrored glass. One end of the station was totally dominated by a huge heroic mural of Lenin addressing a throng of soldiers and workers. Even within the very great limitations of life on Mars, it seemed that the Soviets had maintained their taste for lavish railroad stations.

As the train came to a halt, Casey stood up and took control. "For those of you who haven't been here before, we're about to go through the Soviet entry process. It's a close scrutiny for outsiders at the best of times, and I have a feeling that the KGB has no desire to have us here at all. They are liable to be difficult. They may split us up and interview us separately. Don't let them intimidate you. Our credentials are in order, and we have an absolute right to be here. There are a few tatters of glasnost left, thank God, and both the media and invited law enforcement officers are fully covered by the treaties. Don't let anyone tell you different.''

The umbilical clamped against the port, and there was a loud hissing as the train matched atmospheres with the settlement itself. Hammond noticed that the incoming air smelled rank and metallic, much worse than the air in Burroughs. Was Mars going to make him a connoisseur of air? Finally the port opened. As the five of them picked up their carry-on bags and filed out onto the platform, a badly synthed version of a Tchaikovsky piano concerto was being played over the PA. Then the music was mercifully muted, interrupted by an equally badly synthed voice.

''Please follow the signs to your correct inspection area.'' The message was repeated in Russian and Spanish.

Hammond moved up close to Barstow. ''Don't do anything dumb, okay?''

''Don't worry, I've got a healthy respect for the Russians.''

''I sure as hell hope so.''

They followed the flashing signs in Russian, English, and Spanish that directed nonresidents to their section of customs inspection. It turned out to be a wide, brightly lit tunnel finished in off white stressed polymer. A line of five customs men waited ominously behind a line of steel counters. They were backed up by four uniformed militiamen and a half dozen soldiers armed with Mikhail machine pistols. A trio of KGB agents, in plain clothes but easily identifiable by the loose coats that concealed their weapons, prowled impatiently. At their signal, three of the soldiers approached Hammond and his companions with outstretched arms. The five reluctantly halted while the other disembarking passengers looked around nervously, wondering if something similar was going to happen to them. A bullnecked man with mean little eyes and a boot-camp crew cut stood hunched in a quilted nylon surcoat. He appeared to be the senior of the three agents. He sauntered over to the group and regarded the five men with studied insolence. His English accent was an atrocity.

''You are to be taken for questioning. You will all please follow me.''

They were immediately surrounded by KGB and soldiers. The militiamen seemed to be staying out of the whole affair.

Casey and Chavez pulled out their badges and stood their ground. "We are visiting law enforcement officers cooperating on a case with the local militia. Please do not impede our progress."

The KGB man looked Casey up and down as though wondering how much harassment he would take. The agent must have decided that Casey's threshold was low. He pulled a communicator from his pocket and muttered into it in Russian. After listening for about fifteen seconds, he waved Casey and Chavez through with a peremptory gesture. "You are covered by orders. You may proceed."

Then, as though seeking revenge, the agent rounded on Hammond, Worthing, and Barstow. "You three, however, will not be permitted to enter the settlement."

Hammond was about to protest when Worthing put a hand lightly on his shoulder. "Let me handle this, old boy."

He faced the agent with a look of amused disdain. "I'm afraid you don't really have the authority to keep us out."

The KGB man's neck visibly thickened. "You will not be permitted to enter the settlement. You are going to be taken to a holding area to await return transport."

Worthing did not seem in the least perturbed. He shook his head with great finality. "I don't think you quite understand the situation. It's the middle of the night, and I suspect that, although surly, you are a very low ranking agent. A corporal, probably. My friends and I are operatives of 22C Global. In fact, we're the senior operatives of 22C Global. If we should return to Burroughs and inform Tokyo that a lousy KGB corporal refused us admission to Vostok, can you imagine what might happen to that corporal?"

The agent's eyes shifted from side to side. "You are refused entry."

Worthing enunciated very carefully, as though speaking to a not too bright child. "The Havana and Oslo conventions clearly state that a properly authorized journalist shall not be refused entry to a planetary settlement unless a state of emergency exists. Is there a state of emergency?"

The KGB man's eyes bulged. He knew that he had bitten off more than he could safely chew, and now it was a matter of saving face. He was a little slow at working out how to do that. "You—"

Worthing was one jump ahead of him and determined not to let the man down lightly. "Or maybe Russia rescinded those treaties while we were on the train."

"You will not—"

"In addition, our visit has been fully authorized by Chief Investigator Orlov of the People's Militia."

The KGB man made one last try. "The militia doesn't issue such authorities. That is the responsibility of the Committee for State Security, the KGB."

"That's bullshit and you know it. The militia have always handled press credentials."

"You will not speak to me like that. I can have you arrested."

"Maybe you can, old son, but I really wouldn't recommend it."

The agent's mouth moved like that of a fish out of water. "You—"

"Why don't we get to the bottom line. Contravening the Havana and Oslo conventions could amount to an international incident. Is that what you want, old boy? An international incident?" Worthing's voice was no longer lazy. "Well, is it?"

The agent was too angry to speak. A vein throbbed in his neck. He waved them through with an angry gesture and an expression that clearly said he would have been happy to shoot Worthing on the spot. Worthing nodded curtly and walked through. Hammond and Barstow grabbed their gear and quickly followed him.

The moment they were out of earshot of the KGB man, Hammond caught up with Worthing. "Are you crazy or what?"

Worthing looked at him in surprise. "You can't take shit from people like that. You have to show them who's boss."

Hammond was still angry. "He was KGB, for Christ's sake."

"They don't have absolute power, not quite yet."

"You were pretty damned sure of yourself."

Worthing halted. "Listen, that was just the old routine. That guy had no instructions to keep us out; he'd just been told to give us a hard time and see if we'd cave in. You have to kick these people or they don't respect you.''

Hammond shook his head. ''Jesus Christ. This isn't the British raj, it's fucking Mars.''

''There are certain similarities, particularly in the area of psychology.''

''And suppose he'd psyched out and shot you?''

Worthing treated Hammond to a long, sad look. ''Frankly, Lech, I don't care anymore.''

Hammond was stunned. Worthing was not kidding. His old friend really did not care. The knowledge that he was in no shape to return to Earth was giving him a suicidal edge. His drinking was one thing, but the kind of recklessness he had shown in the encounter with the KGB man was quite another. Hammond was sorry for the man, but he did not want to be dragged into any weird death wish. He glanced from Worthing to Barstow. A fine pair to have at his back.

Militia headquarters, Vostok Settlement—May 19 CEC—8:42 MST.

Irina Orlov sipped her coffee from a wax paper cup with a full-color picture of Minnie Mouse on the side. Despite repeated requests, there had been no disposable plastic cups for the vending machines on the last four supply ships, and as a stopgap measure they had been buying them from the Americans. It was yet another example of *na defitsit*. Irina suspected that having Minnie Mouse printed on the current shipment of cups was some American's idea of a joke. Ideally, her office should have had its own coffee maker, and then they could have used regular china mugs, but that would have created a whole other set of problems—not the least of which would have been maintaining a supply of decent coffee.

Irina had more to worry about, however, than the container in which her morning coffee came. The marshal from Burroughs and one of his deputies were on their way over. That was how she had wanted it. A few days of cooperation between them might well help determine whether the killer of Vera Zasulich was a homegrown maniac native to Vostok or the same one who had been killing girls in the American settlements. But the advantages of working with Lon Casey were counterbalanced by the major problem of the KGB. Even though it was not yet nine o'clock, Melikov had already been on the phone. The call had started with a diatribe against the news crew that had come in with Casey and the fact that she had authorized their entry permits. Apparently the duty agent had tried to keep them out, but one of them, Worthing, the amiable drunk who ran the Fox Global operation on the planet, had known exactly how to deal with him. She wished she had been there to see it.

She hoped that the presence of the news crew might put a brake on Melikov's worst excesses. After about five minutes he had moved onto his second hobbyhorse. He still wanted to put the unfortunate Ewart, Zasulich's last trick before the killer, on trial for the murder, get a quick conviction, and mark the case closed. Although she had stalled, the situation was, at least temporarily, the best thing that could happen. While Melikov treated Ewart as the primary suspect, he actually denied himself access to the case. Ewart was one of theirs, and thus it was a domestic murder. As soon as it came into the open that the perp was a madman out of the American settlements—and all her instincts told her that it would—Melikov would have the excuse he needed to walk all over the investigation. She thanked whatever god watched over cops that Melikov was not yet pursuing that angle. He was still busy agitating to clear the Golodkin and ship its hard-core denizens to the penal colony at Vorkuta. So far she had managed to block him on that, but if Melikov started to pile on the pressure, she would have to let it go. She had more to worry about than the fate of a handful of whores, spivs, and social deviants.

Irina yawned. All she really wanted was a long bout of raw sex and then about two days of uninterrupted sleep.

Boris stuck his head in the door. "Casey's here. There's a deputy called Chavez with him."

Irina sighed. There did not seem to be a chance of either sleep or sex in her immediate future. "Send them both in."

Irina Orlov was not a woman who trusted easily, but she both liked and trusted Lon Casey. Maybe he overdid the slow-walking, slow-talking Gary Cooper bit, but he seemed about as decent and honest as any senior law enforcement officer could be and still hold down his job. There was also something very attractive about his lazy confidence. As he and the deputy entered, she stood up and held out her hand.

Casey shook it warmly. "You're looking very good, Irina, very good indeed."

She smiled. "You're not looking too bad yourself, considering."

She knew that she was looking good. She had made the effort for Lon Casey. Instead of her usual loose coverall, she was dressed in a uniform tunic and short, tailored skirt. She had also done her hair and put on makeup. A flash of flirtation rarely did any harm between collaborators. She never knew when the time might come when she would need a really good friend on the American side.

Casey gestured to his deputy. "This is Ron Chavez. He'll be assisting me while I'm here."

Irina shook hands with Chavez. His grip was not quite as firm as Casey's, and his eyes were cold. She hoped she was not dealing with a Russophobe. Indicating that they should be seated, she relaxed in her own chair, swiveled slightly, and crossed her legs. Casey did not miss the gesture. She was pleased about that. The stockings had cost her a couple of major favors.

She got down to business. "So, did you get the fax?"

Casey nodded. "Sure did."

"And?"

Casey tugged at his earlobe before he answered. "Well . . . you gotta realize that the fax didn't show too many details by the time it reached me, but just on the superficials, I'd say that it was the same one that snuffed our hookers."

Irina took a deep breath. "I was afraid of that."

Casey frowned. "I don't understand. I thought you'd be pleased. At least it spreads the load of catching him."

"It also makes the case more than a purely local business, and that brings the KGB into the picture."

Casey raised a hand. "Hold it there a minute. I can't be getting involved in your internal political problems."

Irina placed her hands flat on the desk. "The way things are going, the KGB may be everyone's problem before too long. Those guys won't be satisfied until they're running Mars."

Casey slowly shook his head. "I'm just here to catch a killer."

"Stick around—you just may get your mind changed for you."

For the next half hour Irina laid out all the details of the crime. She spread out the large color photographs of the body and the crime scene.

Casey studied them for a long time. Finally he straightened up. "It sure as hell looks like the same MO. The configuration of the wounds is so precise that it's beyond the realm of coincidence. It's got to be the same guy. The way he cuts them up has to be nothing less than a ritual, and a pretty elaborate one at that. This shit's too sick to be anything but the work of one guy."

"We're only supposing that it's a man."

Casey smiled grimly. "A mad slay dyke? No, it's definitely a man. There were semen traces at the first killing. I guess since then he's been more careful."

Irina folded her hands in front of her. "So where do we go from here?"

Casey sat down. "We have to face the fact that a serial killer is almost impossible to catch unless we get lucky or he gets careless. By the look of it, he's gotten away clean this time, and we may have to resign ourselves to waiting until he does it again."

Irina nodded. "I realize that. It doesn't sit well, but I do realize it."

Casey cleared his throat. "I hoped we'd left this kind of thing back on Earth. It seems that they can go just as nuts here."

For the first time in a long time, Irina wanted a cigarette. "So where do we go from here?"

Chavez spoke for the first time. "What about the street? Is there any talk? Any other hookers have near misses, weird guys following them, stuff like that?"

Irina shook her head. "Nothing. This sicko seems to have come right out of the blue."

Casey was playing with a pencil. "It occurs to me that we might do well to look for something anomalous in the settlement's entry and exit logs. We can pretty much assume that our boy came in from outside and probably left again after the murder. It's very likely that he used a phony ID. Have you run through the computer records?''

Irina nodded. "Boris is on it now."

"Anything?"

"Not yet." She hit the office intercom. "Boris, do you have anything yet?"

On the other end of the line, Boris Suvorova sounded very pleased with himself. "Yes, I think I've turned up something."

"Bring it in right now."

"Okay."

Boris entered with a sheaf of printouts under his arm. Irina quickly waved him to the last empty seat.

"So what do you have?"

Boris looked uncertainly at the two Americans.

"It's okay," Irina told him. "They're on our side."

Boris's shoulders twitched in the slightest of shrugs. "If you say so. At first there was nothing. I ran a check on anything that might prove to be a phony ID or pass. I was looking for something that was a good enough forgery to pass inspection at the station or any of the air locks but might show up on a deeper inspection. You know the kind of thing—a pass with no previous use, that kind of thing."

"And?"

"Nothing. If there was a forged ID, it was a pretty sophisticated one. I ran this second program that had the capacity to spot backdataing or any other kind of record tampering."

Irina raised an eyebrow. "I wasn't aware that we had a program like that."

Boris avoided her eyes. "We don't. I got it through . . . private channels."

"Should I ask what channels?"

"I'd rather you didn't."

Irina smiled. "So what happened when you ran this?"

Boris grinned.

"I got a name. Liam Flynn, citizen of the Republic of Ireland, free-lance contract with the PRA. There was a bunch of data against his name, but the program clearly showed that it was seeded in by a single backdata squirt. The first time the ID was

used for real was two nights ago, twenty-one fifty at the north
air lock.''

Casey put down his pencil. ''That puts him in the ballpark.''

Boris was looking increasingly smug. ''He left again at five
thirty-seven.''

''Is there anything else?''

''I ran a check on this Liam Flynn. There was no record of
him with any of the agencies and no contract on file at the PRA.
I think we can assume that this is our man.''

''Do the KGB know about this?''

''They know that I was checking the entry and exit logs—I
had to go through them to get access—but they don't know that
I found anything.''

''Let's do everything we can to keep them in blissful ignorance, shall we?''

Boris nodded. ''I'll garbage all traces.''

Irina turned to Casey. ''I think we can also assume that this
makes him one of yours.''

Casey did not seem convinced. ''Don't people go in for electronic forgery around here?''

''Sure, all the time, but there are precious few that are able
to write a backdata squirt onto a simple magstrip. It may be
against the orthodox optimism, but our system sucks. It's anti-
quated. Half the sophisticated stuff that we use we have to get
bootlegged from you guys.'' She smiled wickedly at her assistant. ''Don't we, Boris?''

Boris looked uncomfortable. Irina went right on. ''Computer
time is so stretched that it would be damn near impossible to do
something like that without someone noticing. Besides, we've
nothing like the tradition of jack-in players and cowboys that
you have. I know that this one's from your end of the tracks.''

Casey was pulling his earlobe again. ''If the killer is this Liam
Flynn, he could be one of yours. He might have just bought his
fake ID from one of ours.''

Irina treated Casey to a withering look. ''You really believe
that?''

Casey laughed. ''Not really. I just thought I'd run it up the
flagpole.''

"Nobody's saluting. Either way, the next move would seem to be on your turf."

"That's true enough. Maybe we should have a look around and head back to Burroughs and pick it up there."

Boris raised a hand. "There is one other thing."

"There is?"

"What?"

"I ran a check on all credit spending in the Aquarium Café on the night of the murder. There was another phony there."

"Our boy was using a double ID?"

"Rudi Baum, supposedly a DDR contract worker, the one that left around the same time as Ewart and the victim. The trouble is that he doesn't exist any more than Liam Flynn. More backdataing."

Casey whistled softly. "This bastard isn't only crazy, he's slick as gravy. This isn't going to be easy."

All of them thought about that for a few minutes. Finally Chavez leaned close to Casey.

"There's Worthing's news crew. We have to give them something."

Casey cursed. "Yeah, damn it—if we don't, we'll have them snapping at our heels." He turned to Irina. "What's your attitude toward this? Do you want to talk to the media?"

There was a certain irony in Irina's smile. "Sure. A display of international cooperation always makes for good propaganda. If nothing else, it'll keep the KGB from trying anything really stupid."

Casey looked at her sadly. "You've got the KGB on the brain."

She shot him a knowing look. "You'll find out."

Casey instructed Chavez to call Worthing and get him to meet them at the Golodkin Gallery. Irina stood up and smoothed down her skirt. There was another reason she had dressed up that day. It might have been frivolous individualism, but she wanted to look good on TV.

"Shall we go and face the press?"

U.S. Marine Corps Martian CySec center, Fort Haigh—
May 19 CEC—9:24 MST.

A small display box dropped into the top right corner of the screen. A warning signal was flashing on and off. A cold clutch of fear grabbed at a spot deep in John Whipple Greig's stomach. The warning symbol was instantly recognizable. It was an override from the clandestine monitor line he had hacked into the Vostok records system. Someone in the Soviet settlement had run a check on both Liam Flynn and Rudi Baum. The backdata had been spotted. He had not expected that the Russians would be so smart so fast. For approximately five seconds he sat very still, immobilized by the fear. Gradually he brought himself under control. He wiped the sweat from his palms and killed the warning. He looked around to see if anyone was watching him. As far as he could see, everything was normal in the CySec computer center. The panel lights were hard and bright overhead. Figures in military green and civilian coveralls were bent over consoles and workstations. There was some murmured conversation and the small noises of cybernetics at work, the clack of keyboards and the soft beep and trill of the machines.

Doing his best to look unconcerned, he folded down the perspective projections of the designer virus on which he was working and stood up from the triple display console. Still no one was paying any attention. He walked to his private wall safe and keyed in the lengthy combination. The bolts clicked back, and he opened the round steel door. He hunted through the stacks of printouts, disks, and cones until he found three gold minicones. He took them to a small self-contained workstation that he had set up as an unmonitored disposal unit and quickly garbaged them. There would be no trace of Liam Flynn, Rudi Baum, or the program that had created them. His tracks were covered. He would have to start again from scratch when the entity next stirred, but he could live with that. Security was everything.

Suddenly John Greig felt violently sick—and desperate to get out of the brightly lit computer complex. It was too white and antiseptic, and the walls were closing in. He had to be calm, had to hide in some dark and quiet place. If he did not, the entity might wake before its time. He had to splash cold water on his face. There was no way he could go back to his virus and the routine work problem of jinxing the guidance system on the MiG 90. He logged himself out on a sick call.

As he left the section, the marine guard at the door glanced at him questioningly. "You don't look so good."

Greig was ready with an answer. "I just feel a little queasy. I think I had some bad shrimp last night."

The young marine laughed. "How good can shrimp be after two years in space?"

Greig nodded. "You may have a point there."

Back in his quarters, Greig sat for a long while in the dark, not so much thinking as brooding without words or ideas, relishing the temporary freedom from the entity that followed the kill but, at the same time, dreading its return. Finally he stood up and went into the tiny bathroom. He knelt down and removed the small inspection cover from the wall beneath the sink, reached into the dark recess, and pulled out an airtight plastic box about the size of a cigarette pack. Still on his knees, he opened the box, took out a fragment of black metal, and held it between his flat palms. There was something very comforting about what he had come to think of as his little talisman. He had acquired it during a field trip up to Marsbad, bought it from some crazy old prospector. Coincidentally, that had been just before the entity had first entered his mind. And after the coming of the entity, he had needed a great deal of comfort from whatever source.

*Golodkin Gallery, Vostok Settlement—May 19 CEC—
10:11 MST.*

Hammond, Worthing, and Barstow waited outside the Aquarium Café. Most of the passersby looked at them with open curiosity, but no one approached them. A foreign news crew was not an everyday occurrence in Vostok, but the two figures in bulky topcoats lurking at the end of the gallery were so obviously KGB that they completely deterred anyone from actually speaking to the two Americans and the Englishman. Hammond had become so used to being mobbed on his assignments that he was not sure how he felt about being left alone.

Barstow was looking around uneasily. "If we can't do something to shake these shadows, there's no way we're going to be able to go ferreting on our own."

Hammond was also looking around. The three of them had spent the night in the international visitors' hostel beside the train tunnel—the closest thing to a hotel in the settlement. Hammond and Barstow had breakfasted on reconstituted eggs, salami, and some truly awful coffee in wax paper cups with Minnie Mouse printed on them. Even with that touch of the surreal to lighten the atmosphere, it was still possibly the worst meal Hammond had ever eaten. Worthing must have had advance warning about the cuisine in the Vostok hostel, because he had contented himself with a rather strangely colored Bloody Mary. They had picked up their KGB shadows within seconds of leaving the hostel in response to Chavez's call.

Walking to the Golodkin, Hammond had been quite shocked at the run-down state of the settlement. "Are all the Russian bases as funky as this?"

Worthing had nodded. "Give or take a degree."

"What happened?"

"Basically they stretched themselves too thin in the early days. Colonization proved to be much more expensive than any of the commissars had bargained for. Even with the slowboats, shipping everything from Earth turned out to be monstrously expensive. It started to seriously damage an Earthside Soviet economy that was still only just getting over the turn-of-the-century crash. The Mars colonists tightened their belts as much as they could and started cutting every possible corner. Now they're paying the price. Plus the Russians seem to have a monumental capacity for screwing up."

"And we don't?"

"Nothing in comparison."

"Are these places safe?"

Worthing grimaced. "Pretty much. The basic structures are sound. They've never had a blowout except the one at Pushkin, and that was a construction-related explosion, not a structural failure."

Hammond continued to look skeptically at the ceiling some twenty feet above his head. What would one day be chemical stalactites were starting to form around conduit leaks.

"You're not making me feel any better," he commented.

"This is Mars, not Malibu."

Hammond had a sudden vision of sea and surf. Just as he was wondering when he was going to see surf again, Barstow interrupted his train of thought.

"This looks like our party coming now."

Two of the figures were wearing pale blue militia uniforms. The other two were unmistakably Casey and Chavez. Hammond watched their approach with interest. One of the militia people was a knockout, her uniform tailored to show off her figure to the best possible advantage. Pale skin contrasted sharply with a mass of wavy black hair, and her almost perfect legs ended in the first pair of high heels he had seen in Vostok. By Martian standards she was exotically made up, and her scarlet mouth could have belonged to a porno queen. After the drab functionality of the other inhabitants of the Soviet settlement, she was a sight for sore eyes. Looking at her, Hammond was forcibly reminded that apart from a brief encounter aboard the *Dejah Thoris*, he had not touched a woman since he had left Earth. The woman's companion was a tall muscular young man who looked like a recruiting poster, and Hammond wondered if they were sleeping together. Introductions were made, and Hammond learned that the beauty was Chief Investigator Irina Orlov. He wondered if he would have a chance to get to know her better while he was in Vostok and noticed that Lon Casey also seemed to be making moves in that direction.

For the next two hours Hammond, Worthing, and Barstow were treated to a guided tour of the murder of Vera Zasulich. The tour started in the Aquarium Café, where the big Finn who ran the place protested at first that he had had enough trouble already and tried to ban Barstow's camera but finally relented after Boris leaned on him, pointing out a long list of health and safety violations. As Barstow ran tape, the few remaining customers turned their backs and covered their faces. Apparently rumors had already gone around that the KGB planned to close the place and ship out what they called the "hooligan element" to Vorkuta or one of the other labor camps. From the Aquarium, the tour moved on to Zasulich's blood-spattered cubicle, following the same corridors that had been taken by her and Ewart and, presumably, the killer. Irina and Casey kept up a running commentary for the camcorder but made no mention of the killer's use of phony IDs.

All in all it was pretty routine stuff. The story probably would not have run on the Global News at all if the murder had not taken place on Mars. Even so, a simustruct of the slaying would almost certainly have to be put together before the item was aired. The public back on Earth demanded a good deal more gore in their news stories than was provided by a wrecked cubicle and a bloodstained bed. Hammond was well aware that it was far from being up to his regular news feature standards. He tried to salvage something from the whole sorry business by attempting to get friendly with Irina Orlov, but she easily kept both him and Casey at arm's length. By the early afternoon the news crew was back at the hostel, irritably wondering what to do next.

To simply walk out into Vostok and see what they could see was clearly out of the question. Their KGB shadows dogged their every footstep, and even when they gathered back in Hammond's room in the hostel, they did not feel that they were able to talk freely. Their rooms were undoubtedly bugged.

Worthing seemed to be feeling personally responsible. "Things have seriously tightened up since I was here last. There was always the KGB, but they were never breathing quite so hard down our necks."

Barstow unhitched his camera and put it down on the bed. "So what do we do to stop this thing from turning into a complete fiasco?"

Hammond sighed and pointed to the ceiling to indicate that he was talking for eavesdroppers. "I guess we should stick around until the end of the day and have a talk with Casey. He may have something extra for us. I don't think we were getting the full story just now."

Barstow grunted. "Otherwise I guess we take the next bullet back to Burroughs, right?"

"Right."

"So it's all been a waste of time."

Hammond looked angrily at the cameraman. "You're getting paid whatever happens."

"That's not the point, and you know it."

Hammond took a deep breath. Although he did not care to admit it, he knew that the cameraman was right.

Worthing stood up and reached for his jacket. "Well, I for one don't intend to sit around here all afternoon exuding gloom. I'm going out to see if there's a bar open. Anyone coming with me?"

That gave Hammond a new target on which to vent his frustration. "Jesus Christ, Danny, is that the best you can do in the circumstances? Go out and get drunk again?"

Worthing did a quick pantomime to indicate that he wanted the three of them outside so they could speak with less chance of being overheard.

Barstow quickly picked up on it. "Come on, Hammond, Worthing's right. What else are we going to do?"

The phone chose that moment to start trilling. Hammond picked it up gingerly. The odds dictated that it would be more trouble.

"Lech Hammond, please," said a voice with a heavy Spanish accent.

"This is he."

"Hey, Hammond, remember me? Angel Ramos? We met way back when in Cape Town when the republic was coming apart. I was with the Daniel Ortega Brigade. A few of us saved your ass from those Three Section bastards."

"Sure, Angel, I remember. How are you doing?" Hammond had never heard of Angel Ramos, and the Daniel Ortega Brigade had been nowhere near Cape Town, but he decided that the best thing was to go along with it. It might be a KGB setup, but it might also be someone with an ax to grind who wanted to talk to an outside newsman.

"I'm doing pretty good. I thought, since you were in town, I'd invite you down to the barrio tonight."

"The barrio?"

"That's what we call the Cuban section. I can guarantee it'll be more fun than hanging out and getting depressed with a bunch of morbid Russians.''

"You could be right, at that.''

"So you'll come?''

"If nothing breaks in the story I'm covering.''

Angel Ramos laughed. "Nothing's going to break in that story, Hammond. Stinking KGB ain't going to let nothing break. You come to the barrio.''

"So where and when?''

"There's a café, the Copa Cabana. Anyone will tell you how to get there. Come around twenty-one hundred.''

"Okay.''

"Be seeing you, Hammond. It'll be just like old times.''

"Yeah. I'll look forward to it.''

Angel Ramos hung up. Hammond did the same.

Worthing looked at him questioningly. "What was all that about?''

"Old comrade from the Cape. You remember Angel Ramos?''

Worthing looked mystified but went along. "Yeah, sure.''

Hammond picked up his own jacket. "So what about that drink you were talking about?''

Out on what passed for the street in the underground settlement, Worthing immediately wanted answers. Hammond glanced over his shoulder. Their KGB shadows were some twenty meters behind.

"Let's just walk for a while,'' he said. "Those guys could have a snooper mike pointed at us.''

They walked on, heading in the general direction of the Golodkin. Hammond was looking for something, a piece of a plant or a construction site that was making enough noise to swamp a snooper mike in case their shadows were using one. After about ten minutes he spotted exactly what he wanted. Halfway down an access tunnel that linked two sections, a relay pump, part of the atmosphere recycling system, was noisily malfunctioning, making a loud rhythmic clatter. Hammond halted beside it. Their shadows also halted, pretending to inspect a panel of the tunnel wall.

"I think it's safe to talk here.''

Worthing looked back at the shadows. "So who the hell is Angel Ramos?"

"I've no idea. He claimed to have been with the Daniel Ortega Brigade in Cape Town."

"The Daniel Ortega Brigade wasn't anywhere near Cape Town."

"Exactly."

"So what's this all about?"

"This Angel Ramos wants us to meet him tonight at some place in the Cuban section called the Copa Cabana."

"And you don't know this Ramos?"

"Never heard of him until he called."

Worthing frowned. "We could be walking into a trap."

"Or we could be meeting with someone who badly wants to talk to outside newsmen, someone who has a story. The Russians and the Cubans are supposed to be increasingly on the outs."

"You think we should risk it?"

Hammond nodded. "I don't see that we can afford not to."

Worthing smiled wryly. "I was afraid you'd say that. What time are we supposed to be at this Copa Cabana?"

"Twenty-one hundred."

"I don't have to tell you that we're going to have to tread real carefully."

"That's right, you don't. Shall we go and get that drink you were talking about?"

The three of them started walking again. Their KGB shadows trailed behind like faithful hounds.

Executive landing BD11-20, Vostok Settlement—
May 19 CEC—19:43 MST.

"You want some wine?"

"I'd rather have scotch."

Irina laughed. "You'll be lucky. We haven't seen a bottle of scotch in four months."

Casey raised an eyebrow. "Not even your well-connected apparatchiki?"

Irina snorted. "You have a very old-fashioned idea of how things work here."

"I thought things were getting more and more old-fashioned by the minute."

Irina draped her uniform tunic across the back of a chair. "Can we forget about politics for a couple of hours?"

Casey smiled. "That suits me."

"Do you want some of this wine or not? It's really quite good. It comes in a glass bottle, not a plastic container."

"It's been a while since I've had wine out of a glass bottle."

"Oh, come on, you've got everything over in Burroughs."

"You don't really believe that, do you? We're going to run out of beer next week. *Na defitsit* is universal."

"At least you still have beer. It's been a month here."

Irina produced two glasses and poured the wine. The label said that it was Moldavian. Casey had never drunk Moldavian wine. Irina settled into the couch and indicated that Casey should sit beside her. Halfway through the afternoon, after they had finished with the news crew, she had finally decided that she would sleep with Casey. She had sensed his willingness almost from the moment he had walked into her office, but she had held off making up her mind. Sleeping with an outsider was a pretty sure path to future trouble. The KGB was certain to hear about it, and it would doubtless go into her permanent file to be used against her at some point in the future when the *yedino-obrazie* boys decided to get rid of her and her individualism. There was also the matter of Yuri. He was discreet and dependable, but out of bed he was dull. It had taken half a day for her individualism and craving for adventure to win out over her natural prudence. Damn it all, she was not so far gone that she was going to let the KGB run her sex life. She had called Yuri and told him that she was going to have to work with the Americans that night. For maybe half a minute she had been tempted by the reporter Hammond. He certainly had been coming on to her, but he had been too confident, too sure of himself, and too professionally handsome. She was convinced that at some point he must have had facial surgery, and then there was that ludicrous layered haircut. She wondered how that would look after six months on Mars.

Irina curled her legs under her and sipped her wine. "So, Lon Casey, do you ever think about going back to Earth?"

Casey was not thinking of much apart from enjoying the closeness of this very attractive woman. He knew a number of women back in Burroughs, but the position of marshal tended to set him apart. "I think about it now and then, but I haven't done anything about it. Each time I look, the situation seems to get crazier and crazier."

"And it's not crazy here?"

"Hell, I don't know. Maybe I just like the idea of pioneering. It must be in my genes."

Irina took the initiative and placed a hand lightly on his jeans. "Wyatt Earp, huh?"

"I wouldn't go that far."

Casey was actually looking bashful. Irina found it charming. She removed her hand from his thigh and poured more wine. It would not do to rush this John Wayne.

"Do you like my place, Lon?"

Casey looked around and nodded. "Yeah, I like it."

"Two rooms. A separate bedroom is one of the privileges of rank."

Over the years Irina had gone to a lot of trouble to make her rooms feel as much like a home as possible. It had been hard, and the decor was still very superficial—some wall hangings, a couple of Japanese lamps, some framed prints. The payload allowance for interior decorating was minuscule, and even rank could not do much about payload quotas. It was only with the lights down low, as they were now, that it did not feel like living in a cramped steel tank.

"It must get claustrophobic down here."

"Is it any better in Burroughs?"

"Not much. My place is only a little bigger. If I couldn't regularly suit up and get out on the surface, I think I'd go nuts."

"Them wide-open spaces?"

Casey grinned. His enthusiasm was positively boyish. "I think that's probably why I came out in the first place. The Earth's been ravaged. There's a rawness out here. Humanity hasn't had time to screw things up. You get out into the back much?"

Irina kept a straight face, but she wanted to hug herself in delight. He was so damned adorable. "I get out now and again but not as often as I'd like. The powers that be aren't too keen on us wandering around out there unsupervised."

"That's too bad."

"I went on the volcano tour last year."

"The Martian volcanoes are something else. Can you imagine what it must have looked like when those things were blowing out lava?"

After about another half hour of wine and small talk, Irina decided that it was going to be up to her to make the first move. Casey was just too much of a gentleman to wrestle her to the ground and take her. She slid her arms around his neck and, ignoring his look of surprise, kissed him full on the mouth. He was not too much of a gentleman to respond instantly.

After a long minute they came up for air. Irina smiled and started to unbutton her blouse. "How many police chiefs have you kissed before?"

THREE

Access tunnel D41, Vostok Settlement—
May 19 CEC—20:47 MST.

HAMMOND, WORTHING, AND BARSTOW WERE ON THEIR WAY
to the Cuban section. A new pair of shadows were following
them without any pretense of concealment. When they had asked
directions from the desk clerk at the international hostel, the
man had glazed with nervousness. If he was not actually on the
KGB payroll, he must have had a few sins of his own to protect.
He had gone into his small cubbyhole behind the desk and made
a whispered phone call. Someone must have wanted them to
keep the date with Angel Ramos—when he had come back, he
had pulled up a layout of the settlement on his computer and
shown them precisely where the main Cuban area, the so-called
barrio, was. To reach it, they had to leave the central body of
the settlement and walk down the D41 connecting tunnel, passing through a number of airtight bulkheads as they went. The
barrio was directly under the hydroponic dome.

They had left the hostel with a good deal of unease. Hammond could not shake the idea that they were walking into a
trap. It came almost as a relief when the new shadows fell into
step at the regulation twenty yards behind them.

As they proceeded down D41, Hammond noticed that the
section in which the Cubans lived could be sealed off easily.

Whether by design or by accident, the Soviets seemed to have created their own Hispanic ghetto. They did not find out just how much of a ghetto it was until they passed through the final door. It was like entering a new world. The air was noticeably warmer in the Cuban section. The lights were dim and red. The smell of spice and cooking filled the air, and Cubop poly-rhythms echoed from tunnel walls that were covered in intricate graffiti.

The three guards at the door were all huge, and none seemed the least pleased to see strangers. "You gringos want something here?"

The spokesman was dressed in the traditional Cuban olive-green fatigues. His wide kidney belt, with its whirls of pointed chrome studs, was a lot less traditional, as was the machete that he held loosely at his side. His left-hand companion wore a nylon muscle shirt, red sweatpants, and high lace-up jump boots. He had a baseball bat resting against his shoulder. The one on the other side was an interplanetary version of an East LA cholo with studded vest and leather pants. His bare arms sported a mass of tattoos that included dragons, serpents, and a bleeding heart. A black cotton helmet liner was pulled down over his eyes, and he had a set of folded-back freddy knives attached to the fingers of his right hand. There was a five-kilo drop-forged hammer stuck in the waistband of his pants.

Worthing and Barstow seemed more than happy to let Hammond do the explaining. The trio of Cubans looked as though they would need a lot of convincing. Hammond looked for some sign of receptiveness in the hard faces, but there was none.

"I've come to see a man called Angel Ramos. He asked me to meet him at the Copa Cabana."

"What you want with Angel Ramos, gringo?"

"We knew each other back on Earth. We were together during the fall of the Cape Republic. He helped me out a couple of times."

The one in the fatigues raised a doubtful eyebrow. "You were in the South African Civil War?"

"I was a reporter."

The cholo peered into Hammond's face. "I know you. You're Hammond. I used to see you on TV."

There was a fast conversation in Spanish that Hammond was not quick enough to follow, and then the Cubans stepped aside and indicated that the newsmen should pass.

"You know the way to the Copa?" one of them asked.

Hammond shook his head. The one in fatigues gave him directions. Assured that he would see the lights and that he could not miss it, Hammond started down the tunnel.

Worthing hesitated and looked at the Cuban in fatigues. "There is one thing."

"What's that?"

"There's a pair of KGB spooks following us. They're back down the tunnel."

The three men laughed. It sounded like a mixture of confidence and brutal insanity. Hammond profoundly hoped that he would never be the subject of that kind of laughter.

"Don't you worry about it, gringo. We'll dissuade them from following any further."

As soon as they were out of earshot, Worthing looked at Hammond in amazement. "I never realized that things had gone this bad. This is a full blown no-go area."

"I wonder why the Russians don't come in here in force. It's hardly their style to tolerate something like this."

"It may be that they need the Cubans. There are groups of them scattered all over the planet. If there was an open conflict with the Russians, they'd make formidable guerrillas. The Russians would be sitting ducks. I figure they learned how that feels in Afghanistan and Mongolia. They probably don't want to repeat the experience."

In total contrast to the rest of Vostok, the barrio was, to say the least, colorful, drab surfaces covered with a flamboyant patina of graffiti, a riot of joyous spraywork. About the only wall area that had not been touched was the one at the very end of D41, where a heroic mural showed a mounted Fidel Castro riding into Havana in triumph after the fall of Battista. The place was crowded, tight knots of men and women hanging out in almost every tunnel intersection. Monster pressure boxes pumped out loud latinexo and salsa. On some corners there was even live music—electric guitars and keyboards, amplifiers hooked into lighting outlets, saxophones, and conga drums. A number of sidewalk chess games were in progress, while food vendors hawked pancakes and fried bananas from portable hot plates. When Hammond, Worthing, and Barstow walked by, however, animated faces became as hard and watchful as those of the men at the bulkhead door. Worthing was starting to look uneasy.

"I don't know what you two think, but I'm starting to feel like one of the bad guys."

"The Russians must love having this bunch on their doorstep."

Barstow still had his camera slung over his shoulder in its carrying case. It looked innocent enough, but Hammond could see the turret lens swiveling. The cameraman was covertly running tape. A knot of three- and four-year-old children ran across the corridor in front of them. There was a beautiful fluidity to their low-gravity movement. Barstow's turret lens discreetly tracked them. Presumably they had been born on the red planet, and Hammond wondered if they would ever be able to survive on Earth or if they were the true Martians. He folded them away in his memory. It was not a world-shaking scoop, but it might make a neat little human interest story.

Barstow pointed. "That looks like the Copa Cabana. The guy at the door said to look out for the palm tree."

They were crossing a wide gallery that curved away on either side, and Hammond guessed that it probably followed the perimeter of the dome above them. Fifty yards away to the right, a light sculpture of a palm tree waved against a painted, dark blue sky dotted with tiny stars. Although the sign had clearly been constructed from scavenged parts, there was a true artistry in the way it had been put together.

At the entrance to the bar the three of them were treated to a rerun of the encounter at the bulkhead door. A burly doorman with long greased ringlets and a mirror ripple jacket with the word "Copa" stenciled across the back regarded them with open hostility.

"Only members admitted here."

Hammond was starting to get used to the hostility. "We're here to meet Angel Ramos."

The doorman looked at him with deep, dark-eyed suspicion. "You want Angel Ramos?"

"Right."

"And who wants him?"

"Lech Hammond."

The doorman repeated it slowly. "Lech Hammond?"

"Right."

"You wait here." The doorman turned and went back into the bar.

Worthing looked around with a resigned expression. "The milk of Cuban kindness doesn't exactly run over."

Hammond shrugged. "You can't blame them. They probably think we're from the KGB."

Worthing protested. "Do we look like we're from the KGB? Jesus Christ, I'd never dress that badly."

Barstow grinned. "We sure as hell don't look like we come from around here."

The doorman returned, accompanied by a rotund individual in green fatigues and a full Fidel Castro beard. The newcomer rushed up to Hammond as though the American were his prodigal brother and grasped him in a rib-crushing bear hug.

"Lech Hammond! Amigo! It has been too long!" As he held the newsman close, he breathed urgently in Hammond's ear. "I'm Angel Ramos. Go along with this. I'll explain later."

Hammond instantly fell in with the charade. He held the bearded man at arm's length, as though inspecting the changes that passing time had made on an old and dear friend. "Angel Ramos, you put on a bit of weight since I saw you last."

Angel Ramos's face split into a beaming smile. "You're looking pretty well fed yourself, amigo. What brings you out to Mars?"

"Just doing a story." Hammond gestured to Worthing. "You remember Danny Worthing? We're working together again. It's just like old times."

Ramos began vigorously pumping Worthing's hand. "Of course, of course. How you doing, Danny?"

Worthing shot Hammond one mystified look and then also joined in the game. Ramos, with a nod to the doorman, started ushering them into the bar.

"Come along, my friends. We drink rum and talk about old times, huh? You drink rum, Danny?"

Worthing nodded. "Sure, I drink rum."

Once inside the place, they discovered that the Copa Cabana was, by Martian standards, close to being a full-blown nightclub. The initial impression was one of noise and heat, sweat, glistening bodies, and total chaos. Huge roto speakers and vee-horns filled the jam-packed room with pain-threshold Cubop. Scantily clad dancers in spangles and impossibly tall head-dresses that could happen only in Mars gravity were crowded onto a small stage. One whole wall was taken up by an elaborate foolfeel displaying gyrating erotic abstracts. The sense of dizzy confusion was heightened by a spiral pattern of flashing optical panels that ran around and around on the low nightclub ceiling. The people were a spectacle all on their own. The crowd seemed bent on unashamedly injecting the maximum life into the general Martian austerity. Their costumes, although obviously homemade, were bright and flamboyant and, in many cases, so abbreviated that they left nothing to the imagination. Many of the patrons seemed determined to compete with the showgirls and dancing boys on the stage.

Ramos pushed his way through the mass, shouting back to the three newsmen as he went. "We go to the bar. It's quieter there." He clapped Worthing on the shoulder. "You like this place, amigo?"

Worthing blinked. "It's certainly lively." He seemed a little bemused.

Ramos roared with laughter.

If it was quieter at the bar, Hammond could not tell. The bar was packed three or four deep with drinkers demanding refills. The Cubans seemed to have an unlimited supply of home-brewed rum. Ramos elbowed his way to the front. No one challenged him—clearly he commanded a good deal of respect in the Martian barrio. After a minute or so he returned, clutching a bottle and four glasses.

"Now we drink." He winked. "Nobody can overhear us in here."

Hammond leaned close and shouted into his ear. "You want to explain what's going on?"

Ramos grinned. "Later, my friend, later. First we drink. We drink to old times."

"But there weren't any old times."

Ramos's grin widened as a very beautiful woman in little more than a floral loincloth danced past. "Then drink to her."

Since Ramos did not seem inclined to come to the point, there was nothing to do but wait him out. Barstow, his camera up on his shoulder, was openly rolling tape, and nobody appeared to mind. The stage cleared, and a single spotlight focused on a naked dancer with reflectively bronzed skin. As she writhed and contorted to Passion Mbota's classic "Love Down," the crowd fell silent. The things she did with her body could have been achieved only in Martian gravity, and even then only with great difficulty. When she was through, there was a storm of applause, and then the general dancing and shouting started again.

Ramos took Hammond by the arm. "Now we talk. Follow me and bring the others."

Ramos led them past the Copa's toilets and out a back door that opened onto a narrow, garbage-filled passage. Hammond hesitated at the door. Ramos saw his expression and laughed.

"Don't worry, my friend. I'm not going to hurt you. You are the famous TV news reporter, and I need to talk to you. You must forgive the subterfuge, but the Russians watch me all the time."

Hammond was not quite buying it. "You seem pretty safe in here."

Ramos shook his head sadly. "Even in the barrio there are those who can be bought or coerced."

"So what is this? A back alley conversation?"

"No, Señor Hammond, I want you to come with me up to the dome. We can talk there. If we are seen, I am merely giving you a tour of the hydroponics. We Cubans are very proud of our bioengineering."

"Whatever you say."

Hammond stepped out into the passage. Worthing and Barstow followed him. Ramos led the way through a whole series of back passages until they came to the doors of an elevator.

"This will take us up to the dome."

At the top, the elevator doors opened on a small air lock.

"Are we going out onto the surface?"

Ramos shook his head. "No, just into the dome." He indicated a rack of bubble helmets and air tanks along one wall. "You will each need one of those. The pressure is Earth normal inside the dome, but the atmosphere is largely carbon dioxide."

They arranged the tanks on their backs and put on the helmets. Ramos cycled the lock. The inner door opened, and they stepped through into the Amazon. It was a tropical rain forest, right there on Mars.

Executive landing BD11-20, Vostok Settlement—
May 19 CEC—21:46 MST.

"If you're so worried about the KGB, why don't you just get out of here?"

Irina propped herself up on one elbow. "That almost amounts to solicitation to defect."

"The hell it does. I was just asking."

"And the KGB is most likely just listening."

Casey, who had been lazily extending a hand toward her breast, froze in midreach and blinked at her. "Say that again."

Irina pushed back her hair. "The KGB is most likely listening."

"You are joking?"

Irina shook her head. "Despite a dubious legality, they've got big brother systems all over the settlement. They must have them up here in the executive quarters."

Casey sat up and looked around the tiny bedroom as though trying to spot a camera or microphone. "Are you telling me that there's a strong chance that the KGB could be watching us right now?"

"I should think there's a very strong chance. They've most likely been informed that I went home with a senior American law enforcement officer. It's the kind of thing that piques their curiosity."

"You mean they've been watching us for the past couple of hours?"

"It's probable."

"Jesus Christ."

"After a while you get used to screwing for an audience. You just put it out of your mind."

"You do this kind of thing all the time?"

Irina also sat up. She was starting to get mad. Who the hell did this Casey think he was? What had been slow, old-fashioned John Wayne charm was tilting perilously toward Victorian double-standard prudery.

"What the hell do you mean by that?" she demanded.

"You know what I mean."

Now she really was mad. "If you're asking me if I have an active sex life, you're damned right I do. I'm a cop, goddamn it, not a fucking nun. This is the twenty-first century."

Irina flopped angrily back on the bed and stared at the ceiling. The long silence was broken only by Casey trying to fix the fence.

"I was only wondering if you'd been compromised."

Irina shook her head. "Nothing can compromise me now. I've had too many run-ins with Melikov and his boys. They'll take me out the moment they think they've got the juice."

"I still don't understand why you stick around when you seem so certain that they're going to get you in the end."

Irina turned and faced him. "You really don't understand, do you? I'm a Russian. It's my country, and this is my settlement. I've put half my life into the colonization of this godforsaken planet, and I'm not going to hand it over to the likes of Melikov without at least a fight. Those bastards aren't the natural order of things, they're a disease."

"There are times when a disease can be inevitable. It's called a plague."

"That doesn't mean you don't go on looking for a cure until the very last minute."

"You're that determined?"

"What do you think?"

Casey nodded. "Yeah, I guess you're that determined. Remember one thing, though. If the shit really comes down, you've got a friend in Burroughs."

Irina smiled. "I appreciate that."

She slid her arms around his naked body and pulled him to her. "Let's give Big Brother another show."

Hydroponic dome, Vostok Settlement—May 20 CEC—00:04 MST.

"This is really something."

"That's why the Russians can't get by without us. This is their only hope of eventual self-sufficiency. The day will come when we'll have half of Mars under crop. All we need is the water and the raw materials. We could be doing it now if the damned military didn't get so much of the payload space."

As Ramos led Hammond, Worthing, and Barstow deeper into the jungle inside the dome, it became clear that there was in fact a definite order in the profusion of vegetation. There were plants that were recognizable from Earth—tomatoes, sugarcane, corn—except that they were three and four times their normal size. When Barstow asked about that, Ramos grinned proudly.

"They just keep on growing in low gravity. Of course, they get a little help from genetic engineering. If the stinking Russians would get off our backs, we could be feeding the whole planet inside of five years. It's not only a matter of food." He pointed to sheets of what looked like growing mica. "We're also working on organic building materials."

Ramos still had not given them the slightest indication of what he wanted. It was hot and humid inside the dome, and they were sweating inside the clear Plexiglas helmets. Hammond was starting to become irritable.

"This is all real interesting, but it hardly seems that a guided tour of the dome and a lecture on the future of hydroponics needed so much drama and secrecy."

Ramos treated Hammond to a long hard look, as though sizing him up one last time. "You're right, my friend, it doesn't, but I have to be sure I can trust you."

Hammond raised an eyebrow. "Trust me with what?"

"With the information that the Russians have found something of major significance out by the volcano Olympus Mons."

"We've all heard the rumors."

"This is more than a rumor. Five of my people are dead because of it."

"Dead? I'm not following you. Who's dead?"

Ramos held up a hand. "Before we start, we have to establish the ground rules."

Hammond nodded. "Whatever you want."

"I want your word that my identity will be protected."

"You have it. Both your features and your voice can be electronically disguised."

"I also want you to promise that you won't discuss this matter until you are out of the settlement. I don't even want you to speak about it on the train. You never know when you may be overheard. I'm taking a very great risk talking to you like this."

"I realize that. We'll take every precaution."

Again Ramos hesitated. Finally he appeared to make up his mind. "Okay, start your camera running."

Barstow focused on Ramos, who took a deep breath and began. "As you probably already know, about seven and a half months ago a mainly Cuban survey team discovered something out in the desert. There was a single suit radio transmission, and then the Russians jammed it with everything they had. They even launched a flight of MiG 90 interceptors, and the entire area was cordoned off. It's occupied by KGB and military, and nobody has been in and out since."

"So what happened to the original survey team?"

"As far as we can tell, they're either dead or being held inside the cordoned-off area. Knowing the KGB, I fear that they're dead. We made inquiries and were told that they'd been transferred. That was a lie."

"How can you be sure of that?"

"The Cuban community on Mars is a close-knit one. If these men had showed up at any of the other settlements, we'd have heard about it. They simply vanished without a trace."

"You're sure of this?"

"As sure as one can ever be."

Hammond asked the obvious question. "Do you have any idea what this thing might be out there? Why it caused so much of a flap?"

Ramos shook his head. "I don't know. Like anyone else, I only have a theory."

"And what's that?"

Ramos hesitated. "I think that the Russians have evidence of the existence of intelligent alien life."

Barstow whistled softly from behind the camera. "So the ruskies have themselves their very own hangar eighteen."

Hammond glanced at him. "What's hangar eighteen?"

Worthing supplied the answer. "It was a rumor that persisted during the late twentieth century. The U.S. Air Force was supposed to have the wreckage of a crashed UFO hidden in hangar number eighteen at Edwards Air Force Base."

"Surely that was just tabloid folklore."

"It probably was."

Hammond turned back to Ramos. "And you think the same thing's happening here?"

The Cuban nodded gravely. "I think that's exactly what's happening."

"But weren't you rather jumping to conclusions? Why should it necessarily be something alien? It could just as easily be a unique mineral deposit or a thick layer of permafrost. Something that they might want to keep under wraps but nothing that weird or spectacular."

Ramos spread his hands. "Sure, it could be anything. The trouble is that I did a little checking. The only people who've been sent out there besides soldiers and KGB security are metallurgists and astrophysicists. If it was a mineral deposit, they'd have geologists and mining engineers. Two weeks ago a team of archaeologists arrived from Earth. What does that tell you?"

Hammond frowned. "How do you know all this?"

"When you work with the Russians, you become an expert at reading between the lines."

"Just one more question. Why are you telling us all this? It's surely a terrible risk for something that's really only a theory."

The Cuban's teeth flashed behind the helmet. "Call it a matter of principle. Anything that the Russians want to keep quiet, I want brought out into the open."

Hammond was ready to stop, but Worthing indicated that Barstow should keep rolling.

"There's something that bothers me. If this thing is an alien artifact, why should the Russians go to such trouble to keep it quiet? You'd think they'd be trumpeting it as a triumph of Soviet science."

Ramos shook his head. "Not the way their minds are working at the moment. This isn't the old perestroika Russia. These new bastards are crazy. *Yedino-obrazie* and all the other shit. They want to go back to the days of Stalin. Fear and secrecy. Capitalists under the bed. For them, national divisions are everything. The enemy is at the gates. If there really was solid proof of intelligent life out in the universe somewhere, it would have the effect of unifying humanity. We'd be a hundred times closer to thinking of ourselves as Earthmen first and Russians, Americans, Cubans, and all the rest of it second. That's exactly what these KGB creeps don't want. Believe me, the international brotherhood of man is the last thing they're interested in. Their game is divide and rule."

Hammond signed to Barstow to stop the tape. "So that's it. The question is, Where do we go from here? Despite everything we've heard, this is still a hell of a lot of supposition."

Ramos stretched like a man who had unloaded a great weight. "That, my friend, is your problem. I've told you all I know. Now it's up to you. If you crack this thing, it could be—what do you guys call it?—the scoop of the century."

Worthing was thoughtful. "If we could just get a look inside that base."

Ramos shook his head. "I'd say that was near enough impossible. But you could get close to it without too much trouble. Maybe even get film of the defenses."

Hammond looked at him sharply. "We could?"

"Sure, the site is less than three hundred kilometers from the North Pole Trail. You could follow the trail to the point where it passes Olympus Mons and then head off into open country. The worst that could happen is that you'd be turned back by a Russian patrol."

Hammond nodded. "It's certainly worth thinking about."

That was something they would have to discuss when they were safely back in Burroughs.

As they were waiting for the air lock to cycle, Ramos glanced at the three of them.

"If you do decide to go up the North Pole Trail, be careful. The last stop on that trail is Vorkuta. It's our own trail of tears, and there are some bad people living along its length. You know what loco means?"

Hammond nodded. "I know what loco means."

Executive landing BD11–20, Vostok Settlement—
May 20 CEC—04:02 MST.

There was a pounding on the door. Casey sat bolt upright, reaching for a gun that was not there.

"What the hell is going on?"

The pounding continued.

"KGB, open up!"

Irina was on her feet, stark naked, snatching for the snub-nosed pistol in the shoulder holster that hung beside the bed. So this was it. She had not expected it to come so soon, but now that it was happening, she was beyond fear. Maybe she was a little dazed, but at the same time she was seeing things with a terrible clarity. One thing was certain—her life was going to be irrevocably changed.

"Open this door, Chief Investigator, or we'll be forced to break it down."

It was Melikov himself. He was going to supervise her downfall personally. Casey looked as though he intended to make a fight of it. She held up a hand.

"This has nothing to do with you. Don't do or say a thing. You can only make it worse."

The pounding was renewed.

"This is your last warning, Orlov."

"I'm opening the door," Irina shouted back. "Don't do anything stupid."

Melinkov was there with three of his goons, and Strugatsky was right beside him. Irina wondered why Turchin was missing this. Three Mikhail machine pistols were pointed at her stomach. Melikov made no attempt to enter the apartment.

"The gun, Chief Investigator?"

Irina had a sudden flash of just how ridiculous she must look, naked as a baby and brandishing a pistol. For an instant she thought of shooting Melikov and dying herself in a blaze of machine gun fire. But that was not the way. As long as she was still alive, there would be a chance that she could do something. She dropped the gun onto the couch. The bottle and glasses from the night before were still on the coffee table like a symbol of human vulnerability. The goons lowered their guns, and Melikov stepped inside. Irina faced him down, determined not to be intimidated.

"Are you arresting me?"

"Please get dressed, Chief Investigator."

"I asked if you were arresting me."

Melikov shook his head. "No, Chief Inspector, I'm not arresting you. I'm merely delivering your transfer orders. Now, please get dressed."

"I don't understand. What transfer orders?"

"Please get dressed."

For the first time she noticed that Melikov was sweating and that his voice sounded strained. The man was profoundly uncomfortable. She placed a hand on her hip.

"What's the matter, Major? Do I make you uncomfortable like this?"

"Please, Chief Inspector, I'm asking you for the last time."

"Wait here."

She turned and went into the bedroom.

"What's going on?" Casey asked, pulling on his shirt.

She grabbed her panties from the floor and started to dress. "I'm not sure, but it's nothing good."

"Is there anything I can do?"

"Yeah, stay out of it."

She fumbled into her shoes, threw her uniform tunic across her shoulders, and stalked back into the living room. "So what is all this?"

Melikov smiled coldly. "You're being transferred."

"This is the first I've heard of it."

"The decision has only just been made. You're being transferred to Vorkuta."

Irina's heart sank. So this really was it. "Why don't you stop fucking with me, Melikov? Just come out and say that you're arresting me."

Melikov's eyes were hard and cold, almost reptilian. "Believe me, Orlov, there's nothing that would please me more than to arrest you. Unfortunately, the evidence that I could present wouldn't stand up at a trial. You still have a lot of friends in this settlement. I have, however, been able to bring a certain amount of pressure to bear, and I will be getting you out of Vostok."

"So I'm not going to Vorkuta as a prisoner?"

"No. I wish you were, but you'll retain your rank."

"So what will I be?"

"You'll command the militia."

"There is no militia in Vorkuta. It's a military base."

"There has been some reorganization. The militia will, as of now, be responsible for the civilian prisoners."

"How can the militia be responsible if there is no militia? This is a farce."

"There will be a number of your colleagues going with you."

"So you've broken us in Vostok?"

Melikov's smile was ugly. "Exactly."

Casey came into the room. Ignoring the KGB squad, he put an arm around Irina. "What're these bastards doing to you?"

"They're sending me to the north pole."

"You're kidding."

"I'm deadly serious."

"Marshal Casey," Melikov interjected, "the chief investigator is no longer in charge of the prostitute murder case, and I think you can be assured that whoever takes it over will have no need of your cooperation. I would suggest that you leave the settlement by the first available transport."

"Are you expelling me?"

Melikov shook his head. "Not officially, but for all practical purposes, yes." He looked pointedly through the open bedroom door at the rumpled, disorganized bed. "I might suggest that you reflect on your methods, Marshal. I don't know how you capitalists do things, but the majority of us here are able to tell the difference between cooperation and debauchery."

Irina interrupted. "And when do I leave?"

"Once again, as soon as transport can be arranged. I suggest that you pack. The weight limit is fifty kilos."

Casey quickly embraced Irina. "I guess we won't be seeing each other for a while."

Melikov did not allow her to answer. "That's correct, Marshal. You won't be seeing each other for a very long while, if indeed you ever see each other again."

Irina experienced a sudden terrible sinking feeling. She was quite certain that on the way to Vorkuta or once she was there, the KGB intended to have her killed.

The international visitors' hostel, Vostok Settlement—
May 20 CEC—04:03 MST.

The phone rang. Lech Hammond opened his eyes and had trouble remembering where he was. His head hurt from the rum at the Copa Cabana. The phone rang again. He reached out and picked up the handset.

"Hammond."

"Comrade Hammond, this is the night clerk. Could you please come down to the desk? There are some people here who want to have a word with you."

Hammond looked at his watch. It was just after four. What the hell was going on?

"It's the middle of the night."

"I really would suggest that you come down here, Comrade Hammond." The desk clerk actually sounded frightened.

"Can't it wait until morning?" Hammond growled.

"It's the KGB that wants to speak to you."

Hammond sat bolt upright, unable to avoid the clutch of fear. "I'll be right down."

He dressed quickly. What the hell did the KGB know? What could they have on them? He and the others had not actually broken any laws, but it was hard to tell with the Soviets. Did they know about Ramos? Know that they were interested in the thing out in the desert? Four A.M. was not the time for a social call—it was the hour for terror tactics. It would not be the first time a journalist had been arrested for espionage. He ran into

Worthing and Barstow in the passageway. They had also received a call from the night clerk. Worthing looked like death warmed over.

There were ten of them: nine uniformed thugs with machine pistols at the ready and a tall, pale individual in a leather trench coat who appeared to be in charge. They clearly meant business.

"Lech Hammond?"

"Right."

"Dan Worthing?"

"Barely."

"Rathbone Barstow?"

"That's me."

"I am Captain Turchin from the Committee for State Security. All three of you are under arrest."

Worthing had gone white, and Hammond did not feel much better.

"What are the charges?"

"The charges will be discussed later."

"I demand to know why I'm being arrested," Worthing insisted.

Turchin's lip curled. "You don't demand anything. Prisoners do as they are told."

Two uniforms closed on Hammond. A gun butt was jabbed hard between his shoulder blades. "Move, you scum."

Worthing and Barstow were receiving the same treatment. Like Hammond, they had two uniforms apiece as an escort.

Captain Turchin barked at his three remaining goons. "Upstairs! Search their rooms; bring all of their luggage and anything else that you might find."

The newsmen were hustled outside, where four electric carts were waiting. The prisoners were placed in separate carts, each sandwiched between his escorts. Hammond's brain was racing. There had to be a way out. The problem was that he could not think of one. There was something very humiliating about being so helpless. He glanced at the KGB goons on either side of him. They both had faces of Slavic stone, flint eyes under bushy brows, pug noses, and flat slab cheekbones. There would be nothing forthcoming from them except more jabs from their machine pistols. He imagined that they enjoyed their work.

The tunnels of Vostok were all but deserted. Here and there a night crew was making repairs, and a robot street cleaner moved grindingly down the Dzerzhinsky Gallery, sucking up the debris of the day. Hammond could not help feeling that he was part of that debris. The procession of carts turned into a long descending ramp that seemed to run down into the very bowels of the planet. At the bottom there was a set of heavy-duty steel gates. A sign announced in both Spanish and Russian that entry was strictly forbidden. Hammond could not imagine that anyone in his right mind would casually wander down the long sinister ramp. It was like the path to hell. As the first electric cart approached, the gates slid open with an ominous rasp of metal on metal.

"Abandon hope all ye—"

"Silence!" the KGB goon on his left snarled at him.

Beyond the gates there was an area that seemed to operate as a subterranean parking lot and battery-charging station for more of the electric carts. Hammond, however, was not given a chance to look around. His escorts quickly dragged him from the cart and frog-marched him into a brightly lit holding area. It had the same bare light panels, dirty walls, and the smell of desperation found in prisons everywhere. The boots of the guards crashed echoingly on the concrete floor. The air was filled with a concerto of heavy footsteps and screaming voices. The guards seemed to feel the need to address their charges in something between a scream and a bellow. Signs, again in Russian and Spanish, proclaimed that talking was prohibited and that the possession of contraband was a punishable offense. They did not specify what constituted contraband. A handful of other, terrified-looking prisoners was being processed in. All but one had been stripped naked. It seemed that once a person was in the hands of the KGB, not even the slightest retention of dignity was permitted.

Hammond was quickly joined by Worthing and Barstow. One of the goons who had come in with Hammond pointed to a yellow line painted on the floor.

"Stand on the line and don't move."

A sergeant in his shirtsleeves sauntered over. He was carrying a meter-long billy club and looked eager to use it.

"So what do we have here?"

"Captain Turchin's prisoners."

The sergeant nodded slowly and walked around the three of them.

"You men are in a lot of trouble. We don't like spies here in Vostok." He stepped close to Worthing. "What's the matter? Nothing to say?" Worthing did not rise to the bait, and the sergeant stepped back. "Okay, strip off, pile your clothes on the floor in front of you, ready for inspection."

For the next hour they were put through the introductory mill, which ranged from retinal printing to rectal inspection. At the end of the process the KGB knew more about them than they probably knew themselves, and they were left in no doubt that in that place they were nothing more than lumps of meat headed for the grinder. At the start they were embarrassed, avoiding one another's eyes and covering their genitals with their hands. By the end they had ceased to care. Dignity went fast while one was strapped to a bodyscan or bending over and spreading one's buttocks to be probed by a rubber-sheathed mass detector.

"Okay, back on the yellow line."

Their clothes were gone, presumably taken to be searched somewhere else. As they stood back on the line, a pair of metal double doors at the far end of the holding area crashed open. Two KGB men came through, dragging a limp body between them. It was Angel Ramos. He looked as though he had been beaten half to death. His hair and beard were matted with blood, and there were circular electrode burns on each temple.

The sergeant laughed. "Now there's a coincidence. Isn't that your amigo they're bringing through?"

Hammond was certain that their being allowed to see Ramos and the condition he was in was no coincidence.

"Don't waste any pity on him," they were told. "You may well be a lot worse off when the major's finished with you."

For the next two hours they stood on the yellow line, naked and scared. The KGB men who had brought them in went about their business; although the sergeant with the billy club still prowled the holding area, treating it like his very own sadist's domain, he paid the three of them no more particular attention. Hammond was certain that the waiting period was specifically designed to let fear, confusion, and depersonalization act on the prisoners—but the knowledge of what was being done to him did nothing to inhibit its effectiveness. No matter how many times he told himself it was all part of the psych job, he could not fight down the feeling of sick apprehension that was close to overwhelming him. He kept telling himself that not even the new hard-line KGB would be so dumb as to shoot or imprison a world-famous TV journalist. The problem was that he did not find himself at all convincing.

At some point during the waiting period more prisoners were brought in and made to wait on the line. There were women among the intake. It seemed that the KGB ran an equal-opportunity nightmare. Hammond thought he recognized some of the faces from the Aquarium Café, but he could not be certain. Apparently KGB headquarters was having a busy night. Every ten minutes or so a fresh batch of prisoners was brought in under escort. Hammond could not imagine that every night was like that. If it was, the whole settlement would have been cleared out within a month. He had to assume that some sort of major sweep was going on.

The double doors through which Ramos had earlier been dragged swung open again, and a group of plainclothes agents came swaggering through. They stopped to inspect the prisoners and subject them to a barrage of abuse and ominous gallows humor. One of them seemed to be paying particular attention to Dan Worthing. Hammond thought he had seen the man before. Had he been one of their shadows? The agent appeared to be trying to pinpoint Worthing in his own memory.

"Don't I know you?"

Worthing played it safe and remained silent.

The agent glared at him. "I asked you a question."

"Do I have permission to answer?"

"You damn well better."

Worthing shook his head. "I don't think that you could know me. I'm not from around here."

Hammond suddenly recalled where he had seen the man before. He was the one from the station, the one Worthing had called down. In almost the same instant, the KGB man must have recognized Worthing. He jabbed a finger into the Englishman's chest.

"Sure I know you. You're the bastard that had so much to say for himself at the station the other night. You're ours now, English, and you can forget your fancy airs. The Havana Convention isn't going to help you here. Turn around."

Worthing looked as though he were going to throw up, but he did as he was told. The agent produced a small leather-covered sap from his coat pocket. Calmly, he slapped it a couple of times in the palm of his hand.

Hammond opened his mouth to warn Worthing. "Danny . . ."

The agent glared at him and then, with great deliberation, turned back to Worthing and hit him hard across the kidneys. Worthing screamed and dropped to his knees.

The agent smiled nastily. "That'll teach you to keep your mouth shut."

The sergeant was on his way over, swinging his club threateningly. "What's going on here?"

The agent from the station slipped the sap back into his pocket. "Just settling a score, Sarge."

The sergeant nodded. "Just don't mark them too badly. They belong to Melikov." He turned in Hammond's direction. "Did I hear you speak just now?"

Hammond stiffened. "I . . ."

"Talking is forbidden."

Hammond decided to say nothing. The sergeant hauled off and hit him hard across the thighs with his club. The pain shock exploded through his entire nervous system. His left leg went numb and would no longer hold him up. He crumpled to the ground beside Worthing. The sergeant immediately began to yell at them. The glint of relish in his eyes was strictly that of a psychopath.

"Get up, you miserable little worms. On your fucking feet. You don't lie around on the floor in here."

Painfully, they both stood up. The sergeant seemed to be considering what injury he might next inflict on them. Before he could subject them to any other unpleasantness, however, a large group of KGB men came into the holding area. The whisper immediately went around: "Melikov." Irina Orlov, Hammond remembered, had mentioned Melikov. The KGB major was the leader of the novostroika movement in the settlement and apparently was greatly feared. He was easy to spot by the way everyone deferred to him. Physically he was unimpressive, but Hammond reminded himself that neither Tamerlane nor Himmler had been much to look at. Likewise J. Edgar Hoover. Melikov was a short, slightly balding man with red hair and the kind of blotchy, freckled skin that so often went with it. A black cigarette holder was clamped between his teeth.

To Hammond's horror, the major was walking directly toward them. The sergeant came to attention and saluted.

Melikov looked him up and down. "I hope you're not damaging my prisoners."

The sergeant took on the look of a robot. "No, sir. Just routine discipline, sir. They seem to have a little difficulty accepting their status as prisoners."

Melikov's smile was cold. "That's understandable, Sergeant. These three think they're important men where they come from. They work for Fox Global News and have connections in Tokyo."

"I wasn't aware we had such prominent guests."

"I think they may need a little reeducation before they leave here. They're not quite as prominent as they think they are." He gestured to two of the agents who had arrived with him. "Get them clothes and bring them to me. I'll be in Interrogation Room 14."

They were given only shirts and pants, no shoes or belts; although it was infinitely better than being naked, they still felt like fourth-class citizens as they shuffled, barefoot, with their hands in their pockets, holding up their pants. Interrogation Room 14 was everything Hammond might have expected. It was white and bare, with an easily swabbed down plastic tile floor, and about the only encouraging point was that no obvious instruments of torture were evident, with the possible exception of a mobile MRG scanner mounted on a wheeled dolly. The pilot LEDs still glowed on the ominous headset, and Hammond wondered if it had been used on Ramos. The MRG was officially supposed to be employed only as a physical reaction gauge, but an illegally adapted machine could be set to overload, causing excruciating pain and even actual skin burns for whoever was clamped into the headset. The overload modification could not actually be blamed on the Russians, and their use of it was by no means exclusive. It had originally been the result of an unholy collaboration between BOSS and the CIA in the days of horror immediately prior to the South African Civil War.

Melikov was sitting behind a bare desk. There was an ashtray, a pack of Zimbabwe Marlboros, and an antique Zippo lighter in front of him. Three large spotlights on stands behind him pointed straight ahead. There was another yellow line painted on the floor.

"On the line, please."

Hammond, Worthing, and Barstow stood in a row. Melikov reached for a concealed switch under the desk. The room lights dimmed. There was a brief flare of a lighter flame as Melikov lit a cigarette, and then the spotlights blazed into life, blinding the prisoners.

Melikov let them cook under the lights for a full minute before he spoke. "Hammond, who instructed you to make contact with Angel Ramos?" he asked finally.

Hammond shuffled his feet. "I don't know what you're talking about."

"Please keep still. If you continue to move around, I will have you placed in restraints."

"I'm sorry."

Smoke from Melikov's cigarette drifted into the beams of the spotlights.

"I'll repeat the question. Who instructed you to contact Angel Ramos?"

"Nobody instructed me to contact him. He called me on an open phone line and invited me to see the Cuban section and the hydroponic dome. That was the extent of our meeting. I don't believe there was anything illegal in that."

"You're a liar, Hammond. We have the tape of your conversation with Ramos. You were soliciting information on a classified military installation. That's espionage, Hammond."

Hammond spread his hands. "That's ridiculous. We discussed the possibility of there being some kind of alien spacecraft in the desert. That's hardly stealing military secrets."

"Please keep still. I shan't warn you again."

There was a long silence. Hammond's legs were starting to ache. Melikov sat at his ease, smoking one cigarette after another.

"Do you deny that you're an operative of the Central Intelligence Agency?"

Hammond wished him incurable bronchial cancer. "Of course I deny it. It's absurd. I'm a major broadcast news reporter. There would be no reason for me to compromise myself by working for the CIA or anyone else."

Melikov swiveled in his chair and stared at Barstow. "But you do, don't you, Barstow? You work for the CIA."

Hammond wanted to kick himself. He should have seen the switch coming. Of course Barstow had worked for the CIA. For all Hammond knew, the cameraman might still be technically on the payroll. The Volman Act may have cut Langley out of off-world operations, but that did not mean the company was content to accept blissful ignorance.

Barstow hesitated before answering. When he did, his voice sounded strained. "I've done jobs for a lot of people in my time, the CIA included. It's not easy being a free-lance cameraman. You can get into some strange situations."

"And this is one of them?"

Barstow shook his head. "The only organization that I'm working for now is Global News."

"But you were attempting to obtain Soviet military secrets."

"We were doing a story on prostitute murders."

"What did Angel Ramos have to do with prostitute murders?"

Hammond stepped in. "We were simply following up on the alien spaceship story."

Melikov lit yet another cigarette. "I wasn't talking to you, Hammond."

"I'm in charge of this crew. Barstow was working for me."

"I don't intend to warn you again, Hammond. Answer the question, Barstow."

"It's like he said. I just worked the camera. I don't know anything about Angel Ramos."

"You normally tape discussions about restricted military research stations?"

"I point my camera at what I'm told. I mean, Jesus Christ, if we were spies, do you really think we'd put everything on uncoded tape?"

"Who knows what else you've been doing?"

"You must. You had agents following us everywhere."

"Are you afraid, Barstow?"

"Sure I'm afraid. I'm a prisoner of the KGB. Anyone would be afraid."

Melikov slowly exhaled. He picked up his Zippo and tapped it thoughtfully on the desktop. "Perhaps we should start using the MRG to get down to the full extent of your criminal activities."

Nobody spoke. Melikov continued to tap with his lighter, allowing time for the threat of torture to sink in.

"You realize I could have all three of you shot?"

Worthing spoke for the first time. "That would be a very bad public relations move."

He was still blinded by the lights, and so it was impossible to see how Melikov was reacting.

Melikov put down the lighter. His voice was very quiet. "I'm not particularly interested in public relations."

"It would hardly be a good idea to shoot three members of the international press on trumped-up charges."

"These are hardly trumped-up charges."

"You know we aren't spies."

"I don't know what you are. That's what we're here to find out."

"You must have received reports on everything we've done since we've been here. You know we're legitimate newsmen."

"Are you lecturing me, Worthing? I understand you attempted to educate one of my men on the Oslo and Havana conventions."

Worthing did not answer.

"Are you afraid of me, Worthing?"

"I know I'm in a very precarious situation."

"That's one way of putting it."

For another hour the interrogation went around and around, but although Melikov threatened them twice more with the MRG, he made no attempt to use it. The muscles in Hammond's legs were screaming for him to be allowed to sit, but he was starting to suspect that Melikov was not doing anything but trying to scare the hell out of them. For the first time since they had been roused from their beds, he felt a ray of hope. That hope crystallized when, without any warning, Melikov cut the spotlights and brought up the room lighting. He sat smoking reflectively. The tapping of the Zippo started again. The moment of truth had to be coming.

"I have considered your case, and I have decided to be lenient."

Hammond's legs were threatening to give way. He could imagine that Worthing was in even worse shape.

Melikov took a Marlboro from the pack and turned it between his fingers. "Although I find you the worst scum of the corrupt capitalist media and would personally have you shot, I do not see that it would serve the interests of the Soviet people. I have more important matters to deal with than mere public relations, but I certainly don't wish to give a propaganda weapon to the governments and corporations that conspire against us. Accordingly, you will be expelled from this settlement and banned from all Soviet installations on this planet. If you attempt to enter any area of Soviet Mars, you will be arrested and subject to the most severe penalties. In addition, your tapes and camera will be confiscated. I would also strongly advise you to forget all about this alien nonsense. There is no alien spaceship on Olympus Mons. Indeed, this is the main reason I'm letting you go. Anyone who listens to ravings of a psychotic Cuban criminal cannot be that much of a threat."

Melikov placed the Marlboro in his mouth and thumbed the lighter. It was a gesture of dismissal.

U.S. Marine Corps Martian CySec center, Fort Haigh—
May 20 CEC—11:01 MST.

They were all gathered in the main briefing room. The order had come suddenly, giving them just one hour's notice. All officers from captain up and all CAs with grades above A-4 would assemble in the main briefing room at eleven hundred. No exceptions. As the soldiers and civilians filed into the big underground room with its podium, projection screen, and rows of hard plastic chairs, there was a feeling of suppressed excitement in the air. Something was going down. It was an excitement that John Greig was not able to share. If there was indeed some kind of flap about to break, it might prove a disaster for him. He had already felt the entity move in its sleep. It was still dormant, but he could perceive its form in his mind. That was always the first warning. In a matter of days, certainly no longer than a week, it would wake—and after the initial bout of confusion that always accompanied its arousal, it would begin demanding a victim. If the base went to emergency status during the time the entity was making its demands, he would have no chance, no freedom of movement. He would not even be able to go and hunt in Burroughs, only an hour away on the monorail. He could not imagine what the entity might do if it were denied a victim for much more than seventy-two hours. Unfortunately, he could all too easily imagine what would happen if the entity forced him to take a victim there on the base.

Conversation died as General Elijah walked into the briefing room, flanked by Colonel Osberg, the head of CySec, and Majors Haskins and Schofield. The fact that Elijah was there confirmed that the assembly had definitely not been called for some routine announcement. The military men and women came to attention, and the civilian advisers got to their feet. Elijah held up a hand.

"Please sit, gentlemen. We have no time to waste."

General Saud Elijah was a legend in his own time. Rising through the ranks during the horrendous Yemeni Police Action, he had clawed his way through the Borgia intrigues of the Pentagon. His leadership of the UN peace force at the siege of Cape Town had put him beyond the reach of the enemies who had sent him there in the first place, hoping that he would bury himself. Instead, he had pulled off the brilliant evacuation and rearguard action that had made him the first Muslim general in the history of the corps. If anyone was perfectly suited to be virtual warlord of Mars, it was Saud Elijah.

His style was to come straight to the point. "For the last three to four hours we have been receiving reports from Vostok and other Soviet settlements. It would appear that there is something going on that is little short of a political purge. In Vostok the militia has been virtually dismantled, and a number of its officers are reportedly being shipped to the polar base at Vorkuta. There has been a general rounding up of undesirables. We also have a single unconfirmed report of some kind of siege situation in the Cuban section. Lon Casey, the marshal of Burroughs, one of his deputies, three reporters, and thirteen other Americans have been expelled from the settlement. It would seem as though the KGB has decided to consolidate its position. Although they don't appear to have taken complete control, they have plainly moved a good deal closer to that objective. Fortunately, General Lysenko remains overall military commander, and at least for the moment the moderate group of colonels is still in control of their units. This is not, however, to underestimate the danger of the situation. Any increase in the influence of the hard-liners has got to have a negative effect on the precarious balance by which we coexist on this planet. I have accordingly placed all bases on first-phase alert until further notice."

He paused while his officers digested the information. For Greig, it was the worst possible news. First-phase alert meant that he would be confined to the base. The sleeping entity was heavy in his mind, like an oppressive, clinging fog bank.

Then Elijah was speaking again. "The purpose of the United States Marines is not to sit passively behind a real or imagined defensive readiness. If there is anything we can do to harry, contain, or demoralize the KGB, if we can exacerbate the situation between them and the Cubans or drive further wedges between the hard-liners and the moderates, this is the time to do it. Plainly, any moves that we make against the KGB in Vostok would be, by nature of the emergency, covert operations, and I don't think I have to tell you in CySec that you will be in the spearhead of this endeavor. CySec will be at operational status from now on. I want maximized input and optimum effort. This may well be our best chance to check the rise of hardline communism on Mars. You will be broken down into task groups and briefed on specifics. Are there any questions?''

General Elijah did not welcome questions. The offer was pure rhetoric, and everyone in the room knew it. He slowly looked around the assembled faces and smiled. General Saud Elijah had one large gold tooth on the very front of his upper set.

''To put it plainly, gentlemen, I want you to ratfuck the KGB until its sphincter bleeds.''

As everyone rose to go, Greig continued to sit. There seemed to be no scenario for his future that did not lead to something unthinkable. After a moment he caught himself. He quickly stood up and followed the others. He would remain normal to the last. It was his sole source of pride.

FOUR

"I'M NOT SURE THAT YOU REALLY APPRECIATE WHAT GOING up the North Pole Trail would mean."

"From what you're saying, it's a freezing cold spaghetti western without air."

"That's kind of facile."

Hammond could not quite believe that Worthing actually seemed to be trying to dissuade him from following the story to its logical conclusion.

"For Christ's sake, Danny, what the fuck do you want me to do? File the story from this hotel room?"

"Why don't you concentrate on the KGB expansion story and forget about this Olympus Mons business until some of the dust has settled?"

"Concentrate on what? Press handouts and the odd tidbit from your source in marine intelligence?"

"That's what the other stringers are doing."

"That's exactly why we should be doing something else. I didn't come who knows how many million miles to sit in the bar of the Hilton Hotel. I'm not a stringer, I'm Lech Hammond, goddamn it!"

Worthing got up to pour himself a drink. The argument had

90

been going on half the morning, ever since the two men had met for breakfast in Hammond's suite.

"Listen, I'll run it by you one more time. It's close to two thousand kilometers over rough country. When we reach the trail, we're going to happen across a lot of very weird people—worse than that, there's going to be a lot of Russians. We have to assume that Melikov has the word out on us, and if we're spotted heading for Olympus Mons, they're liable to kill us out of hand. It's like that up the North Pole Trail. There's no law and order up there. We're quite likely to run into people who want to kill us just because they don't like the look of us."

"I still don't see why we can't assume some of the natural cover. It's only another field assignment. We've been in weird places before."

"We've been in weird places on Earth, but usually there was a war on and the press corps had a legitimate role. Out in the back we don't look like anything but greenhorns. I'm a lardass slick out of the settlements, and it shows. You're straight off the boat and can't even walk right. There's no way we can blend into the surroundings."

"We'll just have to try."

"You're really determined to do this, aren't you?"

Hammond nodded. "I'm not letting go of it without a struggle. I've got a reputation to think of."

Worthing shook his head in disbelief. "Damn it to hell. I don't want to get myself killed just to preserve your celebrity status."

"So stay behind."

Worthing sighed. "And let you go up there on your own?"

"If need be."

"Fuck you, Hammond, you know I'll be coming along. I suppose you want me to arrange the specifics. How soon do you want to leave?"

"Could we be ready in forty-eight hours?"

Worthing nodded. "If I push it."

"What about a cam jock? I guess Barstow won't be too keen after the last time."

"Barstow will do it. As far as he's concerned, we're the only poker game in town. He lives for the image drama, and he's a stress junkie. We're the only ones offering a fix. The real question is, Do you want him?''

''Do I want him?''

''He's the best we can get.''

''So I want him.''

''We'll also need a driver. Someone who knows the territory.''

''You have someone in mind?''

''There's a guy name of Travis, experienced outbacker. He'll do it. He may even keep us alive.''

Worthing started making calls. Hammond sagged back onto the couch. He still was not accustomed to sleeping in Mars gravity. Even though he had been in bed for the last twelve hours, he was still weary from the previous five days. After the interrogation by Melikov, the KGB had held them a further thirty-six hours before hustling them to the bullet train and, with further stern warnings never to return, dispatching them back to Burroughs. Casey and Chavez had also been on the train, also expelled by the Soviets. The ride back to the American settlement had been taken up by the kind of maudlin, angry drunk that was exclusive to men who felt they had been screwed, humiliated, and possibly outsmarted. Toward the end of the trip the Russian cabin attendant had come in for a good deal of unwarranted abuse.

Even after he had slept it off, Hammond was still angry. He had lost his tapes and had been run out of town with his tail between his legs. That kind of thing did not happen to Lech Hammond. Although he hated to admit it, his professional pride had been massively bruised, and it hurt like hell. The only response that would allow him to live with himself was to ignore Melikov's warning and get straight back on the case. It was not merely the same principle as climbing back on the horse after one had fallen off. Hammond was quite convinced that there was something of great importance up on Olympus Mons, and he wanted to find out what it was. It might not have been anything as exotic as an alien artifact, but he had a powerful gut feeling, over and above bruised pride, that the Soviets were hiding something up there that needed to be revealed to the world. All through his career he had gone with his gut feelings, and despite Worthing's protests, he was not about to stop.

It was partly pride that had prevented him from reporting back to Tokyo about what had happened. He certainly did not want the front office to know that he had screwed up so abjectly his first time out on Mars. He was also motivated by a good deal of pragmatism. The corporation already had its own problems with the Russians. The hard-liners were doing their best to shut down the main satellite feeds, and the situation was, to say the least, precarious. If they knew that he intended to go toe to toe with the KGB, they might very well attempt a measure of remote braking.

Worthing's first move was to rent a small storage dome out on the surface, in the direction of the spaceport, where he started assembling supplies for their journey. His first and most important purchase was a vehicle—a twin-pod White Marsman with front and back electrorotary engines and huge flexible steel-cage wheels. Solar panels on the roof recharged the power batteries during the hours of daylight. Outwardly it did not look like much—a sand-scarred tan paint job had made it appear to be on its last legs, and Hammond had questioned just how long it was supposed to hold up in the desert. Worthing had patiently explained how the exterior had been deliberately aged, while the engines, the electronics, and the life support were all working perfectly. He and Travis seemed highly pleased with the purchase.

Travis was a spare leathery individual from the badlands of Kentucky. His family was probably of coal-mining stock, and his sweat-stained cowboy hat appeared to be a permanent fixture. He spat in the dust before he shook hands with Hammond.

"It may look funky, but it'll get us anywhere we want to go. It even has a turn of speed if we get into trouble. If anyone sees us, they'll probably assume that we're nothing but down at the heels indie prospectors. With luck, they'll also assume that we're not worth robbing. Only a damned fool goes up the north pole in a factory-fresh rig."

The vehicle had one further deterrent against marauders in its small concealed weapons system: .40-caliber miniguns, mounted fore and aft, that commanded a 360-degree sweep of the surrounding landscape.

By the second day of preparations, a stream of packages was being delivered to the small dome. Worthing was treating the whole thing like an unscheduled Christmas.

Hammond watched with some amazement. "Do we really need all this stuff? Anyone would think we were going up the Amazon."

Worthing grinned. "Believe me, going up the Amazon is a stroll in the park compared to what we're planning."

"And what's all this costing the company?"

"Plenty. Even with your track record, we'd better come out of this with something to show, or you're going to be the biggest journalistic nonevent since Geraldo Rivera opened Al Capone's vault."

The most dramatic delivery had come when an unmarked flatbed had rolled up carrying three coffin-shaped crates. Rat Barstow had turned up at the same time.

"What in hell are those?"

"Our suits."

"Really? Let's get them uncrated and take a look."

Travis and Barstow prized open the first case and hauled out the suit. Hammond had expected some state-of-the-art number straight off a supply ship, maybe one of the new General Dynamics softsuits. The one Travis was holding up was a Straus, solid polymer armor, maybe five years old, and as beat up as the Marsman. Originally it must have been a bright scarlet, but it had been sun-bleached to the color of old dried blood. A flat triangular crest curved over the top of the helmet, and an equally faded love-bomb bikini babe had somewhere along the line been airbrushed across the chestplate.

Hammond slowly lowered his raised eyebrows. "Only a damned fool goes up to the north pole in a factory-fresh suit?"

Travis nodded. His face was impassive. "You're starting to get the idea."

Hammond wondered if Travis was the man's first or last name. Later he would learn that it was a leftover from the time when the surface vehicle handlers, the truck drivers of Mars, had gone in for naming themselves after characters from classic motion pictures. The outbacker had worn a Mohican and called himself Travis Bickel back then. The vehicle handlers still used a lot of phony names. Most stayed constantly one jump ahead of a string of safety violations that, if they ever had to be paid, would bankrupt them.

Hammond ran a hand over the suit. It had been worn to a high sheen by years of Martian sand. "Who's expected to wear this?"

Worthing kept a totally straight face. "You are. It's yours."

"Picking my clothes for me now, are you?"

"It was all they had in your size."

The next suit was brought out. It was an old Honda Startrooper, reinforced plastic plate with rubber joints. The custom knife-blade crest on the helmet was designed to give the wearer the look of a conquistador. It was finished in dark blue with burgundy trim.

"Who gets this one?"

Worthing smiled. "I do."

"Very dashing."

"I just got lucky."

"I hope those rubber joints are good."

"All new. I saw to it myself."

The third suit was a bulky Zil that had been sprayed black with a suede finish. Large metal studs had been bonded to the torso and arms and along the leg seams. The helmet had been chromed.

Barstow look at it dubiously. "Is that mine?"

Worthing nodded. "Your very own."

"I'm not sure I want to look like a leather queen."

"There's method in this madness. The studs hide no less than four minicams. They can run auto or be controlled by a neck ring in the helmet."

"Pretty slick, although I still think I'm going to get weird offers in the bars."

After letting the three of them have a few minutes to examine their suits, Travis called them to order. "Okay, here's what we're going to do. We'll all suit up and go voidside to surface-test these suckers. Make sure you all know where your slap-on patches are stored. They're the only things that'll save you if you spring a leak.''

Travis vanished inside the Marsman. He emerged five minutes later wearing a suit so customized that it was a piece of folk art. It more than amply demonstrated the outbackers' traditional attitude to their suits. An outbacker lived in the thing for the majority of his working life, and that life was completely dependent on it. The obsessive customizing was a form of bonding between a man and his life support. The human did his very best to make the austere hardware something personal, something that reflected his personality. In many respects it was just like the old-time mountain men beading their buckskins. Decorations were totems against a scarcely known and hostile environment. Travis's suit was a GE Bodytight, but much of it was concealed by a sleeveless duster he wore over the top of it. Most of the work had gone into the helmet. It was covered by a camouflage net held in place by a wide snakeskin band. Trailing feathers, crystals, and silver coins were sewn on and woven into the net. The suit changed the withdrawn Martian cowboy into a primitive spacegoing Indian. Hammond realized that if Travis was any measure of the norm out on the desert trails of Mars— and he had no reason to think that he was not—the newsmen would not look at all outlandish in their secondhand pressure armor.

Travis checked each of their suits' seals and made sure the heat and air systems were on-line. ''Don't be putting no blind faith in the suit computer. Check everything before you hit the void. For the duration of this mission we'll work it on the buddy system. Hammond and Worthing will check each other, and so will me and Barstow. I want it to be second nature. Always check each other.''

Hammond peered at Worthing through the faceplate of the red pressure suit. ''You better watch your drinking.''

Assured that the suit radios were functioning, Travis shepherded his party of what he clearly thought of as greenhorns to the air lock.

U.S. Marine Corps Martian CySec center, Fort Haigh—
May 24 CEC—14:45 MST.

"It's defended. You've never seen such ice. Thick crude Russian ice that there's no way to gimmick through, short of a full kamikaze."

"That's why we have to go in with a patrol."

Whittaker slowly nodded. "A two-person cyber team and a rambo."

Colonel Osberg pursed his lips. "The corps doesn't refer to them as that. We prefer the designation HT7. The term 'rambo' is something the media cooked up."

Whittaker returned his stare. "A rose by any other name. I hadn't realized there were any rambos on Mars."

"We don't exactly advertise the fact."

The three of them were alone in the small windowless office. It was prepped for security, and they knew they could speak freely.

"I also thought the HT conversion process had been outlawed by the Spanio McLaine Act."

"That's why we have them on Mars."

Whittaker pushed her hair out of her face. "I'm sorry, Colonel, but I don't know about all this. A field operation is well out of the normal range of my experience. I'm a technician, not a commando."

Osberg did not take her reluctance particularly well. He came from the same blood-and-guts background as Elijah.

"I realize that since you're a civilian adviser, I can't order you into the field, but we badly need to know what the opposition is up to out on Olympus Mons. As part of the backup team, you'd be doing a major service to both the Marine Corps and your country. Damn it, woman, I'm not ordering you into combat." He looked at Greig. "You're very quiet. Do you feel the same way?"

Greig started, realizing that he had been totally preoccupied, lost in his own mounting fears, and had missed a large part of the conversation. He quickly shook his head. "No, I'll go. I don't mind. It'll be refreshing to work on a practical problem for a change."

All Greig cared about was that he had been offered a chance to get off the base before the entity forced his mind to the wild place. Any potential danger on the mission paled into insignificance beside what the entity could do if driven to extremes of unrequited blood love.

Whittaker looked at him in amazement. "You'll go? Just like that? Half the way up the North Pole Trail and then try and infiltrate a secret Russian base? Are you crazy, Greig? We're not marines. Let some of them go."

Greig knew why he and Judy Whittaker had been selected for the mission. Whittaker was good, but she was also one of the principal jocks among the CySec staff, star of the track team and the gym. She had more than enough stamina for scrambling around in the desert. Although he kept himself reasonably fit with solitary workouts, Greig was no jock. He was simply the best ratfucker they had. He faced Whittaker calmly.

"There really isn't that much risk involved. A surface journey of that length and duration can be hazardous, but we'll have an HT7 for protection."

Greig found that he was starting to be able to divide his mind into separate layers, a sure sign that the entity was ready to wake. While he talked rationally to Whittaker, a second part of him was fantasizing how he might slip away from the team somewhere along the trail and make the kill.

Whittaker was still looking at him as though she did not believe he was real. "God, you're a cold fish."

"I just try to be objective."

The colonel grunted. "A little more objectivity on your part might not be a bad thing, CA Whittaker."

Greig went on. "Even when we reach the object, we would hold off at a very safe distance. The HT7 would be taking all the risks. Our job is to monitor and control, not to make a frontal assault. The infiltration we'd be doing would be strictly cybernetic."

"We could always run into a Russian patrol."

"I'm sure we'll be given a cover team to run interference and make sure we get away safely." Greig was actually sure that Osberg had not intended to use such a team at all, but it was worth a try.

The colonel hesitated. "I suppose that might be possible."

Whittaker was still resisting. Greig sensed, however, that she had started to waver. In the end she would go with them.

"If I don't volunteer for this mission, are there likely to be any repercussions?"

The colonel gave her a cold look. "Of course not. Refusing to volunteer isn't a crime, it's a right. How people might interpret the fact in the future when they see it on your record is entirely up to them."

Judy Whittaker looked angry. "You're really trying to pressure me into this."

"Only because you're the best qualified."

Whittaker was silent for a long time. "It's not that I'm afraid. It's the idea of a rambo. Even the thought of one of those things disturbs me."

"They're not things. They're just ordinary soldiers with a few adaptations."

Whittaker's eyebrows shot up. "A few adaptations? Those things are a mess of grafts, implants, steroid growth, and God knows what else. They're Frankenstein jobs. They're . . . weird." The final word came out as a shudder.

"Have you ever been in the same room as one?"

"No, but—"

"You'll get used to him very quickly. His name is Booth, by the way. He normally works in the warehouse section. No one in his company suspects that he's anything but big, strong, and dumb."

Greig had a moment of anxiety. "Dumb? But I thought . . ."

"In fact, he's highly intelligent, but he has to maintain a certain cover."

Whittaker was frowning again. Finally she sighed. "Okay, I'll go, but there better be a backup team ready to haul us out at the first sign of trouble. And I want a damn great bonus for this."

Osberg smiled. "A bonus can be arranged."

She looked at Greig and shook her head. "Him, me, and a rambo. This is going to be some trip."

As she stood up to leave, a thought occurred to the other part of Greig's mind. If worse came to worst, Whittaker might suffice as the victim.

*Federal Building, Burroughs Settlement—May 24 CEC—
17:06 MST.*

Chavez came through the door clutching a swatch of printouts. "I've been doing some checking."

Casey was lying back with his Stetson pulled down over his
eyes and his boots up on the desk. He pushed back his hat and
focused on Chavez. "And?"

"I think I've actually made a little progress. On the hooker
murders."

"That would make a change."

"Am I supposed to take that personally?"

Casey swung his boots off the desk. "Hell, no. None of us
has performed too outstandingly over the last few days. So what
have you got?"

Chavez spread out the printouts on the desktop that had been
so recently vacated by Casey's lizardskin Tony Lamas. "Okay,
you remember how we tried to get a breakdown from Marine
CySec to see if any of their wunderkinds was away from his
post or on leave or absent for any other reason at the times of
the murders?"

Casey nodded. "And the marines refused to play ball. I spoke
to Elijah himself. He said that the release of that kind of information to civilian authority would compromise his entire operating procedure. He sounded like my asking was an invasion of
his personal privacy."

Chavez grinned. "After that, I started thinking. Maybe there
was another way to get this information. Would it be on file
anywhere that wasn't as well secured as the CySec personnel
records?"

"I assumed that there was one from the way you're gloating."

"They get paid."

Casey peered at Chavez from under his eyebrows. "Say that
again."

"They get paid. They have pay records. Everyone's such a
glutton for data these days that I figured that absences, official
and otherwise, might well be attached to the basic pay records,
along with overtime and sick benefits and all the rest of it."

Casey nodded. "That makes sense, although I doubt the marines would volunteer their payroll information, either."

Chavez avoided Casey's eyes. Casey knew what was coming next.

"You cut a couple of corners?"

"Just in the interests of the investigation."

"It would make any information, to say the least, a little extralegal."

"Hell, chief, I was just looking for background, not evidence," Chavez protested.

"Okay, okay, enough of the disclaimers, there are only the two of us here. What did you get?"

Chavez held up a hand. "You got to realize I didn't do this myself. There's a bright boy over in the MarCo computer section that I work out with at the gym. I just gave him a few ideas, and he followed them up. It's not my fault if he stepped over the line a little in the process. You know how these guys are. They live in a world of their own."

Casey slowly closed his eyes. "Just covering your tracks there, Ray?"

"I figure it pays to be discreet."

"So what was the outcome of all this covert hacking around?"

"Well, first of all, this buddy of mine goes directly into the paymaster files, but they were too well covered. So then he decides to take one individual and backtrack through his bank. He figured that there was probably an interface between the bank and the pay office that he could bluff his way through."

Casey sat up, eyes wide. "You went into the banking system?"

"In a kind of oblique way. It's really very simple. Something ought to be done about their lack of security."

"Do you know what you and your good buddy could get for that, oblique or otherwise?"

Chavez looked down at his hands. "About four years. But that's only if we were detected. We weren't."

"What happened?"

"To make a long story short, we've got three names: Timothy Earle Brookes, Adam Katz, and John Whipple Greig. They were all away from the base for all of the murders."

Casey was interested. "I guess it's a start."

Chavez rubbed his chin. He needed a shave. "Well, let's not get carried away. It may be a start. They're all covered for at least one of the murders. Brookes was sick in a Bradbury hospital, Katz was on an organized climb of Arsia Mons, and Greig was twice on assignment. So there's no single one that's a complete suspect."

Casey was thoughtful. "Any one of those alibi incidents could be a plant. We know that our boy is a master at backdating. It seems to me that the next thing we have to do is have a talk with this trio. How would your workout buddy feel about running the same kind of check on the men in his own department?"

"I think he'd probably balk. I'll try and figure out another way around it."

"So when do we talk to these marines?"

"Actually, one of them—Greig—isn't a marine. He's a civilian adviser."

"When do we get to talk to them?"

"There's a problem there. We can't get to them."

"Why the hell not?"

"The base is on alert since the start of this KGB business. Nobody in, nobody out."

"At least they aren't going anywhere."

"Nothing we can do but wait."

Casey looked down at the printouts on the desk. "Any word about what's happening in Vostock?"

Chavez shook his head. "Nothing new." He smiled knowingly. "You worried about Chief Investigator Orlov?"

Casey glanced up and caught the smile. He gave Chavez a hard look. "Yes, I am."

Soviet Ground Transport K197 on the North Pole Trail, ninety kilometers out from Vostok—May 24 CEC—19:17 MST.

There was more than five thousand kilometers to go, over some of the least hospitable terrain on the planet. It could take them up to two weeks to get there. The crawler lurched and swayed along at a steady twenty k. The seat was hard, and there was a smell of anxiety, even dread, in the chill, chemical air. Irina Orlov stared out through the dirty window at the Martian darkness. The sun had gone down in the fast, almost nonexistent sunset, and neither of the moons was visible, but the starfields did throw enough light to give the passing landscape a faint, ghostly form. The only thing moving out there was a probing spotlight from the crawler itself as the guards in the observation dome on top of the second car scanned the area through which the transport was passing. Although the army boasted that it had complete control of the polar trail, it was not unknown for a transport to be attacked and hijacked. Although it was not likely that an attack would come while they were still so close to Vostok, the guards were still vigilant. There was a second purpose to the roving spotlight. It was supposedly looking for escaped prisoners who might have dropped off the train, although it was a mystery to Irina where an escaping prisoner would get a pressure suit. Whatever its real function, if any, the searchlight certainly gave the transport the air of a prison camp.

The transport was a very old K-class crawler, the kind that had been used for all transportation on Mars before the rail lines had been built. Now it only made the sad run to Vorkuta and the northern polar cap. It was made up of four heavy, rust-streaked cars joined by massive articulated steel couplings. Each one was supported by its own set of caterpillar tracks, but they shared a common low-yield pressure drive system. The lead car housed the control room, the crew, and the noninmate passengers. The second car was for the prisoners. It had a projecting skirt of razor wire, just above its tracks, that would slice the pressure suit of any prisoner trying to jump off. Like the searchlight, its effect was mainly psychological. There were no windows in the prison car from which a prisoner might jump. The third car contained cargo destined for the camp at Vorkuta and other points along the way. The rear car housed the turbine and the miniature cold reactor and its shielding.

An infectious sadness had boarded the crawler with the passengers. Except for the crew and maybe a handful of replacement guards, none of them could be sure that they would ever be coming back again. Even among the staff, the mortality rate at Vorkuta was frightening. At the most minimal, they were all leaving a way of life, and they could be fairly certain that they would never come back to anything quite the same.

There was a Red Army lieutenant over on the other side of the car who kept looking at her. He had a stupid arrogant face and she knew that she'd have trouble with him once he got drunk. She was also certain that he was the kind that would get drunk as soon as he could. Fortunately the strange hunched individual who'd been tagged with the name Igor and who sold the vodka, the tea, and the indescribably greasy snack food moved very slowly and would only serve one drink at a time so the process of getting drunk on the crawler, unless you'd brought your own booze, was a slow one. Irina had brought her own. She had brought a lot of things. Favorite books and microchips had been given away or stored with friends and her weight allowance had been devoted to dried food, vitamins, antibiotics, and the best vodka that she could find. As she'd been leaving, one of the air lock guards had offered to accidentally lose one of the prisoners' belongings so she could take an extra weight allowance and bring on more stuff. From the way he made the offer, it seemed like a routine scam on the Vorkuta run. She'd remembered how he'd grinned when she'd declined the offer. He'd seemed so confident that no one on their way to Vorkuta was going to report him and his racket.

"I wouldn't worry about them, Comrade Chief Investigator, back in the old days they used to make them walk up to the pole. This bunch has got it easy."

She had declined a second time. She did not doubt that she would learn enough corruption when she reached the camp. She did not want to start, however, before she had even left Vostok.

She thought about the bottle in her carry-on bag and sighed. Maybe that was the only way to handle the journey. It certainly had all the trappings of a slow ride into hell. She could stay drunk for as much of the journey as was humanly possible. What, after all, did she have to lose? She took her bag down from the overhead rack and pulled out the bottle. Yuri had given her six of them as a farewell gift. The rest were in her cases in the freight car. They were supposed to have come from a friend who made only small quantities and took fanatical trouble with his still.

Irina quickly learned that it was perhaps the vodka that she had to lose. The army lieutenant had spotted it and was coming across. He put a hand on the back of her seat and leaned over. His eyes were bloodshot, and his breath could have stripped paint. One day the army would have to learn that the policy of exiling the fools and failures to Mars was counterproductive. This idiot had probably spent the previous night bidding farewell to his buddies in any bar that had survived the purge of the Golodkin. He grinned at her, revealing an incomplete set of yellow teeth.

"Hello there, little lady. What do they call you?"

Irina looked him up and down. It was only his blind stupidity that stopped him from being frozen where he stood. "Most people of your rank call me sir," she said.

She was very put out when the grin did not falter. Instead, he dropped uninvited into the seat next to her.

"Don't give me that shit. You're on your way to Vorkuta, same as everyone else."

"I realize you're drunk, Lieutenant, and if you go back to your seat right now, I'll forget this whole incident."

He completely ignored her. "You're going to need a few friends, darling, when you get up on the eightieth parallel. I could be a real good friend to you."

"Please go back to your seat, Lieutenant."

He leaned closer and put a hand on her arm. "Why don't you just give me some of that vodka, and I'll tell you about all the things that I can do for you."

"Listen, asswipe, go back to your fucking seat or I'll call the commander of this bucket and have you put on a charge. You understand me?"

He half rose but then paused and leaned back toward her. She again caught the full blast of his grinning breath as he thrust his face into hers.

"Oh, yeah, I understand you, sweet thing, except I don't think you know what's going on. It's all mapped out. Before too long you're going to find yourself a prisoner, and when that happens, a babe who looks like you do will need all the friends she can get. You think about that—sir."

He lurched back to his own seat, along the way making a

remark she could not hear to another soldier. They both laughed. Irina took a hard hit of vodka. She should have been angry, but suddenly she was very frightened. Drunk as he was, the lieutenant was horribly plausible.

White Marsman, forty kilometers out from Burroughs on a 315 bearing—May 24 CEC—21:08 MST.

> If the whiskey starts working
> And the pain starts to ease,
> Then love lies there bleeding
> And becomes a disease . . .

The speakers were pumping out Rhet Holmes and his Jailhouse Nightingales, and Travis, bent forward over the big steering wheel, was singing right along with "Patsy Cline's Lighter." Country music was big on Mars.

> Can't beat out the fire,
> Can't extinguish the spark,
> And Patsy Cline's lighter
> Still flares in the dark.

There was something almost cozy about the cabin of the Marsman. In the time that they had had for the conversion, Worthing had spared no expense on the interior comforts. With the exception of Travis, who peered fixedly through the windshield as he sang and drove, they lounged back in deep blue velour contour chairs. The entertainment bank was state of the art, and the air system was brand new and circulated something that actually tasted like air. The bar was as well stocked as any bar on the red planet could hope to be, and their food supply had severely drained gourmet resources in Burroughs. The roof-mounted sweep scope showed nothing threatening. In fact, it showed nothing at all. Despite their previous trials, there was a definite feeling of well-being. They were admirably set up in their mobile home, and they were off on an adventure. Every now and then they were bounced around a bit, but for the most part the big cage wheels made for an excellent ride.

Travis turned in his seat. "For those of you who are interested, we're making a healthy fifty k, running parallel with the bullet track and a little to the north of it. I figure that we'll hold this course for the best part of tomorrow."

Hammond levered himself into a sitting position. With nothing to see beyond the Plexiglas, he had been stretched out, lost in his own thoughts. "You want to keep going nonstop?"

Travis nodded. "Hell, yes. We've got almost a day's worth of flat, boring bullshit to go through before there's anything at all—nothing to look at except stinking desert and the tip of Arsia Mons sticking up over the horizon. That's why we left after dark. I wanted to spare you guys a view that makes Nebraska look scenic. You know what I mean?"

Worthing swiveled in his chair and looked at Travis. "We left after dark because we wanted to sneak away like conspirators. That's the way we do things, we corporate ronin. Always creep-crawling around in the night."

Hammond looked offended. "Who are you calling ronin?"

Worthing was sitting in the shotgun position up beside Travis. The navigation console was in front of him, but he had become bored with playing with it quite soon after they had left Burroughs. Hammond and Barstow were in the rear positions, with no function except to sprawl and drink and watch the vid and, when the sun came up, look out the window.

Worthing swiveled around to face Hammond. "What makes you think that you're not ronin?"

Hammond blinked a couple of times. "I assumed I was something a little more elevated."

"Gajin ronin, dear boy. Just like Barstow and me. Only higher-priced."

"How do you figure that?"

"Tokyo isn't going to cradle-to-grave you any more than us. Once they have no more use for us, that's it. Benihana for leftovers."

Hammond shook his head. "You've got a weird attitude."

Barstow looked up. "He's right, though."

Hammond got to his feet and moved up behind Travis. "Are you going to want me to spell you with the driving?"

Travis shook his head. "I figure me and Barstow got it covered. You ain't ready to be driving an SV all over Mars. And him—" He jerked his head toward Worthing. "He ain't never going to be ready. Just sit back and relax."

"What's the first thing we come to after all this flatland?"

"If all goes well, sometime before sundown tomorrow we'll see the south walls of the crater Biblis Pater. That's when we turn north for the Tjanath Valley. That'll take us through the ridges. I ain't too keen on running through the Tjanath in the dark, but we gotta keep moving."

"What's wrong with it?"

"There're some scalawags out in them ridges. Pirates and wreckers, the kind that prey on travelers who stray off the trail. Crazy and fucked up and just plain desperate. Hopefully we can scoot through in the dark, and in the morning we'll see the North Pole Trail."

Federal Building, Burroughs Settlement—May 25 CEC—11:07 MST.

The phone warbled. Casey picked up the handset. "Yeah?"

"Something really strange has fallen into our laps." It was Chavez.

"What are you talking about, Ray?"

For a moment Casey thought there might be word of Irina, but he was quickly disappointed.

"You remember those CySec names that the computer spit out?" Chavez asked.

"What about them?"

"There's one of them in Burroughs right now."

"Which one?"

"Greig. He just came in on the monorail from Fort Haigh."

"How is that possible? Has the alert been lifted?"

"No, that's the weird part. A single monorail came in with only three passengers. Greig was one—there was also a big man and a girl. They had all this luggage. I swear, they looked like a mission team.''

"How did we catch on to them?''

"Quite by accident. Monroe was riding the snoop board at the monorail terminal, and he just got idly curious about this trio coming in from Haigh and ran a hard image.''

"Thank God for idle curiosity. Do you have a make on the other two?''

"The woman's another CySec CA, name of Judy Whittaker. The third one's a bit of a mystery. There's a need-to-know block on his profile in the central register. It makes me even more convinced that they're a marine mission team.''

"Where did they go when they left the terminal?''

"The marines have a pressurized warehouse out toward the power plant. It's registered in the name of Kingdom Freight-lines, but it's an open secret that it's a marine front for covert operations.''

Casey nodded quickly. "I know it.''

Chavez went on. "I pulled Monroe off the snoop board and had him follow them.''

"Good work." Casey thought quickly. "Listen, I want to talk to brother Greig before he goes anywhere. Where are you?''

"Down at the Times Square deputy post.''

"How soon could you be at that warehouse?''

"I don't know. Maybe twenty minutes.''

"Make it noon. I'll meet you close to this warehouse at noon.''

"I'll be there.''

Casey hung up. For two minutes he just sat, deep in thought. It did not make him comfortable when things just fell into his lap. He had an instinctive distrust of free rides. Finally he stood up. He walked to the closet where his suits were racked. There were two in there: a plain unmarked soft suit for when he did not want to be noticed and the blue and white marshal's armor with the gold star bonded to the chest. Which one? What the hell, he'd high-profile it. It would take some intimidation to get past the marines and their passion for secrecy. He stepped into the blue and white armor. After he suited up, he strapped on a gun, an air-jacketed .375 magnum. There was no harm in going loaded for bear.

As he walked through the outer office, Rhoda, his secretary, looked up. "You going out?"

"For a while. I'll call in."

A VW electric buggy was waiting, parked in the tunnel outside the Federal Building. Casey climbed aboard, placed his helmet on the seat beside him, keyed on the drive, and headed for the John Glenn air lock. He cursed under his breath as he joined the line of vehicles waiting to be cycled through the lock. As Burroughs grew, it was developing a traffic problem. Inside the air lock, he clamped and sealed his helmet and waited as the air was pumped out. As the doors rolled open, light streamed in. He darkened the faceplate of his helmet. Outside on the surface it was bright midday, with a white sun blazing from a pale pink sky. He turned onto the flat, fused sand surface of Industry Boulevard. On either side of him the sunlight gleamed from the surfaces of aluminum silos and pipe complexes. Suited figures swarmed over the scaffolding that shrouded a half-constructed smelting plant. A crane was dropping a giant solar panel into the framework of a new suncatcher. In the middle of the day, with work going on all around, Burroughs looked like a boomtown. It was all too easy to forget that Mars had its darker side, and it scarcely seemed real that he was on his way to talk to a possible psycho killer.

Even out on Industry Boulevard, the traffic was heavy and slow-moving, and Casey became impatient. He cut in his siren and pulled out onto the center divide. In view of the fact that there was no real emergency, the action was totally illegal, but who was going to call him on it? He was the marshal.

Spotting a sign for Kingdom Freightlines, he turned onto a service road. Two other police VWs were parked a hundred meters back from the warehouse gates. He pulled in beside them. Chavez and Monroe came over to greet him.

Chavez looked at Casey's official armor and whistled. "Dressed up, aren't we?"

"Figured we might have to put on a show." Casey pointed in the direction of the warehouse. "What's going on in there?"

"They're still inside."

"You got anything on the big guy?"

Behind his faceplate, Chavez was shaking his head. "Not a damn thing. He's totally blocked."

"That's interesting in itself. Do you have the pictures of the three of them?"

Chavez went back to his own buggy and returned with a large plastic envelope. He spread out a set of color prints on the hood of Casey's VW. As he had said, they were routine snoop camera printouts of three people in off-white coveralls coming from the monorail, pushing a trolley loaded with a number of bulky aluminum travel cases. The woman was a drab blonde with a resentful expression. Casey turned his attention to the smaller of the two men. So that was Greig. The man did not look like anything. The prematurely gray hair was a little unusual, but otherwise he scarcely merited a second glance, a short, bookish mouse of a man who could scarcely have been farther from the popular image of a ravening sex killer. Casey, however, was well aware that very few sex killers looked like the popular image. The big man was something else. He was huge, and even in the loose coverall it was easy to see that he had the super-developed physique of a beach god. Unfortunately, the godliness did not extend to his features. He was an ugly brute.

"What does that face say to you?" Casey asked.

"He has trouble getting dates?"

"Think about it."

"Jesus Christ, steroids?"

"Fucking A steroids. Look at that face, the oversized jaw, the spread nose, the bony ridge across the brow. This joker's been taking steroids for years. It's probably only constant exercise that stops him from ballooning up to three hundred pounds."

"How the hell did he stay in the marines?"

Casey drew a long breath. "I imagine the marines must have been giving them to him. I think what we're looking at here is a rambo."

Chavez's voice was soft in the suit radio. "No shit?"

"Right."

"I thought rambos had been outlawed," Monroe put in. "I sure as hell never heard that there were any on Mars."

"I think that's what you were supposed to never hear."

Chavez leaned on the hood of the VW. "It's got to be some mission if they've taken a rambo out from under wraps."

Casey stared at the blank silver plastic walls of the warehouse. "You're not kidding."

"So what are we going to do?"

"Just walk up to the gate, nice and polite, and ask to see Mr. Greig."

"You think that's a good idea with the possibility of a one-man army being inside?"

Casey squared his shoulders inside the suit. "Why not, dammit? I'm the law around here, and no goddamn marine is going to intimidate me, no matter how many implants he's got."

"Whatever you say. I'll be right behind you."

Casey walked down the road toward the Kingdom Freightlines security gate with Chavez and Monroe slightly behind him. A guard in a Brinks pressure suit sat in the sealed gate house, helmet off, watching television. As the marshal approached, he looked up and spoke into a radio mike that was tuned to the standard suit radio frequency. "What can I do for you, Marshal? Is this an official visit?"

"I'm afraid it is. I want talk to an individual called John Greig."

"I'll check." The guard put down the suit mike and talked into an intercom that was presumably linked to a system in the warehouse. There was a short conversation, and then he turned back to Casey, shaking his head. "No John Greig anywhere in the facility. Not even a record of a John Greig. I think you gotta have bad information, Marshal."

Casey scowled. "I think I'm getting the runaround, that's what I think."

"Listen, Marshal—"

"Listen nothing. You get back on the horn and you tell them that the marshal of Burroughs wants to talk to John Greig. He's the little guy that just came in from Fort Haigh with the woman and the big guy and all the fancy luggage. You can tell them that it's part of a major investigation. You can also tell them that if I don't see Greig, my next call will be to Saud Elijah to talk about obstruction of justice."

The Brinks guard held up a hand. "Hey, don't get on my ass. I just work here." He turned back to the intercom, and there was a longer conversation.

"They're sending someone out here to talk to you," the guard said finally.

"It'd better be Greig."

It was not Greig. Instead, they had sent the rambo. He came toward the gate in a plain stainless steel suit that must have been custom-made and cost the corps a fortune. Up close, he was massive. Casey was by no means a small man, but the hulk towered head and shoulders over him.

When the rambo spoke, his voice was flat and dead, without inflection. He sounded like a robot. "Marshal Casey?"

"Where's Greig?"

"For the time being, Marshal, John Greig doesn't exist. He is engaged in a matter of planetary security. Nobody talks to him until further notice."

"Greig could be a material witness in a major criminal investigation."

"I'm sorry, there's nothing I can do. As far as you're concerned, Greig is no longer on the planet."

Casey was beginning to get angry. "The hell he's no longer on the planet. He's right there in that building."

The rambo glanced back at the warehouse. "That building is private property, Marshal."

"I just want to talk to Greig, and this is starting to amount to obstruction of justice."

"Do you have a warrant, Marshal?"

Casey knew that the ice had melted under him. He did not even have room to bluster. There was no hard evidence to justify a warrant on Greig. "Do you really need me to get one?"

"It's the only way you'll get in here."

"I only have to call a judge."

"So please do that."

The conversation was clearly at an end. Casey turned and walked back toward the cars. He glanced back at Chavez. "I want a watch on this building. Twenty-four hours."

"Greig may not be the one."

"I know that, but the marine attitude pisses me off. They

think that all they have to do is holler national security and we all roll over. I want a watch on this place, and if Greig leaves, I want him followed. Okay?''

Chavez shrugged inside the rigid shoulders of his suit. "Whatever you say, chief."

Kingdom Freightlines warehouse, Burroughs Settlement—
May 25 CEC—12:19 MST.

Booth stepped out of the air lock, brushing ice crystals from his suit. He twisted off his helmet. Greig's heart was in his mouth. Why did the marshal of Burroughs want to talk to him? What had gone wrong? He had hunted only that one time in Burroughs. He had been very careful. What could have gone wrong?

The rambo unsnapped his gloves. "So I got rid of the marshal."

Judy Whittaker looked up from the inventory she was checking. "What did he want?"

"He wanted Greig. I told him he couldn't have Greig." He looked at Greig. "So what did you do?"

Greig was having a lot of trouble controlling his expression. His hands wanted to shake. "Nothing I can think of."

Booth did not appear to notice Greig's nervousness. "You didn't murder anyone?"

The rambo grinned broadly. He looked almost human when his face was at rest, but there was something hideous about him when he smiled. Greig had never seen him angry, and he was not sure he wanted to. The grin was turned on Whittaker.

"Maybe our Greig is the Martian Ripper."

Whittaker did not smile. She just looked sharply at Greig as though actually considering the possibility.

*Soviet Ground Transport K197 on the North Pole Trail, 570
kilometers out from Vostok—May 25 CEC—18:58 MST.*

Irina woke with a start from an anxiety nightmare. The crawler
was lurching more than usual. There was a series of loud metallic bangs. The sound of the crawler's drive was not right. It
was high-pitched and seemed to be racing. There was something
definitely wrong. Now the rest of the passengers were awake.
Some were looking around in alarm. There was another flurry
of bangs. The drive coughed and cut out for a second. When it
resumed, it sounded a little closer to normal, although it still
seemed to be laboring. After five minutes without any more
bangs and with the drive running at some approximation of normal, the concern in the cabin subsided a little. Irina decided that
she was going to use the bathroom. Outside the passenger cabin,
she discovered that there were no lights along the corridor that
led to the toilets. Three light panels had burned out.

"Yeah, right, all at once," she muttered.

She pushed her way into one of the stalls. At least there was
light in there, although the toilet stall probably could have done
without it. The place was filthy, and the bowl was stuffed with
sodden paper. She wondered if the bathroom was deliberately
left like that to remind the user that she was on her way to
Vorkuta. A thought closed on her like an icy cloud. Oh, God,
what was Vorkuta really like? Despair swirled around her
feet. She tried to fight it back.

As she came out, the army lieutenant was waiting for her.
She was momentarily blinded, but she could smell his breath.
She was outraged. He had actually followed her to the bath-
room. Damn the man.

"What the hell you do want?"

He did not say a word. He simply grabbed her, ripping at her
blouse. His fingers grabbed at her hair and twisted. He was
trying to force her to her knees. For a second she was too shocked
and outraged to do anything. She tried to kick him, but he turned
slightly and blocked the kick. His fingers were still locked in
her hair. She took a deep breath, preparatory to screaming at
the top of her lungs. The scream never came. The hand that did
not have hold of her hair went to his pocket and came out hold-

ing an American gravity knife. He held it in front of her face, letting her take a good look at it.

"One sound and I'll cut your fucking throat."

A wave of panic hit her. Oh, Jesus Christ, was this the one who had murdered the prostitutes? His fingers were still locked in her hair. He was pushing her down. The knife was right in front of her eyes. Go with it, she told herself. Don't resist.

"Even if you did scream, it wouldn't do you any good. The men in there would just come out and watch." He laughed, but his voice was strained. "It's never too early to teach a snotty bitch like you the way things are in Vorkuta. You hear me?"

She kept silent. Don't resist. Wait for an opening. There had to be one. He twisted her head back. Her hair felt as if it were coming out at the roots.

"You hear me?"

"Yes, I hear you."

"Unzip my fly."

The knife was against her cheek.

Suddenly the crawler lurched. There was a loud bang from one of the rear cars. The whole vehicle seemed to bounce in the air. The lieutenant staggered backward. Irina came up swinging her knee. This time she connected. The lieutenant's scream was drowned by another bang. She ran. The crawler tilted danger-ously, and she was flung against the wall. The lights went on and off in the passenger cabin. The drive was screaming. The crawler swayed violently from side to side. They had to be out of control. She clung desperately to a seat back. The lights came on in the cabin and then went out altogether. The vehicle seemed to be hitting things—rocks, boulders. There was the scream of metal and some kind of explosion in the rear. The crawler slammed into some invisible thing in the darkness, and she was thrown the length of the cabin. Black.

FIVE

Soviet Ground Transport K197 on the North Pole Trail, 580 kilometers out of Vostok—May 25 CEC—19:32 MST.

THE BLACK FADED AND WAS REPLACED BY A BLINDING PAIN in her head. She tasted blood in her mouth. Was she hurt badly? There was a flashlight moving through the cabin. The floor seemed to be tilting at an impossible angle. How long had she been out? Oh, shit, the crawler. Was the air leaking out? Irina grabbed a seat back and tried to haul herself up. It hurt, but she could move. There did not seem to be anything broken, but as she straightened up, she felt dizzy and started to fall. Someone held on to her arm and steadied her. It was one of the crew.

"What's happened?" she asked.

"We're still finding out."

"The air?"

"The air's okay, and we'll have the lights back on any time now."

As he spoke, the cabin lights came back on. The cabin was a mess. People and luggage had been thrown all over by the impact. A number of people were still unconscious. The crew and some of the soldiers were giving what first aid they could. She noticed that the crew had radstrips clipped to the front of their jackets, the kind that changed color from pink to blue in hard radiation. Mercifully, they were still pink, but the fact that they

117

were wearing them had to indicate that they were not ruling out the possibility of damage to the reactor. She looked around for the army lieutenant. There was no sign of him. Maybe he was still stretched out in the corridor. She hoped he was dead.

"This is your captain speaking."

The PA was back on.

"We have suffered a major breakdown, and although we are still assessing the damage, it seems that we won't be going anywhere in a hurry. The life-support system is functioning, and Vostok has been informed. A relief vehicle is being sent, and in the meantime, there is nothing we can do except sit tight and wait. It may not be comfortable, but it's comparatively warm, and the air is breathable."

Irina wondered if the prisoners were hearing the announcement or were being left in the dark with their fear. It was an hour before they heard from the captain again, although crewmen in pressure suits came and went in and out of the air lock. Irina recovered her carry-on bag. The bottle of vodka had not shattered, and she passed it around to the others in the cabin. Spirits improved with the application of alcohol, but they were quickly dowsed when the captain came back on the PA.

"I'm afraid I have some rather bad news. There is considerable damage to the reactor shielding, and we cannot risk staying with the crawler. Accordingly, we are going to leave a skeleton crew to wait for the relief vehicle, and the rest of us are going to walk up the trail to the next settlement. We estimate that it should be a ten-hour march. If everyone will move to the air lock, the crew will issue emergency pressure suits. Once you have been processed through the lock, all passengers will assemble in front of the prison car."

The emergency suits proved to be minimal, little more than heavy-gauge plastic bags cut to shape, with tuck and roll ribbing at the joints. A high-impact plastic yoke and collar supported the air tanks, radio, and heater and provided a seal for a tinted, softbubble helmet. When Irina reached the head of the line, one of the crewmen handed her a folded suit. She shook it open and then pulled it over her clothes.

The crewman quickly checked the seals and then slapped her on the shoulder. "Okay, into the air lock."

Once outside, even in the dark, it was possible to see just how badly the crawler was damaged. The front car had thrown a tread and then, after being pushed along by the uncontrolled power of the cars behind, had charged down the trail for about a mile before it had veered off to the side, run head-on into a rocky outcrop, and jackknifed. The second and third cars had stayed on their treads, but the fourth one, the one containing the reactor, had slewed around, smashed into the car in front of it, and rolled. The crew had already set up banks of floodlights that threw the area around the prison car into stark relief. Even in the throes of a disaster, they were worried about escapes. Thick cables ran back to the crawler's external power outlets. With the reactor on emergency dampdown, they had to be running everything, including the life support and the outside lights, straight off the storage batteries. Irina wondered how long the batteries could stand up to that level of demand.

She had little chance to think about it, however. An army sergeant in an olive drab, fully armored combat suit hurried up to her and pushed a spare AK-110 into her hands.

"You know how to handle one of these?"

Irina gave him a bleak look that seemed to be wasted on his darkened faceplate. "Of course I know how to handle one of these."

With the deftness that comes only with long experience, she checked the magazine, the power pack, and the gas jacket that was essential for operating in the Martian near vacuum. Apparently satisfied that a major in the militia knew what she was doing, the sergeant pointed to a group of guards who were circling the air lock of the prison car.

"Go and reinforce them. If the prisoners try anything, shoot them out of hand. This is an emergency. There's no time to screw around with procedure. I want to be away from that reactor as soon as possible."

Irina could empathize with the final statement. If one thing really terrified her, it was radiation, the idea of something silent and invisible lancing through her body, killing her without her even knowing it. After the meltdown crises of the 2000s, fear of radiation had been inculcated into every Soviet child of her generation.

The prisoners were already being brought out. The air lock

on the prison car was directly below the faded and rust-streaked
red star that was painted on its side. They emerged from it in
threes. In fact, they were secured in threes. Someone, somewhere along the line, probably in some KGB back room, had
devised a truly fiendish system for moving prisoners out on the
surface of the planet. Three prisoners marched side by side.
They were dressed in suits that were even more minimal than
the emergency model Irina was wearing. The prisoner in the
middle carried a single life-support unit. Three plastic hoses ran
from the unit to each of the suits. To uncouple the hose was to
die of explosive decompression, and so there was no way, short
of deliberately killing his two companions, any one prisoner
could run without taking the other two with him. It was a fun-
damentally Martian adaptation of the basic chain gang principle.

The sergeant came up behind Irina. "Keep a sharp eye on
them. If three of them decide to jackrabbit, they can put on quite
a turn of speed in Mars gravity."

Irina was becoming extremely irritated at the way the sergeant
was treating her like some raw recruit. She had had quite enough
of the army for one day. "I've seen more than enough of Mars-
grav jackrabbiting in my time, Sergeant."

This time the message seemed to get through. "Yes, sir. Just
checking. Since the lieutenant got his head stove in, I'm responsible for this bunch. They shouldn't be much trouble,
though. Their air supply is loaded with prefrontal blockers."

"Will they be able to walk?"

"They'll have to walk—they have no choice."

Members of the crew were unloading containers from the
unpressurized freight car. The containers were being broken
down, and the prisoners were being made to carry essential
supplies. The two of each three who were not carrying the life-
support unit were laden with makeshift backpacks containing
food and water. A half dozen of the most burly prisoners had
been singled out and equipped with the same suits as the passengers. They were designated to pull two heavy sand sleds that
carried spare air tanks; extra food, water, and medical supplies;
and a large inflatable dome that could house them if they needed
to stop and sleep.

It took about twenty-five minutes to get all the prisoners out of the car and formed up into orderly ranks. Finally the sergeant was satisfied. Then, just as he was about to give the signal to move out, one of the prisoners' suits ruptured. He was on the outside of the third rank in the column. A passenger ran to him with a pressure patch, but it was too late. The prisoners' suits had only receiving sets. No one could have heard him cry out. Blood was already boiling from the exposed skin of his face and hands and splashing on the inside of the transparent suit. His legs gave way, and he dropped to his knees. The woman next to him, the one in his trio who was carrying the life-support unit, appeared transfixed. She stood rigid, doing nothing, probably screaming, too. The man at the end of the row pushed her to one side, turned off the victim's air supply, and ripped out the hose. The guards were nervous. They were gripping their machine pistols and anxiously waiting for someone to give them an order. If a single prisoner did anything stupid, it would start a massacre.

Then the sergeant was roaring in their helmets, breaking the terrible silence. "Nobody move! Everybody stand exactly where you are!"

The tableau froze, casting long black shadows under the bright floodlights. Almost in slow motion, the victim fell forward on his face. He twitched a number of times, and then it was over, apart from a plume of blood that fountained from the punctured left leg of his suit.

One of the passengers looked at the sergeant. "Should we do something about the body?"

The sergeant looked very deliberately at the reactor car. "We don't have time. We're moving out." He raised his arm. "Come on, let's move out! Let's move out now!"

The sorry column started forward. From the fourth rank back, every prisoner on the outside had to step over the fallen victim before heading out into the Martian darkness, away from the lights of the crawler. Irina cradled the AK-110 in the crook of her arm and walked alongside the lines of stooped prisoners. It seemed impossible that her life could have changed so radically in such a short period of time. They had been on the move only five minutes when the lights behind them went out. Although Irina knew it was just the skeleton crew conserving the batteries, there was something desperately final about it. They could no longer feel that they had any kind of home base. There was no turning back. They were alone in the night, and all they could do was trudge forward.

White Marsman on the North Pole Trail, three kilometers from the Silver Locust Settlement—May 26 CEC—01:23 MST.

They had been peering through the windshield at the lights for maybe twenty minutes. The Marsman was rolling down from the high ground with a clear view of the flatlands.

"The Silver Locust Motel, Bar, and Grill?"

"That's what the sign says."

Travis grunted. "The sign may be the best part of the whole place."

"So what's it like?"

"Kinda wild and woolly."

Hammond shaded his eyes against the glare of the spotlights. "You think we should give it the go-by?"

Travis shook his head. "No, we're going to have to stop sometime. You guys look about ready to stretch your legs."

Hammond nodded. "We've been in this damned capsule for a day and a half."

Travis looked at Hammond as though there were no hope for him. "That's nothing by Martian standards."

"It's enough for me."

Worthing quickly stepped in to prevent yet another old hand against rookie confrontation. "It's enough for me, too. Let's pull over."

Hammond and Travis did not seem to be hitting it off. They both had egos of roughly the same size, and they manifested them in direct opposition to each other. Hammond was the superstar who expected to have things his own way. Travis, on the other hand, was the hard-bitten specialist who did not expect his word to be questioned. Worthing hoped they would resolve their differences before too long. If they did not, the expedition could rapidly become a disaster.

The sign that announced the Silver Locust to the world was

huge, maybe twenty meters high, a giant cartoon cowboy smoking a cigarette, constructed from neon tubing, fiber optics, and interlocking light panels. It was so far the most ludicrous thing Hammond had seen on Mars, standing as it did in the middle of barren rocky desert, an alien invader from a very different planet. As they got closer, they were able to see the settlement itself. As usual, the bulk of it was under the sand: only an unpressurized aluminum hangar, a circular fuel tank, and the air lock entrances to the lower levels were visible on the surface. There were a number of smaller signs around the foot of the big one.

FOOD
FUEL
ROOMS
WATER BEDS
LIQUOR
GIRLS
ROULETTE, BLACKJACK, AND POKER

Worthing blinked. "They really have all that stuff down there?"

Travis grinned. "They got it all, and a few other things besides, but I doubt you're going to find it quite as appealing as you're probably imagining."

His statement proved to be absolutely correct. The Silver Locust Bar and Grill was little more than a big, almost empty room covered by a fine layer of Martian dust. Two longrangers played three-card stud on a table covered by a dirty green baize cloth, and the roulette table looked as though it had not been used in years except as a surface on which to stack crates of empty bottles waiting for recycling. The owner was a fat Hispanic man who lounged behind the bar in a sweat-stained T-shirt with the name of the bar printed across the front. He had the resigned air of a man who had long ago given up hoping for anything better. Later they would learn that he was called Ramon Silver. Despite his seeming fatalism, there was an old pump shotgun in easy reach on the back of the bar.

Guns seemed to be the rule up on the North Pole Trail. Before they had left the Marsman parked beside the other three vehicles in the Silver Locust's hangar, Travis had insisted that they break out weapons of their own. Hammond had been surprised.

"Weapons? I'm a journalist—I don't carry a gun. The most dangerous thing I've ever carried is a sign saying 'Prensa.' "

Travis had gone on opening the armory cases. "You're undressed out here without a gun. Worse than that, you attract attention by being different, and that's the last thing we want. I suggest you forget your principles, partner, and strap on a piece. Nobody's asking you to go pulling it out and waving it around."

Hammond had nodded. "Whatever you say. You're the expert."

Travis had laughed. "That's right, I am."

Worthing frowned. If Hammond and Travis did not quit riding each other, there was going to be serious trouble. And serious trouble was something he wanted kept to a minimum out there in the wilderness.

Travis was holding out a pair of Heckler and Koch Starmasters. "You and Worthing should take these H&Ks. They fire solid fuel, so you can use them on the surface without gas jackets."

They took the pistols, and Travis fished out a pair of army-issue webbing holsters. "Wear them in these. They won't peg you as gunfighters."

Worthing nodded. "That's the last thing we want."

Travis turned to Barstow, who was holding up a Mossberg regulator with a pistol grip and a cut-down barrel. It hung from a simple leather loop attached to a ring in the bottom of the butt.

"You wanted this?"

"Figured it'd be appropriate."

Worthing raised an eyebrow. "Kind of aggressive, isn't it?"

Barstow shrugged. "After the shit we got into in Vostok, I feel more comfortable with something solid."

"It's solid, all right."

It was thus that the four of them had walked to the air lock of the Silver Locust, sealed in their new suits and as heavily armed as any Martian backrat. The two poker players had looked up as the newcomers came out of the lock, and Ramon Silver watched them with lazy indifference as they removed their helmets and brushed off the frost that immediately formed on their suits. Doleful guitar music, probably a piece by Estavez, sobbed over a muted sound system.

Silver flashed gold teeth in something that was closer to a sneer than a smile. "You here to drink?"

"That was the general idea. What have you got?"

"I got vodka, and I got something that might be scotch."

"You got any beer?"

"Ain't seen beer in two months. I got Coke, and I got Orange-O."

"Give me a vodka with a Coke back."

The others indicated that they would have the same. Silver did not move.

"What do you intend to use for money?"

Worthing fished in his pouch and hauled out a roll of bills. There in the wild, credit devices like cones and magstrips were not accepted. Outbackers expected currency.

"U.S. dollars."

"No shit."

The owner started pouring liquor. Travis leaned close to Worthing and hissed at him. "You want to be careful of flashing your cash like that."

"Sometimes it can be handy for them to know that you've got the cash to back it up."

"Sometimes it can be fatal."

There were three girls in the place, and they were already homing in on Worthing's money. When the four men had come in, two of the girls had been idly watching the poker game, while the third had been sitting at the bar talking with the owner. Now they surrounded Travis and his charges, teeth and smiles and pretty much anything one could want on resigned display.

"Hey, boys, you come far?"

Travis nodded. "Far enough."

Even by the standards of Burroughs, the women were not much to look at. One was a tired redhead in corset and fishnets who could have come out of a Lautrec painting. She had a Cuban accent.

"Hey, boys, call me Theresa," she said.

The second was a country blonde in cutoff coveralls, an overfilled push-up bra, and an accent that must have come straight out of the twilight streets of Atlanta's Shanktown.

"Hi, boys. You can call me Cilla."

The last one was bad—bad, as in the running gangs on the old interstates. She had a purple box cut, a bike jacket that from the lettering on the back had once belonged to Pepe, a black-gloss rubber miniskirt just like the whores in Vostok were wearing, jumpboots, and makeup of the living dead. She probably took care of the more outlandish requests. She seemed to have her eye on Worthing. "You can call me Max."

The men carried their drinks to a table, and the women followed them. After being shut up in each other's company for what had started to seem like an eternity, it was quite a relief to swap smutty small talk with complete strangers. It did not, however, sit too well with the two longtimers at the poker table. There was some muttering and hard looks. Only Travis noticed the hostility, however, and he did not think it wise to make it known right then to the others. The longrangers' resentment slowly smoldered as Hammond, Barstow, and Worthing became better acquainted with Theresa, Cilla, and Max. The sound system was playing Marty Robbins.

Finally one of the locals stood up and walked slowly over to the table. The top half of his suit was off, revealing the gun belt slung over one shoulder of his Rockee b'Chokee T-shirt. He leaned down and whispered something to Max. She routinely brushed him off.

The longranger straightened up. He seemed about to deliver the first inflammatory remark on the path to escalation and drunken bloodshed when the air bulkhead at the end of the bar slid open with a whoosh. It opened on the corridor that led through to the motel rooms. The man who came through had a girl on each arm and a half-empty bottle of whatever passed for whiskey clutched in his fist. He was sallow and unshaven, and the chestplate of his worn black armor was hanging open. He was very drunk and was being half supported by the two women. They led him to a table as far as possible from both Hammond's team and the remaining poker player. The girls sat down with the drunk newcomer, but he angrily waved them away. He wanted to pass out on his own. He pulled out a thick roll of both rubles and dollars and, in a very final gesture of payoff, threw a handful of bills on the table. The girls shrugged and went back to the bar. They proved to be the perfect face-saving solution to the longranger's problem. He followed them to the bar, and very soon his companion joined him.

Although Cilla was whispering breathy obscenities into his ear, Hammond was half watching the drunk in the black armor. The man hardly seemed typical of someone who had just finished romping with two women. He was sitting on his own, drinking whiskey with what was close to a look of hunted terror on his face. His eyes were sunken, and he shook as though he had been running on Methedrine for days. Then he glanced up and caught Hammond's eye.

"What the fuck are you looking at?"

Hammond said nothing, quickly transferring his attention to Cilla, who seemed intent on pushing her left breast into his face.

The drunk leaned forward belligerently and bellowed across the room. "You look good, buddy! You take a fucking good look! You tell everyone tomorrow that you saw Slate Yablonsky on his last night."

After that he was quiet, back in his horrified introspection. It was more than an hour before they all discovered that the drunk's fear was the result of something a great deal more substantial than mere alcohol devils.

Worthing was throwing back vodka like there was no tomorrow and playfully slipping bills into the waistband of Max's miniskirt when the air lock started to cycle. The door opened, and two men came in. On their own either one would have been cause for a second look, but together they were formidable. All conversation stopped. One of them was the size of a sumo wrestler, and his pressure suit was high-gloss polymer with dragons like blood-red tattoos painted on the arms and chestplate. The other would have been over six feet tall if it had not been for his hunchback. His purple Starflash softsuit was custom tailored to the curve of his spine. A tattered dust cape hung limply from his shoulder.

Worthing blinked. "Holy shit, it's the baddest cats in the valley."

Travis hissed at him. "Will you shut up."

Neither man attempted to remove his helmet. The hoarfrost gathered thickly on their suits, as though they had been out in the cold for a very long time. They advanced on the drunk and halted in front of him. He slowly raised his head. He had the face of a man who had thought the unthinkable and was resigned to the worst.

"So you finally got here."

The hunchback pulled a small MA laser from under his cape. His voice hissed from an external speaker. It had a noticeable Korean accent. "Are you ready?"

Ramon Silver was leaning forward with the shotgun leveled across the bar. "No lasers."

The hunchback did not turn. "This is my business, Ramon. Stay out of it."

"No lasers in my place. I ain't having you cut through the outer plates. You can take care of your business. I'm sure Yablonsky has it coming, but no lasers, else I blow your head off."

The hunchback's helmeted head nodded. He handed the sumo wrestler the MA, and that man in turn passed him a sawed-off Remington Elite. The hunchback hefted the shotgun and stared down at the drunk. "I asked if you were ready."

The drunk raised a warning hand. "Don't shoot me—I ain't going for a gun." He pulled out the roll of mixed bills and flipped it onto the table. "There's the money, most of it. Does that get me anything?"

"It gets you nothing. You know that. Nobody steals from Kim Modo and lives to boast about it."

"I'm not boasting."

"I have a reputation to maintain."

The drunk nodded. "I realize that. I guess I just ran out of road."

"I'm glad you understand."

The drunk looked down at the table. He had nothing left to say.

The blast of the Remington seemed to reverberate through the room forever. The drunk was thrown backward, blood spurting from a fist-sized hole in his chest. His chair bounced as he sprawled across the floor. When the echoes had died away, the sumo wrestler looked around the bar. Everyone had frozen.

"Does anyone have a problem with this?"

No one moved or spoke until the owner stood up. "You killed him, you pay to bury him."

The hunchback picked up the roll of bills, peeled off about half of them, and dropped them on the table. Without a word, he and the sumo wrestler walked back to the air lock.

Worthing slowly let out his breath. "Jesus Christ."

Barstow nodded. "Amen to that."

Ramon Silver opened the bulkhead and shouted down the corridor. "Hernandez, Chuck, get out here quick!"

Once Hernandez and Chuck had hauled out the body, the party never really got going again. Only Barstow seemed unaffected by the killing. He actually seemed elated. It was only after the dust had settled that he leaned forward confidingly. "I got it all on tape."

"The shooting?"

"Every last gruesome detail. In slowmo, it'll look like fucking Peckinpah. We'll put on voice-over in the morning, squirt capsule it back to Burroughs for relay to Tokyo. Frontier justice on Mars. It ain't earth-shattering, but it's sure as hell Lech Hammond in the thick of it."

Hammond stared into his drink. "Christ."

Barstow looked surprised. "You don't like it?"

Hammond shook his head as though he were trying to clear it. "No, no, I like it. It's just a bit soon after the real thing to be thinking about exploiting it."

Barstow grinned. He seemed to be enjoying the spectacle of the great Lech Hammond in a moment of drunken weakness. What was the matter with Hammond? He had seen people killed before. Maybe the big time was making him soft. "Remember what they say, chief. Don't get too close to it."

At that point the party was beyond all resuscitation. Barstow slipped away with Theresa, and Travis just vanished.

Finally Worthing got unsteadily to his feet. "Max and I are going to take a room."

Hammond nodded drunkenly and looked at Cilla. "I guess maybe we should do the same thing."

"Whatever you say, baby."

Holding on to each other, they headed for the bulkhead door.

Although Cilla did her level best to take his mind off it, all through the night that followed the bloody image of frontier justice kept replaying itself in his head. He kept seeing the body of the drunk flying backward with his chest exploding. In slow motion it did look like Peckinpah.

Police Cruiser A-17 in high-speed pursuit in Mars 5, the unfinished highway north out of Burroughs—May 26 CEC—05:07 MST.

The word had come. Greig and his party were on the move, apparently having slipped out of the settlement in the darkness before dawn. Lon Casey had been asleep in the chair in his office. Chavez was sacked out on the couch in the outer office. Stumbling blindly, they hurried to the garage where the department's fastest cruiser was warmed up and waiting. Once inside the cruiser, they both woke up. Chavez accelerated the cruiser up the ramp and out of the garage. Once clear of the Kennedy air lock, he sped through the surface-level settlement at speeds approaching two hundred k. The cruiser's computer fed them constant updates of the target vehicle's position. Greig, the woman technician, and the rambo were on Mars 5, heading north. Presumably, when they reached the end of the unfinished highway, they would start out across open country. They were riding in a compact, three-man Jeep ATV. It was fast on a paved road but not fast enough to outrun the cruiser.

Chavez was less than happy about the whole business. "You realize that what we're doing doesn't have even the slightest basis in legality?"

Casey grunted dismissively. "If I can't come up with an excuse to stop a vehicle in my own jurisdiction for a routine check, I'm losing my touch."

"But this isn't a routine check. You're harassing the man. You know it, and he knows it. You don't have a warrant, not the slightest shred of evidence, nothing. You really want to get into a beef with the marines?"

Casey scowled. "Just do the driving. I'll worry about the marines."

Chavez refused to shut up. "You're crazy, Lon. You've never even seen the man. He's just a name thrown up by a computer search."

They were just ten kilometers behind the Jeep and closing fast. When the gap had been narrowed to five, Casey got on the radio.

"This is the Burroughs Marshal's Department broadcasting on a closed hailing channel. Please pull over. I repeat, please pull over."

The voice of the rambo came from the dashboard speaker. "Is this Marshal Casey?"

"I'm ordering you to pull over."

"Listen, Casey, I don't know what bee you've got in your bonnet, but you're way out of line. You're interfering in a matter of planetary security, and there's sure as hell going to be an official complaint about your behavior."

They were just two and a half kilometers behind the Jeep. "Just pull over."

"Back off, Casey, or you'll be in serious trouble."

Casey played his final card. "I'm broadcasting on a closed traffic band. It's of limited range, and I doubt that anyone but you and me can hear, but I could switch to an open channel any time I like. You want the surrounding world, including any listening Russian satellite, to hear that you're a marine covert mission team heading up-country?"

"You wouldn't—"

"Pull over."

"I'm pulling over, but I'll get you for this, Casey."

Chavez shook his head. "You do realize you're fucking with a rambo here? He could probably crush your head with one hand."

Casey sealed his helmet. "It's too late to back down now."

Deciding that his boss was so far out of line that he might as well make it look good, Chavez cut in the flashing lights. Casey shot him a glance but did not say anything. The headlights picked up the Jeep and were reflected from the pressurized bubble canopy. It was small for three people and a full load of gear. If it was, as it seemed, a covert combat team, they were doing things the hard way.

The cruiser pulled up alongside the vehicle. Casey got on the radio again. "Please step down from your vehicle."

"We'll do what you want, but only under the strongest protest. I'm going to have your badge, Casey." The rambo sounded dangerous.

"Just step down."

"We're coming out, but the Jeep has only a small air lock. We'll be coming out one at a time."

Casey nodded. "I understand."

He swiveled the cruiser's spotlights so that they were trained on the Jeep's air lock. As Casey had expected, the rambo came out first, the woman came next, and finally Greig climbed down. Seeing them, Casey was left in no doubt that they were a mission team. They were dressed in full-combat dust-camouflage suits. Fortunately, they were not carrying weapons.

Casey waited until the three suited figures were out on the road surface before he depressurized the cruiser and popped the canopy. He eased himself out of the seat with one last look at Chavez. "Cover me, okay? Just in case the rambo goes nuts on me."

"Rambos aren't supposed to go nuts."

"I wouldn't care to bet on it."

Ignoring both Whittaker and the rambo, Casey walked straight up to Greig. "John Greig?"

"I don't believe I have to talk to you."

Casey tongued on his helmet light and directed it straight into Greig's faceplate. The man blinked nervously. The pictures from the monorail terminal had not lied. Greig really was one of the most nondescript individuals Casey had ever encountered. The man's eyes flickered from side to side like those of a frightened rabbit. Casey could not imagine how Greig had even come up with what it took to make it to Mars.

"Where were you on the night of May 17, Greig?"

"I'd have to consult my journal."

Casey sighed. "It was only just over a week ago."

The rambo cut in. "He doesn't have say anything."

"I'm not talking to you."

"He still doesn't have to stand still for this."

Casey peered intently into Greig's face. "You didn't happen

to be in Vostok, did you? Maybe had a couple of drinks in the Aquarium Café?''

The man looked ready to jump out of his skin. Casey suddenly knew. The man worked with the marines. Just being interrogated by a cop should not have scared him that much. Casey was certain that his cargo had shifted somewhere along the way and that there was something inside him that would eventually blow him apart. It was a gut feeling: Casey was sure he was looking at the Martian Ripper. Of course, proving it would be something else entirely.

"Come on, talk to me, Greig. Let's get it all out in the open.''

The rambo lost patience. He turned to face Casey. "I've had enough of this, Casey. There's no reason for Greig to talk to you.'' He started to advance on Casey.

Chavez's voice snapped from the suit radio. "Please stay exactly where you are. I have you targeted on this vehicle's weapons system.''

The rambo halted, but Casey knew that he could not press it any further. He took one last look at Greig. "Just remember, I'm going to be right behind you. I'm going to stop you in the end.''

He turned and walked back to the cruiser with just a single glance at the rambo. "You're free to go.''

"Your badge, Casey.''

"Yeah, right.''

He dropped into the cruiser, banged down the canopy, and repressurized the interior. Both he and Chavez removed their helmets. Casey stared straight ahead.

"So say it.''

"I hope you're satisfied, because you're sure in a shitload of trouble.''

"It's him. I could swear it. I know it's him.''

"Are you sure you're not getting a bit obsessive about all this?''

Casey shook his head. "I swear to God, Ray, it's him.''

Jeep ATV, forty kilometers north of Burroughs—
May 26 CEC—06:12 MST.

As the police cruiser had pulled away, Booth had hurried Greig and Whittaker back into the Jeep. He had eased it into gear and driven in silence for twenty minutes, and then he had pulled over. Half of Greig's mind was screaming. The cop knew. He had looked into his face, and he knew. How had he even gotten close to him? The trail was covered. He was certain the trail was covered. Somehow that man Casey had stumbled onto the truth. It was impossible, but Greig had heard him and seen his eyes. Casey knew. He had sensed the entity. It was only with the greatest difficulty that Greig maintained his composure. Even so, his hand went to the piece of black metal in the leg pouch of his suit. He found a certain comfort in having it close to him.

When the Jeep had come to rest, Booth took his hands from the wheel and turned in his seat. "So what's going on, Greig? Why is this cop going apeshit all over you?"

Greig shook his head. "I really don't know."

The rambo's eyes were hard slits in the gross, devil-mask face. "Is that the best you can come up with?"

"I swear, I don't know what the hell this marshal is talking about."

Whittaker did not look at all convinced. "So where were you on the night of whatever?"

Booth, drawing on his enhanced memory, supplied the accurate date. "May 17."

"Right. May 17. Where were you?"

Greig did his best to look angry and innocent. "What is this? You're both as bad as that goddamn cop."

Booth looked thoughtfully through the windshield. The dawn was starting to come up over the Martian desert. "I want a satisfactory conclusion to this matter before we proceed with the mission."

Greig was shaking his head. "I really don't know what to tell you."

Booth's face was like stone. "A major civilian police involvement is more than adequate reason to abort the mission. That's the book. I have to decide if this is in fact a major civilian police involvement or if it's merely a misunderstanding. I have to say out front that it's already looking a good deal more complicated than a simple misunderstanding.''

Whittaker looked aghast. "You can't abort the mission. It'll go on our permanent records like a black mark.''

The rambo smiled coldly and ran a hand over his overdeveloped arm. "I don't have to worry about my record. I'm in something of a fixed mode.'' He seemed to reflect on that for a moment; then he suddenly turned on Greig. "So, okay, Greig. Where were you on the night of May 17?''

"I was in Burroughs; I was trying to get some blind data medium on the black market. Something that couldn't be traced back to the unit. There's this guy I use who hangs out in one of the Times Square bars, the Alfredo Garcia. A lot of people saw me, both in Burroughs and on the monorail.''

Greig knew he was safe with that story. He had ratfucked his own records, and he knew that the phony log entries would stand up to everything but the most intensive examination—and if it came to that, the whole record would dump itself. Of course, no one had seen him in Burroughs, but that was impossible to prove.

Booth nodded. "I can check on that.''

"I know.''

Booth unfastened the neck of his undersuit to reveal three neural plug implants set in his neck, just above the collarbone. He pulled a line from the special unit that was built into the dash and plugged it into one of the implants. His eyes closed. In about ten seconds he opened them again.

"You check out, although I am quite aware that you could have planted the data. However, I also ran a three cross on May 17, Vostok, and the Aquarium Café.''

Greig's stomach turned to ice.

Whittaker made an impatient gesture. "And?''

"There was a prostitute murder in Vostok that night. The last place the victim was seen alive was the Aquarium Café.''

Whittaker's mouth fell open. "Jesus Christ, he is the Martian Ripper! I thought it was a joke.''

Greig did a masterful job of keeping his voice from breaking up. "I'm not the Martian Ripper, goddamn it!''

"Marshal Casey would appear to think that you are."

Greig kept repeating to himself: Don't sound desperate! Don't sound desperate! "He's got to be wrong."

Whittaker and Booth were both staring at him as though they expected something more from him.

"I don't know what I can tell you. I don't know any more about this than you do." A thought occurred to him. "Unless . . ."

"Unless what?"

"Unless what's happening here is that we're getting ratfucked ourselves."

"What do you mean?"

"I mean that the information on which Casey is basing his suspicions was fed to him by the KGB. Rat versus rat."

Booth was thinking. "Go on."

"It would be quite possible for a KGB countercyb team to circumloop the names of specific individuals to a civilian police investigation. God knows, we've done it ourselves. We've fed the Vostok militia all manner of crap. It's easy with them; they're always in the market for bootleg soft."

"Could they do that to us?"

"Easily. It's not like they needed to penetrate CySec. All they'd have to do is get hold of some of our names and then hack into the databanks of the marshal's department. It'd be child's play."

Booth thought some more. "It's plausible. I'd prefer to blame the KGB than believe that you're a serial killer." He turned and looked at Whittaker. "What do you think about this?"

"I really don't know."

"Do you want to go on with the mission?"

She hesitated for a long time. "How much would it affect the mission if he was this criminal?" she asked finally.

"But I'm not," Greig protested.

"That doesn't matter. For the purposes of the mission, we have to assume the worst."

"What is the worst?"

Booth did not seem particularly perturbed. "That one of our team is a prostitute killer. I don't see that it would affect us at all. Neither of us is a hooker."

Whittaker looked grimly at Greig. "I'm a woman."

"These things are usually very specialized. You have very little to worry about. About the only factors that could jeopardize the mission is if he starts to offend our sense of morality or aesthetics and we cease to function efficiently as a result. There is no room for that and we have to control it."

Greig felt sick. "I find this all very offensive."

"Logic dictates that we discuss it."

Whittaker treated Greig to a long appraising look. "The prospect of being shut up in a small surface vehicle with a rambo and a sex killer requires a little thought."

"I'm not—"

Booth cut Greig off. "That's already been noted. It has to become irrelevant. I think, taking everything into consideration, we have to go on with this mission."

He looked at Whittaker. She slowly nodded.

The rambo did not say another word. He put the Jeep back into gear, and in a moment they were rolling again. Greig felt as though he had been granted a temporary stay, except that Whittaker would no longer look him in the eye.

The Silver Locust Settlement—May 26 CEC—12:56 MST.

Worthing's wrists were secured to a pair of rings set into the frame in the water bed. His ankles were pinned in a similar way, leaving him spread-eagled on the undulating surface. Max was crouching over him, wearing purple stockings and a vibraglove on her right hand. It was set all the way up, well past the pain threshold, and each time she touched him with it, he groaned out loud.

When they had first gotten to the room, they had fallen asleep very quickly, too drunk for anything but the most fumblingly rudimentary sex play, but now the two of them were making up for lost time. Max had been working him over for the last half hour. When the vibraglove got too much for him, she exchanged it for an ice bag and feathers and then moved on to the short lash made of electrical cables. Worthing could not quite figure out what he might have told her to make her think that he would enjoy that kind of mistreatment. Maybe it was just her instincts, or perhaps he had said something the previous night that had been washed out of his memory when the floodgates of alcohol had opened. Either way, he had not protested when, with a knowingly wicked grin, she had produced the wrist restraints from her bag of goodies and set to strapping him down.

She grabbed him with the vibraglove again and slowly tightened her grip. His whole body convulsed. He was so immersed in the waves of pleasure-pain that he did not even hear the banging on the door. His first realization that something was wrong came only when Max suddenly let go of him and exclaimed angrily, ''What the hell is going on?''

Barstow's voice came from beyond the door. ''Come on, Worthing, get up!''

Worthing raised his head and looked down at himself. ''That might be easier said than done.''

''This is serious. Get out of there. There are Russians all over the place.''

Worthing let his head flop back on the water bed. His last brush with the Soviets was still far too fresh in his memory. ''God almighty, doesn't it ever stop?'' He looked up at Max. ''Get these things off me. I've got to see what's happening.''

Max did not need any second urging. She began deftly stripping off the restraints. Within three minutes he was out in the corridor in full pressure suit, with his helmet under his arm. Travis, Hammond, Barstow, and the other two girls were waiting.

''What's going on?''

''A bunch of Russians marched in here about half an hour ago.''

''What kind of Russians?''

''Mainly prisoners with a military escort,'' Travis told him. ''They were on their way to Vorkuta, that camp up inside the arctic circle. Apparently their transport's broken down and they've been on a forced march all night.''

''So what do we do?''

''I suggest we get out of here while they're still stumbling around looking dazed and confused.''

Hammond nodded. ''I'll go along with that.''

Barstow was still thinking business. "What about the voice-over for last night's tape?"

"We'll do that along the road someplace. Let's get clear of the Russians first. The less I have to do with them, the better."

It was then that Theresa spoke up. "Take us with you."

Travis looked at her in amazement. "What?"

The other two women joined in. "Yeah, come on, take us with you. It can get hairy with the Russian military around. Those guys can be animals."

"You've got to be fucking crazy."

Worthing was much more prepared to be reasonable. "Why not? I can't see the harm in it. They could be the natural cover we were looking for."

Travis did not like the idea at all. "And what would we be disguised as? Traveling pimps?"

"It would take attention away from us."

"The owner might have something to say about us running off with three of his main attractions."

Max shook her head. "He won't notice until we're gone. He's too busy making sure that the Russians don't commandeer the place. Besides, he's still got Beverly and Bonnie."

Travis was shaking his head. "Sweet Jesus Christ, we can't go up the North Pole Trail with a truckload of whores."

"Why not?"

Travis shrugged off the question. As far as he was concerned, the gig was going to hell in a basket, and he was not fighting anymore. "It would seem to be Hammond's decision."

Everyone looked at Hammond.

"Well?"

Hammond's brow furrowed. He was too hung over to think clearly. "Oh, what the hell. You girls got suits?"

"Of course we got suits."

"So get them quick, or we'll leave you behind."

Once the women had gone, Travis faced Hammond. "Do you have any clue what you're doing?"

"Come on, Travis, what harm can it do?"

"Shit, Hammond, don't ask me, I'm just the hired help."

"You got an attitude problem, Travis."

"At least I ain't crazy enough to be packing a parcel of bimbos."

At that moment the women came back in their suits. They were a sight to be seen. Theresa's gold suit was pulled skintight by a network of inflated hose seams. The arms and shoulders were made from a transparent material tinted to protect her from the sun's UV. Cilla's was a Sears Slimline in shocking pink polymer, with a chestplate that had been custom-molded to the contours of her bust. The ensemble was topped off with a purple-tinted hardbubble helmet. Max was more sinister in an old and extremely customized suit: the chestplate was white; the arms and shoulders had shaggy nylon fur bonded to them, giving her the look of a skinny but dominant panda; the legs were leather finish; and the rubber crotch joints were covered by a loincloth of steel mesh. A Valkyrie touch was added by the gold wings attached to her glossy black helmet.

Barstow let out a whistle. "I didn't know they made cocktail armor."

Max glared at him. "Listen, asshole, on slow nights we hustle the trail. Advertising is everything."

Travis cut in. "We need to get out of here. Are you women sealed in?"

"Sure."

"Checked each other?"

"Listen, Travis, we know the buddy system."

The men sealed themselves into their own suits and checked one another out, then Travis took control.

"What we're going to do is walk out of here as normally as we can manage. We go straight to the Marsman, we get in it, and we drive away. Don't look back."

"And if the Russians stop us?"

"Who the hell knows? We improvise."

The bar area was full of Soviets, both soldiers and civilians. Most were drinking vodka as though it had been a long hard trail. Their suits were crusted with dust and ice, and their faces were drawn and weary. Silver was trying to work out a roster of rooms to accommodate the sudden influx and demanding to know who was going to pay for everything. Nobody said a word to Travis and his party as they walked to the air lock. A few of the soldiers stared at the women, and there were a couple of reflex whistles, but that was all.

The air lock could take only four people at a time, so Travis, Barstow, Hammond, and Cilla went first, leaving the other three to go through on the next cycle. As he waited with Theresa and Max, Worthing looked around idly and was amazed when he spotted a familiar face. Chief Investigator Orlov, the militia commander from Vostok, the one who had been getting friendly with Lon Casey, was standing over by the poker table waiting to be assigned a bed.

"I guess she must have fallen foul of the KGB purges," he mused.

Max looked at him. "You say something?"

"Just talking to myself."

Out on the surface, in the midday sun, the three women looked even more outlandish, particularly when contrasted with the drab, dirty Red Army men and their wretched prisoners in cheap plastic suits who formed ragged, exhausted lines on the flat parking area in front of the air locks and the hangar. Hammond's heart sank when a Soviet sergeant started signaling to them.

"Here we go again."

The sergeant was walking toward them, a machine pistol slung over his shoulder. "You traveling in the Marsman?"

"That's right."

"Move it."

"Say what?"

"You'll have to move it. We're inflating a protective dome in the hangar to house the prisoners. You'll have to get it out of there."

Hammond's heart was restored to its normal location. "Sure, no problem. Right away."

The forward cabin of the Marsman was crowded with six passengers and a driver as Travis backed it carefully through the mass of Russians on the parking area. Hammond peered out of the side window, then turned to Barstow. "Are you shooting?"

"Sure thing."

"Look at those prisoners' suits. They're so damned flimsy. If they marched all night in those things, how many do you think made it?"

Max supplied the answer. "Those suits aren't worth shit. They could have lost a bunch of prisoners over twelve hours."

"Jesus."

Travis swung the Marsman around, and then they were back on the trail, rolling away from the Silver Locust. The others treated him to a round of applause, which he acknowledged with a nod.

"We made it out."

Worthing began stripping off his suit. "There was someone we know in among that bunch."

Hammond looked up. "There was? Who?"

"Irina Orlov, the militia chief from Vostok."

"No kidding. What do you think she did?"

"The way things are, you don't actually have to do anything anymore. It's quite enough if someone like Melikov doesn't like you. She wasn't a prisoner. More like she was being sent into exile up in the frozen north."

"That's too bad."

Worthing unfastened the legs of his suit. "I was wondering if we ought to pass the word back to Lon Casey. He was kind of friendly with her."

Travis glanced back. "Not on an open channel. If the KGB picked it up, it could drop her right in the shit."

Barstow grinned. "We could put a message in the squirt for Burroughs, put it on the end, after the voice-over on last night's tapes. Sandoz can call the marshal and tell him."

Hammond nodded. "Yeah, tell him. Maybe he'll jump on his white horse and go rescue her."

Worthing laughed. "He might, at that. Lon Casey's a real John Wayne underneath it all."

Federal Building, Burroughs Settlement—May 26 CEC— 16:23 MST.

The phone trilled. It was Rhoda.

"There's a guy called Sandoz wants to speak to you. Won't settle for anyone else."

"Sandoz?"

"Dan Worthing's second banana over at Global."

Casey placed the man: a piece of goshwow weirdware from a dark corner of the valley with plugs in his neck. Normally he handled the tech stuff, but when the need arose, he could be a nit-picking background investigator.

"I've got nothing to talk to the media about."

"I don't think this is media as such. He says he has a message for you."

"What message?"

"Your ears only."

Casey was curious. What was Sandoz so secretive about? "Okay, put him on."

"Marshal Casey?"

"What's up?"

"I got a squirt back from Lech Hammond and Dan Worthing, out in the field."

Casey half smiled. So those two were out getting into trouble again. He wondered where exactly they were. Hopefully a long way from Burroughs.

"Tacked on the end was some footage of Dan with a message for you," Sandoz went on. "It concerns a Russian called Orlov."

Irina. Casey was quite surprised by the strength of his reaction. "What about Orlov?"

"You want to see the clip? Like, get it from the horse's mouth?"

"Sure."

"You got an s-code on your AV?"

Casey entered a sequence into the keyboard on his desktop. "On line."

"Sending."

The desk screen snowed and cleared. A figure in a fancy blue pressure suit was standing in front of a ghosted-in background of the Silver Locust Motel. Worthing's voice came from it.

"Hi, Lon. I'm just passing along a bit of information, for what it's worth."

Worthing must have been standing in a cut-paste that Hammond had been using. So the two of them were up the goddamn

North Pole Trail, no doubt going for the Soviet base. They had to be fucking crazy. But what about Irina?

"We just left the Silver Locust. As we were leaving, a party of Russians came in, mostly prisoners, poor bastards, on their way to Vorkuta. It seems that their transport had been totaled and they'd had to walk all night. Irina Orlov was among them. She wasn't a prisoner, but I figure that if she's on her way to Vorkuta in any capacity, she has to be under a pretty dense cloud. I don't know if this is of any interest to you—I knew that you and her were friendly. I'm sending this by a roundabout route so there's no chance of the Russians picking it up. That's about all I can tell you. I didn't think that it was a particularly good idea to go and talk to her, so I didn't. She looked okay, if a little tired. May 26, 13:49 MST. This is Dan Worthing signing off."

Sandoz was back on the line. "Does that cover it?"

"Yes. Thanks a lot. Thank Dan for me. Tell him I owe him one."

"We just aim to please."

Casey slowly hung up the phone. He knew what he wanted to do, but he also wanted to sit for a couple of minutes before he started doing it. Finally he picked up the phone.

"Rhoda, where's Ray?"

"He's in his office."

"Ask him to come in here, will you."

When Chavez came in, Casey waved him to a seat.

"I need to take off for a couple of days."

"How many days?"

"Maybe a week."

"A fishing trip, or have you made a new friend?"

"I just need to follow something up on my own."

"You want to talk about it?"

"You'll tell me I'm crazy."

"Try me."

Casey shrugged and ran a copy of the message from Worthing. Chavez watched intently and then shook his head.

"You're crazy."

There was a long silence.

"I've got to go up there and see what I can do for her."

"You're planning on springing her?"

"I don't know."

"Sure you do. You're thinking about the full white horse job."

"Maybe."

"Like I said, you're crazy. It'd be an international incident. They'll have your badge."

"Only if I get caught."

"They're real good at catching people who stage jailbreaks."

"I thought you were on my side."

Chavez held up his hands. "I am. That's why I'm telling you that you're crazy. Shit, Lon, I'll cover for you if that's what you want, but this is a crazy scheme."

"I just don't want her going to Vorkuta. She'll die up there."

"So you're going? A man's gotta do, etcetera."

Casey nodded. "I guess I am."

"You want me to go with you?"

Casey shook his head. "No, this is my problem."

"When do you want to leave?"

"As soon as I can. How long do you think they'll keep this bunch of prisoners at the Silver Locust?"

Chavez thought for a moment. "It's only a guess, but I figure they'll be hanging about up there for a while. Prisoners ain't going to be a major priority. It could be a couple of weeks before another transport shows up for them. What they might do, though, is march everyone up the trail to one of the Russian refueling stops. They probably won't want them at the Silver Locust for very long. For that matter, I doubt Ramon Silver wants his place jammed up with Russians and prisoners."

"I'm going to get a couple of hours of sleep and head up there."

"You want to use an aircraft?"

Casey was tempted, but he turned the idea down. Aircraft were prohibitively expensive to operate in the thin Martian atmosphere. "I could never justify the fuel cost."

"So what's the cover story?"

It was Casey's turn to think. So far, he had just been reacting. "Hell, tell them that I'm off on a lead in the Ripper investigation. That's the one that's getting all the heat. Maybe it'll get the media off everyone's back for a couple of days."

Chavez hesitated. "Listen, be real careful, okay?"

Casey put a hand on his shoulder. "I'll do my best."

*White Marsman on the North Pole Trail, twenty kilometers
south of Marsbad Caverns Settlement—May 27 CEC—
17:09 MST.*

The sandblasted, sun-bleached sign by the roadside read
"Only Twenty Kilometers to MARSBAD CAVERNS—the freetradingest town on the whole damn trail!" The word *HELLHOLE*
had been scrawled across it in fresh red spray paint. With Travis
and Barstow spelling each other, they had covered a lot of ground
in the twenty-seven hours since they had left the parking area of
the Silver Locust. The first leg of the journey had been quite
festive as the nondrivers had cured their hangovers with more
of the same.

As the hours had passed, the camaraderie in the forward cabin
had become increasingly sluggish. Even the low-key fondling
that had been going on started to grow tiresome. At the start,
Worthing had found it quite amusing to travel with a scantily
clad Max sitting in his lap. After ten hours, however, she had
become dead weight, and his legs were in pain. They were facing the fact that the vehicle was overcrowded. Maybe Travis had
been right, after all.

Around one in the morning, they had pulled into a SunServe
Robot Roadhouse. Travis had decided that they were going to
get a few hours of static sleep. Nobody argued. The SunServes
were the closest thing Mars had to a franchise. Owned by National Food in Chicago and serviced out of Burroughs, Bradbury, and the new settlement in the Herschel crater, they dotted
most of the major trails across the planet, red and white Per-
mapod Doubledomes, squat and indestructible, which reliably
supplied a minimum of food, water, fuel, and sleep. The fully
automatic pod incorporated a multiple fuel line, clean but expensive water and liquid air dispensers, and a rack of coffin-
shaped bed boxes. SunServe supply freighters were a familiar
sight on the Martian roads and trails. The SunServes refused to
handle cash. It was their first line of defense against the danger

of becoming the nightmare haunts of backrats, leftovers, and worse. The second was the scanner disk on top of a pylon that stood like a spindly sentry beside the low dome. It swiveled to observe them as Travis backed up the vehicle and the passengers started climbing down from the air lock. The CC laser mounted in the center of the dish would cut them down if they did anything that the unit's protection program did not sanction, and the service crew, when they next came by, would bury the bodies. It might have seemed a touch of overkill, but it was standard operating procedure for the National Food Corporation. It was no accident that it was referred to worldwide as Nazi Food.

Worthing was ready with credits in a bunch of phony names. "You never know who might be paying attention." He grinned at Max. "In our business, it doesn't always pay to advertise."

Travis fueled up the Marsman and then crawled into a bed box, declaring that he was going to catch a couple of hours of sleep. Hammond and Theresa fitted themselves into one of the doubles, and after buying a couple of packs of Rockee b'Chokee Tips'n'Wings from the vending machine, the other four went back to sleep in the vehicle.

Travis's couple of hours stretched to five, but the dawn saw them back on the trail. It also brought Hammond his first glimpse of Olympus Mons. The huge conical crag seemed to stretch to the sky even when its base was far beyond the horizon.

"Do you realize that sucker's twelve miles high? Over twice as tall as Everest. The summit's as good as in outer space. It's fucking amazing."

Hammond was quite surprised that Travis had condescended to give the running commentary. The closer they came to the volcano, the more Hammond came to realize just how big it really was. There was nothing like it on Earth, nothing to even compare it with. It could be judged only according to a totally alien scale.

Even the awesome size of the volcano could not keep them from noticing that the cabin was extremely cramped. Barstow had screwed up the microwave during an attempt to make a hot dinner from a package on which the instructions were in Hindi and that had turned out to be self-heating. The air was thick with greasy smoke and the smell of exploded murgha tikka makhani. Barstow was fanning the smoke with his hat to little effect.

"It's getting bad in here."

"There's too many of us."

Hammond scowled. "So who do we drop overboard?"

"Shit, this ain't overcrowded," Max said. She had just done a whole deck of blind tiger, which she had produced out of nowhere. "One time, you know? Me and these three other girls went on a forty-eight-hour freefall jag in a little two-man survey ship. These two Japanese were crazy. They just wanted women floating all around them. They liked it so they could reach out in any direction to touch someone. Claimed they were full *denshi*, but we didn't believe them. It was kinda fun until one of the girls threw up. You know what happens when you throw up in freefall? Anyway, we got a thou apiece."

The blind tiger hit, and she stopped. She looked blank and then mystified. "Now what in hell was I talking about?"

A second sign announced that Marsbad was only ten miles away. This one had FLA arrow symbols painted over it. The Fuji Liberation Army, the first truly corporate terror group, seemed to have the ability to get everywhere, Hammond reflected. After it passed out of sight, he glanced at Worthing.

"What the hell does the FLA want on Mars?"

Worthing shrugged. "Who knows? There's probably some obscure passage in the Book of the Five Rings that advises strategic conquest. You have to calculate that a bunch of sweating fanatics whose idea of fun is to read Ayn Rand and then go out on a suicide mission can't be dealing from the same deck as the rest of us."

"I thought we'd left that shit behind on Earth."

"Frontiers always attract the unstable."

Travis glanced back. "You're all here, ain't you?"

Barstow picked up the thread. "I ran into a bunch of FLA in Amsterdam one time. You know the kind—headbands, Ray-Bans, and the Plexiglas mouthbreathers. Being a creature of habit, I up the camera and away we go. The trouble was that the moment I look at the frame display, I know I'm in deep shit. They're coming for me with the expressions of men who feel that someone's been screwing around their defensible mortal space."

"So what did you do?"

"I dropped the camera and I ran. My mother didn't raise this kid to not recognize a no-win situation when it's waving a meat cleaver at him. I ran and I ran all over Dam. Feets don't fail me now. They chased me for about half a mile and my lungs are about to cave in, and then I see this pornodrome. You know, the kind they have over there. So I dive inside, and to my true relief, it stops them dead in their tracks. It seems that they can't look upon the lusts of the flesh without communal ritual cleansing and a couple of sacrimental martinis. Mind you, I had to wait in there for nearly four hours before they gave up waiting for me and went away. That's a hell of a lot of pornodrome."

"Rugged."

"Maybe they came to Mars looking for you, Barstow."

Barstow laughed. "That would be a little extreme."

"Extreme's their middle name."

"What's this place Marsbad all about?"

Travis sniffed. "It's another wart on the planetary body. Bad booze, lying women, and thieves."

The three girls bristled at the phrase "lying women," but Travis did not appear to notice.

"It's bigger than most of the other spots up the trail because it handles the bulk of the traffic to and from Olympus Mons," he went on. "There's a lot of communications up on the mountain, and new stuff is being installed all the time. There's always engineers and such passing through, even tourists now and again, and all ready to get clipped for their rolls."

"The Russians don't control the whole mountain?"

"Hell, no. Olympus Mons is too big for any one corporation or country to control. Right at the beginning of colonization, it was declared a common planetary resource. Access to everyone and no mining. The Russian base isn't on the mountain itself at all. It's at the bottom of the cone on the northeast side, in an area that's hemmed in by foothills. The worst they can really do is make it uncomfortable for people walking around on bits of the volcano that overlook the base. I wouldn't, on the other hand, try getting into the valley. It's posted. Go in there and you're dead."

"Marsbad will be enough for a start."

"You even have to watch your ass in there. I don't know if it's the fact that it's built in an old deep metal mine or if the settlement is just too close to the volcano, but there seems to always be a high level of craziness in there." He looked toward the three women. "Oh, yeah. Marsbad's the end of the road as far as you ladies are concerned. It's going to be all work for us from there on in."

Cilla pulled a face. "I guess it's as good as anywhere."

Theresa was polishing her nails. "If we can stay clear of that pervert Marky Proust."

The final sign marked the exit for Marsbad, although the idea of an exit from a dirt trail seemed a little incongruous. The settlement itself lay about two kilometers off the trail.

From the surface, Marsbad still looked like a mine. The slag heaps and ore silos had never been flattened or removed. The wheel and the cage winding gear were still in use, still taking the inhabitants up and down from the lower levels. There was an extensive parking area behind the disused ore silos. There were maybe a couple of dozen SVs there, mostly the dilapidated vehicles of hard-core backrats.

Barstow peered through the windshield. "Looks like a fun place."

Travis nodded grimly. "Oh, yeah. A bundle of laughs."

Before they suited up, Travis drew Hammond aside. "How long do you plan on staying here?"

"I don't know. I thought, since this is as far as civilization goes in this direction, we'd stick around and see what we can hear."

"Well, like I said, be careful. Keep a particular lookout for the KGB. After your last escapade, you may be on some sort of list."

"There's KGB down here?"

"They spook through on a regular basis. In the freetradingest town on the whole damn trail they can come and go the same as everyone else."

The Marsbad air locks were below ground level. The first descent was made in the old creaking miners' cage. Hammond looked around at the scarred, dented metal of the elevator car. Back in the days when the mine had been in full production, its output must have been enormous. The cage alone was quite capable of holding a couple of semitrucks.

As the gates closed on them and four other travelers, Barstow looked around dubiously. "You think this thing's safe?"

"It hasn't crashed so far, and it's been going for a few years. You got a phobe on elevators?"

"It ain't a phobe. I just don't trust them."

Once they had cycled through the air lock and stashed their suits in the entrance lockers, they emerged into a long, high gallery that was part natural formation and part excavation with steel support columns and polymer liners. It was what served in Marsbad as a main street, but it seemed a shadowy place for a main street, a perpetual nighttime with little overhead lighting. What little light was there spilled from the booths that ran along its length and the mosaic of glowing signs that advertised each one's individual attractions. Lasers stabbed up to the cavern roof and were reflected back again. Hypnos and uncle tubes revolved and flashed, and hologram dancers cooched and cooed in the columns of colored vapor that drifted up around the entrance to a place that called itself the Lovezone. An electronic flame dragon reared over a Szechuan noodle stand. Ghostly optic filaments danced abstract patterns in the circulating air and drew the customers to a Dreamscape. Only Mars and a couple of the sleazier Earth-orbit environments still had Dreamscapes—the cort-stim parlors were illegal everywhere else. Before they had been forced out by the SEC and the UN, the Drexa Corporation had attempted to market their direct pleasure-center feeds under a number of different names—Dreamscape, Ectsat, Sooth, and a half dozen more—always ignoring the fact that it gave the habitual user something not unlike Parkinson's disease and reduced him or her to a single quivering twitch. By all accounts, becoming habituated was all too easy. Ex-Dreamscapers who had been straight for years would still smile wistfully and use words like "perfection" and "ultimate."

The air in Marsbad was a long way from perfection. Where in Vostok the air was just rank and stale, here there was the bite of chlorine and maybe a touch of ammonia, as though the scrubbers were malfunctioning. No one seemed to care about what contaminants poured into the system, either. Plumes of vapor rose not only from the main street stalls but also from pipe joints and ruptured conduits.

A crowd of people moved between the light and the shadows. Up on the surface it might have been late afternoon, but down there it was the wee, wee hours. A strange blend of music from a dozen competing sources filled the air. People drifted with the aimlessness of men wondering why the fun had not yet started. There was the usual percentage of staggering drunks, swaggering troublemakers, and calculating predators in among the blank, sweating faces and the empty eyes of those on the grailquest of the elusive good time.

Max stopped and planted her hands on her hips, taking it all in. "Well, goddamn it to hell, here I am back in the city of the mole people."

A lot of the men moved in groups—survey teams, ice crews, work gangs—sticking together come what might. There were also those who moved in pairs. They were Marsbad security: gold badges and shoulder flashes, peaked caps, and nylon bomber jackets with fur collars. They had stun prods hanging from their wrists and Galil needleguns in strapped-down holsters.

Hammond and his crew and the three women, who did not seem to want to part company with the newsmen quite yet, joined the rest of the aimless strollers. They walked down one side of the main street, looking over the line of booths just like any other bunch of tourists. The whores plied their trade, the numbers men hawked lottery systems, and the smell of fried food came in bursts, some of which were strong enough to make Worthing want to gag. Pitchmen and come-on girls tried to lure them into a half dozen joints, but the new arrivals were not at the stage where they wanted to settle somewhere. There was a long line outside the Dreamscape. Some of those waiting already had the shakes.

Max looked around in weary distrust. "The shit don't change."

Worthing eyed the Dreamscape speculatively. "You know, I always wanted to try that, just once."

"Don't you have enough problems already?"

They continued down the main street. A souvenir stand

wanted to sell them towels with "I love Martians" printed on them. Also on sale were Marsbad T-shirts, red planet tote bags, and tiny plastic models of Olympus Mons, each in a transparent globe with its own snowstorm. A bunch of rent boys shot Barstow and Worthing come-hither looks and were rewarded with dour scowls.

They paused for a while to watch the teaser video displays outside a place called the Crash Palace. A pair of converted mining robots were battling it out in a small ring. They were about one meter tall and squatly humanoid. Whoever had customized the original miners had gone for maximum aggression. Fists had been turned into ferocious armored clubs. Heads and bodies were armed with stubby horns and sharp steel spikes. Every movable surface that could be employed to crush, puncture, rip, or gouge was put to destructive use.

Hammond looked a little puzzled. "Isn't this kinda tame compared with cockfighting or pit bulls or even rink hockey? Nobody's getting hurt, no blood or anything."

Worthing pointed to a pair of auxiliary screens. There might have been no blood, but the suffering was plain to see in the two sweating faces on the screens.

"They used to run these things with a crude pseudointelligence, but the novelty quickly wore off and people stopped coming. It was then that they started using human handlers, and the sickos came back for the pain."

The handlers, a man and a woman, both young and attractive, were linked to their respective robots by direct neural interface. The woman had a DNI band around her forehead; the young man had gone all the way and had the permanent implants. Each time a blow fell, agony registered in one of the faces. The handlers registered pain that the robots could not even conceive. There was no physical damage, but the mental scarring was massive.

"You have to be real relentless for Crash Palace. Even the best go mad in a couple of years. You make a lot of money while it lasts, though."

They walked on. The girls stopped to talk to a couple of Marsbad security men. From the animation of the conversation, it was clear that they all went way back. Hammond and the others waited at a distance. After the recent brush with the KGB, Hammond was a little leery of off-world law enforcement. Travis agreed.

"You don't want to be tangling with those guys. Justice is a tad rough and ready around these parts."

Piano music was coming from a place with an electric blue sign that read "The Cool Cave." Worthing stopped to listen. "That's 'Monk's Groove' he's playing."

Travis shot him a warning look. "You get a high percentage of Russians in bop joints."

Worthing did not seem particularly daunted by the idea of Russians. "Ah, what the hell? I just want to check out the music. Let's go have a drink."

The others looked less than enthusiastic, but then a drunk started whooping and hollering and firing his pistol into the roof of the gallery. Cascades of dust fell on the passersby. He was immediately surrounded by a half dozen security men, who, without any formalities, commenced to club him bloody. Getting off the street for a while suddenly seemed like a very good idea.

The Cool Cave was aptly named. It was essentially a low-ceilinged side tunnel that had been driven off the main gallery. The lights were dim, and the fittings were black and chrome. The only bright spot in the room was around the pool table, where three local bopniks shot nine ball while a girl in a leather dress watched them. The piano player was a traditionalist in a shark-skin slimjim with a watch chain and a white silk shirt with a Mr. B collar. Half his face was hidden behind insect glasses. He was playing an old-fashioned acoustic grand that must have cost a fortune to ship out from Earth. His only audience was a booth full of SV drivers who were close to the comatose phase. Worthing took a seat at the bar, and the others, including the girls, who had followed them in, did the same.

Worthing grinned at the bartender. "You got any scotch?"

The bartender shook his head. "I think scotch became extinct."

"How come all the bar owners on this sorry planet don't get together, rent a ship, and bring in some decent booze?"

The bartender grinned. "They did. Eighteen months ago. Just six more months to wait before it gets here."

"So what you got?"

"I got beer."

Worthing's face brightened. "That makes a change."

"It's brewed right here in the settlement."

Worthing's face fell. He could imagine what Marsbad beer was like. "Okay, give me a beer and a shot of vodka. You got vodka, right?"

"We've always got vodka."

The piano player finished his set with "Round Midnight" and then came over to the bar and sat two stools down from Worthing. Worthing indicated to the bartender that he should give the man a drink on his tab. The piano player nodded.

Worthing leaned toward him. "You play very nicely."

"Thanks." The musician glanced back at the drivers in the booth. "It's nice to be appreciated."

"If it's not a rude question, what's a guy who can play Monk the way you do—"

"Doing in a place like this?" The piano player was grinning. "It's a long story, friend. A long sad story."

He took off his sunglasses, revealing the extremely bloodshot eyes of someone with a blind tiger habit. "You might not believe it, but five years ago I was playing at Birdland in Moscow."

"I can believe that—you sure as hell play sweet enough."

"Well, thank you, friend, but that didn't help me when novostroika came in and they started closing down the bop joints and looking real close at the working papers of cats like me. You dig?"

Worthing nodded. "So how did you get out here?"

The piano player downed his shot in a single gulp and signaled to the bartender for another. "Hell, that was another dumb mistake. I was back in New York, and the only thing they were listening to there was industrial noise, and I don't play industrial anything. I got this agent, see, and he tells me that he's got me a residency at this club in Vostok. So I ask myself what I've got to lose, and I ship out to Mars. The moment I arrive, I start to find out what I've got to lose. For a start, Vostok's a toilet, and then I'm told the gig's been canceled. Novostroika got out here

decisions. Despite that, however, Perovsky was looking more and more to her for direction. When Silver had delivered his ultimatum about the Americans, the sergeant had taken her to one side.

"I can't let him bring the Americans into this. There's no knowing what might happen if they got involved. The only thing that's certain is that it'll be my head."

Irina had been cautious. Her own head did not feel exactly secure on her shoulders. "Have you tried Vostok again?"

"They don't give a damn about us."

"What about Commander Reyleyev? Doesn't he have any ideas?"

"He just wants to get out from under. He's strictly the commander of the transport. He says the prisoners are the army's responsibility. He's worried about losing the cargo that's still in the wreck. If a relief vehicle doesn't leave Vostok by tomorrow, he's saying that he's going to take what's left out of his crew and go back to the crawler to protect it from looters. He says the cargo's more valuable to him than the prisoners."

Irina wished she had a way out from under. "How are the prisoners?"

"They're quiet at the moment, but another day or so of this and they'll be ready to try something."

"You've got enough guns to stop them."

"Shooting prisoners on independent territory could create a serious incident. Silver could get U.S. Marines up here. It's the way wars get started."

Perovsky looked profoundly unhappy, but Irina did not know what to say to the man, particularly as she was little more than a prisoner herself. Thoughts about using the situation to try to escape had already crossed her mind. The same ideas must certainly have occurred to at least some of the prisoners.

"One thing's for sure," she said. "There's nowhere we can go without transport."

"I've been thinking about that."

Irina looked at him bleakly. She did not like it when the army started thinking. "You have?"

"There's one of our refueling stations about a hundred klicks up the trail."

"So why can't they come down and help us out?"

"It's unmanned. Just a supply base and emergency living quarters."

"So what good is it to us?"

"We could wait there until we get a relief transport."

"What do we do about the hundred kilometers?"

"We can walk it in two days."

"Are you serious?"

"I don't see any other alternative."

"You lost nine prisoners on the way up here. How many more are going to die on a two-day forced march in those emergency suits?"

Perovsky's face became stiff and professional. "That's not a problem."

"It isn't?"

"Listen, Chief Investigator, I have to bring in these prisoners or a corresponding death count. That's it. That's my job. All they care about in Vorkuta is that the numbers tally."

"And you want to start a death march on the basis of arithmetic?"

The sergeant's face closed up. He had clearly decided that he would get no help from Irina. In his book, that probably made her as expendable as any prisoner. "I'll do what I have to do."

Irina was silent.

Perovsky seemed to have a final need to justify himself. "How long do you think they're going to last once they get to Vorkuta?"

In that moment the idea crystallized. If the chance presented itself, she was going to escape. She did not care what it took. She wondered what would happen if she appealed to Silver, the owner, for political asylum. Then she dismissed the idea. Silver was not the kind to take pity on a damsel in distress. He and Perovsky would probably flip a coin to see who got to shoot her.

"So when do you want to start this walk up the trail?" she asked.

"At dawn. I thought I'd let everyone sleep through the night and then move out at dawn."

Irina nodded. From that point on she was going to be looking out strictly for herself.

Jeep ATV on the North Pole Trail, 580 kilometers north of Vostok—May 27 CEC—21:04 MST.

Greig had slept for a while, but then the evil dream had forced him to wake. The evil dream came only when the entity was stirring. In a day or so it would be starting its demands. At first it was hard to make the transition from the horrors in his subconscious to the clinical interior of the mission vehicle. A dark cloud from the depths still lingered, and nothing seemed quite real. He had to force himself calmly to take stock of his surroundings. They were running through the Martian night as fast as they could on the uneven surface of the trail. The cabin was dimmed out, and the racked equipment was an arrangement of bulky shadows. Whittaker was driving, and Booth was quietly reading Maltin's *Yesterday* by the light of a small penlite.

The cloud in Greig's mind slowly cleared, but normality did not quite return. He found that he was hyperaware of the sound of the engine and the other small vibrations in the cabin. The green displays around the driver's seat glowed like bright emeralds. He viewed everything with the heightened awareness that always came when the entity was ready to emerge.

Whittaker turned in her seat. "There are lights up ahead."

Booth looked up from his book. "The Silver Locust?"

Whittaker shook her head. "Not unless the navigation program is way off. We shouldn't be at the Silver Locust yet. Besides, these lights aren't that stupid cowboy sign. You can see that thing for miles around. These are just a couple of small lights in the darkness."

Booth put down the book, turned off the penlite, and leaned forward. "There are a lot of vehicle hijackings along this stretch of the trail. It could be a trap." He turned to Greig. "Arm the exterior weapons system."

Without a word, Greig turned to the weapons board. He did not trust his voice. Nothing in the Jeep's cab seemed quite real. Whittaker had the forward scanner up. "There's some kind of vehicle up ahead. It doesn't seem to be moving . . . Wait a minute, I'm getting a better picture. It looks like a Russian crawler, probably the old K class. There seems to be something wrong with it. The front and rear cars are at a weird angle. I think it's a wreck.''

"Don't slow down."

Whittaker looked back at Booth in surprise. "We don't stop? It's a wrecked surface vehicle. The code demands that we stop and give assistance.''

Booth shook his head. "We don't stop, particularly for Russians.''

"What about the code?''

There was something in the rambo's face that was scarcely human. "We're operating on a different code.''

Burroughs Marshal's Department's high-speed pursuit vehicle, forty kilometers north of the crater Biblis Pater— May 27 CEC—21:35 MST.

Casey knew that he should stop and sleep, but he made no attempt to pull over. The pursuit vehicle roared through the night with its headlights blazing. He had been driving for just under twenty-four hours, and his eyes were starting to play tricks on him. He was going too fast for the uneven surface of the open desert, but he was past caring. He was determined to catch up with Irina at whatever cost. The bootleg drynamax he had been swallowing had helped somewhat. The pills had been in the drawer of his desk ever since he had taken them off a crazy Kenyan in a weapons bust a couple of months earlier. He guessed that he had been saving them for whatever passed on Mars for a rainy day, and now that day had come. He did not particularly like drynamax, or most drugs, for that matter. His mouth was dry, and the peripheral hallucinations were very irritating. He was jittery and kept starting at imaginary objects just beyond the beams of the headlights.

"You have really got to start looking for a SunServe, boy, or you're not only going to go nuts but also run out of fuel and air.''

He had been pushing the PV so hard that he had been burning fuel way over the econopoint. He still had half a tank left, but he had taken off across open country to avoid coming close to Vostok, and he had no real idea where the next fuel supply might be. He also realized that he was talking to himself out loud. Maybe he was nuts already. He wondered, after all, if he should have used one of the department's two rocket planes. Short-range aircraft were one of the least cost-effective methods of travel on the red planet and were avoided except in the direst emergencies. Without enough atmosphere to allow wing lift, all flying, with the exception of some experimental giant microlites the marines operated, had to be done on full burn, and the fuel consumption verged on the absurd.

An amber light was flashing on the instrument display.

"Now what?"

He set the communicator to proximity sweep. An automatic distress signal pulsed from the speaker.

"Goddamn it to hell!"

There was no way he could ignore the emergency call, but it was the very last thing he needed. Any kind of delay increased the risk that Irina would be gone when he got to the Silver Locust. He slowed the PV and turned in the direction of the signal. He was heading into rock-strewn uneven terrain, and he had to be careful. There was another reason for caution: Al-though the North Pole Trail was reasonably well patrolled, the highlands north of Vostok were notorious for particularly vi-cious hijackers and bandits, the ones who had been dubbed martacheros. It was common for them to use a distress signal to lure their victims off the trail and into some blind canyon where they could be robbed and murdered with ease. Some of the martacheros were plain blind desolation crazy, the kind who liked to cat and mouse their victims in a variety of unpleasantly creative ways before they finished them and after they were dead. There had even been rumors of cannibalism.

The forward scanner was showing the outline of a vehicle. It looked like an old Citroën Gyrodyne lying on its side. The single-wheeled, supposedly all-terrain vehicle had turned out to be the Edsel of Martian surface craft. The huge balloon tire with the two-man cabin mounted in its hub had bounced too much in the low Martian gravity for the gyroscopes to keep the thing stable. In the end, the French had virtually been forced to give them away. Casey had not seen one in at least nine months, but if he was going to come across one of those mechanical dinosaurs, the highlands and ridges beyond Biblis Pater were the place. It could be some old-time prospector in trouble, or it could just as easily be a setup for a hijacking.

The PV's speed was down to walking pace. It was unlikely that any potential highjackers, even hard-core martacheros, would be dumb enough to jump him once they saw the federal marshal shields on the sides of the pursuit craft, but Casey had not lived as long as he had by overestimating the prudence or intelligence of criminals, particularly the kind who prowled those dead hills, out of their minds on loneliness and bad booze.

Casey halted the vehicle and flicked off the headlights. There was nothing moving on the forward scan. For about a minute he sat in the darkness just watching and listening. Still nothing moved as the distress signal pulsed on.

"I guess this means I've got to go the full fucking route."

The first thing he did was swallow two more drynamax. If he was going into something bad, he needed a chemical backup. After the pills, he ran through the book sequence for entering a threat situation. Helmet on, depressurize the cabin, bring up the weapons system. The PV carried two small heat seekers in the prow nacelles and had a rotating solid-fuel minigun mounted above the cabin. When everything was in place, he opened a broad hailing channel.

"Breaker, breaker, I'm picking up an oh five niner out here. If you're in trouble, please acknowledge."

There was nothing except the distress signal, and still nothing was moving around the old Citroën on the radar. He repeated his message. No response. He would have to go look in person. He was tempted simply to split and forget the whole thing, but he knew he could not do that. The code was too strongly in-grained in him.

He shook his head. "I really don't need this shit."

He set the headlights on dim and eased the PV forward. When the Gyrodyne was within range, he flashed on the hibrights, and the military spots brilliantly illuminated the desert in front of him. The Citroën was right in the beams, leaning over on one side, tilted on its one huge balding tire. Suddenly suited figures in ragged dust capes began to emerge from holes in the ground. The nearest one had a red skull painted on the visor of his helmet, and a second wore curved Viking horns.

"Fucking martacheros! I've walked into this one."

He hit the minigun control, putting it through a 360-degree sweep. The martacheros hit the dirt, scrabbling for cover. They clearly had not expected such a fast and aggressive response. One of them was up on one knee aiming some kind of shoulder-held missile launcher. Casey jammed the machine into reverse. The wheel cages spun, throwing up fountains of dust, and the PV's drive screamed as it went backward at full speed. He kept his thumb down hard on the minigun's firing button, letting go with a sustained burst. The martachero's missile launcher puffed flame and smoke. At first the missile seemed to be traveling very slowly, but it quickly gathered speed. Still in reverse, Casey spun the controls. The PV bucked as the right rear wheel hit a rock. The missile flashed by the windshield, its gas plume less than a meter away. It had missed on the first pass, but if it was a heat seeker, it would turn and come back.

Then Casey got lucky. The missile slammed into the Gyro-dyne, and the whole thing exploded. Casey braked hard. The martacheros were running for an old Ford Astro that was half-hidden in the rocks. Casey loosed one of his own heat seekers. It streaked away, and the Astro exploded. He breathed out hard and slumped back in his seat. He was sweating inside his helmet, and his nerves were jumping from adrenaline and dryna-max. He had to force himself not to throw up. Very carefully, he repressurized the cabin, removed his helmet, and took a deep breath of the fresh cool cabin air. Finally he eased the PV into drive and started back for the trail.

"I really have to pull over for a couple of hours."

The Cool Cave, Marsbad Caverns—May 27 CEC—
23:49 MST.

It was five hours before Crazy Mouly drifted through, and when he did, he was stumbling drunk. As the old backrat blundered in through the entrance, Worthing glanced at the bartender. Was this the one? Worthing had tipped the man a fifty to give him the nod when Mouly showed his face. The bartender nodded.

Worthing let the backrat settle into a booth on his own, and then he leaned close to Hammond. "That's our man."

Hammond covertly glanced around. "The ragged-assed old geezer? We've been waiting for him?"

"It ain't no beauty contest."

Hammond shrugged. "It's your idea."

Worthing treated Hammond to a bleak look. "You got a better one?"

"Hell, no. I'm just the star. How do you want to play this?"

Worthing picked up his drink. Hammond did not seem to be firing on all cylinders, and the Englishman was starting to worry. "I thought I'd let the girls soften him up first and then go over and see what I could get out of him. If he's worth taping for background, we can get him out of here and you can do a full interview for the camera."

Hammond nodded. He seemed willing to go along with anything. "Sounds good to me."

Theresa and Cilla were still hanging around, drinking on Worthing's money, although Max had vanished sometime earlier, promising to be back in ten minutes. Worthing turned to the two of them, jerking a thumb in the direction of the old man. "You think you could soften up the ragged-assed old geezer?"

Theresa did not look too enthusiastic. "Why would we want to do that?"

Worthing laid a pair of hundreds on the bar. "The milk of human kindness, or because he reminds you of your dear old daddy."

The two women picked up the hundreds. Cilla giggled. "Honey, I'm so drunk, I could soften up a concrete block."

"So let's go to work."

The Cool Cave was fairly crowded, and so there was plenty of cover. No one in the bar seemed to be paying any attention to Crazy Mouly. The piano player was beating out one of his own compositions, something dissonant with almost a rock 'n' roll rhythm. The title was "Stranded in the Sprawl." There was a brief confrontation as Theresa and Cilla homed in on Mouly. An older woman with thick pancake makeup also seemed to have designs on Mouly, and she was clearly amazed that a couple of girls like Theresa and Cilla should want to have anything to do with him.

The older woman's voice came clearly across the bar. "He isn't even worth robbing."

In a very fluid movement for one who had drunk so much, Worthing was off his bar stool and moving. He bore down on the older woman and, without breaking stride, grasped her arm and propelled her along. He held a hundred in front of her eyes.

"Don't say a word. This is a security matter. Just go to another joint and don't make a fuss."

Her eyes popped, but she took the C note. "What are you? KGB?"

Worthing did not answer. Any smoke screen would help. When the woman was gone, Worthing looked around the bar. The incident did not seem to have caused a ripple. Cilla and Theresa were in the booth cozying up to Crazy Mouly. Worthing wiped his face and went back to his stool. He judged that he should give the girls maybe ten minutes with Crazy Mouly before he joined the party. So far things seemed to have been going fairly well. The newsmen had their first line on the Soviet base. There had been a few moments of anxiety an hour or so earlier, when three men who had a certain KGB look about them had come into the place, but when the three had left after a couple of drinks, Worthing had relaxed again, dismissing it as paranoia.

After a suitable period of time had elapsed, Worthing got to his feet and, looking as casual as possible, sauntered over to Crazy Mouly's booth.

The old man looked up and glared at him. "What the hell do you want? I don't recall inviting you over."

Worthing knew that he was dealing with an ingrained curmudgeon. "I thought I might buy you a drink."

Crazy Mouly's bright beady eyes squinted at him suspiciously. "Why?"

"I wanted to talk to you."

"Why in hell should you want to talk to me? Most people call me crazy."

"I heard you know more about Olympus Mons than anyone around."

"You heard that, did you? Well, I'd like to talk to you, but—" He indicated Cilla and Theresa. "—I've got my hands full right now."

Casey nodded. "So I see."

Mouly's jaw jutted pugnaciously. "So, if you see, why don't you shove off?"

Worthing smiled. "The thing is, old boy, it was me who sent these two lovelies over to sit with you in the first place."

Crazy Mouly resembled nothing more than a beat-up, even more weathered version of Popeye the Sailor. One busy eyebrow went up, and the other came down, while the deeply etched lines in his face could have been a relief map of the planet itself. "And why should you have done that?"

"Like I said, because I want to hear all you know about the volcano."

"And you thought a couple of Marsbad whores might loosen my tongue?" He pronounced the word *hoors*, rolling the "r."

Worthing's grin broadened. "And as much as you can drink. You had a better offer lately?"

Mouly was a picture of distrust. "And who might you be, anyway?"

"The name's Dan Worthing, out of Burroughs."

"And why do you want to know so goddamn much about the mountain?"

"That'll have to be my business, for the moment."

Mouly grunted and muttered something inaudible into his beer. Worthing maintained his amiable smile.

"So, do you want to talk with me or not?"

The old man's expression changed from distrust to backrat cunning. He made a fast gesture, indicating the two girls. "What about them? Will they still be around when we get through talking?''

Worthing nodded. ''They could be. If everything goes the way I want it to.''

Theresa's eyes narrowed. ''Who says? Who's paying?''

Cilla joined in. ''Right, who's paying?''

Worthing looked at them both with annoyance. ''I'll be paying. Remember me? The bankroll that got you out of the Silver Locust and that's been keeping you in booze for the last few days.''

Mouly cackled. ''Ain't it always the way with whores?''

Worthing nodded. He had the old man where he wanted him. ''Ain't it always? You mind if I sit down?''

Crazy Mouly was suddenly expansive. ''Sit down, Dan Worthing. Sit as long as you like if you're paying the tab.''

Worthing glanced at Cilla and Theresa. ''Can you be back here in an hour?''

''You're asking a lot.''

''I'm also paying a lot.''

When the women had gone, Worthing settled himself across the booth from Mouly. The backrat was still watching the girls walk away.

''Are you sure they're coming back?''

''If they don't, I'll buy you two more.''

Mouly nodded. It was a deal. ''So what do you want to know about the mountain so bad? You're laying out a lot of money.''

''I want to know what the Russians have got out there that's making them so nervous.''

Mouly was watchful again. ''Who says I know what they've got there?''

''I heard you'd been all over Olympus Mons long before the Russians set up that base.''

''Me and Boogie Boy been all over the big mountain, that's true enough.''

''Who's Boogie Boy?''

''Boogie Boy was my partner. Now he's inside of me.''

Worthing knew that he was getting his first glimpse of why they called the guy Crazy Mouly. ''What do you mean by inside of you?''

"I mean that when Boogie Boy died out there, he came inside of me. You sure ask a lot of questions, mister."

Worthing said nothing and signaled to a waitress for more drinks. This time he had her bring a whole bottle. He gave the old man a couple of minutes before he started questioning him again. "People say you claim there are aliens out there."

"People say a lot of things. I ain't responsible for what people say."

"But are there aliens?"

Mouly was vigorously shaking his head. "No aliens. No live aliens. Not here. Not on Mars. You gotta look farther than here for your aliens, and even then you won't see them. You won't never see them. Not unless they want you to."

Mouly seemed to be watching Worthing's expression. Worthing kept his face impassive, even though he was starting to wonder whether he had wasted everyone's time just to listen to some brain-damaged old prospector.

"What about dead aliens? You and Boogie Boy ever see anything like that?"

"It wasn't my fault."

"Of course it wasn't."

"He went crazy. They call me crazy, but they don't know what crazy really is. He was going to kill me. We'd shipped out from Earth together. That was back in the old days when you had to do it the hard way, before the coldsleep. He was going to kill me, and I had to shoot him. He blew up inside his suit. You ever watch a partner go into explosive decompression? That's why I had to take him into my mind. First to stop the pain, and then so he could go on living inside of me."

Mouly quickly grabbed for his drink. There was desperation in the way he sucked it down.

Worthing immediately poured him another one. "You want to tell me about it?"

Mouly stared into the middle distance. His lips were moving soundlessly. When he finally found his voice, he seemed to be talking more to himself than to Worthing. "It was five years ago. You know how long five years can be?"

Worthing nodded and let the old man go on.

"Boogie and me had been sounding for permafrost around

the northwest base of the mountain. We figured that there might be deep frost down under the lava folds. We started up this valley, and then we saw it.'' He paused as though, even after all that time, he still could not believe the memory. ''It was black, black as sin and almost as old as the rocks. Bits of it all over the far end of the valley. Just bits and pieces. The skeleton and other stuff.''

''A dead alien?''

Mouly looked at Worthing as though he were an imbecile. ''No, dummy, it was a ship. An alien ship, half-buried in the sand and looking like it was from the dawn of time. At first Boogie and me thought we were rich. We thought we'd hit the big strike.''

''Did you tell anyone about it?''

''Are you crazy? You hit it big, and you don't start shouting about it over an open channel. You hit it big, and you keep very, very quiet about it. Otherwise you get what those Cubans got.''

''So what did you do?''

Mouly suddenly looked up straight at Worthing. The look in his eyes was not madness, just a horror that had been long in maturing.

''We sat on top of it planning how we were going to spend the money.''

''The money?''

''The money we were going to get for having discovered the very first alien artifact.'' Mouly's eyebrow shot up, he let his mouth drop open, and his eyes were wide. ''There were tons of it. It was the Dead Sea Scrolls and the Lost City of the Incas and Sutter's Mill all rolled into one.''

Worthing decided that Mouly looked more like Charlie Manson than Popeye. It was a wild story, but he was drunk enough to start believing it. ''So what went wrong?''

''The smoke in the head. The black smoke. That old black smoke in the head.'' Mouly cackled. ''Yes, sirree, we started seeing it 'bout the third day. It came out of sleep at first, creep-crawling away once the sun was up and you were out and moving around. You know what I'm talking about, Dan Worthing? The creepcrawl into the concious, the old black smoke in Crazy Mouly's head.''

Worthing did not answer. Mouly was off to the weird country.

"It wasn't no radiation, fuck no. We knew better than that. Out in the back you don't start fucking with nothing without running a rad count over it. We checked that shit and rechecked. We selected and dissected and inspected that shit. It was metal. That was the best that our truck's little lab could come up with. It was fucking metal. Beyond that it was fucking alien. And the more we looked at it, the more alien it got. And that's what we did, we started to look at it. We looked and we looked and we looked. We sat on our asses and we stared at that shit like a couple of dummies. We just sat and stared until the helmet LEDs went on to tell us that our air tanks needed filling."

Mouly grabbed the bottle and splashed vodka into his glass. His hands were shaking, but he did not look mad at all.

"It was feeding on us. We sat on our asses and watched as it drew us in. Feeding on us and making us mad, and there wasn't a damn thing that we could do about it. We couldn't even raise the idea. It was only that time when I went to fill the tank that it came to me. Just drive the hell out of there and not stop until I couldn't feel the smoke anymore. And I yells out to Boogie Boy. I yells to him to get in the truck. I yells that he don't got to think about nothing. And he's coming, running and leaping, he's coming for the truck, but he's got this heavy rockchopper. He didn't ought to have the rockchopper, except I know that he's coming for me. The black smoke's got him, and he's coming for me, so I go for the gun, and the gun comes up. It's a big old motherfucker Hatfield Electroblaster, and when I squeezed the trigger, it just motherfucked Boogie Boy. Fucked him up good, and I didn't really care that I was killing my partner and pal because the black smoke was in my head, too. And he's flying backward and screaming in my helmet, right in my head, and there's this hole the size of a basketball in his chestplate, and blood's boiling out like a fountain, smoking and curdling, and it's filling up his helmet inside the visor, and there's more of it splashed all over the front of my suit, boiling off in this vapor. And then, very slowly, I walk over to where Boogie Boy's lying and ask him, 'What you have to go and do that for, Boy?' And as I speak to him, he comes out of his body and into mine. In like the smoke. And I'm running and I'm screaming. This time I don't look back. I slam that truck into drive, and I go and I go and I keep on going, burning gas for I don't know how long. Then I came to this drilling camp and went into shock. The miners brought me to Burroughs. Me and Boogie been wandering ever since.''

His head dropped, and he stared blankly at the bottle in front of him. He seemed drained and forlorn.

"Wandering ever since, me and Boogie.''

He roused himself and poured another drink. "You heard enough of Crazy Mouly's story, Dan Worthing?'' Making an even further recovery, he winked. "There ain't a word of truth in it, mind.''

Worthing still said nothing, and for two, maybe three minutes they drank in silence. Worthing's thoughts were in a slow reel. He was almost set to believe the old man's story, but he was not sure what frightened him most, the idea that there might be an alien spacecraft under the volcano or the fact that he was entertaining the idea at all. It could be a terminal case of longing for the alien.

"Did you ever go back?''

Mouly scowled and shook his head. "Are you kidding?''

"Did you bring any of the alien metal with you when you took off?''

Mouly hesitated before answering. "There was one piece. It was in the truck's lab. It was the bit we'd run tests on at the start.''

"Do you still have it?''

"I kept it for a long time. Seemed like Boogie Boy didn't want me to get rid of it. He seemed to like the lump of metal. Then this guy from the marines at Fort Haigh came to see me. Little mousy feller with ferret eyes. Said he'd heard my story and wanted to buy the bit of metal.''

"And you sold it.''

"Sure I sold it. Sold it just like that. It was a relief to find that I could. Boogie seemed to have just stopped caring about it. He wanted the mousy little guy to have it, so he'd get the black smoke, too. When I handed it over, the little mousy guy held it for a minute or so like he was having a religious experience. Then he put it in the lead-lined box, and that was the last I ever saw of it. Never heard a thing. Stayed drunk for a month on the money, though."

Worthing slowly refilled his glass. "It's a hell of a story."

"Ain't it just. Do I get the whores now, or are you going to welsh out on an old man?"

"Anything you want. Dan Worthing never welshed on anyone."

Mouly was all backrat again. He looked around at the women in the bar, slowly licking his lips. "I get two, right?"

Worthing nodded. "If you think you can handle two."

"Don't worry about me none."

The way Worthing put the next question made it sound like an afterthought. "Would you go back up there if I paid you? Maybe get us to a spot where we could see the Soviet base?"

Crazy Mouly firmly shook his head. "Boogie Boy wouldn't like that."

North Pole Trail, ten kilometers north of the Silver Locust—
May 28 CEC—07:42 MST.

Irina Orlov put one foot in front of the other. She stared fixedly down at the red dirt of the trail and tried as hard as she could to think of nothing. The fast flash of the Martian dawn had come and gone, and the sun was already climbing into the relentlessly pink sky. Toward the horizon, there were the faintest wisps of early morning ghost clouds. The scenery gave the illusion that the prisoners were marching straight toward the enormous bulk of Olympus Mons, which, although still hundreds of kilometers away, totally dominated the landscape. It seemed to loom over them like some sinister eventual fate, but in reality their eventual fate was a long way beyond Olympus Mons.

They had marched away from the Silver Locust in the first light and long shadows, feeling that they were once again leaving even the most minimum shelter of civilization and walking into a hostile unknown. The seemingly endless expanse of drab red dirt and washed-out pink sky that lay in front of them exactly matched the dead resignation they felt inside. The march itself was not particularly strenuous in the low gravity—it was the constant fear that proved to be the most exhausting factor. The flimsy emergency suits were simply not designed to stand up to the prolonged stress of a march across the Martian surface. As she walked, Irina waited for the first tear or rip or puncture, the resulting rush of air to the near vacuum, and the sudden and final eruption of foaming blood and pain that was explosive decompression. Already, in the first two hours out of the Silver Locust, one prisoner had gone down. He or she—Irina knew absolutely nothing about the day's first victim—had simply been left to lie, covered by the fine red spray of his or her own blood. The body would remain there, perfectly preserved, until some passerby took pity and buried it or the void crazies who prowled the trail carried it away for their own weird purposes. With death such a regular occurrence, no one could forget how fragile and vulnerable they were.

The fear might have been the exhausting part, but the silence was the eeriest: a mass of people moving together in unison but without the background of small sounds that made them human. Even in their misery, there should have been sighs, cries, and quiet groans. Instead, there was nothing. It was as though they were already dead spirits. After they had left the Silver Locust, Perovsky had ordered radio silence among the nonprisoners. Irina could not see the point of the order, but she had noticed that when in doubt, Perovsky tended to issue orders. He seemed to take a certain comfort from the action. Back at the Silver Locust, she had watched Perovsky carefully, telling herself that if she was observant enough, she would spot some flaw that she could exploit to form the basis for an escape plan. But out there on the surface, under the pink sky, she could no longer pretend that the idea of escape was anything but futile. Even if a miracle happened and she was able to slip away unnoticed, how far would she get on foot in a disposable pressure suit?

Irina Orlov put one foot in front of the other and tried not to think.

KGB headquarters, Vostok Settlement—May 28 CEC—08:30 MST.

"Good morning, Comrade Major."

Melikov was in the foulest of moods. There had been a heat reduction in his quarters during the night, and he still felt chilled to the bone. Some maintenance engineer was going to pay dearly. "I didn't notice anything particularly good about it."

"I'm sorry, Comrade Major."

Melikov settled himself behind his desk. "Well, just don't stand there, man. I can't imagine that the night was a totally uneventful one."

Turchin stiffened. "There was a signal from that transport that was wrecked on the way to Vorkuta. The sergeant in charge is moving the prisoners from the Silver Locust up to one of our supply depots to wait for a relief crawler."

Melikov looked bored. "They can walk all the way to the pole for all I care. We don't have a relief transport to send. Anything else?"

"I had Estavez brought in for questioning."

Melikov nodded. "Good, I'll talk to him later. Let him sweat for a while. Is that all?"

"There is one other thing. The local field officer in Marsbad filed a report that Hammond and his news crew are up there asking questions about the Olympus Mons facility."

Melikov compressed his lips. "I should have disappeared that man when I had the chance."

"He and the other one, Worthing, have been seen talking to the man known as Crazy Mouly, the old prospector who rants about there being an alien spacecraft near the mountain."

Melikov regarded Turchin bleakly as he stubbed out one cigarette and lit another. For several seconds he was wreathed in a halo of smoke.

"I fear that the time has come to rectify my initial mistake. Who do we have up there who could do a covert job?"

"A prejudicial pass?"

"Fully prejudicial."

"There are any number of hired guns in Marsbad at any given

time. Hammond and his people could be taken out for a few thousand rubles, and there'd be nothing to connect it to us."

"So arrange it. Make it look as though Hammond and his team were killed by a gang of drunken martacheros."

Turchin looked sideways at his boss. "Should I arrange it myself?"

Melikov shook his head. "Let the field officer do the dirty work. If anything should go wrong, we want all the distance and deniability we can get."

The Lucky Strike Hotel, Marsbad Settlement—May 28 CEC—11:24 MST.

Dan Worthing had expected to be the first down to the hotel bar, but Rat Barstow had beaten him to it. The cameraman looked up blearily from a weird-looking yellow drink when Worthing joined him.

"Have you noticed how much we're all drinking? Hammond's practically a zombie."

Worthing shook his head and signaled to the bartender. An analysis of their collective drinking habits was the last thing he needed right then. He pointed at Barstow's drink. "What the hell is he drinking?"

"A Bloody Mary."

Worthing blinked. "How do you account for the color?"

The bartender gave him a look that dared him to make something of it. "It's a taste synth. What did you expect, fresh tomato juice?"

Worthing did not have an answer. He took one of the dubious yellow drinks.

When the bartender had moved off, Barstow leaned close. "The booze here is real bad."

Worthing grunted and held up the yellow Bloody Mary. "I noticed."

Barstow shook his head. "No, I mean real bad. I had this kind of mist in my head this morning."

Despite his hangover, Worthing looked sharply at Barstow. "What?"

"A mist . . . in my head."

"Mist?"

Barstow looked confused. "Something like that. I don't know how else to describe it. It seemed to come out of sleep with me. It was gone before I could really focus on it. I figure they've got to be doing something really evil to the booze."

Worthing kept his thoughts to himself, but he could not stop thinking them. Barstow's mist was just too much like Mouly's smoke for complete peace of mind.

Silver Locust Settlement—May 28 CEC—14:13 MST.

Casey came out of the air lock. His boots rang on the floor of the almost empty barroom, and icy crystals cascaded behind him like an angry trail. He had not bothered to remove his helmet. Ramon Silver's hand went toward the shotgun behind the bar but stopped when he recognized Casey's suit.

"What are you doing here, Marshal? Aren't you a tad out of your jurisdiction?"

"Where are the Russians?"

"What do you want with these Russians, Casey? They're just the regular prison detail on the way up to Vorkuta."

Casey brought his gloved fist down hard on the bar. "Damn it, Ramon, don't fuck with me. I'm in a hurry."

"They're walking."

"Walking where?"

"Walking to some fuel dump on up the trail. Perovsky, the sergeant in charge, figured that it would be a two-day march."

"So where will they spend the night?"

Silver started to look angry. "What do you want from me, Casey? How the fuck should I know where they're going to spend the night? I didn't ask. I just wanted them out of my place."

"When did they leave?"

"Listen, Casey, slow down. You're sounding crazy. They left at dawn. You can catch up with them in one of your cruisers in under an hour. You gotta take off your helmet and have a drink before I answer any more questions."

Casey exhaled. Silver was right. He was going to burn himself out if he kept going at that rate. He unsealed his helmet and started pulling off his gloves.

Silver looked at him in some surprise. "Jesus, Marshal, what bad speed have you been taking?"

Casey ignored the question. It was none of Silver's goddamn business. "You got any whiskey?"

"That's a dumb question."

"Vodka, then."

Silver leaned forward as he poured the vodka. "You wanna sit right here until sundown, Casey. I don't know what you're up to and I don't want to know, but if you're going to pull anything with them Russians, you want to wait until after dark. There are more than enough guards on that detail to make a mess out of you. And those bastards don't care—they shoot first and check it out later."

Casey slowly nodded. He was suddenly very weary. "I guess you're right."

Silver flashed his gold teeth. "Sure I'm right. You know I'm right."

Casey quickly looked up from his drink. "You wouldn't be thinking of sending out a warning to the Russians, would you, Ramon? I wouldn't like to think that you weren't on my side."

Silver's grin broadened. "Why would I do a favor for the Russians? What could they do for me in return? No, my friend, I don't need no stinking Russians."

The Lucky Strike Hotel, Marsbad Settlement—May 28 CEC—16:17 MST.

"It's just the ravings of this old lunatic."

"That doesn't mean that there isn't a core of truth."

"Hardly enough of a core to go chasing about all over that fucking mountain."

"We were going to do that anyway."

"Yes, but up to now we've been talking in terms of this mysterious Soviet base. Now, on the sole say-so of some wino, we're into aliens."

"Very old, long-dead aliens."

"They're still fucking aliens."

It was the middle of the afternoon, although the passage of time was pretty much academic in the perpetual night of the Marsbad Caverns. The four men had gathered in Hammond's hotel room to discuss their next move. Hammond was in a filthy mood, and almost immediately he and Worthing had clashed head on over Crazy Mouly's story while Barstow and Travis had watched the confrontation in silence, Barstow looking worried and Travis looking disgusted.

"You've got to admit that it all kind of fits."

"Fits what? It's nothing but an alcoholic fantasy."

"Just for a moment, try and imagine the story's true. Mouly and his partner are prospecting round the base of the mountain. They come across the remains of an ancient alien spacecraft. Very quickly, they realize that the material of which the remains are composed is having a very destructive effect on their minds, but they're unable to do anything about it until the moment Mouly tries to make a run for it. His partner goes berserk and tries to kill him."

"How do we know that this Boogie Boy character even exists outside Mouly's fevered imagination?"

"I checked. He exists."

"What do you mean he exists?"

"I went out to the truck and ran a computer check."

Irritated by the Englishman's smartass certainty, Hammond had an irrational urge to punch Worthing. He fought it down and contented himself with a terse question. "So you ran a computer check?"

"Up to two years ago, Carl Moulin and Vincent Gotti were partners in a number of ice claims. They weren't getting rich, but they were doing okay."

"And you figure that this Gotti was Boogie Boy?"

"He had an arrest record in Burroughs for public drunkenness and disturbing the peace, the usual prospector stuff. The fact that he answered to the nickname of Boogie Boy is down there in black and white."

Hammond wished Worthing would shut up. He could not remember the last time that he had felt so bad. He could not understand it. He did not think he had drunk that much the night before. The booze up in Marsbad had to be really bad. The way his vision had been blurred when he had woken up that morning had scared him a little. He had felt as if there were a thin mist inside his head. He had never experienced anything like it before. Worthing, unfortunately, showed no signs of shutting up.

"Mouly's killing of Boogie Boy is also a matter of record. It seems that eighteen months ago, Carl Moulin was brought into Burroughs raving about how he'd killed his partner. Lon Casey conducted an investigation, but lacking any hard evidence, no charges were brought, and the whole matter was written off to isolation stress."

"Maybe that's exactly what we should do."

Hammond was aware that he was behaving like a petulant child, but he did not seem able to stop himself.

Worthing looked at him with an expression that was more concerned than angry. "Why don't we spend a few minutes riding this thing to the end of the line?"

Hammond hated Worthing for his concern. "Okay, if you have to. Ride it. I personally think it's going nowhere."

Worthing took a deep breath but refused to rise to the bait. "So our alien ship stays up there undisturbed with Boogie Boy Gotti's body laying beside it until our Cubans come along. The Russians freak, and the whole thing is surrounded by a massive security screen. It seems to upset the Russians when informed guesses keep mentioning the idea of an alien artifact."

"Is that the end of the line?"

"There are a couple of questions we ought to consider."

"There would be."

Worthing let out his breath in exasperation. "What's with you, old boy? I thought brainstorming was a respected technique of our profession."

Hammond avoided his eyes. "Just get on with it."

Worthing's expression became tight and formal. "The first question, still supposing that Crazy Mouly's story is basically true, is, what's happening to the Russians up on that base? The alien metal made Mouly and his partner quite nuts. Is there any reason to assume that it wouldn't do the same to the Russians?

Maybe worse if they've been doing experiments and generally fucking around with it.''

Hammond started to show a grudging interest. "You're talking about this radiation stuff?''

"I'm figuring that we have to think of it in terms of an influence of a totally unknown kind. Mouly was very insistent that they'd checked the metal for all the basic types of measurable radiation.''

"So we've got an influence?''

"I've been asking myself, How far does this influence, if it exists, extend? Up close, it seems to have completely deranged Mouly, but I've been wondering if it has a diminished effect over a much greater area.''

Travis looked up and spoke for the first time. "What makes you wonder that?''

"These hills round here are full of weird characters and worse. Why should they be concentrated in this particular area?''

Travis was thoughtful. "This is sure getting weird.''

"What else do you expect on Mars? It's fucking weird being here in the first place.''

Travis shook his head. "Damned if I know.''

Hammond was also thinking. "It seems to me that if this alien metal is as dangerous as Crazy Mouly claims, something would have happened to this guy from Fort Haigh who bought the piece from Mouly. Nothing's been heard of him.''

"That doesn't mean he wasn't affected. If he started acting strange, the marines' first instinct would be to hush it up. He might also have done something quite unspectacular, like simply offing himself.''

"I suppose you checked on that?''

"There have been seventeen suicides at Fort Haigh in the last two years.''

"It's still too weird.''

Worthing looked at each of the other three in turn. "I could even make a case that we're being affected.''

The other three looked back at him in total disbelief.

"You're crazy.''

"Think about it. The farther up the trail we've come, the more we've been drinking and becoming generally disorganized.''

Worthing decided that it was time to lower the boom. "I mean, look at you, Lech. You're turning into a dead weight. Where's the old spark and enthusiasm? We've gone after stories on much more slender threads. Look at yourself, man. You've lost all spirit of adventure. I thought that was what we were in this for. All you've been talking about lately is your bloody reputation."

Lech Hammond knew inside that Worthing was right. A strange deadness had come over him lately, but he was not ready to admit it. "That's bullshit."

"The hell it is."

"Okay, okay, you're right. I have been a bit below par for the last few days, but it's hardly proof of alien intervention. It's more likely to be planet lag or something like that. This started far-fetched, but now it's completely out there."

Worthing decided to play his final card. "Mouly described the influence as a black smoke in his head. This morning Barstow was suffering from something that he described as a gray mist in his brain. You have to wonder if they're related."

Worthing had expected Barstow to look shocked, but he had not thought that Hammond would go white. Hammond, for his part, had no desire to believe any part of either Crazy Mouly's fantastic story or Worthing's rationalization of it, but the mention of gray mist was like a kick in the stomach. Waking with that mist in his head had scared the hell out of him. It really had felt like something foreign trying to infiltrate his mind. He still wanted to disbelieve Worthing's hypothesis, but he found that he was no longer so easily able to reject it out of hand.

"That leaves us with the perennial question: Where do we go from here?"

Travis and Barstow both nodded.

"That's the big question."

Hammond made a helpless gesture. "I guess we go on."

Barstow frowned. "Yeah, but if Worthing's right and the influence gets stronger the nearer we get to the thing, aren't we all going to wind up crazy?"

Travis agreed with Barstow. "He does have a point there."

"You want to turn back?"

Both Travis and Barstow shook their heads.

"No, but I think we've got to start going real careful."

Worthing looked very serious. "I think we can only hope that an up-front awareness that something could happen to us may minimize its effect."

"That ain't much of a consolation."

"It's the best I can come up with at short notice."

An electronic warble came from the phone. Hammond picked it up. "Hammond." He paused. "Uh huh . . . okay . . . yeah, right, thanks for calling up. I appreciate it." He looked around at the others. "That was the desk. Apparently Crazy Mouly came by and left a message. I quote: 'Boogie Boy changed his mind, and we're willing to go to the mountain with you.' "

Travis sighed. "He's just the one we need to complete this team."

Surface parking lot, Marsbad Settlement—May 28 CEC—17:48 MST.

The Jeep rolled to a halt, and Whittaker cut the drive. It was the end of the brief Martian sunset. The sky was deep indigo, and the stars were showing through. At any moment Phobos would rise. Whittaker had parked the vehicle between a GM half-track and a White Marsman that despite a drab exterior looked as though it meant business. There were lights on inside the cab of the half-track, and people seemed to be moving around. There was a sense of normality about it that was very strange and distant after the ride up there. For at least three hours not one of them had said a word, Booth because he habitually lapsed into long, unembarrassed silences, Whittaker because conversation with Booth was pointless when he went into one of those withdrawals and she had no desire to talk to Greig, and Greig because the entity was almost free and he no longer trusted himself to speak.

Whittaker removed her hands from the controls with a flourish of finality and flopped back into the padding of the control chair. "Okay, Booth, we made it to Marsbad. What's the plan now? Do we spend the night here? I for one could use a drink."

Booth nodded. "Yes, it'll be our last rest stop before we hit the mountain. We might as well make the most of it."

"So let's suit up and go down into town. I feel like I've been in this tin can for a year."

Booth made a gesture indicating that he would pass. "I'll stay here in the vehicle. I'm too noticeable in a crowd. There has to be KGB down there, and we don't need to advertise ourselves."

Whittaker suspected that the rambo was also uncomfortable around strangers. How the hell did a man let himself be altered the way Booth had been? She glanced around at Greig, who was in the rear seat. "So it looks like it's you and me, or are you going to stay with the vehicle, too?"

Greig shook his head. "No, I'll go down into Marsbad."

Greig was all too hideously aware that he had no choice but to go down into Marsbad. In a couple of hours the entity would be fully awake and demanding that he find a victim in the underground settlement. There had been a time when he had hoped that the entity would wake somehow changed. Now he no longer hoped. It was always the same—always the same demanding appetite. For the last few hours Greig had been feeling particularly awful. The waking of the entity was always unpleasant, but this one seemed to be shaping up to be particularly rough. The toadsquirm was spreading through his whole nervous system, and although there were no visible signs, his skin felt as though it were crawling around his body with a will of its own, stretching and contracting like a mass of inchworms and forming and re-forming invisible welts. His senses were so amped up that he was living in a world that was all but hallucination. Lights and colors were so bright that they were close to pain, and even the smallest sound was an assault on his senses. He knew that it would not be any better down in Marsbad, but at least he would be out of the cramped cabin of the Jeep and away from the watchful eyes of Booth and Whittaker.

Whittaker was already climbing into her pressure suit for the short walk to the elevators. She looked at Greig with scarcely concealed distaste.

"C'est la guerre."

He and Whittaker rode down in the elevator without speaking. When they stepped out of the air lock, she immediately removed her helmet and lit a cigarette.

"You don't have to feel obliged to hang out with me. You do realize that, don't you?"

Greig nodded. "Oh, yes. It would probably be much better if we went looking for entertainment on our own."

Burroughs Marshal's Department's high-speed pursuit vehicle on the North Pole Trail, forty kilometers north of the Silver Locust—May 28 CEC—20:14 MST.

Casey had them on the radar. At first he had wondered if the three images were a small vehicle convoy, but as the gap had narrowed, he could see that they were not moving and also that they were not as substantial as vehicles ought to be. It had to be the Soviet prison detail camped for the night, probably in one large inflatable dome and two smaller, folding plastic igloos. When he was still a mile from them, he stopped the cruiser and sealed his helmet. He was going to go in on foot.

Overhead the starfields were bright and unwinking, and the dust under his feet was crisp with cold. He moved cautiously. He doubted that the Soviets had any kind of scanning equipment, but he was not taking any chances. Despite the air-jacketed Mossberg he had slung over his shoulder, he was well aware that in a direct confrontation, the Soviet guards would have him outnumbered and outgunned.

The first problem was how to locate Irina and get her out of the camp while causing the minimum disturbance. He knew that it was not going to be easy, and to make matters worse, he had far too little information about the layout to formulate a definite plan. He was not only going in on foot but playing it by ear all the way.

There was a low rock-strewn ridge in front of him, and as far as he could estimate, when he reached the top he should be looking down on the Soviets. Just before the crest, he dropped to his hands and knees and crawled the final few meters. Both moons were up, and the starfields were so bright that a man could be seen plainly if he skylined himself.

Casey had guessed right. The three domes were on a stretch of sandflat in front of him, and as he had expected, there were two small igloos and a larger blowup. The igloos were close together on the west side of the dome. A pair of supply sleds were parked between them. There were dim lights in the igloos, but the dome was in darkness. Obviously, the prisoners were penned up in the dome, and the guards occupied the igloos. The report from Dan Worthing had said that Irina was not actually a prisoner, and so he could only assume that she was in one of the igloos. There were five guards patrolling the perimeter of the camp, but from the way they moved, it was clear that they were concentrating their attention on the dome and the possibility of the prisoners trying for a breakout. They had obviously not anticipated an attack from the outside. After all, who in his right mind would mount an attack on a Soviet penal column?

He glanced back in the direction of the cruiser. He did not particularly want to return, but it was clearly too far away if they had to make a run for it. He would have to bring the machine closer. He slid down the ridge and walked quickly back to the cruiser. He figured that he could bring it right up to the bottom of the ridge without any of the guards seeing it. He eased the cruiser into drive. Although he knew intellectually that the sound could not carry to the Soviet guards, he still drove at less than walking pace and with the maximum possible care. It felt like an eternity before he made it back to the bottom of the ridge. He left the cruiser running on idle and once more climbed the ridge. Again he went over the top on all fours, feeling like an Apache scout stalking a wagon train.

A few minutes of observation showed him that the guards were not actually circling the camp. Each one had been assigned an individual quadrant. Focusing on the one pacing the quadrant that included the igloos, Casey mapped out a route by which he could reach that guard without being seen. It went along the ridge, down a gully, and behind an outcropping of rock. From the rocks to the guard was just two five-meter, low-gravity bounds. The best part was that when the guard in question was at the point on his patrol where he would be nearest the rocks, he would also be out of sight of the other four.

Once Casey had reached the rocks, he waited and watched for another couple of minutes. The guards definitely had a casual attitude. They looked bored and tired, and trouble was the farthest thing from their minds. If they had been back on Earth, they would have been carrying on whispered conversations and holding cigarettes in their cupped hands.

The guard was approaching Casey's hiding place. Casey switched his suit radio to receive only, drew his side arm, and tensed. The guard had three paces to go. Then, on the second one, he halted and stared at the inflatable. Casey accepted that gift from the gods and jumped. He landed silently behind the guard. His left hand grabbed for the radio connections in back of the guard's helmet and yanked them loose. His right hand brought the pistol up in front of the man's visor, where it could be seen very clearly.

He touched his helmet to the guard's. "Do exactly as I say or I'll blow your head off."

The guard nodded. Casey maintained the contact between their two helmets.

"Do you know Irina Orlov?"

The guard nodded again.

"You can speak up," Casey whispered tersely. "I can hear you while our helmets are touching."

The guard sounded frightened. "Yes, yes, I know her. What's this all about?"

Casey ignored the question. "Where is she?"

The guard pointed. "She's in that igloo there."

"How many in there with her?"

"Ten, maybe."

"Armed?"

"Some have weapons, but they're off duty."

"You'd better be telling me the truth, boy."

"I am, sir. I swear it."

"Okay, here's what we're going to do. Are you listening?"

"I'm listening."

"First of all you're going to place that machine pistol of yours very carefully on the ground."

The guard placed his weapon on the ground.

"Now kick some dirt over it so no one spots it."

The guard kicked dirt.

"Now you and me are going to walk very slowly to that igloo. If anything happens, you do exactly as I tell you." Casey removed the gun from the guard's visor. "My pistol will be right in the small of your back. You understand?"

"I understand."

The two of them walked toward the igloo with Casey setting what he hoped looked like a relaxed pace. When they reached it, Casey indicated the structure's small air lock.

"Can you get two in there?"

"It's difficult."

"We'll do it."

They waited tensely for the air lock to cycle. When the outer door opened, Casey motioned the guard inside. The air lock started to fill. Eventually the light went on, indicating that the pressure was equalized and that it was possible to open the inner door. Casey holstered his pistol, hitched the Mossberg off his shoulder, and took a deep breath. He opened the door and sent the guard staggering inside. Then, flicking on his suit's external speaker, he stepped through, jamming the muzzle of the riot gun against the roof of the igloo.

"Everyone freeze, or I blow the dome."

Looking at the ten shocked faces, Casey realized that he must have been a fearsome sight, with the frost melting from the hard surfaces of his suit. Some of those inside had obviously been asleep. The interior of the igloo was, as the guard had indicated, an uncomfortably cramped billet for ten people. To his relief, Irina was one of the ten. A Red Army private inched a hand toward a weapon, but Casey pointed a warning finger at him.

"Wouldn't try that if I were you. Not unless you want everyone in here to die."

When he was satisfied that the message had sunk in, he gestured to Irina. "You, Orlov, get over here."

She was sitting in a corner, but as he waved his hand, she scrambled to her feet and came over to him, picking her way across the people who were stretched out on the floor, the stacked pressure suits, and the wrappers and cans that were the remains of a recent evening meal. She looked shocked and scared, but he could not risk letting her know who he was until they were away from the camp. He turned his attention to the guard who was now picking himself up out of the confusion of bodies into which he had fallen.

"You, take that helmet off."

The guard busied himself unsealing his helmet.

Casey glanced at Irina. "Okay, get suited up."

She reached for her emergency suit, but Casey shook his head. "Not that piece of garbage. Put on one of those military suits of armor."

He waited, with his gun still against the roof of the igloo, while she struggled into an overlarge military pressure suit. Finally she sealed the helmet and faced him as if waiting for further instructions.

"Okay, what I want you to do now is to pick up all the helmets in the place and throw them into the air lock. Make sure you get all of them."

Irina did as she was told. When all the helmets were piled in the bottom of the air lock like a collection of high-tech skulls, Casey indicated that she should step inside herself. Then, with a final warning to the remaining occupants of the igloo not to try anything, he eased in beside her. It had been a tight squeeze with the guard, but with the addition of the helmets, it was almost impossible; they had to press tightly together in order for the inner door to close.

As the air wheezed out of the lock, Casey issued a final order. "Turn your radio to receive only. If you want to talk to me, touch your helmet to mine."

The moment they were out of the air lock, Casey started tossing out the helmets, indicating that Irina should stack them beside the sleds, where they could not immediately be seen. While she was doing that, he noticed that a small satellite dish had been up on one of the sleds. It was probably the detail's link with Vostok. He quickly ripped the leads out.

"That should slow them down a bit."

He looked around cautiously. None of the guards seemed to be taking any notice of them. He touched his helmet to Irina's.

"We're going to try and walk out of this camp without attracting any attention. Try and look as normal as possible, but be ready to run if I give the word."

"Who are you?"

Casey shook his head. "Later."

They strolled past the large dome, for all the world like two friends taking a walk in the light of the two moons. They were all the way to the camp perimeter before they were challenged. The voice roaring from their open suit radios reverberated in both helmets.

"Halt! Stop and identify yourselves!"

Casey gripped Irina's arm and forced her to keep on walking as though they had heard nothing.

The guard shouted again. "Halt!"

The other guards were turning to see what the problem was. The first one was unslinging his machine pistol. Casey tongued open his radio and added his own voice to the growing confusion.

"The dome! Look at the dome! The prisoners—"

Instinctively, every one of the guards turned and looked at the inflatable dome.

Casey grabbed Irina's wrist. "Run! Run for that ridge over there!"

In huge reckless leaps, they covered the ground as fast as they could. There was the strobing flash of a machine pistol from behind them, and over on their left, bullets kicked up silent puffs of dust. The near slope of the ridge was in deep shadow, and as they scrambled up it, the shooting from the camp came nowhere near them. They rolled over the top and slithered down the other side. Casey could hear his breath rasping inside his helmet. He was getting too old for that sort of thing.

"Quick, into the cruiser!"

Irina looked at him in amazement. "You!"

"Can it! Get in the cruiser!"

There was a figure on top of the ridge. A machine pistol flashed, and bullets spattered around them. Casey fired a blast from the Mossberg. He deliberately missed the Russian, but it had the desired effect: The soldier ducked for cover.

Casey slid behind the wheel. "Hang on tight!"

He threw the cruiser into full-throttle screaming reverse. More figures were coming over the ridge.

"Get into your seat belt."

They were slammed back into their seats as Casey braked hard and then were slammed into them again as he accelerated forward. He put a high-speed ten miles between them and the

Soviet camp before he pulled up to seal and pressurize the cabin. When the two of them finally did remove their helmets, they sat unmoving, just looking at each other for almost a minute.

"We're in a lot of trouble, Lon Casey."

Casey grinned. "We can handle it."

"I thought you were a KGB killer."

"I thought it best if they didn't know who it was."

Then the spell that was holding back emotion was broken, and despite the bulk of their suits, she flung her arms around him. Their lips met, and her tongue slid into his mouth. With the restraints gone and the reaction to fear and danger setting in, they seemed to want to eat each other alive.

SEVEN

THERE WAS A GUNFIGHT ON MAIN STREET. TWO OLD BOYS in slouch hats and ragged dusters who probably no longer remembered how the beef had started had decided to take it to the street. Marsbad security quickly gathered, but when they saw that it was going to be a formal gunfight, they held off, content merely to control the crowd. Marsbad had a long tradition of formal gunfights that went back, if not to the American West of the nineteenth century, at least to twentieth-century television. The epithets and final insults were exchanged, and then at the peak of it all, hands flashed, a shotgun and a machine pistol roared simultaneously, and the good old boys went down together, ripped by bullets and buckshot. There was shouting and a couple of screams from the crowd, and then it was all over, as brief as it had been pointless. Encouraged by the security men, the crowd went on about its business. The clean-up crew, in their dirty white coveralls, flopped the two old boys into black plastic body bags and poured sand over the puddles of blood.

Even the entity had been briefly interested. The undertow of its constant demand had slackened, and it had allowed Greig to pause for a moment in his search for its victim and watch as the two drunken prospectors gunned each other down. The entity

192

seemed to be obsessed with death, as though it somehow gained nourishment at the moment when a human being gave up his or her life.

Once the bodies had been carted away, the wild place reclaimed Greig. The noise and pressure in his head came back like a black tide, swamping what was left of his personality and turning him into a searching automaton, driven by the entity. The chill, the numbness in his fingers, and the sense of unreality and detachment were also back. All that he had left of his own was the fear. This waking of the entity had come without planning or protection. He had no fake ID and no way to cover his tracks. He felt exposed and vulnerable, although he suspected that if trouble came, Booth was sufficiently fixated to get him out so that they could complete the mission. Greig wished that the entity would pick a victim so that he could get it over with. Despite its insistence, the entity seemed to be in no hurry. It continued to have him search as though savoring the possibilities. It pushed him on in a precise quest for the unknown quality that separated the victims from all the others.

There were a great many prostitutes in Marsbad. Indeed, that was the only reason the place existed at all. The biggest way station on the North Pole Trail, looking straight across at the huge bulk of Olympus Mons, Marsbad supplied fuel and air to travelers, but beyond that, it was nothing more than a giant bordello, a shopping mall for sex and booze and gambling. Greig could feel the unhealthy heat of the women as he moved through the crowd. Beneath the flesh and the paint and the costumes, there was always the heat, the sweet unhealthy heat, which Greig guessed was in some way related to whatever it was the entity had him searching for. A woman in a scanty stretch tube of acid yellow smiled at him with orange lips and poked out a sharp pink tongue. No, she was not the one. The entity wanted him to go on.

He went through a set of Lucite doors. He was not exactly sure why. The sign read "House of Blue Light." Inside, the sexual offers were a good deal more direct than they had been out on the street. A Nordic blonde in a red satin garter belt and black fishnet stockings cupped her hands under white melon breasts and offered them to him as though they were ripe fruit.

She was not the one, either. All around him women beckoned, beamed, or smoldered from beneath hooded lids. Some bent over, exposed in a moment of scarlet flash. They smiled constantly and laughed with every part of their bodies but their eyes, hot, willing, but ultimately calculating or just plain dead. Diamond points of light sparkled from beads of sweat and bright teeth. Greig sweated, too. Inside the gloom of the House of Blue Light, he was walking in a tank, a cloud chamber of cloying, oppressive scented hallucination. It clung to his skin like a warm, oily residue.

"Hey, baby, you want to go out?"

"Hey, honey, you looking for a date?"

"Hey, baby, you want to go upstairs with me?"

Questions and propositions floated by him on wafts of cheap perfume, alcohol breath, and cigarette smoke. He was suffocating. Could there be something wrong with the atmosphere systems? His head was spinning. His senses were stretched taut against the jagged edge of overload. The air in the House of Blue Light, coupled with the sweet heat of the women, made him want to gag. For pity's sake, pick a victim and let's have done with it.

"You can call me Max."

She was strange, but the aura was around her: This was the victim. Her hair was purple and box-cut, and she was wearing an old black bike jacket and a blackgloss rubber miniskirt. What was left of John Greig was surprised. The woman was skinny and muscular and looked as though she belonged in some kind of street gang. She was nothing like the entity's usual selections. The aura was there, though, and there was nothing he could do but go through with it.

"Can—can we go somewhere?"

The woman smiled at him knowingly. "Nervous?"

"A little."

"Don't be nervous. Just keep thinking how interesting I'm going to make the next hour or so. Just keep thinking about what you'd really, really like me to do to you."

"Where can we go?"

She took hold of his hand. "Don't worry, I've got a place upstairs."

The woman Max started leading him through the crowd toward a flight of stairs that led to an upper level. "What's your name?"

"John."

Max snorted. "That's kind of apt."

There was heavy traffic on the stairs. Men and women were constantly coming up and down. There were so many people who might know him, might remember his face. Greig wanted to turn back and forget the whole thing, but the entity had too firm a grip on him. If he stopped now, his head would explode.

"My room's down at the end of this corridor."

It was so much like the last time—the narrow corridor with its rows of cubicles. In Vostok there had not been the dim red lights and the hologram nudes decorating the walls, but in all other respects the layout was identical. He was traveling back into a nightmare. Greig was walking behind the woman; unseen by her, he removed the aerosol of stun gas from his pocket and patted the ribbon knife. It would have to be fast and soundless.

The woman ran a keystrip through the lock. "This is it, John. Have you decided what you want?"

The cubicle was small and dim, decorated in black and red. There was very little in it—a small steel locker and a narrow bed upholstered in black plastic, like something one might expect to find in a hospital. The bed was fitted with restraints, and there was a system of pulleys set into the ceiling. Greig, however, had no time or even the mind to wonder about the equipment. He was running on automatic. The woman was ushering him inside and closing the door behind him. She was taking off her leather jacket.

"So tell me what you want, John."

The gas canister was in the palm of his hand. It should have been one smooth movement. He turned and brought up his hand. He would never know what made her suspect.

"You bastard!"

The karate chop was swift and skilled. The hard edge of her hand struck his wrist with enough force to make his arm go numb. He jumped back to avoid a follow-up kick. The ribbon knife was out. He pulled off the sheath and thumbed on the power. The thing made its characteristic high-pitched whine.

"I'm sorry, but I have to kill you."

The woman's hands flashed again and produced a length of razor chain. She dropped into a fighting crouch.

"I'm going to have your balls, you bastard." She swung the chain and at the same time started shouting at the top of her voice. "Somebody help me! I've got a weirdo in here!"

The entity gave up, releasing Greig and leaving him reeling. Everything in his makeup screamed for him to run. The girl was advancing on him, swishing the chain. She seemed quite capable of killing him. He went through the flimsy door shoulder first. Two burly bouncers were coming down the corridor. He ran in the opposite direction, deeper into the maze of corridors. Max was still yelling.

"Stop the motherfucker! He wanted to kill me! Stop him!"

Without the entity, Greig had no protection, no buffer against the pumping adrenaline and the awful reality. He could not grasp how he had come to that place. He had tried to kill a prostitute named Max, and the alarm had been given. He was being chased by people who, if they caught him, would most probably kill him. It was not right, it could not be he. He might be a little strange, a little withdrawn, a little too studious—but he was not a maniac.

There was a door at the end of the corridor. Mercifully, it was not locked. He went through it and found himself in a long, curved service tunnel. In contrast to the previous corridor, with its seductive lighting and ghostly nudes, it was a place of bright lights and the whir of machinery. From the brisk breeze that was blowing down the tunnel, he assumed that it was part of the air circulation system. He went on running. He could hear the bouncers, and probably others, as well, somewhere behind him, but he could not see them. He reached a vertical shaft with a steel ladder bolted to the wall that would take him down to street level. That was his only idea: get back to the main street, get to his suit, and get out of the huge underground whorehouse. Beyond that, he could not formulate a plan. In a matter of minutes they would have a make on him. He had dropped the stun gas aerosol when the woman had hit him, and his fingerprints were on it.

At the bottom of the shaft there was more machinery, what

looked like relay pumps. There was also a metal inspection door with a bolt on the inside. At first the bolt stuck, but on the fourth try it started to move. He pulled the inspection door open and, to his surprise, found that he was looking out at the milling crowds on Main Street. He slipped through the door and gently closed it behind him. No one seemed to have noticed him. He mingled with the crowds, walking as calmly as he could, heading for the main air lock and the suit check. He glanced back in the direction of the House of Blue Light. Security men were milling around in the entrance, but there did not seem to be any kind of search being conducted on the street. They probably thought he was still somewhere in the back corridors and tunnels.

Greig kept on walking. He was close to the entrance to the suit check, the one that led on to the main air lock. There were security men standing around, routinely scanning the crowd, and at least one in every pair had his eyes hidden behind insect-eye infrared spotters. Greig's first instinct was to freeze, but both common sense and his CySec training dictated that he go on walking as though everything were normal. It was much too early for a detailed description of him to have been circulated.

To his infinite relief, the security men ignored him. As he went through the open bulkhead doors on his way to the suit check, he had to pass close to two pairs of them; they glanced at him only briefly before switching their attention to the others who were coming in and out.

The suit check presented another problem. He had checked his pressure suit under his own name. He doubted that they had managed to get a make on him from the fingerprint on the aerosol yet, but he could not be absolutely sure. He had to count on the assumption that in any matters more complicated than rousting drunks and busting heads, the Marsbad security men would be fairly slow and inefficient. That Fort Haigh was still, as far as he knew, on red alert should also help—they would have a hard job getting any information from that source. He took a deep breath, walked up to the counter, and handed his magstrip to the bored suit check girl, an over-the-hill dancer in torn fishnets. She sashayed into the racks, swaying her hips, and came back with his suit, with no comment at all. Greig tipped her twenty and began pulling on his suit. That was the last immediate obstacle out of the way.

The entity had totally vanished. It seemed to be nowhere in his mind, either asleep or awake. Had the shock of failure driven it out? Dare he hope that it had gone forever? There had been very little for which to hope in the last few months. The relief of getting out of Marsbad intact and the freedom from the weight of the entity made him feel almost optimistic. Perhaps there would not be a full investigation. Nothing had actually happened to the woman. It was not as if this were Burroughs, where that goddamned marshal would already be running comparisons with the other killings. Deep inside, though, he knew he was in a great deal of trouble. Once the mission was over, there would be a whole mess to be faced. His only protection, he thought as he rode up in the elevator, was to concentrate on nothing more than the immediate future. He was going back to the surface vehicle to lie low until Booth took them out onto the mountain. He could only pray that no one would come looking for him.

Greig left the elevator, and then was out in the open under the bright, cold starfields. He stood for a moment, suddenly aware that his whole body was shaking with delayed shock. He had to get control of himself—he had his mind back, and he had to put the past firmly behind him. It was a long time before he finally walked over to the Jeep and entered it. As he emerged from the air lock, Booth appeared to be sleeping in the command chair, but as Greig moved into the cabin, the rambo's eyes opened.

"I thought you were going to spend the night down in the settlement."

Greig flopped into one of the other chairs. "It got a little claustrophobic down there."

The Lucky Strike Hotel, Marsbad Settlement—May 29 CEC— 10:19 MST.

"Word is that the Ripper tried for a hit in Marsbad last night. Max was his intended victim."

Worthing blinked. "Say what?"

"By all accounts, the Martian Ripper tried to take out Max last night."

"Max? Our Max?"

"Our Max."

"Was she hurt?"

Hammond shook his head. "Apparently she fought him off."

"Well, good for her."

Burroughs Marshal's Department's high-speed pursuit vehicle on the North Pole Trail one hundred kilometers south of Marsbad—May 29 CEC—10:21 MST.

An amber light was flashing on the control panel. Irina looked at Casey.

"What's that?"

"It's a coded message coming in."

Casey reached out and keyed a nine-digit code into the cruiser's computer. The monitor screen snowed and then cleared. The words RECORDED MESSAGE flashed three times, then were replaced by an image of Chavez.

"Okay, so I don't know where you are and I don't think I want to know what kind of trouble you're getting yourself into, but if you haven't gotten yourself shot and you're still at all interested in police work, the Ripper surfaced again. He had a crack at a Marsbad hooker last night. Apparently she was a whole lot faster on her feet than the others have been, and she ran him off. We haven't been officially notified yet, but from the information requests that have been flying around, it sure as hell sounds like your pal Greig. He's still on the loose, but Marsbad security seems to have a partial make on him. The only thing that's jamming up a positive is that the marines at Haigh are refusing a confirmation because the base is still on red alert. I don't know what, if anything, you want to do about this, but call in if you can. We'll wait on your orders. Message timed at ten-twenty standard."

Chavez's face faded. MESSAGE CONCLUDES flashed up, and the screen went black.

Irina sighed. "That qualifies as duty calling, Lon."

Casey slowly nodded. "Yeah, that's the truth."

"So what are you going to do about it?"

"I don't know."

"You want this guy, don't you?"

"Sure. I'm still a cop. I want any maniac who's running around killing people."

"From the way Chavez was talking, it seemed to me that it was a bit more personal than that."

Casey hesitated before he answered. "Listen, I got my ass tossed out of Vostok because of this goddamn freak, and then I narrowed it down to this character Greig, but he turned out to be attached to the marines, and instead of turning him over, they started running interference for him. I want that bastard, but it doesn't look as if I'm going to be able to get him."

"Why not?"

Casey looked at Irina in surprise. "We got a few other problems going for us at the moment."

Irina waved the idea aside. "I'm the one with the problems. There's no reason why you shouldn't head up to Marsbad and go after him. You could make it by sunset in this thing."

"And what about you? You think I'm going to leave you somewhere where the KGB can pick you up all over again?"

Irina started to get annoyed. "Give me a break, Casey. I'm a cop, too. I was the police chief of Vostok, goddamn it, until Melikov fucked me over. I understand how you feel. I'd also like to see this creep nailed. I can also look after myself."

"What are you suggesting?"

"First thing you should do is call Chavez on a closed channel and get filled in on the details. After that we can decide on a course of action. If you want, we could go to Marsbad. You could stash me there while you go and look for Greig."

"After what we've just been through, I don't want to stash you anywhere."

"Come on, Lon, I know you just did your knight on a white charger act, and it was very romantic and I'll be eternally grateful that you saved me from Vorkuta, but I'm hardly a helpless damsel in distress. If I can't vanish into the crowds inside Marsbad, I don't deserve to survive."

"Are you sure?"

"Of course I'm sure. Get Chavez on the line. You could ask him one thing to satisfy my curiosity."

"What's that?"

"Ask what someone attached to the marines is doing all the way up in Marsbad."

Surface parking area, Marsbad Settlement—May 29 CEC— 10:22 MST.

"You tried it again last night, didn't you, Greig?"

Whittaker had come out of the Jeep's air lock, helmet off and face like a thundercloud. Greig started. It had not occurred to him that Whittaker might hear about the aborted killing and connect it to him. He silently cursed himself for his carelessness and did his best to bluster.

"What are you talking about?"

"You had yourself a shot at some little hooker, didn't you, Greig?"

Booth turned in his seat. "Is this true?"

"Of course not. She's out of her mind."

"For your information, Greig, I talked to a security man. He filled me in on all the details."

Greig's lip curled nastily. "I suppose you spent the night with him?"

"As a matter of fact, I did. You have a problem with that?"

"Whatever's appropriate."

"Screw appropriate, Greig. You're a homicidal maniac."

"How in hell do you figure that out?"

Whittaker turned to Booth in a gesture of appeal. "Sometime around midnight this creep here goes after one of the girls at a bam-boom joint called the House of Blue Light with a stun can and a ribbon knife. Fortunately, she beats him to the punch and he jackrabbits out of there."

"You really sound like you've been sleeping with peace officers."

Booth was watching Greig with narrowed eyes. "You were back here soon after midnight."

"I told you, it was too claustrophobic down there. I couldn't handle it."

Whittaker was not finished. "Yeah? You're as good as nailed, Greig. You dropped the stun can, and there was a partial print. They've run it down to the fact that the owner of the print is U.S. military personnel, but they can't get any farther because of the red alert. What have you got to say about that, Greig?"

Greig was emphatically shaking his head. "We're being rat-fucked, for Christ's sake!"

It was strange. Half of him actually believed what he was saying, while the other half was feeling considerable relief that a full identification had yet to be made.

Whittaker was glaring at the rambo. "Face it, Booth, we have to abort the mission and get some kind of guidance from CySec. This bastard's got to get what's coming to him."

Greig realized that both he and Whittaker were appealing to Booth as if the rambo were the judge or something. He was pleased to see that the judge was shaking his head.

"We can't break communication silence, and cooperating with the local security is quite out of the question."

Whittaker looked shocked. "You can't mean that."

"We can't afford to be caught up in a civilian investigation. We could find ourselves detained as material witnesses. I am certainly not going to be detained under any circumstances. Don't forget that I'm highly classified."

"Christ, you can't mean it. Next you'll be saying that we should go on with the mission."

"I think that's the best option."

"What?"

"I believe that we should go on with the mission."

"You're crazy. What about him?"

"It really doesn't matter, if you think about it with a little detachment."

Whittaker was holding her righteous fury in check only with the greatest difficulty. "Would you like to explain this piece of detached logic?"

The rambo lowered his head, and the overhead light caused his eye sockets to be filled with shadows. He looked scarcely human, and it became easy to believe that he really was a highly classified weapon.

"As I see it, the situation has actually been the same ever since the marshal from Burroughs stopped us. We have only two belief scenarios. Either, as Greig says, we have become a target for a ratfuck attack—"

"You can't believe that," Whittaker protested.

Booth looked at her coldly. "Will you let me finish?"

"Okay, go on."

"The other alternative is that we have to go with your contention that Greig here has some very extreme ideas of recreational sex."

"You're sick."

"And you're losing track of your priorities. If Greig is a killer, it hardly matters in the context of the mission so long as we don't let it affect our performance in the field."

"You're out of your mind if you think I'm going up that mountain with a killer."

"I don't see that you have any choice in the matter."

"What's that supposed to mean?"

"You may not be a marine, Whittaker, but you are certainly subject to marine discipline. We are currently on a covert mission, and that is the equivalent, by the book, of being in a combat situation. I suspect you know the penalties for refusing a direct order in combat."

"Are you threatening me?"

"I'm warning you."

"Jesus, Booth, this bastard kills women for fun, and I'm the one getting threatened?"

"I don't kill women for fun."

Booth ignored Greig. "I'm only going to say this once, Whittaker. Get with the program. You're a fully trained civilian adviser, and you should be as aware as I am that from the moment we started on this mission, we put moral niceties aside. Our only responsibility is to complete the mission."

"You call murdering four or five women a moral nicety?"

"Believe me, Whittaker, I've had to cooperate with individuals who have done far worse."

Whittaker was silent.

"We will move out for Olympus Mons after sunset," Booth went on. "Greig, you are confined to the vehicle until that time, unless I order otherwise."

"Very well."

"And Whittaker, I want you to be in no doubt that if you do anything to jeopardize this mission, I will have no hesitation in shooting you out of hand. Do you understand me?"

Whittaker became very stiff and formal. "I understand, but I lodge a formal protest."

Booth nodded. "Your protest will be noted."

Lucky Strike Hotel, Marsbad Settlement—May 29 CEC—11:37 MST.

Hammond had called everyone into his room.

"I figure we should pull out of here sometime after sunset," he said. "You think we can locate Mouly by then?"

Worthing nodded. "It shouldn't be a problem."

Barstow nodded, too. "Getting him sober will be the problem."

Travis scratched his earlobe. His beat-up Stetson was pulled down over his eyes. "It'd be easier to get him drunk and let him sleep it off as we drive out of town. Be much less trouble unconscious."

Relations between the four men had improved greatly since the previous afternoon's confrontation and the resulting release of pressure. Hammond had made an effort to regain some of his energy and start thinking about the job at hand. The night's drinking had been drastically reduced, but once again he had awakened with the gray mist in his mind. Checking with Barstow, he had learned that the cameraman had had it, too. Even though it had vanished almost immediately, he hoped to hell that Worthing was right and that it would disappear once they got away from that damned mountain. Hammond was developing a quite illogical dislike of Olympus Mons, which at least was an improvement on his previous limp apathy. He stood up and got himself a soda from the room's small fridge, feeling that he could have killed for a bottle of branded beer. He had to climb around Worthing to get it. His room at the Lucky Strike was the best that could be bribed out of the desk clerk, but it was still small and cramped, and the en-vee system made strange noises when he tried to sleep.

Barstow looked up. He had been staring at the TV that was playing the delayed feed from Earth with the sound down. Earlier there had been a piece on the Kristy Karoway murder. The LAPD was trying to nail the singer's live-in girlfriend for the bludgeon slaying. The follow-up was a report of an explosion on the JAL lunar shuttle. It was being claimed by the FLA. Then the news finished and was replaced by a Rockee b'Chokee cartoon. Barstow could not imagine why Rockee b'Chokee should go out on the feed.

"If we've got the time, what would you say to getting an interview with Max about the Ripper?" he suggested. "It looks like they're going to nail the guy, so there could be a story in it."

"We lost all the other Ripper footage in Vostok."

"It doesn't matter. We can put together a reconstruct. That Sandoz ain't as dumb as he looks. He does good work."

Hammond nodded. "Sure, so let's do it if we have time. The first priority, though, is to find Crazy Mouly and get him safely on the truck. Is there anything else?"

Travis pushed back his hat with his index finger. "Small point of information."

"What's that?"

"I've been in and out a couple of times this morning, and I couldn't help but notice some characters across the street who seemed to be watching the front of the hotel."

"What kind of characters?"

"Characters that I wouldn't particularly want to be tangling with. They looked like they were local guns for hire."

Worthing frowned. "They could be looking for anyone. There are a lot of people in this hotel."

"It still doesn't hurt to be careful."

By six that evening, everything was together. They had taped the interview with Max, and they had Crazy Mouly safely stashed at the hotel. Finding Mouly had involved a fairly lengthy tour of the bars, but finally they had come upon him in a bottom-rung joint called the Redline. Mouly had protested that he did not want to go to the mountain, that it was a bad day for the mountain. What he had not done was claim that Boogie Boy had changed his mind, and Worthing had taken that as a hopeful sign. His technique for persuading Mouly had been elegantly simple: He had produced a roll of two-hundred-dollar bills and peeled them off one at a time until the old man agreed to make the trip.

With their gear packed and everything ready to move out to the truck, they once again assembled in Hammond's room.

"So this looks like it."

Worthing nodded. "Don't see any reason to linger."

Hammond glanced at Travis. "Have you checked the street? Are those two characters still hanging around?"

Travis shook his head. "No. Those ones have gone, but there are two more in their place."

"I guess we better hope they're not waiting for us. Is there anything we can do about them?"

"Can't shoot them for just hanging about."

"So let's get going."

They emerged onto Main Street suited up, grips and helmets in hand and guns strapped to their hips. As Barstow had remarked, "Might as well go out looking superbad."

As they walked away from the hotel, Worthing took a covert look at the men hanging out on the other side of the street. They were typical of the trailtrash that came and went from Marsbad. They were squint-eyed and unshaven, with leather coats and wide-brimmed hats, and he would not have wanted to tangle with them any more than he would have wanted to go head to head with Travis. Fortunately, they seemed to be showing absolutely no interest in the five of them leaving the Lucky Strike.

They went straight down Main Street directly to the entrance that led to the big air lock and the surface elevator. Up on the surface, the stars were out. Olympus Mons was a huge black shape against the bright night sky.

Hammond stopped for a couple of seconds. "I really don't like that goddamn mountain."

Mouly came up behind him. "Only a damned fool or a mad-man would like that mountain."

Travis started herding his charges. "Let's get in the truck, shall we? I filled up with fuel and air this afternoon."

It was immediately after he spoke that the shooting started. The worst part was that it happened in total silence: silent puffs of dirt around their feet and silent muzzle flashes from behind a parked truck over on their right and from under another to their left. The equally silent red beam of an MA laser swept the parking area. The only sounds were their own voices yelling in their helmets. Travis was the one who took control. He grabbed Mouly and pushed him toward the safety of a parked vehicle.

"Down! Everyone down! We're under attack!"

Surface parking area, Marsbad Settlement—May 29 CEC—19:03 MST.

Booth eased the Jeep up to the fuel and air bouser and stopped. "I'm going outside to fill up."

Greig and Whittaker both nodded. Booth snapped his helmet closed and sealed it. He went through the air lock, swung down to the ground, and started fueling up the Jeep. He had just about finished topping up the air when the firing started. Instinctively, he dropped the air hose that was connected to the tanks at the back of the Jeep and ducked underneath the vehicle. His training told him that whenever firing started near him, the first assump-tion should be that he was the target. He crawled on his stomach to a vantage point behind one of the Jeep's wheels. His own side arm was already in his hand.

A quick survey of the area made it clear that he was not the one under attack. It was five figures in the center of the parking area who seemed to be the ones getting themselves bushwacked. He spotted two shooters and a third operating a laser. Miracu-lously, none of those under attack had yet been hit. They were scattering for cover, moving fast in the low gravity. At any min-ute he expected one of their suits to explode as it took a bullet or was sliced by the laser.

One of them had rolled under a parked truck and was returning fire. Booth slid his own side arm back into its holster. No way was he going to play the hero and get involved in it. A second gun opened up, fast blasts from what was probably an autoload. The attacker with the laser flipped over. His weapon arced in the air, striking showers of sparks from the hood of a GM hauler. His two companions were moving as though they were having second thoughts about the attack. One of them broke cover and ran, firing as he went. A sleek high-speed vehicle came across the parking area with its headlights blazing. Although it had no specific markings, it was clearly a police pursuit cruiser. The man who had broken cover seemed to have decided the same thing. He changed course and headed in the direction of the elevators. The cruiser slid to a stop in a cloud of dust, and after a couple of seconds, the top popped open and a man jumped out.

Booth decided it was time to get out of there. He cautiously emerged from cover and disconnected the hose. The firefight was still going on, but it was impossible to tell who was on what side. He ducked under the truck again and took the ladder to the air lock in one smooth motion. Once he was inside the cabin, Greig wanted to know what was going on outside. Booth settled behind the controls and brought the drive on-line.

''Nothing that concerns us.''

Surface parking area, Marsbad Settlement—May 29 CEC—19:07 MST.

Casey turned into the Marsbad settlement and ran straight into a gunfight.

''Jesus Christ, what is this? The OK Corral?''

Old habits did not die at all. He stamped on the brakes just as though he were on patrol in Burroughs. At the same time, he yelled at Irina, ''Close your helmet and seal it! I'm going to pop the canopy.''

''I'm ahead of you.''

Casey was out of the cruiser, shotgun in hand and yelling into his helmet radio. ''What the hell is going on here?''

Surface parking area, Marsbad Settlement—May 29 CEC—
19:09 MST.

Worthing was under a truck, flat down in the dirt. He had drawn the H&K, but he was not clear about what he should shoot at. There were flashes and dark figures all around him, but in the confusion it was impossible to tell who was who. There was a bright flash of flame, and the attacker with the laser went down. Worthing was grateful. The deadly beam had been sweeping uncomfortably close to where he was huddled. Suddenly a pair of bright headlights slewed across the parking area in a cloud of dust. The headlights stopped, and first one figure and then a second came out from behind them. There was a voice in his helmet's headset.

"What the hell is going on here?"

"I know that voice. Lon Casey?"

"Dan Worthing?"

Another of the attackers broke from cover. Casey's shotgun belched fire, and the man went down. There was no more firing. Worthing gingerly scrambled out from under the truck.

Casey walked toward him. "What's been happening here?"

Worthing straightened up. "I think this bunch of guys was trying to kill us."

"What are you doing here, anyway?"

"I could ask the same of you."

At that moment a Jeep SV started pulling away. Casey quickly turned. "Damn it to hell! That's them."

Worthing was mystified. "That's who?"

Casey watched the Jeep drive away. "That's who I came here for. And I don't have the fuel to go after him."

By that time Barstow, Travis, and Hammond had joined them, and Hammond suggested that they go to the truck and talk. When they were all inside, the shocked exclamations came thick and fast.

"Lon Casey?"

"Crazy Mouly?"

"Chief Investigator Orlov?"

"What the hell is going on here?"

"Who were the people in the Jeep?"

"I need a drink."

"Who's going to start explaining first?"

It took a good fifteen minutes for the stories to be sorted out, even though everyone was too shocked to do very much lying. Not that lying would have served any useful purpose. Their separate tales had become so intertwined that it was not hard for each party to guess broadly what the other had been up to. When the questions finally stopped, Hammond did his best to sum up. He started with Casey.

"So, if I've got all this straight, the moment Worthing slipped you the word that Ms. Orlov was on the chain gang, you came Lone Rangering up here to save her from the gulag."

Casey nodded. "Picturesque but basically correct."

Worthing grinned. "Isn't that kind of precipitate for one of the top law enforcement officers in the U.S. colonies?"

Casey looked a little uncomfortable. "I'm doing this on my own time."

"I doubt the KGB would see it that way."

"I'm not answerable to the KGB."

"That's only because they ain't caught up with you yet."

Casey went for the high ground. "So what about you guys? Planning to break into a top-secret Soviet military installation isn't exactly the summit of cool, either."

Hammond found himself on the defensive. "We weren't planning to break into the place. We just wanted to know what was going on up there."

"So you picked Crazy Mouly as a native guide?"

"The choice of personnel wasn't exactly vast."

Casey sighed. "Well, I guess you're going to have to forget all about that now."

The three newsmen looked at him in amazement.

"What are you talking about?"

"I would have thought that it was obvious. Those three in the Jeep are clearly on some weird CySec covert operation that's aimed at the base. That alone has got to be reason enough to keep the hell away from Olympus Mons."

Worthing was shaking his head. "Seems to me that it's all the more reason to get up there."

Casey snorted. "That's a goddamn rambo leading that trio.

Those guys aren't answerable to anyone. He'll grease your ass as soon as look at you if you get in his way. I'm well aware that you're intrepid news hawks protecting the public's right to know and all that stuff, but realistically, it's time to back off.''

Irina joined in the discussion for the first time. "It's more than likely that the KGB is already aware of your presence here.''

Travis glanced at her sharply. "How do you figure that?''

"Who do you think hired those men to try and kill you just now?''

Travis nodded thoughtfully. "Maybe we should think about this.''

Worthing glanced sideways at Casey. "I guess you'll be going straight back to Burroughs.''

Casey was almost indignant. "The hell I am. I'm going after Greig. I want him.''

"You're not worried about the rambo greasing your ass? You're almost certainly going to get in his way.''

"It's my job.''

Worthing's voice was very soft. "It's our job too, Marshal.''

Hammond backed him up. "We're going up there.'' He glanced at Travis. "Unless you want to drop out.''

Travis shook his head with the expression of a man who suspects that he's making a terrible mistake. "No, I'll see it through.''

Hammond grinned and turned to Casey. "Then I suggest we work out some area of cooperation.''

White Marsman, in open country, forty kilometers west of Marsbad—May 29 CEC—21:18 MST.

They were on the last leg of the journey to Olympus Mons. They had nothing in their future except raw rock-strewn desert and whatever dangers the Soviets and the marine covert operation team might present. Some fifty meters in front of them they could see the lights of Casey's pursuit vehicle. The two parties were maintaining strict radio silence. Casey led; Hammond's larger truck followed. If Casey spotted something up ahead on his ground radar, he would flash his lights, and Hammond's party would pull up alongside. They were proceeding with caution. In front of them the huge volcano blotted out a whole section of the sky. Inside the cabin of the Marsman, the lights were turned down. Barstow was driving, and Worthing was sitting beside him, peering through the windshield. Crazy Mouly had passed out, and Travis was eating a microwave chicken burrito.

Hammond seemed to be lost in his thoughts. When he spoke, it was to no one in particular. "Anybody ever read Stephen King?"

Worthing glanced back. "Sure. Couldn't get enough of it when I was a kid."

Barstow took a hand off the wheel and rubbed his left eye. "Wasn't he the guy who vanished back in the nineteen nineties?"

Worthing nodded. "Yeah, right. He was driving across country. His Camaro came off the road, somewhere off Interstate 70, going through the Rockies. The car was buried in the snow, and they never found it until the spring thaw. He must have crawled away or something, because his body never turned up at all." He looked at Hammond again. "Why do you ask?"

"He wrote this book called *The Tommyknockers*, where this big-ass flying saucer was buried under this little town in Maine."

Worthing shrugged. "So? According to Stephen King, there was something nasty buried under every small town in Maine."

"This saucer gave off some kind of chemical or radiation that turned the town's population into mutant aliens."

"You telling us that this thing the Russians have got is going to turn us into mutant aliens?"

"Of course I'm not. I was just thinking about the parallels."

Worthing scowled. "At least it's not Arthur C. Clarke's monolith."

Travis swallowed the last mouthful of the chicken burrito. "Are you suggesting that we're heading into a Stephen King novel?"

Hammond shook his head. "I wish I'd never mentioned it in the first place."

*Burroughs Marshal's Department's high-speed pursuit
vehicle, in open country, 255 kilometers west of Marsbad—
May 30 CEC—02:06 MST.*

Casey was close to exhaustion. It seemed as though he had
been driving forever. First there had been the dash from Burroughs and then the actual rescue of Irina and the run up to
Marsbad, and now he was off after Greig with little more than
an hour stop that had been spent in discussion with Hammond
and Dan Worthing. He wondered if he could chance taking any
more drynamax, but he dismissed the idea. He was already on
the verge of hallucination. Any more and he would start seeing
Martian bats flying alongside the car in formation. Irina was
asleep behind him. She had offered to drive, but he had told her
to get what sleep she could. He was too wired to relax. He
wanted to go after Greig. He realized that it was turning into an
obsession, but there was not a damn thing he could do about it.
When a person was driven, he was driven, and that was it.

There had been quite an argument with Irina as to whether
she was going to come with him at all. He had wanted to stash
her someplace safe in Marsbad until he came back. She had
flatly refused to go along with that plan. He had pointed out the
dangers that might be involved, and she in turn had pointed out
that she was a fully trained and highly experienced peace officer
and that he could not have wished for a better partner. Further-
more, if he thought that she was going to sit around in some
Marsbad hotel room like the docile little woman, waiting to hear
that he had been killed or arrested by the KGB, he had to be
crazy. After that speech, he had had no choice but to give in
and let her come with him.

He glanced into the rearview mirror to make sure Hammond
was keeping up. The lights of the Marsman were right there, a
hundred or so meters behind. Next he checked the long-range
forward radar. It was showing a line of low hills ahead of him
that curved around the base of the volcano. If Hammond's information was correct, the Soviet base was between the foothills
and the lower slopes of the volcano itself, in a small lava valley.
Of course, the bulk of Hammond's information had come from
Crazy Mouly, and so there had to be some doubt about its ac-

curacy. What bothered Casey more was that there was so far no sign of the Jeep carrying Greig. Even if they were making better time than he was, they could not be more than an hour and a half ahead of them, and a trace should have shown up on the outer limits of his radar. Unless, of course, the Jeep was equipped with some kind of stealth device that was hiding it from him. The other alternative was that the Jeep was not headed for Olympus Mons at all, that the Soviet base was not the target of the team's mission. If that were the case, he was off on a wild goose chase with this bunch of suicidally crazy newsmen, and Greig was getting away from him. That was something he did not even want to think about.

He fed the radar plot into the car's computer to enhance the contours of the ridge. It was typical terrain for that part of the planet, a line of sandblasted volcanic rock jutting from the desert. Suddenly there was a blip in what looked like a narrow pass between two low peaks. It was too far away to have any real configuration, but it looked like something metallic, and it appeared not to be moving. Casey blinked and rubbed his eyes to reassure himself that it really was a blip and not a hallucination produced by wishful thinking.

The blip was still there. It was vague and unsteady, but it was definitely there and about the right size for a three-person ground vehicle. He flashed his lights and slowed to a stop. Hammond's truck pulled up beside him, and Dan Worthing's face peered out from one of the side windows. Casey signaled that he was coming across. Worthing nodded that he understood.

Casey shook Irina awake. "You'd better seal your helmet. I'm going across to the truck."

"What's going on?"

He pointed to the radar blip. "I think we may have spotted Greig's Jeep."

"You want me to come with you?"

Casey shook his head. "No. Stay here and keep an eye on that blip. If it does anything, start flashing the lights."

Irina nodded and sealed her helmet. Casey popped the canopy, climbed out, and walked across to the Marsman. The truck's air lock had already vented, so he climbed straight in. He waited for it to refill with air and then ducked into the cabin in a flurry of ice crystals.

"Did you see anything on your radar?"

Worthing, who had the navigation console, shook his head. "Not a damn thing but rocks and sand."

"I think I've picked up Greig's Jeep. I guess I've got a better range."

"Where?"

"Are you picking up a low ridge up ahead?"

Hammond moved up beside Worthing. "You got a ridge?"

Worthing made room so that Hammond could take a closer look at the forward radar screen.

"Barely," the Englishman said. "There's something, but it's right at the limit of our range."

"Well, I got it on mine, and the question is, What are we going to do with it?"

Just then Crazy Mouly woke up. The old-timer shuddered, coughed, and looked around as though trying to remember how the hell he had arrived in the strange truck. Then he seemed to remember—and he did not like the situation at all. "Jesus Christ, we must be getting close to that Russian base. Boogie Boy has been walking around in my dreams."

Casey sighed. It was not exactly the kind of confirmation he had been looking for.

Travis moved in and poured the backrat a shot of vodka. "Here, old man. Drink this and take a load off your mind."

Crazy Mouly stared gratefully into the shot glass while the others faced Casey.

Worthing voiced the question. "So, Marshal, you have a plan?"

Casey shook his head. "I've been kind of playing it by ear up to now."

"You say the blip isn't moving?"

"As far as I can tell, it's just sitting there."

Travis looked over Hammond's shoulder at the radar screen. "If you spotted them, there's a damn good chance they've spotted us, and if they are some kind of military team like you figure, they're going to have state-of-the-art scanning hardware. They may even be getting satellite pictures. In fact, they may be looking at us right now."

Old Mouly put down his glass. "You guys got a map?"

Casey wondered what the old coot wanted. Worthing, on the other hand, took Crazy Mouly quite seriously and put up a one-centimeter map of the area on the computer monitor. "Can you read one of these things?"

Mouly regarded him with disdain. "I may be crazy, but I ain't stupid, boy. I made some of the maps of this area."

The others made room for Mouly to see the screens. He looked from the radar to the computer map and then glanced back at Hammond. "You say there's a ridge up ahead?"

Casey nodded impatiently. The backrat was just wasting time. "That's right, top screen, just beyond the edge of the radar range."

Crazy Mouly pointed to the map and looked at Barstow. "And we're here."

"Right."

Mouly traced a map contour with his finger. "So this must be the ridge, and right beyond it is your Russian base."

The drynamax was making it hard for Casey to wait out the old man's geography lesson. 'I think we pretty much figured that for ourselves."

Mouly shot him a look of scarcely concealed irritation. "Just hold your water, Mr. Policeman, and hear me out."

Worthing realized that it was all too easy to think of Mouly as just a loony old drunk and forget that in his lucid moments the old man knew more about the Martian outback than did the rest of them put together.

Mouly waited until he had everyone's attention before he went on. "Now, it seems to me that if anyone wanted to sneak up on that base, their best plan would be to stash their vehicle in along that ridge, where it would be hidden from the base's scanning gear, and go the rest of the way on foot, hoping to be too close to the ground to be noticed."

Travis nodded. "He's got a point there."

Worthing looked amused. "It still doesn't tell us what we should do."

Mouly cackled. "For a bunch of bright boys, you guys are kinda slow."

Casey scowled. "You got a plan?"

Mouly was grinning from ear to ear. "I got a bit of an idea, if you all got the time to hear it."

"Okay, let's hear it."

Mouly leaned forward with a conspiratorial grin. "I'd do exactly what those people up ahead seem to be doing. I'd hide these two units up on the ridge and go on from there on foot. Of course, I'd pick a spot a few miles along the ridge. Then, if they do spot us, it won't look as though we're tracking them."

Worthing had to stifle a laugh. Both Casey and Hammond seemed to be having trouble accepting the notion that Crazy Mouly was the only one with an acceptable plan.

Mouly looked at Casey. "Your woman talks Russian, don't she?"

Casey nodded. "Probably on account of the fact that she *is* Russian."

"You?"

Casey nodded again. "I'm pretty fluent."

"Anyone else speak it?"

Worthing raised a hand. "I can get by."

"So I suggest, while we're heading for the ridge, you make a bunch of Russian radio small talk. It might help convince those folks up ahead that we ain't following them."

Casey had to admit that incredible as it was, the old-timer was on the money. "What do we do when we hit the ridge?"

Mouly shrugged. "We stash the truck and the cruiser as best we can, and then you go about your business. You go get your man, and these boys get their pictures of the Soviet base or whatever other damn-fool thing they have in mind, and we all hope we get out in one piece. It ain't hard to figure. The trick's in the doing it."

Jeep ATV, close to Olympus Mons—May 30 CEC—
02:07 MST.

"There are two vehicles behind us. They're too far out to make a configuration, but they're definitely coming in this direction."

It was the first time in hours that Whittaker had spoken to Greig. It took Greig so much by surprise that he twitched. They had parked the Jeep in a narrow canyon that the vehicle's computer had pinpointed. It was on the far side of a rock ridge from the Soviet base and had been selected because it afforded close to total protection from Soviet scanning. There was even a sand-carved overhang along one wall of the canyon, which would conceal them from satellite inspection. That was just as well. The stealth unit that had made them electronically invisible during the last leg of the journey produced such a power drain that their storage batteries were dangerously depleted and they could not risk running the thing for very much longer without jeopardizing the vehicle's other functions.

Whittaker was waving to Booth through the Jeep's windshield, indicating that he should come inside. That close to the Soviets, they were maintaining absolute radio silence. Greig leaned over and looked at the radar screen. There were two blips on the outer edge coming from exactly the same direction from which they had come. At first the blips seemed to be slowly crawling across the flat desert, but then they halted abruptly.

Greig called out to Whittaker. "They appear to have stopped."

Whittaker glanced around. "Check the radio. See if there are any intervehicle radio transmissions."

Greig keyed through the ground transport communication bands. "There's nothing."

"That doesn't look good."

The air lock ready light was flashing. The hatch slid open, and Booth came through with hoarfrost forming on his suit. "What's the problem?"

Whittaker showed him the blips on the screen.

Booth removed his helmet and stared thoughtfully at the radar plot. "We won't know their real intentions until they start moving again. In the meantime, we maintain readiness and do everything that needs to be done before we leave the vehicle. We won't, however, actually move out until it's clear what these things on the screen mean to do. We'll have to put a time limit on it, though. It's two already, and I want to be inside the base before dawn. If they haven't moved inside an hour, we'll have to review the situation. Does anyone have a problem with this?"

Whittaker shook her head. Greig had a problem, but he was not about to voice it. Ever since the victim had escaped from him back in Marsbad, the entity had been punishing him with a hellish unchecked anger. After the bungled murder attempt it had briefly left him, but then it had quickly returned with a vengeance once coast and host were clear. Only by looting the morphine supply from the Jeep's emergency kit while praying that neither Booth nor Whittaker would notice had he enabled himself to pull enough of his mind together to run through the preparations for the final phase of the mission. The lower levels of his consciousness were being stormed by a rolling scarlet blood pain that coursed through them like a flow of molten lava. The entity raged inside his mind; cheated of its due sacrifice at the crucial moment, it howled out its insatiable hunger. Greig had no idea how he was going to get through the mission that lay ahead. There was no hope that the entity would relax its grip on him until its agonized need for blood was satisfied.

"They're moving again."

Booth and Whittaker quickly turned to the scanner.

"Plot a projected course," Booth ordered.

"They are making for the ridge but not coming directly after us."

The next moment there was a burst of Russian from the radio speaker.

Whittaker looked relieved. "Seems like they're on regular course for the base from Marsbad."

Booth looked dubiously at the speaker. "Or someone's trying very hard to convince us that that's the case."

"Should we call up satellite images for a closer look?"

Booth shook his head. "Absolutely not. We can't afford to break radio silence under any circumstances."

"So what do we do?"

Booth looked at each of the other two in turn. "We go right ahead. We move out as planned."

EIGHT

The foot of Olympus Mons—May 30 CEC—03:19 MST.

FIVE SUITED FIGURES WERE ASSEMBLED IN FRONT OF THE parked cruiser. It was the parting of the ways and the start of the culmination. They had divided into three groups: Hammond, Barstow, and Mouly were going to work their way as close to the base as they could; Casey and Irina were going to follow the ridge in search of Greig; Worthing and Travis were to stay at the truck. Worthing would handle the backfeed from Barstow's camera and instantly relay the signal to Burroughs via satellite squirt, while Travis would be ready to drive if they had to make an emergency getaway. The air was filled with the kind of tension that surrounded any group of people who knew, without a doubt, that they had passed the point of no return. Radio silence made it doubly hard for the five on the outside. They were sealed in their suits, alone with their thoughts and fears. Hammond shook hands with Casey, and all five started walking away from the ground units. Worthing and Travis watched them go.

Worthing sighed. "I'm beginning to wish we'd never started this thing."

"It's kind of late to be thinking like that, isn't it?"

"You never think like that until it's too late."

"I guess we can count ourselves lucky we got the easy job."

"I hate waiting. At least they're out there doing something."

"Waiting's just a matter of setting your mind to it." The others were out of sight now, and Travis stood up. "You want a drink?"

"Just a small one. This is no time to get shitfaced."

At first the two groups moved up the ridge together. As they climbed, the Soviet base was still out of sight on the other side of it. Olympus Mons itself dominated everything, blotting out half the sky. Now that they were so close to it, its size was truly impossible to grasp. It defied all Earth-conditioned senses of scale or perspective. The enormous cone seemed too vast, too tall even to exist.

Mouly was the first to crest the ridge, and even he, with his long experience, stopped and took a long look at the spectacle. The others came after, one by one. They all stopped and stared, standing close together in an awed, mutually protective group. A wide, flat valley extended out in front of them and spread all the way to the lower slopes of the volcano. No particular effort had been made to hide the Soviet base. Acres of camouflage sheeting might conceal from prying eyes what went on inside, but the fact of its existence was no secret at all. The roughly square perimeter was floodlit and surrounded by a high triple fence of razor wire. There was a pressurized gun tower on each of the four corners, and a light, Martian-modified T-40 tank patrolled the ground immediately outside the wire. Casey could well imagine the battery of other, unseen defenses that also surrounded the camp. Hammond and his cameraman had to be out of their minds to go anywhere near it.

It was harder to make out what was behind the wire. They could see a small vehicle park that contained two more light tanks, some heavy trucks, and a handful of small runabouts. The rest of the base seemed to be made up of a collection of camouflaged huts and low, single-story buildings. As with most other installations on Mars, the operational heart of the base was no doubt underground. Barstow raised the large portacam to his shoulder to tape a preliminary long shot of the base. Hammond signaled him not to. The backfeed to Worthing was all too detectable. They could not risk shooting until the very last minute.

Mouly was gesticulating that they should start down. Casey indicated that he and Irina would head along the top of the ridge. Hammond, Barstow, and Mouly watched them go for a few minutes and then started down. The temptation when descending a steep incline in Martian gravity was to take it fast in long, bounding leaps. They had to force themselves to go slowly.

It took about twenty minutes for them to get down. When they were finally on the floor of the valley, they paused again. For about a minute the three men looked at each other in silence. Then they started cautiously forward.

The base of Olympus Mons—May 30 CEC—04:04 MST.

Greig put one foot in front of the other. Inside the suit, sweat was running down his body. Despite the fact that he had shot up the last of the morphine, the entity was still filling his head with pulses of blinding pain. The radio silence decreed by Booth was something of a mercy. With their radios turned off, the other two could not hear his labored breathing and agonized gasps.

Booth was up ahead, scouting for a sheltered place such as a gully or a small crater in which to set up the relay point. Whittaker was a few paces in front of Greig, bending forward, as was he, under the weight of the equipment on her back. The plan was for them to move as close to the base as they could, using all possible cover and at all costs avoiding detection. They were sticking close to outcroppings of exposed rock, and their suits were covered by mattlar ponchos and hoods that would disguise the heat leakage from the suits and produce confused and shapeless reflection images on electronic scanners. If the base defenses did pick up an image of them, the mission planners hoped that it would be so confused that the Soviets would dismiss it as ground clutter or shimmer. In that way they would cover about half the distance from the ridge to the base perimeter. At the halfway point they were supposed to find a concealed position where Greig and Whittaker could set up the relay hardware. When the equipment was on-line, Booth would advance on his own and attempt to break into the base, using all the considerable weapon technology at his disposal.

If Greig had not been thoroughly briefed on the rambo's exact capabilities, he would never have believed that a single man, no matter how powerful, could have made it through the defenses and into the base. Everyone who had even so much as looked at a comic book or watched a grunt snuff movie knew that rambos were strong. Military buff folklore told how three CIA rambos had held off over three hundred assault troops during the siege of Cape Town. Nobody, however, outside of a small cadre of senior marines and civilian technicians, was aware of just how much damage Booth was capable of doing when he went operational. He had something like three times the firepower of the old-style rambos like the ones who had been in the U.S. embassy in Cape Town. And it was not just a matter of his weapons and ultrasouped strength and reflexes. The titanium steel pressure suit was so gimmicked with cyberware that when he hit the perimeter of the base, it would start putting out a scream that could upset, if not actually garbagedump, every major electronic defense system in the installation.

While Booth went to work, Greig and Whittaker would crouch in their makeshift foxhole, monitoring Booth's every impression of the interior of the base through direct neural interface. Whittaker would run the satellite squirt and the recording rig, while Greig would actually be jacked into the link with Booth. The DNI pickups were already taped to his neck and forehead. Over and above his other pain, Greig had a deep hollow-gut trepidation about what would happen when his mind parasited onto Booth's. Would Booth be aware of the entity? An evil thought seeped through. Maybe the entity would be able to crawl along the link and take over Booth's mind; maybe Greig could finally be rid of it. He shivered. He was not sure where the thought had come from. Did he himself want to get rid of the entity, or was it actually the entity wanting to move on to new pastures?

They seemed to be coming uncomfortably close to the base perimeter, and Greig was growing increasingly nervous. Finally the rambo raised a hand and pointed to a small, fairly recent crater. Breathing a sigh of relief, Greig clambered over the raised rim of the crater and crouched down in the curved bottom. Then he slipped out of the webbing of his pack and began breaking down the load. As he worked with Whittaker to hook the relay gear together, Greig tried desperately to distance the surface layer of his mind from the swirling inferno and raging entity beneath. The effect was not unlike the way he had always imagined madness to feel.

Strangely, however, the distancing worked, and the setup was smooth and swift. Within fifteen minutes the relay unit was on-line, the ground antenna was rolled out, and they were ready. Booth checked every function himself. When he was satisfied, he faced the other two and silently raised a thumb. Then he turned and crawled up the side of the small crater. Just below the lip, he tensed into a sprinter's crouch. Even through the rigid steel armor, the energy building inside him was obvious, growing in surges like a hot rod on the line, revving before the clutch was popped. Then he kicked dust and was gone, stealing low across the ground, heading straight for the nearest section of perimeter at the inhuman, superman speed run that was unique to rambos.

The base of Olympus Mons—May 30 CEC—04:32 MST.

The three of them ran in fast, short bursts from one piece of cover to another, an exercise in rudimentary commando tactics that Hammond knew was essentially pointless. There was an outside chance that that kind of tactic just might fool a nodding human guard, but it could certainly not deceive a computerized scanner or even the most elementary heat scope. There were probably alarms going off inside the base at that very moment. About the only thing that could be said for spending ten seconds running and then two minutes lying panting like a dog in the shelter of some weird Martian rock formation was that it provided the release of tension and generated some handy endorphins.

To Hammond's complete surprise, the crude tactic actually seemed to be working. They reached a dark gray rock less than a hundred meters from the base perimeter without anything in the base showing any visible interest in them or any kind of alarm sounding. The light tank with the large red star on the turret that was patrolling the outside of the base did not deviate from its established circling pattern.

Hammond crawled up close to Barstow and touched helmets with him so that they could talk without using the radio. "It's weird. Are they all asleep in there? I thought we would have been busted by now."

"So, now we're here, what do you want to do?"

Hammond glanced behind him. Mouly was back behind some boulders, keeping a safe distance. He thought for a moment. "I guess there's no way around it. It's kamikaze time."

Behind his faceplate, Rat Barstow blinked. "Say what?"

"I want you to start shooting exteriors of the base. I'll be in the shot, and I'm going to start walking toward the base. I want you to follow me at a safe distance, shooting with a telelens. If there's any response from the Russians, take off. Save yourself as best you can."

"Are you crazy? There's no need to stick your neck out. We can fake it."

"I've got to do this one for real."

"What are you trying to do, provoke a response from the Russians?"

"It may be the only way."

"How far do you think I'm going to get if the Russians come after us?"

"It's the best I can do. Unless you want to pull out right now."

Barstow raised a reluctant gloved hand in mock salute. "I'll be right behind you. Don't sweat it."

"So let's get to it."

Hammond slowly stood up and stepped out into the open. Barstow crawled around the rock outcrop, shooting from the last of the cover. Hammond took three paces in the direction of the base and turned to face the cameraman. He tongued open his radio.

"Am I centered against the base?"

Now there was no turning back. The Soviets could not have missed the transmission.

Barstow nodded. "Right on the money."

"Okay, here we go." After a momentary pause, Hammond slipped effortlessly into his on-screen persona.

"This is Lech Hammond reporting direct from the Martian outback. Behind me is the huge bulk of Olympus Mons, the great Martian volcano that is over twice the height of Mount Everest. It isn't this natural wonder, however, that has brought us to this desolate stretch of Martian desert. Also behind me are the lights of a secret Soviet base that has become, in recent months, the red planet's greatest man-made mystery. Despite a growing storm of rumor—" He broke off. "Now, what the hell is that?"

There was something streaking across the desert way over on his left. It looked like a sprinting human figure, but it was running at a speed far in excess of any normal human capability.

Hammond gestured quickly to Barstow. "Get a fix on that thing! Maximum magnification!"

Barstow's voice cursed over the radio link. "Jesus Christ! That's a fucking rambo. It's got to be going against the base!"

Perimeter of the Soviet installation at Olympus Mons—
May 30 CEC—04:34 MST.

Booth hit the wire. Cutters extending from the first and second fingers of his left glove began slashing quickly through the steel razor strands. He could feel the blood pumping in his head. The world around him had slowed to a crawl. He could remember how fear felt, but he was not able to experience it. He was a machine with an objective: he was in the unbreakable hold of a burning need to get to the object, to hit the target square on, to hit, to tear, to destroy. The exultation of power swamped all other emotions. The ribbons of steel were coming away in handfuls. Inside the metal suit, their razor edges could not hurt him.

It was always the same when he went into the combat state. Anger and motivation were everything. When he went into combat, he was finally and ultimately the perfect soldier, the end product of his training, of the months of surgery and the endocrine and electronic systems that had been grafted into his flesh and, last of all, the drugs that he had shot into himself before leaving the Jeep. But deep inside a part of his original personality continued to maintain a cold knot of resentment. He might be the ultimate soldier, but he was also ultimately expendable. It was not simply the fact that after all that had been done to him he was not likely to live past forty. The batteries of psychs and drill sergeants who had rebuilt his character had long ago brought him to the acceptance that he had traded longevity for power. It was the way the chemical cocktail that neutralized his fear also turned combat into a headlong stampede that totally ignored any consideration for his own safety. Damning the torpedoes was the built-in weakness of all rambos.

The tank must have spotted him—it was changing course, and the turret was turning, bringing the battery of lasers and PLs to bear. In a smooth practiced motion, Booth pulled a dull steel tube from the weapon rack on his back. The pair of one-time-use Ward rockets launched themselves in a single, silent puff of flame. Moments later two points of blinding white light blossomed on the tank as the slow-burn thermal warheads burned through the porous outer armor. Seconds later the tank itself exploded. The ground shook, and dust and debris flew past Booth. The laser on the nearest watchtower was turning in his direction. There was a second miniature rocket launcher in his hands, and a second puff of flame, and then another silent blast as the watchtower's canopy burst.

Then he was through the wire and on the open floodlit ground between the perimeter and the nearest building. There was an air lock over on his left that looked big enough to hold four or five men. He swung the multifunction M180 into its operating position on the sediharness that projected from the chestplate of his suit. It was linked to a servo system in his helmet. All he had to do was look at the target and tongue the fire bar in front of his mouth. His hands were free to create other kinds of destruction. He sprinted toward the air lock but stopped dead a few yards short of it. The external indicator showed that it was cycling. In a couple of seconds there would almost certainly be a Soviet fire team coming out of the lock. Since there could not be more than five of them, he was ready. He armed the M180.

The air lock opened, and even Booth's hyped-up reactions were taken by surprise as a fountain of blood and exploding flesh blew out from it. A bloody AK-90 was on the floor of the lock. The man had indeed been armed. His mistake had been forgetting to put on his suit. That was the last thing Booth had expected. What the hell was going on inside the base to make a trained professional cycle an air lock without a suit on?

Foot of Olympus Mons—May 30 CEC—04:37 MST.

The quality of the picture diminished as the bloody air lock door closed behind Booth. There was a slight snowing of the monitor screen that Whittaker was watching, and Greig's subjective DNI images faded a little.

"This isn't good," Whittaker said, shaking her head. "I hope to hell we don't lose him when he goes deeper into the base."

Greig had more on his mind, though, than the reduction of his signal. If anything, the loss of the signal from Booth would be a merciful relief. His brain was on the edge of overload. At first the entity had been intrigued by the audio and visual impressions from Booth that were being fed into him by the DNI link. For a few minutes it had simply observed, but then its mood had abruptly changed. It had started to grow angry. In a rage, it had started to hurl waves of pain and confusion at him. It wanted the strange intrusion gone, and it wanted a victim. It seemed vicious and petulant. Greig tried to send back that there was nothing he could do. There was no way he could remove the DNI jacks without first removing his suit, and there was no way he could provide it with a victim out there in the wilderness. If the entity kept up the levels of rage and pain it was currently throwing at him, it would kill him. The entity either did not understand or did not care. The pain grew worse. He had never had much success in communicating directly with the alien thing that had taken up occupancy in his mind. A small detached portion of Greig's rapidly fragmenting personality wondered what would happen to the entity if he died. Would it die with him, or would it be able somehow to move on to another host?

Booth was through the air lock and moving down a bare interior corridor. Suddenly there were figures at the other end of the passageway, figures in green Soviet uniforms that were carrying automatic weapons. Instantly there was a crash of gunfire. Bullets ricocheted from Booth's hardened-steel armor. The bark of the M180 was deafening. The Soviet soldiers spun and fell, and for a moment there was silence. Booth continued his careful progress down the corridor, stepping over the dead and looking for stairs or an elevator that would take him deeper into the base.

Greig was under a fresh attack of his own. A name was being repeated in the pain: *Whittaker, Whittaker.* The entity had found a voice and was hammering at him with the word. Greig realized with a brand-new horror that it had solved its own problem. It wanted Whittaker as a victim, and it wanted her now. But that was absurd. He could never get away with killing her.

"I can't do it to Whittaker. It's simply not possible."

His own voice in his helmet startled him. He was actually pleading with the entity, begging it to let him off the hook. He thanked God for the imposed radio silence. Whittaker could not hear. The entity presumably could hear him, but it was not taking any notice. It continued to jabber the name at him: *Whittaker, Whittaker, Whittaker.*

Booth had reached the doors to an elevator. He spoke to them along the link. "I hope you're getting this. I'm going on down."

He pressed the call button. The elevator doors opened, and he stepped inside, half turning to get the M180 through the door. The elevator was empty, and the control panel indicated that there were three levels beneath him. He pushed the button that would take him to the lowest level. The doors closed.

Inside Greig's head, the voice of the entity had become a rasping scream: *Do it to Whittaker.* Greig could hold out no longer. Hands that scarcely seemed to belong to him reached for the small console in front of him and cut the DNI connection. Whittaker turned sharply and looked at him. She did not activate her radio, but her question was clear: What the hell did he think he was doing? There was a familiar roaring in his head. He was going to make the sacrifice. He could not avoid it. He pushed back the mattlar poncho that was draped over his shoulders and slowly stood up. He walked toward where she was bent over the monitoring and relay equipment, trailing his DNI leads in the dust. Confined as he was in his suit, it could not be an elaborate kill. He would do the minimum that would satisfy the entity.

Whittaker started to get to her feet as he approached her. Her movements signaled alarm. Greig did not hesitate. His fingers reached for the locking toggle on her helmet seal. She grabbed his arm but could not break his hold. In the grip of the entity, his strength was enormous. He twisted the toggle twice, one twist to unlock it and override the safety and one more to actually unseal the neck ring. Warning lights came on inside her faceplate. The air jetted out. At first it was a white spray of condensing, freezing water vapor, but it quickly turned blood-red. Whittaker's body spasmed and then sagged. He lowered her to the rocky ground. The next task was to remove her suit, exposing her flesh to complete the ritual. He lifted off the helmet. Her face was unrecognizable. It was as though her head had been turned inside out. He threw the helmet aside and started to unfasten the suit's chestplate. At that moment the entity had mercy on Greig and took over his mind. He knew nothing more about what he was doing.

The foot of Olympus Mons—May 30 CEC—04:39.

When the tank had exploded, Casey and Irina had thrown themselves flat, oblivious to the risk of puncturing their suits on a sharp rock. Casey quickly crawled up beside her and touched helmets.

"That's got to be the rambo," he told her.

"What does he think he's doing, staging a one-man frontal attack?"

"Anything's possible with a rambo."

"I find it hard to believe that any of those things still exist. How could anyone subject themselves to that?"

Casey shrugged. "It's like the muscle boy steroid craze back at the turn of the century. There is a certain kind who can't resist taking the superman treatment, no matter what it costs."

"You Americans are crazy."

"Oh, yeah, and I suppose your comrades are paragons of enlightened logic."

The conversation was halted by the second explosion.

"What is this?" Casey wondered. "The first Martian war?"

"That would complicate our situation."

Casey grunted. "You're not kidding."

After the blast that destroyed the watchtower, they waited in silence. When ten minutes had passed with no more explosions and no Soviet troops had come charging out of the base, Casey got to his feet and indicated that they should move on. They continued in their original direction, walking parallel to the ridge that overlooked the base. At regular intervals they would glance over at the blazing floodlights of the Soviet installation. All seemed quiet. Only the fallen watchtower and the blackened tank, canted over on one side, testified to the recent violence. Casey also kept stopping to scan the surrounding area with his night scope for some sign of Greig and the woman. Concern for his suit's batteries stopped him from using the redscope all the time, but he figured he could flash it once every five minutes or so without running them down too badly.

It was on his third scan after the explosions that he spotted something beside a small recent crater. He placed a hand on Irina's arm and leaned forward once again to touch helmets. "There's something out there."

"What is it?"

"I don't know. It's hard to make out. Seems to be one figure on the ground and another one bending over it."

"What do you want to do?"

"I'll go closer and take a look. You stay back here and cover me. Okay?"

"Shouldn't I come with you?"

"No. Stay put and cover my back."

Irina was doubtful but in no mood to argue. If Casey wanted to play the hero, then let him.

Foot of Olympus Mons—May 30 CEC—05:06 MST.

When Greig came back to himself, he was on the ground on all fours. Both moons were up, and he could plainly see the naked corpse of Whittaker sprawled beside him, mutilated like all the others. Worse than that, there was a pressure-suited figure standing over him. The figure was tall, over six feet, wearing one of the latest American civilian-model suits and holding a weapon that was pointed directly at the faceplate of Greig's helmet. Greig's first instinct was to scrabble crablike away from the threat, but he realized that that was about the stupidest thing he could have done. Whoever was holding the gun on him was quite liable to think that he was going for his side arm and shoot him dead. The entity was quiet after the kill, so at least Greig was able to think for himself.

"I know how this must look . . ."

"How does it look?"

Greig recognized the voice. It was Casey, the marshal from Burroughs. He must have followed them all the way out there, and he sounded as though he would have been delighted to shoot Greig down right where he was. Greig glanced down at himself. There was blood all over his gloves and down the front of his desert camouflage pressure armor. He realized that he must have looked like some unholy thing there on his knees in the dirt. In most respects that was exactly what he was—except he was not the one responsible for the blood and the elaborate wounds all over Whittaker's exposed torso.

"You have to understand. It wasn't me. I couldn't help myself."

"Can it, Greig. We know exactly what you are. We've been following you for a long time."

"Do you mind if I get to my feet?"

"You stay right where you are, Greig."

"I'm not dangerous now that the entity is dormant." It was important that Casey understand the situation as quickly as he was able. The lawman had to realize that it was not Greig who had done these things.

From his tone, Casey seemed in no mood to understand anything. "Shut up, Greig. You've probably already brought the military in that base down on us by breaking radio silence."

"I think the people in the base have plenty to do right now. Booth is already in there."

"The rambo?"

Now the marshal was listening to him. Greig raised himself slightly. "That's right. He's in there, and he'll take some stopping."

Greig started to come up on one knee. Casey motioned with his gun.

"Any farther and I drop you here and now."

Greig eased back down onto all fours. The gun did not waver. "What are you going to do with me?"

"I've been wondering that myself." Casey's voice betrayed no emotion.

"And?"

"The book says I have to take you back to Burroughs for trial. Except it's a long way to Burroughs, and you could pull all kinds of shit on me along the way. The alternative would be to drop you right here, a bit of frontier justice. I tell you what, Greig. Why don't you try for that side arm of yours and solve my moral dilemma."

"Make your day?"

"Exactly."

Suddenly the entity was back, violent and angry, roaring hate and protecting itself, intent on survival. And yet it was not roaring the hate at Greig. It was screaming at Casey. Above the noise in his head, he heard Casey gasp over the radio. Greig knew instinctively that somehow the entity was inside Casey as well. He would never know if it was the entity or his own sense of self-preservation that made him claw for the side arm. All he knew was that the air-jacketed Colt was in his hand and that Casey had not fired his own weapon. The marshal seemed paralyzed. Greig squeezed the trigger. The first impact hole was small, but it immediately exploded outward. More blood splashed over Greig's suit. Casey's body flipped backward and hit the ground. The joints of his suit went limp as it lost the last of its pressure.

Foot of Olympus Mons—May 30 CEC—05:08 MST.

Irina had monitored the conversation between Casey and the killer over her radio.

"Make your day?"

"Exactly."

At that point she left cover and started walking toward the two men, even though Casey had told her to stay put. Everything seemed secure, and she wanted to see what Casey was going to do. Did he really intend to go by the book and drag Greig all the way back to Burroughs? The killer was down on all fours, apparently groveling at Casey's feet. It could not have been more suitable. Casey clearly did not need any help. Then, just as she relaxed her grip on the spare shotgun Casey had given her, both men gasped almost simultaneously, a brief weird chorus in her helmet. A fraction of a second later there was a puff of smoke from the ground. Casey was blown backward with red vapor streaming from his chest.

Irina froze in horror. The little bastard had shot Lon Casey.

She was out of her shock in an instant, bounding toward Greig. Rage had replaced all thoughts of her own safety. Greig was up on his feet, turning in her direction. There was a pistol in his hand, and she saw a second puff of smoke. The shot went wild. Irina's feet hit the ground, and she loosed a blast from the shotgun. Greig spun but did not fall. The spent orange cartridge case jumped from the ejector. She pulled the trigger again. This time Greig exploded.

The perimeter of the secret Soviet base at Olympus Mons— May 30 CEC—05:07 MST.

"The situation here is exceedingly confused. As far as we can tell, and we have no hard information beyond what we have seen for ourselves, some kind of U.S. special forces unit has breached the perimeter of this ultrasecret Soviet installation and is now inside the base. We can only guess at what this action will do to the already strained condition of U.S.-Soviet relations here on Mars."

Hammond refrained from mentioning that the U.S. special forces unit was a unit of one, and that one a full-blown rambo. There was journalistic integrity, and there was plain stupidity. Even in the most absurd situations the press had to coexist with the military, if only because the military had all the firepower and tended to turn bitter and twisted if one gave away too many of its nasty little secrets.

He and Barstow were on the outside of the Soviet wire, right by the hole that had been torn by the lone intruder. Barstow dropped to one knee to get a dramatic low angle of the festoons of tangled wire, then panned around to the other evidence of destruction.

Hammond picked up the commentary. "Already a guard tower and a Soviet tank have been destroyed, and we can only guess at what can be taking place inside the installation itself."

Barstow signaled that he was going to stop shooting. "That's it for out here. What do we do now?"

Hammond indicated the hole in the wire. "We go on through. Follow our supersoldier."

Barstow hesitated. "Are you sure about this?"

"Are we shooting news, or are we shooting news?"

Barstow suddenly laughed. There was an edge of hysteria to the sound. "Shit, you should have told me that we were shooting news."

Before he ducked through the hole in the wire, Hammond paused and looked around. "You seen anything of Mouly?"

Barstow hefted the camera back onto his shoulder. "Not a thing. I was sticking close to you. He probably went to ground when the trouble started. I wouldn't fret about him too much. He can take care of himself—he knows most of the ratholes in this wilderness. It's us we ought to be worrying about."

White Marsman in a ridge canyon at the foot of Olympus Mons—May 30 CEC—05:09 MST.

"Christ, they're going inside. Those two have got to be crazy."

The moment the pictures from Barstow had started coming back, Dan Worthing had set down his drink and started watching the input feed monitors with rapt concentration. Travis stood behind him, peering over his shoulder. At regular intervals he glanced up at the satellite signal response. It was indicating strong, clear reception.

"It's a miracle that either the Russians or the marines ain't jamming us by now. This stuff's starting to run too close to the bone for either of them. All this looks a mite too much like the start of Mars War I."

Worthing also looked up at the display. "That's the joy of a direct squirt. It goes straight up. Virtually no lateral spread. Neither side may have detected it yet. Shit's going to hit in about eighteen minutes, when they start getting this back on Earth."

The situation alarm on the radar sounded. Travis quickly turned to it. "I hate to tell you this, but I think some sort of shit is hitting right now. We've got aircraft at about two hundred klicks and closing. They're making about e-mach three. I figure they'll be over us inside of five or six minutes."

"Good guys or bad guys?"

"Can't tell yet."

"Better warn Hammond."

Travis shook his head. "I don't think so."

"It could be an air strike on the goddamn base."

"The rule was one-way contact only. There was no talk about better or worse scenarios. If we pipe up now, we'll be a sitting duck."

Worthing reached for the talkback. "Fuck that. We stick together. I'm warning Hammond."

Travis shook his head. "I admire your loyalty, but I can't let you do that. We're going to keep things just as they are."

Worthing blinked. To his complete surprise, he found that he was looking down the black and very menacing barrel of his own Heckler and Koch Starmaster. Travis had produced the gun out of nowhere.

"Have you gone nuts?"

Travis sighed. "I don't want you to take this personal, Dan, but the CIA are paying me a whole lot more for this jaunt than you guys are."

*Interior of the Soviet installation at Olympus Mons—
May 30 CEC—05:11 MST.*

The vast underground cavern and the thing it contained stopped even Booth in his tracks. The thing itself was roughly a hundred meters long. It lay cold and blackly cadaverous beneath lines of bright, remorseless floodlights and amid a jungle of power cables and spindly aluminumwork gantries that attended it like an infinitely complex life-support system in some vast medical facility. It looked like nothing less than the fossil remains of some Leviathan sea beast from the billion-years-gone Martian oceans. And yet that was impossible. Every kid on Earth knew that life, as Earthmen thought of it, had had only a brief and ultimately unsuccessful flirtation with Mars. It had never risen to any level beyond minimally bright algae and certainly had never spread on the scale needed to support something as awesome as this. Monsters needed massive food chains. So what the hell was this thing stretched out in front of him, this thing that was now being probed by thousands of patch contacts like the barnacles on a whale?

Clearly, the thing had been literally mined from the desert. It lay in the bottom of its own excavation between walls that were shored up by a latticework of steel beams and hastily sprayed polymer. There was a makeshift urgency to the work, as though the pressure had been cooking as the dimensions of the thing were progressively uncovered. The cavern effect was a product of the pressure-sealed steel and plastic roof that had been built over what was nothing more than a big rectangular pit. The roof had presumably been covered with a layer of rocks and dirt to make it look like flat desert from above.

An added edge was given to the already disturbing picture by the fact that the cavern was deserted. There were no people moving around the thing. No lab coats or coveralls. No soldiers on guard. LEDs twinkled on banks of outboard hardware and blue-gray monitors flickered, but no one was there to watch them. Booth struggled to think like a marine. There was no place for anything this bizarre in his training. Without resistance, without something to fight against, he was stranded—and after that first brief firefight, he had encountered no resistance whatsoever. That disturbed him almost as much as the thing in the pit did. Someone was playing him like a rat in a maze. As he had advanced down the bottom-level corridors that led away from the elevator, weapons at the ready and prepared to kick ass, doors had kept closing on him, leaving him no choice but to follow a route that was being laid down by an unseen opposition. Booth could imagine some chickenshit Ivan in sealed control, afraid to face him but dicking around with his head by remote control. A rambo did not function well in such situations, and the frustration tended to tilt him off center.

The condition of the corridors themselves had given him quite enough to wonder about. He had passed three places where the walls, roof, and floors were scarred by the black blast prints of thermal grenades and pitted with bullet holes. There had already been fighting inside the installation. Mutiny? Madness? Surely he would have been briefed if there had been a previous marine incursion. He had been raised on marine deviousness, but leaving him quite so much in the dark would have been beyond all reason—unless, of course, he was only the sacrificial pawn.

And then a door had opened, revealing the cavern. And Booth had been stopped dead in his tracks. Whoever was running him allowed him two minutes to stand and stare. Then a voice echoed around the man-made cavern.

"The real question is, Are we showing it to you, or are we showing you to it?"

White Marsmen in a ridge canyon at the foot of Olympus Mons—May 30 CEC—05:12 MST.

Travis seemed to be treating it all rather lightly. "Spooking ain't what it used to be, boy."

Worthing treated him to a walleyed stare. "Are you going to put down that gun and let me warn Hammond?"

Travis shook his head for the second time. "I said I can't do that."

Worthing was disgusted. "The CIA?"

Travis grinned.

Worthing was filled with a deep sense of betrayal. Hell, he had always liked Travis. This was not the first time they had worked together. The feeling of betrayal was tinged with not a small degree of panic. The unidentified aircraft were only minutes away.

"I really didn't expect this of you, Travis. I mean, you don't even look the type."

"Hell, I'm not the type. I'm strictly local talent, an occasional hired gun. This deal was too good to pass up."

"So you're dumping Hammond and Barstow just for the money?"

"Get real, Dan. There's nothing we can do for them, anyway. If it is an air strike, they're not going to be able to outrun it."

There was a certain logic to his argument, but Worthing was not about to accept it. The situation light on the radar scope was flashing in double time.

Travis shifted his gun to his left hand and tapped out a command on the keypad. "Looks like we have a make on these planes."

An identification schematic came up on a side screen.

Travis turned back to Worthing. "They're Russian. MiG 90s. It doesn't look as though there's going to be an air strike, not unless the ruskies are going to bomb their own base."

Worthing grunted. "Stranger things have been happening lately. Hammond's still in deep shit whichever way you slice it."

"He walked into it of his own free will."

Nothing Travis could say was going to change the way Worthing felt. He glared at the feed monitors. "Just keep watching those planes."

Open country at the foot of Olympus Mons—May 30 CEC— 05:15 MST.

Irina was in shock. There were three bodies on the ground in front of her: two in their split and ruptured suits and the third, the American woman, stripped and mutilated just like the prostitute back in Vostok. Even with her experience, the scene horrified her. She could not detach herself from it. One of the bodies was that of the man who had so recently been her lover, now unrecognizable behind a blood-covered faceplate. Even her training deserted her. After being arrested by the KGB, the wreck, the march up the trail, and now this, she had no reserves left. She simply stood and stared at nothing as the first purple hint of dawn began to show in the eastern sky and a long shadow started to form behind her. She seriously believed that she might

have remained standing there forever, or at least until her air ran
out, if it had not been for the planes.

It was only by chance that she spotted them so early. She
happened to look up toward the dawn and saw that there were
three dots against the lightening sky, close to the horizon. They
were coming in low and fast. As they rapidly closed, she could
make out details. Their rocket exhausts flared an angry red, and
white contrails blossomed behind them. Their gossamer wings
were fully extended to gain every ounce of lift from the thin air;
the wings gave the aircraft the appearance of weird geometrical
moths, except that no moth ever came on with such speed and
deadly purpose.

''MiGs.''

She was surprised by the sound of her own voice, so dead and
expressionless. Everything had ceased to signify. It was all
meaningless. Even the arrival of the aircraft did not move her at
first. She just stood transfixed. The fighter planes could only be
the heralds of a new phase in the horror, and she had taken all
she could take. They could do what they liked to her.

''MiGs?''

The spell was broken only when it became clear that the planes
were not just coming in her general direction but actually were
rocketing straight at her. She was not sure if it was training or
just old-fashioned instinct that kicked in, but without thinking
she dropped flat on the ground. The three MiGs passed almost
directly overhead. They could not have been more than fifty feet
in the air. It was possible to make out every detail of the flimsy
mica wings with their cantilevered leading edges and delicately
complex support frames. She could see the cluster missiles belly-
slung beneath the squat gray shark bodies, the bold red stars
painted on the sides of the fuselage, and even the heads of the
two-man crews inside the high-mounted bubble canopies.

As the MiGs completed their approach to the base, their forward retros fired; keeping formation, they executed a slow banking turn, obviously making a low, circling inspection. As they
came around and passed overhead for a second time, Irina instinctively pressed herself to the ground. The MiGs went around
for a second pass at the base. They seemed to have failed to

notice or were paying no attention to either the suited figure flattened on the barren surface or the corpses that lay beside her.

"I have to get away from here."

She was coming alive again, and she wanted to survive. Her air was down; she would have to get a move on if she was to make it back to the vehicle. The MiGs definitely seemed to be ignoring her. She slowly got to her feet.

Inside the perimeter of the Soviet installation at Olympus Mons—May 30 CEC—05:15 MST.

The arrival of the three aircraft took Hammond and Barstow completely by surprise. Following the trail left by the marine rambo, the two of them had made it to the nearest of the low buildings and had been creeping slowly toward the air lock, pressed furtively to the wall. For them, the MiGs came out of nowhere. The approach of the planes had been hidden from them by the building. On Mars, there was no warning scream of engines. The MiGs suddenly appeared right above them, filling the sky, a silent and menacing visitation, so low that the two men could see every rivet on their undersides. It was as though they had come right out of nowhere.

Hammond stopped dead, frozen in shock, and even the normally unshakable Barstow stood stock still for a full five seconds, camcorders running pointlessly, aimed at nothing. Pure fear. It was all too easy to assume that they were the quarry of those sleek hunter killers with their red stars, their missile pods, and the batteries of lasers and rocket cannons.

Hammond finally found his voice in an involuntary gasp. "Holy shit!"

Barstow was quicker to recover. The camcorder was up and filming the planes as they sped away and started into their turn. "That remark went out on the feed."

"Screw the feed. Let's get under cover."

"As far as I can see, the only cover is inside the air lock."

"So let's get inside the air lock."

Already they were running for the air lock in great bounding leaps, making no pretenses at hiding.

Barstow was panting. "Isn't there something about fires and frying pans in this picture—" He came to an abrupt halt in front of the air lock. "Jesus Christ! Will you look at that."

There was a body, or at least what was left of a body after explosive decompression, sprawled in the entrance to the lock. It was a mess, kneeling forward with its head pressed to the ground almost in an attitude of prayer, as it must have come to rest after it had either toppled or been pushed from the lock. Blood and tissue had been sprayed for a good ten feet all around.

Barstow whistled. "He wasn't wearing a suit."

Hammond ignored the body and pointed to the air lock. "Can you open this?"

Barstow inspected the controls. "There's a heavy-duty admission code, but there's probably also a distress override."

He tapped the keypad experimentally. The cycling indicator came on immediately. "The barn ain't even locked." He glanced down at the corpse. "Maybe nobody cares."

The inside of the lock was also spattered with blood. Barstow hesitated before stepping inside. "This is a terrible idea."

Hammond nodded and looked back at the aircraft silhouetted against the rapidly breaking dawn. "I know it is, but I don't have another."

*Interior of the Soviet installation at Olympus Mons—
May 30 CEC—05:17 MST.*

They had finally shown themselves. There were ten of them. Hardly the Soviet's finest, but four were armed with Zhukov lasers, and the rest carried heavy automatic weapons. As they advanced on the gantry where Booth was standing, he did nothing. He just stood his ground on the high, wide gantry that overlooked the alien thing in the excavation. Although he probably could have outgunned the whole bunch of them, he held off and made no move. The lasers could make a mess of his armor at close range. Even though its polished steel surface would deflect maybe fifty percent of a direct laser blast, there was still the other fifty to worry about. Also, Booth was curious.

He had come to the base to find out what was going on. It was not just another demolition job.

The individuals who were cautiously approaching him with nervously leveled weapons fitted perfectly with everything else Booth had seen since he had entered the Soviet base and tended to confirm that something violent and bizarre had occurred there. They looked like something out of a snuff pack video. The three women and seven men were gaunt and haggard, red-eyed and dressed in mismatched clothes that indicated, if nothing else, a major breakdown of normal military discipline. One of the women was all but naked. Her marcam pants and T-shirt were cut down to a bikini brevity, and her body was daubed with ocher and tan camouflage grease. The effect might have been attractive except that she was little more than skin and bone, like something out of the Peruvian famine. One of the men was even more far gone. A walking skeleton, he had made matters worse by shaving his head and dressing in nothing more than a woman's torn and filthy red silk slip. Another man had completely hidden his face behind a black Arab-style burnoose, while the only laser-wielding woman had a cross apparently burned into her forehead.

"You'd make us very happy if you'd refrain from moving. We are very tense people, and if we all start shooting, I doubt that anyone will survive. That would be a pity, because then no one would know for sure what happened here."

It was the longest version of telling someone to freeze that Booth had ever heard, but one look at the speaker was enough to show why. The group's apparent leader looked like the captain of some damned and haunted U-boat that had been in limbo since the end of World War II. He huddled into the three-sizes-too-large leather greatcoat as though he were freezing. There were filthy rags wrapped around his heavy moonboots, and his dirty blond hair was pushed up into greasy spikes. He also had an unpleasant running sore on the left side of his mouth. The hands that held the solid-fuel street sweeper with the big drum clip shook as he pointed it at the rambo. Booth knew immediately that this man was the one who had been dictating his actions since he had entered the base. While promising himself that he would make sure the freak paid in full for his games before the mission was over, he set his vocal delivery to calm and authoritative.

"And what has been happening here?"

The ten of them had formed a half circle around him. The freak was right. If anyone started shooting, it would be a massacre. Booth certainly would not survive. He noticed that the scantily clad woman's jaw muscles kept flexing as though she were constantly grinding her teeth. Booth knew he needed to tread carefully around these people.

The leader made a twitchy gesture with the street sweeper before he answered. "It probably didn't occur to you that the security you assumed was there to keep you out might actually be more concerned with keeping us in."

The leader's voice had the flat, dead inflection of someone who had been cracking for so long that there was nowhere left to crack to. What the hell had been happening there?

Booth let his arms hang loosely at his sides. Do nothing to spook these weirdos. "And is that the case here? You're prisoners?"

"Let's say that after what's happened, they can't afford to have us running around loose. Both Vostok and Moscow have an overwhelming interest in keeping us here. They will want to keep you here, too, now that you've been contaminated."

"Contaminated? What do you mean contaminated?"

That word struck fear into Booth's heart. Even a rambo was helpless against a silent, invisible destroyer.

The freak leader smiled and pointed to the thing lying there in its pit. "It's already started working on you. You'll go the same way as the rest of us."

Booth was having trouble maintaining his calm. "You want to explain what you're talking about?"

The leader shook his head. "I will in time, but not right now. You are not our only uninvited visitor." He gestured to a single audio plug in his left ear. "I've just been informed that there is a flight of MiG 90s directly overhead. I've repeatedly told Vostok that blowing up this place would only succeed in scattering the contamination over half the planet, but it may well be that they've stopped listening to us. It'd be understandable. About the only thing they know for sure back in Vostok is that those of us who've survived are hopelessly insane."

Open ground at the foot of Olympus Mons—May 30 CEC—05:21 MST.

The MiGs were coming in to land. After they had slowly circled the base for a full five minutes, their wings had started to retract and their downward thrusters had cut in, blowing up clouds of dust as they gently settled to the surface of the desert. Irina watched from behind an outcrop of rock. The Soviet aircraft had not landed at the base as she might have expected. Instead, they had come down at a point a kilometer or so outside the wire. Their engines died, but no one from any of the three crews made a move to climb down from the cockpit. The planes simply sat with furled wings like huge guardian insects while the rising sun turned the hoarfrost on the upper slopes of the huge volcano a vibrant pink.

Irina had paused for a moment to watch them come down, and then, when it was clear that the fighters were not about to do anything particularly dramatic, she had turned away and continued on her solitary trudge toward the ridge where the vehicles were hidden. She felt dead inside. She was using the single fixation on getting where she was going to shut out the pain. It worked very well as long as she did not think.

Interior of the Soviet base at Olympus Mons—May 30 CEC—05:27 MST.

There were more bodies inside the corridor, but they had died the old-fashioned way, riddled with bullets. The rambo appeared to have been leaving his mark. After a cursory inspection Hammond removed his helmet and cradled it under his arm. He wiped his face with his free hand. He was sweating, and he felt a little dizzy. Inside his head, he could hear soft weird murmurings. Was he getting sick, or was this the way it had started with Old Mouly? He looked at Barstow. It was hardly the time to say anything.

The cameraman had made no attempt to unseal his own suit. He just stood looking at Hammond. "I hope you know what you're doing."

Hammond grinned sourly. "Just high profiling for the maximum viewer identification."

"Tell me that when they toss you out of an air lock like that other poor bastard."

Hammond ignored him and faced the camera. "We are now inside this highly secret Soviet base, and clearly things have been happening here that are far from normal. So far, all we have seen is the aftermath of violence and carnage. I don't know how long we're going to be able to stay on the air, but we're going to go on bringing you this exclusive report until we're physically stopped."

He signaled for a cut. "How's that for brave talk?"

Barstow was stepping over the bodies, peering on down the corridor. "Personally, I think we're out of our minds."

They walked on down an empty corridor.

"Deeper into the base?" the cameraman asked.

Hammond nodded. "Now we've come this far."

"I hate to say this, boss, but it's too damn quiet."

"Who do you think you are, John Wayne on some late-show western?"

"There's a goddamn rambo inside this place. There ought to be all hell breaking loose."

"Maybe he's already got the place secured."

"And maybe he got himself creamed, and we're going to have to face a bunch of very angry Russians."

"There isn't a happy ending in this."

They were approaching the door to an elevator shaft. When they were just a couple of paces away from it, the door slid silently open. The two men stopped dead. No one came out, and the doors remained open. They moved closer. The elevator was empty, just standing there as though it were inviting them to step inside.

"I think we just left the late show and entered the Twilight Zone."

*Interior of the Soviet base at Olympus Mons—May 30 CEC—
05:32 MST.*

"That's Lech Hammond," the rambo said.

"So there are more of your people."

Booth started to get impatient. "Don't you watch TV? He's a news reporter. Works for the 22C-Fox satellite network out of Tokyo."

"We watch a lot of TV. Old TV. It helps to focus on something."

They had taken him to the base's main control room. He had allowed them to remove his helmet and take away his heavy weaponry, although there were still enough hidden gimmicks built into the suit for him to take the ten of them any time he wanted. There was one more freak on duty in the control room, quite as weird as any of the others. That made eleven. Were these all that were left alive in the place? The leader in the leather coat had indicated that Booth should sit down, away from the main action. The woman with the cross burned into her forehead stood behind him with the lens tube of her laser just inches from the back of his head.

The leader made perfunctory introductions. "I'm Number Two."

"Huh?"

The others also identified themselves by numbers, Two through Twelve. It was far too freaky for Booth.

"What is all this? What's with the numbers game?"

"It focuses on names. It's one of the ways that it takes control. It doesn't seem to handle numbers too well."

"You talk about this thing as though it were alive."

Number Two shook his head. "No, it's too old to be alive, but it's something."

"I don't understand."

"Neither do we."

Booth shook his head. He was out of his depth. "Maybe I should talk to Number One."

"There is no Number One." A weird smile spread over Number Two's face. "Unless, of course, you're Number One."

Number Two saw his confusion and actually volunteered some

information. "It was an idea that we took from an old British TV show. I told you that we watch a lot of old TV. We have had to adopt some very unorthodox behavior patterns in order to survive."

"You still haven't told me what you've been surviving."

"All in good time."

The main action in the control room seemed to be a matter of watching. One section of a wall of multiple view screens showed the aircraft sitting, doing nothing, out in the desert; another followed the progress of Lech Hammond and his cameraman as Number Two ran them through the maze just as he had previously run Booth. There was also a big brother unit that showed other parts of the base. As far as Booth could see, the rest of the place was deserted. By far the bulk of the screens, however, showed different angles and views of the thing in the underground cavern.

The explanation finally came as Number Two, using a computer schematic, moved Hammond through the lower corridors of the base, opening doors in front of him and his cameraman and closing doors behind them. Number Two seemed to do all the talking. Booth had yet to hear any of the others utter a word.

"There were originally over a hundred of us, some sixty military and over forty specialists. After the artifact was first discovered, Vostok put together the best possible research and evaluation team that they could gather in the time. We had geologists, metallurgists, mathematicians, organic and inorganic chemists—just about every kind of expert you could imagine. I was an alien-life-form theorist."

Number Two paused to lock Hammond and his companion into another section of corridor.

"We started noticing the effect almost immediately, but we tended to dismiss it at the time as something that would pass. We were all too excited to think that the artifact could harm us. We had a true alien object that, although strange, was clearly the product of some kind of intelligence, a builder and space traveler. It was what we'd always dreamed about. It was still being dug out of the desert, and we were just getting our first inklings of how big it was. The effect was fairly mild at first. There was the weird brain fog when we first woke up. Some people experienced headaches. Some started acting a little strange. There was a brief wave of religious mania, but that was put down to the shock of realizing that somewhere out there there was another intelligent and technically adept species. The problem was that we were still thinking about the artifact in terms of Earth life models. We tested it for radiation, chemical toxins, and even microorganisms, but it came up clean each time. After that we simply went on with our work, running our tests and cataloging our data, hoping that the effect would pass. We were working on the naive principle that what we couldn't measure couldn't hurt us.''

It was time to let Hammond into the next section of corridor. On the monitor screens the two newsmen were looking around in mystification. They were obviously starting to realize that someone was screwing around with them. For his part, Number Two played the game with the relish of a behaviorist going one-on-one with a lab rat.

''The effect didn't pass, of course. It got worse. Every night there was someone screaming in their sleep. After two suicides and three catatonic withdrawals, there was no more room for self-deception. Something coming off the artifact was seriously impairing the functional capacity of our brains. We couldn't detect it, but we also couldn't pretend that it wasn't happening. The thing was driving us crazy. Some of us tried a lateral approach to the problem. We tried fringe sciences; we tested it in terms of Reich's orgones and Frechetti's miso particles. We placed tomato plants next to the thing. We even exposed a cageful of canaries to it.''

''What happened to the tomatoes?''

''They died.''

''And the canaries?''

''After twelve hours they went mad and started killing each other. It was only a matter of days before we were doing the same thing. The military came unglued first. A group of noncoms took it into their heads that it was we, the scientists, that were causing all the trouble. They went on the rampage one night and butchered twenty-seven of us. The rest of us barricaded ourselves in here and were able to fight them off with the remote weapons systems. When they couldn't get us, they started slaughtering their officers. For about seventy-two hours they declared a soldiers' Comintern, whatever that was supposed to mean. After the Comintern collapsed, one small group of sergeants decided that they alone were the only ones who deserved to survive. They started a massacre of the other soldiers. They claimed that an alien entity was making them do it, that they were its chosen ones. We were running out of food and water in the control room, and in desperation we put together a suicide squad to gas bomb the sergeants.''

"How come you guys didn't become victims of the effect?''

Number Two smiled wearily. "Oh, we did. Believe me, American, we did. We all saw the hallucinations; we felt the pain and the violent, irrational compulsions. Many of us also thought there was an entity in our minds. No one was immune.''

"So how did the eleven of you manage to save your collective ass?''

"There was a degree of natural immunity, a variation one to the other in how susceptible we were. And then one of the chemists came up with a cocktail that enabled us to resist the effect.''

Booth looked up sharply. "Chemicals? You mean there's a cure for this thing?''

"Not a cure, just an aid in resisting.''

"So what is this stuff?''

"Just a mixture of parallel tranquilizers. Diasapan, mellomax, thiasol, largactal.''

Booth raised an eyebrow. "That shit'd turn a man into a zombie.''

"Being a zombie is infinitely preferable to taking the full brunt of the effect without a cushion. In addition, we've been taking large amounts of methamphetamine. We've discovered that the effect can be minimized if we sleep as little as possible. Sleep seems to allow it to deepen its hold.''

"Old-fashioned speed?''

"It's crude, but it works. Right now I've been awake for nine days straight.''

So that was why the eleven were in such terrible physical shape. They were speed freaks. Booth had a thought. "Maybe if I started taking the stuff right away, I could avoid the worst of the effect.''

Number Two looked at him coldly. "And why should we aid you? You're an enemy, an intruder. You've already killed a number of our people. We have only limited supplies of these chemicals. Why should we waste them on you?"

Booth took a deep breath. "I'm not talking charity. I just thought that it might be in your interests not to have someone with my potential for violence going mad all over you."

The woman behind him with the laser, Number Five, nodded in agreement. "He has a point there. The last thing we need is an insane homicidal rambo running around the place causing trouble."

Booth glanced back at her. "I prefer the term artificially enhanced person."

Number Five scowled at him. "As far as I'm concerned, Yank, you're a rambo."

Booth turned back to Number Two. "Seems like the only alternative is to let me get out of here before anything starts to happen to me."

Number Two shook his head. "That's out of our hands. Although they've so far refused to acknowledge our signals, those MiGs are not about to let anyone out of here. You may be"— his lip curled—"an enhanced person, but they've got more than enough firepower to vaporize you."

Booth wondered why the freaks had not thought of simply killing him. They seemed to have a need to tell their story to someone. "What you're saying is that we're all prisoners here together."

Number Five was not having any of that common ground stuff.

"Some of us are more prisoners than others."

Booth appealed to Number Two. "So start giving me the dope so I don't get weird on you."

"It's probably too late already."

"What do you mean by that?"

Number Two moved Hammond into another corridor before answering. "For almost three weeks now, Vostok has been jamming our communications with the outside world. Before that, however, we were already getting indications that the effect was spreading. We received reports of it being felt in Marsbad, at least in some kind of reduced form, and our own sensors showed that increasing numbers of backrats and other marginals were being drawn to the ridges on the east side of this valley.''

While Booth was wondering if Greig's alleged attack on the hooker in Marsband might have had something to do with the effect, Number Eleven, the man who had been minding the control room when the others had brought the rambo in, looked up from a bank of display monitors.

''The sensors show an unusual level of marginal activity tonight. A large number of them seem to be massing at one particular canyon. Do you want to take a look?''

Number Two shook his head. ''We have too much to deal with here without worrying about what the marginals may be up to.''

Booth had another question. ''You have any idea why the effect should be spreading?''

Number Four, the bald man in the woman's slip, answered. ''I fear we may have, in some way, woken it up. We dug it out of the earth and exposed the surface. We've chopped bits off it with lasers. We've tried to melt it, and we've cooled it with liquid nitrogen. We've passed high-voltage current through it and run every kind of chemical test we could think up. If that's not the equivalent of ramming a stick into a hornets' nest, I don't know what is.''

''So what you're telling me is that I was already contaminated even before I broke into this place.''

''You were certainly getting the effect all the way across the valley.''

Booth needed time to think, but he did not get it. Number Two held up a hand.

''Everyone be quiet, please. Hammond and the cameraman are going into the artifact area. I think we should watch their reaction.''

On the monitors, Hammond and the cameraman were standing in front of the final door that led to the underground cavern and the artifact.

Booth looked sharply at Number Two. ''You're going to let them in there?''

''It's what they've come to see.''

"They're reporters, goddamn it. They'll photograph the thing. They've got cameras. Shit, they could be feeding everything back to those fucking Nips on the satellite. Your secret could be out."

"It might be the best thing that could happen. It was secrecy that got us into this mess. Maybe if the thing's existence is brought out into the open, Vostok will be forced to do something."

Booth was adamantly shaking his head. "Don't do it. Think about it for a minute. Can you imagine what would happen back on Earth if all this became public?"

Number Two looked hard at the rambo. There was a bitter amusement in his bloodshot eyes. "Funny thing, American. That's exactly what the KGB said."

He hit the control that opened the door.

*Interior of the Soviet installation at Olympus Mons—
May 30 CEC—05:59 MST.*

"Good God, what is that thing?"

Hammond had completely lost his professional detachment. He stood and stared like a wide-eyed kid. Barstow was equally awed. His hand went to the release toggle on his helmet. He wanted to take it off for a better look.

Barstow placed his helmet down on the gantry. "Not of this Earth."

"What?"

"Just thinking aloud. I mean, this is really it. All the flying saucer movies, all the things from outer space. Keep watching the skies. Two thousand light-years from home. Christ, Hammond, this is the big one."

"This isn't even of Mars."

"A galaxy long ago and far away."

Hammond winced. "That's why you're behind the camera and I'm in front of it."

"When the clichés all come true, boss, that's when you know it's getting serious. How are you going to describe this baby in a thirty-second sound bite, anyway?" Barstow was already loading auxiliary recording disks. "This is the big one, Hammond. This is fucking destiny. Imagine the Russians sitting on this for so long. And the size of it. Can you imagine what the footage of this thing is going to fetch? Damn, I can write my own ticket from here on out."

Barstow was starting down the steps that led from the gantry to the floor of the man-made cavern, shooting as he went. "You realize that Old Mouly must have only stumbled across the tip of the iceberg? This bastard's enormous."

Hammond was coming down the steps with a great deal more caution than Barstow. "Remember what happened to Old Mouly."

Barstow halted. Nothing had been farther from his mind. He looked nervously at the artifact and then quickly shrugged. "So we don't stick around. We get film on this thing and then get the hell out of here."

"You aren't wondering why there aren't any people in here? Why we seem to have been getting the runaround since we got inside this place?"

Barstow refused to be further deflected from his enthusiasm. "So we get the images and we're gone."

Barstow moved down the length of the thing in the cavern. He seemed to be trying to record every inch of it. Hammond did not quite share his cameraman's childlike delight over the mysterious black object. Barstow was right. There was no way he could describe the monster in a thirty-second sound bite. There was no way he could describe it in a three-hour special. He simply did not have the words. It was too overwhelming and too alien. Maybe he should just let the images speak for themselves, let the world see the first evidence of life other than their own just as he was seeing it. It defied editorializing. The thing filled him with a sense of helpless awe, and along with the awe there was also a terrible foreboding. Then Barstow halted for a second time. He turned back to Hammond with a look on his face that was close to horror.

"The feed's out."

"Are you sure?"

"Positive. No reception readings at all. The link with Worthing's been broken."

"Jammed?"

Barstow shook his head. "Clean break."

"So shoot to disk and we'll try and sort it out later."

"I admire your confidence that there will be a later, Mr. Hammond." The voice came from the gantry behind them.

Five of the strangest individuals Hammond had ever seen were coming down the steps toward them with leveled weapons and expressions that scared the hell out of him.

White Marsman in a ridge canyon at the foot of Olympus Mons—May 30 CEC—06:01 MST.

Worthing and Travis were busy watching each other and the images that were coming back from Hammond and Barstow. They were too preoccupied to notice the figures coming up the canyon, moving furtively from one jumble of rocks to the next, taking every advantage of the long black shadows that were created by the Martian dawn. Then suddenly a violent rocking shook the rear cab of the Marsman. Heavy blows were being rained on the air lock, as though a number of people were trying to bust it open with clubs and crowbars.

"What the hell?"

Travis lunged past Worthing and activated the exterior scanner. "Holy shit! Dawn of the dead!"

There was a whole crowd outside the truck, maybe thirty dust-covered figures with ragged ponchos thrown over their pressure suits, weirdly decorated helmets, and an assortment of mismatched but adequately deadly weapons. Although only blank faceplates looked out of the screen, it was all too easy to imagine the dull eyes and slack jaws and yellow teeth. These were the worst of the terminally Marsdamaged, the ones who had lost their minds and personalities to the red planet and had slunk away to live as scavengers in the outback.

Worthing stared at the screen as though he could not believe his eyes. "Martacheros don't run in packs as big as this. They don't have the social mechanisms. Six or seven together, maybe, but not a couple dozen of them."

He flicked on the wide-beam suit radio receiver and got a

cacophony of grunts and obscenities on the speaker. He flicked
it off again.

Travis was already pulling his suit out of the rack. "Seems
like they do now, so suit up and let's get out of here."

Worthing reached for his own suit and started hauling on the
leg sections. The beating on the air lock had taken on a mea-
sured rhythm.

"You think they could get in here?"

Travis, who was about to seal his helmet, nodded at the screen.
"I figure that that big sucker could do anything he set his mind
to."

A huge individual, all of seven feet tall, with loose chain-mail
armor over his suit and what looked like a dog's skull mounted
on the top of his helmet, was swinging a huge iron hammer,
repeatedly smashing it into the seal of the air lock. More of the
marginals were trying to prize open the canopy of Casey's PV.
Travis slid into the fire-control seat and quickly armed the exterior weapons system. Worthing got behind the wheel and
started the engine. Travis's first move was to run a high-voltage
charge through the truck's outer skin. The next time the giant
swung his hammer, there was a blinding flash, and he staggered
backward.

Travis rubbed his hands and flexed his fingers. "That takes
care of you, asshole."

He flipped the safety covers of the trigger toggles of the fore
and aft Straus miniguns. He directed the first burst over the
hands of the matacheros. That was enough for most of them.
The twin bursts of fire sent them scampering away from the
truck in every direction and diving for cover behind the canyon's
litter of boulders. One small knot of about seven of the backrats
was not quite so easily intimidated, however. They backed off,
but it was an orderly retreat. The giant in the chain mail was on
his hands and knees, seemingly wondering what had happened
to him. Suddenly one of the knot of seven darted forward. There
was something in his hand that looked unpleasantly like a satchel
charge.

Travis hit the toggles again. "The bastards have got explo-
sives."

The man exploded as twin streams of .40-caliber slugs smashed into him.

Travis signaled to Worthing. "Okay, let's go before they get any more smart ideas."

Worthing gunned the motor, and the truck lurched forward. Gaining speed, it bucketed from side to side as the tracks repeatedly hit rocks.

Travis grabbed for a handhold. "Don't roll us over, for Christ's sake!"

Worthing fought the bucking controls. "I'm doing my best."

They were running fast, hairpinning down the canyon, the marginals a long way behind them. Worthing had to struggle with the manual gearshift to keep the truck from running away from him. They were heading for a narrow section of the canyon. It was a bottleneck and the ideal place for an ambush, but it was also the only way down to the flatlands at the bottom of the ridge.

"Oh, no!"

Travis's head whipped around. "What?"

Worthing did not answer. He jammed on the brakes. Travis was flung from the fire-control chair and sent sprawling across the floor. Rocks had been piled to the height of a man across the narrow bottleneck. Worthing had seen them in the nick of time.

"How the hell did these backrats get so organized? It must have taken them hours to set that up. What has got them so stirred up?"

He slammed the truck into reverse, spun it around, and started back, cramming on all the speed he could risk on the rock-strewn surface. Travis was just getting to his feet, but the sudden maneuver sent him flying again. He crashed to the deck. This time he did not get up. He just lay there, nursing his leg and cursing loudly. Worthing was enjoying himself. It was a minimal payback for Travis's selling them out to the CIA.

"Quit bitching and get back in the fire-control chair. We're going to be running back into that gang of backrats any minute. They may have figured out some kind of surprise for us. They seem to have become really good at figuring of late."

An explosion to their rear shook the truck.

"What?"

"One of the bastards must be up in the rocks with a missile launcher."

"Let's hope he's only got one rocket."

There was a second explosion, this time in front of them.

"That's two."

"And he's got us bracketed."

"Here come the infantry!"

What looked like the entire gang of marginals was racing toward the oncoming truck, firing every weapon they had. Travis was back in the fire-control seat. This time there were no warning shots. He cut down the leaders of the ragged charge at waist level. Blood splashed the truck's windshield as their suits blew.

There was a third explosion, so loud that it sounded as though it were right inside the truck. The Marsman staggered as Worthing wrestled to regain control. Papers and small unsecured objects spiraled into the air and were sucked back into the rear cabin. The joints on their suits suddenly swelled as the cabin pressure dropped to nothing.

"We're hit!"

"We're holed."

"Close the connector."

Worthing hit the control, and the iris door between the two cabins spiraled closed. He glanced at the dash display. "At least the power's holding."

"Can we dump the rear pod?"

"Not at this speed."

There were no more explosions. The marginal in the rocks seemed to have run out of rockets.

"You realize that we've lost the satellite feed?"

"We'll have to worry about that later. How about the gun controls? Are they still working?"

Travis tried the toggles. "Negative. They're locked solid."

"So we can't stop and hold them off."

"So we keep on going."

"Also, we've left Casey's cruiser for the goddamn martacheros."

"That's something else we're going to have to worry about later."

"You realize that the way we're going is taking us straight to the Russian base?"

"We don't have a lot of options."

NINE

"**W**AIT UP!"

The voice seemed to have come out of nowhere, and it stopped Irina in her tracks. She turned quickly. There was no one there. The only object anywhere near her was one of the spiky rock formations that had been given the somewhat misleading name of Martian coral by the early explorers. As she was suspiciously unslinging her shotgun, a figure stepped out from behind the coral. She immediately recognized the beat-up suit.

"Mouly? You scared the hell out of me."

"What are you doing out here all on your lonesome? Where's Casey?"

"Casey's dead."

"What happened?"

"He was killed by the bastard he was trying to bring in."

"And what happened to the bastard?"

"I shot him."

"Well, good for you, little girl."

Irina ignored the old fool's chortle. "What are you doing out here, Mouly?"

"I asked you first."

"I'm going back to the vehicle. I want to get out of here."

260

"You can't do that."

Irina was still holding her shotgun loosely at her side. "Are you thinking of stopping me?"

Old Mouly raised a calming hand. "Hell, no, lady. I didn't mean anything like that. There are some, though, who'd do a lot more than just stop you."

"What are you talking about?"

"Martacheros."

"What about them?"

"There's a whole pack of them in the canyon where we left the vehicles. Worthing and Travis have been forced to run."

"How do you know this? You haven't had time to go back there, and anyway, martacheros don't run in packs."

"Boogie Boy told me."

"Cut the crap, Mouly. It doesn't work on me. I know you can think straight when you make the effort."

Mouly sighed. "I've been listening on the suit radio. I heard the whole thing. They hit Worthing and Travis with a hand-launched rocket."

Irina was still suspicious. "I heard nothing of this."

"That's because you weren't tuned to the same band that the martacheros use. They tune through a range that's all but off the dial."

"Are Worthing and Travis okay?"

"They lost their air, but they're still mobile. They're headed for the Russian base."

"This is going from bad to worse."

"I figure our only chance is to do the same thing."

"The base?"

"Ain't got the air to do anything else. There ain't no Sun-Serves out here."

Irina could not argue with that. The air gauge on her helmet display was well below half-full.

"But I can't go to the base," she protested. "As far as the Russians are concerned, I'm a fugitive."

Mouly wiped off his faceplate. "At least you'd be alive."

Control room of the Soviet installation at Olympus Mons—
May 30 CEC—06:34 MST.

"When we were first recruited, we were led to believe that
the preliminary on-site examination of the artifact would be under civilian control. Of course, we were aware that the military
would be in on it. They'd be responsible for site security, and
we knew that they'd assume a much greater level of involvement
if the thing proved to be a threat of any kind or if it demonstrated
some sort of weapons potential. I suppose, with the wisdom of
hindsight, we were innocent to the point of negligence. It really
didn't take very long, though, for our innocence to be rudely
deflowered. Within a matter of days it became perfectly apparent
that the KGB was going to be in sole and absolute control of the
whole operation. There was something about the artifact that
made them extremely uneasy."

Booth looked up. "The effect?"

"No, long before the effect became noticeable, it was plain
that the KGB, as an entity, was profoundly frightened by the
whole idea that an alien anything had been discovered."

Hammond stared at the ceiling. "They probably felt that it
diminished them. Secret policemen yearn for a small, tidy world.
That's why they invent so many paranoid fantasies."

The three newcomers were starting to realize just how crush-
ingly tedious life inside the Soviet base really was. The eleven
survivors were exactly that—survivors. They had no other function and nothing to do except resist the effect. They took their
drugs and waited without too much hope for the situation to
resolve itself. Work on the artifact had long since been abandoned, and they existed in a perpetually doped limbo, trying to
retain the last shreds of their collective sanity. Booth, Hammond, and Barstow had also discovered that Number Two, probably on account of the speed that kept his brain constantly
dancing, wanted nothing more than to conduct a nonstop monologue. Their arrival seemed to have given him exactly the captive
audience he needed. Maybe that was the real reason he was
keeping them alive.

"Before the effect was discovered, the KGB was all over the
base. In fact, two of them were among the first to die as a result

of it. They even overrode the most basic guidelines. We'd decided, at the very start of the examination, that until we knew more about the artifact, no part of it would be removed from the site. The KGB decided that this quarantine rule didn't apply to them. They started taking pieces of the artifact back to Vostok.''

Booth stared at Number Two with a shocked expression. "Bits of that thing went away from here?"

"Over half a ton of fragments was removed from the site in the first month of the operation. For all we know, some of them may have been shipped back to Earth.''

"Aren't they liable to contaminate anyone who comes in contact with them?''

Number Two nodded vigorously. "Indeed they are. In fact, we have a good deal of evidence that being in a confined space for a prolonged period of time with a fragment of the material can produce higher effect levels than general exposure to the whole artifact. The mind invasion delusion has been particularly prevalent among those who have handled fragments.''

Hammond leaned forward in his chair. "Doesn't that mean that the KGB in Vostok is riddled with people who are becoming progressively crazier?''

Number Two nodded. "It may not be confined just to Vostok. It is quite possible that Earth already has its own share of effect victims. Before we were cut off, we started to hear rumors that they were having problems at the Leningrad Institute after some of the fragments were sent there.''

"What did the KGB do when the effect was discovered?''

Number Two's mouth twisted. "They got the hell out of here as fast as they could. They also stopped taking souvenirs away with them. Their next idea was to nuke us. Fortunately, we managed to talk them out of that.''

"How?''

"We pointed out that since the artifact was composed of a completely unknown material, subjecting it to the heat of a fusion reaction could produce completely unknown isotopes that would be spread all over the planet in the form of radioactive fallout.''

"How many KGB people do you think are contaminated so far?"

Number Two shook his head. "It's impossible to estimate. It could be as many as a hundred."

"Christ."

Number Two smiled archly. "It would explain a lot."

Hammond stared at Number Two. The man was clearly on his psychiatric last legs, yet he was totally plausible. Booth, on the other hand, did not seem to share the newsman's opinion. The rambo regarded Number Two with only barely disguised contempt.

"Now who's talking paranoid fantasies?"

Number Two's eyes narrowed. "What's that supposed to mean?"

"Well, let's get real, shall we, pal? I know you and your buddies are hard up against this thing, but isn't blaming it for all the troubles of two worlds getting a little extreme? I mean, you told us yourself you've been doing amphetamines for God knows how long."

Number Two treated the rambo to a long hard look. Finally he sniffed. "I think I detect the military mind at work."

Booth's lip curled. "Fuck you, you freak."

The woman with the cross burned into her forehead stiffened. Her grip tightened on the laser, but Booth sagged back into his seat. Hammond eyed the rambo speculatively. He was certain that Booth had the resources to cream everyone in the room, so why wasn't he doing exactly that? Hammond could only assume that the supersoldier was keeping quiet and biding his time for reasons of his own. His best guess was that he was letting Number Two go on running off at the mouth until he had gleaned all possible information. Only then would he make his move.

Booth caught Hammond looking at him and returned his stare with an expression of absolute loathing. Was it just an enhanced version of the natural enmity between military and media, Hammond wondered, or did it go deeper? Was the effect already working on Booth? Would a rambo be more or less able to resist? Whatever the answer, Hammond knew that he could look for no help from that quarter, even though they were nominally on the same side.

Barstow was also quiet, but it was not from fear of the effect. His natural what-me-worry, it-ain't-going-to-happen attitude protected him from that. Rat Barstow was quiet because he was getting it all down for the record. When he and Hammond had first been brought in from the artifact area, the large shoulder cam had been confiscated, but the concealed system built into his suit had gone undetected. The search conducted by Number Two and his people had been downright sloppy. Barstow had even managed to hide two of the disks he had shot of the artifact. If he ever got out of the base intact, he was going to be a very rich man. As he kept a low profile and discreetly lensed everything that went down in the control room, he explored the fantasies of what being very rich and successful was going to be like. He decided quite early in the process that he was more than prepared to handle it.

As time passed, the eleven survivors seemed to adjust to the presence of the three outsiders. They seemed to relax, if "relax" was a term that could be applied to them even in a relative sense. Number Four stared vacantly into space. Number Nine, the woman with the camouflage paint and very few clothes, was drawing on a small notepad with determined concentration. Number Ten, a worried-looking young man in a T-shirt with a picture of Beethoven on the front, was moving his lips as though silently talking, either to himself or to an invisible companion. Number Two continued to talk. Barstow decided that it was not unlike being locked up in a mental institution.

Every so often Hammond would interrupt Number Two's monologue with a question. "I've been assuming that you eleven are the only survivors. Is that in fact the case?"

Number Two shook his head. "No. There are maybe a half dozen others. Loners and recluses. We haven't seen any of them lately."

"You don't check on them?"

Number Two looked puzzled. "Should we? They wouldn't welcome it, and it wouldn't be of any advantage to us. Some of the loners get violent when they feel that they're being intruded on."

Number Eleven seemed to be exceedingly interested in the ground radar screen. He turned and called to Number Two, breaking in on his flow. "There seems to be something going on out here."

Number Two's head snapped around. "What?"

"Some kind of ground vehicle has come down from the east ridge and is heading this way. It must be doing something like its top speed."

"Can you make out what it is?"

Number Eleven shook his head. "It's too far away to tell. It could be some kind of backrat flipping out. We've been speculating how the effect may be getting to the marginals on the ridge. One of them has probably gone vehicle crazy."

Number Two got up and walked over to the radar display. "Just keep watching it. There's nothing else we can do."

As he spoke, a red light started flashing on the communications unit. Number Nine looked up from her drawing.

"It looks like there's an incoming transmission. I can only guess that it's from Vostok. They seem to have put us back on the mailing list." It was the first time any of the outsiders had heard her speak. Her voice was slurred and sleepy, as though she went heavier on the tranquilizers and lighter on the speed than did either Number Two or Number Eleven.

Number Two slowly exhaled. "Turn up the audio. Put it on the PA."

There was a brief burst of static.

"This is Workers' Paradise calling Stargrave. Please acknowledge."

Number Two had clasped his hands in front of him. The knuckles of his interlaced fingers turned white as he squeezed harder and harder.

"Vostok finally decided to talk to us."

Booth's face was like a mask. Number Eleven was looking at Number Two expectantly.

"Do I acknowledge?"

The arm sweep was wide and dramatic. "Oh, yes, acknowledge."

Number Nine leaned forward into the microphone. "Stargrave to Workers' Paradise. We copy."

"Please stand by. General Lysenko will be speaking with you shortly."

The eleven survivors looked at each other with a good deal of consternation.

"Lysenko?"

It was hard to tell whether they feared a death sentence or hoped for a reprieve. They certainly seemed to be expecting something. The last time Hammond had checked, Lysenko had been supreme commander of the People's Forces on Mars. Whatever was coming, it was practically guaranteed to be portentous.

Number Two was the first to recover from the shock. He rolled his eyes at Hammond. "Three and a half weeks of silence and now this." He turned to Number Nine. "Put up the video."

Eight communication screens lit up red. PLEASE STAND BY was spelled out in Cyrillic letters across each screen. Ten of the eleven were staring at the screens, waiting for the next shoe to drop. Number Eleven was the exception. He was still glued to the radar. With great reluctance he turned to the others.

"I hate to tell you this, but a second flight of aircraft is coming this way. They're coming from the direction of Burroughs, so I think it's safe to assume that they're American."

Damaged White Marsman in open country at the foot of Olympus Mons—May 30 CEC—06:58 MST.

"How the hell did they get there?"

Running at full tilt, the Marsman had roared out of the canyon, plowed through an area of dunes, crested a low rise, and then run straight into three MiG 90s. They were parked side by side on the open desert less than a kilometer away. There was absolutely no chance that the Marsman had not been spotted.

Worthing cursed the blank screen in front of him. "Why did the goddamn radar have to go out?"

Travis clung to the handholds on the sides of the observation bubble as Worthing slammed on the brakes. "At least we're still alive."

"That may only be a postponement. I'm going to turn back, try and lose the marginals in the canyons."

Travis swung down from the Lucite bubble. He nodded in the

direction of the Soviet aircraft. "There's no way we could out-run one of those babies to the ridge if it took a mind to come after us. Besides, there's something following us. I've seen its dust."

Worthing got out of the driver's chair and climbed up into the dome. Travis was right. There was a plume of dust back in the dunes.

"With our luck, it's got to be a couple of marginals who got Casey's cruiser started."

"That cruiser comes with miniguns and a couple of heat seek-ers."

Worthing got behind the wheel again. "I have a bad feeling that we're screwed. Have one more shot at getting the radio working. Maybe we can surrender to the Russians. As far as they're concerned, we're only a couple of travelers on the run from martacheros."

"And we just happen to be on the run right by a highly sen-sitive Soviet base."

Worthing slipped the truck into gear. "So we got lost."

"Which way are you heading?"

"If in doubt, go straight on."

No sooner had the truck gathered speed again when Travis's worst-case scenario started to come true. Dust billowed from beneath the nearest MiG as its downward thrusters started. Its furled wings slowly extended to half stretch.

Worthing winced. "I think one of those babies is taking it into its head to come after us. How're you doing with the ra-dio?"

"The receiving circuits are out, but it claims to be ready to send."

"So send. Make it a distress signal."

"Betting everything on the code?"

"Just send it."

The nearest MiG was majestically easing itself into the air, nose up, thrusters belching flame, and wings half-spread.

Travis spoke calmly into the microphone. "Mayday, Mayday. Ground vehicle under attack. I repeat, Mayday, Mayday, ground vehicle under attack by martacheros. We have sustained rocket damage and are losing our air. Mayday, Mayday."

"You could put a bit more feeling into it."

"I don't even know if I've got an audience. How is our air, by the by?"

"We've got about forty-five minutes, if we're lucky."

The MiG 90 had made height. Its forward rockets cut in, creating a giant's smoke ring. It accelerated quickly, streaking silent and low across the desert. The sun was now well clear of the horizon, and the ghostly day image of Phobos was right overhead. Ten kilometers out, the MiG went into a full 180-degree turn, extended its wings to the maximum, and started back, coming directly toward them like a huge bird of prey.

"Oh, my God!"

"I think this is it."

Control room of the installation at Olympus Mons—
May 30 CEC—07:01 MST.

Eight video images of General Sergei Lysenko stared out of the communications unit. The general was a squat, tough, self-made peasant from the Nikita Khrushchev school of doing it the hard way. He had moved to the front of the Soviet power stage when he had been one of the few who had kept their heads and done nothing during the collective insanity of the face-down with China. When the Soviet media, most of the country, and nearly all of the Central Committee had been howling to go thermonuclear toe to toe with the bastards, Lysenko had held the line. He had even gone so far as to order his tank divisions into three of the most unstable Siberian missile bases to make absolutely sure that nothing was fired. For his pains, he had received the Order of Lenin and been made military commander in chief on Mars. The Martian appointment had been something of a backhanded reward. He was king of his own planet, but it was a small planet and a long way from Moscow. He was off Earth and away from the mainstream of Soviet politics. He had ceased to be a player in the big game, and that was the way the cold-eyed *yedino-obrazie* kids wanted it. Individuals like Lysenko were too independent and uncompromising in their thinking to be trusted with the real power.

"This situation cannot be allowed to continue."

The anxiety in the room was like glass about to shatter.

"A solution has to be found and found quickly."

Number Two faced the screens. "We would prefer it if it was a solution that involved us remaining alive. It's not our fault that we're crazy."

It was a bizarre confrontation. On one side of the screen was the squat, scrubbed career officer with his immaculate green tunic, his gold epaulets and medals, and the red flag in the background. On the other stood the emaciated, unshaven drug-ravaged scientist in his leather coat and dirty rags, someone who had abandoned even his own name. There was, however, a strange equality between the two men. Just as Number Two was refusing to be intimidated by Lysenko, the general appeared not to be prejudiced by what he was seeing on the screens in Vostok. He nodded to Number Two.

"We seem to be thinking along the same general lines."

"You have a proposal?"

"We want to bring you out of there as soon as possible."

"And then what?"

"You would be hospitalized and treated for the traumas that have occurred during your ordeal."

Number Two took a step back from the screen. "We've all heard about KGB medical facilities."

Lysenko's face was impassive. "The KGB will have nothing to do with this."

Number Two's eyes narrowed. "I find that hard to believe."

"I have been forced to take certain measures to maintain order in the colony. One of those measures was to relieve a number of KGB officers of their duties."

The look of suspicion on Number Two's face did not diminish. "How many have been relieved?"

"Seventy-three, so far. One of them was Major Melikov. I believe he took a personal interest in your project."

There was a buzz of whispered conversation around the control room. Number Two waved a hand for quiet.

"We've had experience with Major Melikov. And, having had experience with Major Melikov, how do we know that he isn't right beside you telling you what to say?"

Lysenko's eyes glinted. "I'm a general and a Hero of the People. How could a mere major tell me what to do?"

"That's never seemed to have bothered the KGB."

The glint almost became a twinkle. "In the final analysis, you'll have to take my word for it. Isn't life always a series of risks?"

"We might consider your proposal less risky if there weren't three MiG 90s waiting just outside the base."

"Those planes are there for your protection. We have reason to believe that the Americans have started taking an unhealthy interest in your installation."

Number Two glanced briefly back at Booth. "We have reason to believe that there are American aircraft on their way here right now."

Number Two clearly did not intend to give Lysenko the full picture. Lysenko seemed to be doing his best to be reassuring.

"Let me worry about the Americans."

"Isn't life a matter of doing one's own worrying?"

Number Two looked questioningly at Number Eleven. Number Eleven answered in a voice that was too low to be picked up by the communication mikes.

"They're still coming, but slowly. Earth subsonic. As far as I can make out, it's a C30 transport and a pair of MF12s."

General Lysenko might not have heard Number Eleven, but Booth had. He knew what the C30 was. No regular cargo plane would be coming up there with a pair of MF12 interceptors. It had to be the specially converted C30 that was Saud Elijah's personal command center. The general himself was coming. The rambo glanced at the communication screens. If Elijah was on his way, it also put Booth under the gun. It was a matter of honor. He was going to walk out of there to meet his commander on his own feet and carrying his weapons. Semper fi, you bastards. It was getting to be time for him to move. He glanced casually around the room. The woman behind him still had the laser pointed, but like everyone else, she was watching the exchange between Number Two and Lysenko.

Number Eleven was waving for Number Two's attention. "One of the MiGs is lifting off."

Lysenko was looking off-screen as though he were also being told the news.

Number Two's voice showed the strain. "Why is one of the aircraft taking off? I thought you said they were here only for our protection."

"There are unidentified ground vehicles heading in your direction."

Number Two looked to Number Eleven for confirmation.

Number Eleven nodded. "I've got them on the screen. There's two of them, some distance apart."

"American?"

"I can't tell." A light started flashing. "Wait a minute. One of the ground craft is sending on the emergency band."

"Put it on the PA."

The control room was filled with noisy static.

". . . I repeat, Mayday, Mayday, ground vehicle under attack by martacheros. We have sustained rocket damage and are losing our air. Mayday, Mayday."

Hammond was on his feet. "Those are my guys, my backup team."

Number Four snapped to life and thrust a gun into his face. "You! Shut up!"

Hammond froze.

Number Two faced Lysenko. "Did you get that message?"

Lysenko nodded. "We received it."

"I'm going to let those people into the base."

Lysenko shook his head. "I don't think that's a very good idea."

"There have been enough deaths."

"I still don't think it's a good idea to have outsiders in the base at a time like this."

Lysenko did not know how many outsiders were in the base already. Number Two's voice was starting to shake. He was clearly nearing the end of his rope.

"General Lysenko, this is all getting very complicated. I'm breaking this connection. I will talk to you again later."

He signaled to Number Eleven to break the connection, then faced the others. "I just hung up on a general."

Booth took that as his cue. He was out of his chair, reaching forward for the flat .22 boot gun that was hidden in a secret compartment in the armor that covered his left thigh. Before he could hit the concealed button, though, a laser burst scarred the floor at his feet. Number Five was out of her chair.

"Next one cuts you off at the knees. You want to be a cripple, rambo?"

Booth raised his hands and slowly turned. "You're fast."

"We have very bad nerves."

Damaged White Marsman in open country at the foot of Olympus Mons—May 30 CEC—07:24 MST.

The MiG was huge and was coming straight at him. It looked as though it were going to fly right through the windshield. Worthing could make out details that he did not want to see: the cannon and laser ports in the nose, the pilot's head inside the cockpit canopy. He closed his eyes and gripped the wheel as hard as he could. Seconds passed, but there was no explosion blowing him to oblivion, just the roar of the engine and Travis shouting something about watching where he was going. He opened his eyes. The fighter plane had gone, but the Marsman was speeding straight at a jumble of large boulders. He wrenched the wheel around.

"What happened?"

"It went right over us."

The explosion rocked the truck, but it was some distance behind them. Travis swung himself up into the observation dome and hung there like a monkey.

"They took out Casey's PV. Hit it with a missile."

"The Ivans saved our asses?"

"Sure looks like it."

"What's the MiG doing now?"

"Turning."

"Is it coming back?"

"I'm afraid so."

"Jesus Christ."

This time Worthing did not shut his eyes. He waited. His palms were sweating, and the hairs on the back his of neck were quivering. Again, there was no explosion. The MiG was suddenly right over him, darkening the sky. It waggled its wings, cut in its afterburner, and streaked away.

Worthing slumped in the driver's seat. "The Ivans really did save our ass."

"So let's get to the base as fast as we can and see how far their hospitality extends."

"Wait a minute. What the hell is this?" Worthing was peering through the windshield.

Travis was once again trying to make the radio work. "Whatever it is, ignore it. Don't stop for anything."

"It looks like two people up ahead, on foot."

Two figures appeared to have scrambled out of a small crater. They were running to intercept the truck. Travis came forward and peered over Worthing's shoulder.

"They're probably more martacheros. Try and run them down if you can." He paused and leaned forward. "Hold up." He whistled under his breath. "Sweet Jesus, that's Mouly!"

"Who's that with him?"

"It looks like the Russian broad that was with Casey."

Worthing was already slowing the truck. Travis looked at him in surprise.

"What are you doing?"

"Picking them up."

"We don't have time."

Worthing gripped the controls with grim determination. "I'm picking them up."

"I wouldn't advise it."

Worthing turned on Travis with a look of total contempt. "What are you going to do, shoot me?"

Travis deflated. "Do what you have to do."

Worthing braked the truck beside the running figures, and Travis leaned out of the damaged hatch. "Get in quick. We're almost out of air."

"So are we."

Irina and Mouly scrambled aboard, and Worthing accelerated away. Travis did not even bother to redog the useless air lock.

"Where's Casey?"

"He's dead."

"Oh, Christ."

*Control room of the Soviet installation at Olympus Mons—
May 30 CEC—07:47 MST.*

"I've got a line of sight on the American aircraft."

"Lock a telecam on them and put the picture up on the big screen."

While the rest of the control room watched tensely, Number Eleven keyed in a series of commands. The control room's big main display screen flickered into life. The slightly blurred image of three planes showed dead center. A big C30 painted in brown and orange Martian camouflage wallowed through the air, propelled by its four big rocket motors on the underside of the tail section, seeming too heavy and bulbous to be in the air at all. On either side and slightly above it a pair of sleek sky-pink interceptors watched over it, coasting at only a fraction of their combat speed, their delta membranes fully spread. The MF12 was the U.S. counterpart of the MiG 90, a thoroughbred fighting plane. Where the Soviet interceptor was snub-nosed, slab-sided, and bulky, the MF12 was a light and almost elegant weapon. Comparing the two was like comparing a rapier and a club.

Number Two glanced at Number Eleven. "How are the MiGs responding?"

"The two on the ground are staying put, but the one that's already in the air is on an intercept vector."

There was a burst of plane-to-plane chatter. Hammond's Russian was good, but not good enough to keep up with the pilots' high-speed jetspeak. The MiG in the air came onto the main screen. It took up a position above the three American aircraft but made no overtly hostile act.

The pilot's warning to the Americans came over the control room speakers. His English was heavily accented. "You have entered proscribed Soviet military airspace. Please alter course immediately."

There was no response from the Americans.

The MiG pilot tried again. "MiG 90-47 to unidentified American aircraft. Do you copy? Please acknowledge."

The Americans continued to ignore his signals.

"MiG 90-47 to unidentified American aircraft. I say again, you have entered proscribed airspace. Please acknowledge. Failure to acknowledge will be interpreted as hostile intent."

There was still nothing from the Americans.

"MiG 90-47 to unidentified American aircraft. This is a final warning. Alter course immediately or I shall open fire. I say again, I shall open fire."

"Marine task force to MiG 90-47. I am unable to alter course. I have people lost on the ground in this area."

"You have invaded Soviet military airspace. Leave immediately or I shall open fire."

"Marine task force to MiG 90-47. I repeat, I am unable to alter course. I have missiles targeted on the ground installation in front of us. If you fire on us, we shall release the missiles." The American's voice changed. "Let's face it, Ivan, my birds will be away and locked on before yours hit."

Number Two leaned over Number Eleven's communications chair. "It seems like we have the makings of a standoff."

For people who were facing the possibility of being blown up at any moment, the survivors were weirdly detached. Hammond wondered if they simply did not care anymore. For himself, he was terrified. His palms were sweating, and he felt a little sick.

Number Two straightened up. "I think it's time we took a hand in this. We've been pawns in this game for far too long. Open me a channel to the American aircraft."

Number Eleven nodded. It was impossible to read his expression.

Number Two faced the multiple screens. "Soviet installation to American marine task force. Do you copy?"

Hammond spoke half to himself. "For Christ's sake, don't do anything stupid."

Number Two heard the remark and stared coldly at him. No visual appeared, but a voice came from the audio speakers.

"We copy, Soviet installation. Go ahead."

"This is the commander of the installation. I wish to speak with the commander of the task force."

"Stand by."

In just a matter of seconds the eight screens flickered and then showed a marine officer, a hard-eyed black man with an air of authority but no visible insignia of rank on his pressure suit. The visor of his combat helmet was pushed back. None of the survivors seemed to recognize him, but Hammond and Booth did. It was Saud Elijah himself.

"With whom am I speaking?" asked the marine corps' top man on Mars.

Number Eleven reached across the communications board to turn on the video send, but Number Two shook his head. "That really doesn't matter. The important thing is that I have a warning for you. It would be a very bad idea to attempt to destroy this base. It contains an alien artifact. It is an extremely dangerous alien artifact. Exposure to it is ultimately fatal to human life. If it should be blown up, serious and possibly lethal contamination could be spread all over the planet."

Saud Elijah's face did not change. "Please turn on your video. I like to see the person with whom I'm talking."

"I'm unable to do that right now."

Number Eleven looked up. "Vostok's sending."

Number Two placed a hand over the microphone. "Let them wait."

Elijah looked coldly from the eight screens. "I refuse to hold this conversation with someone I can't see."

"I'm afraid you may not like what you see."

"There's a great deal that I don't like already."

Number Two shrugged. "I don't have the time left to play games. I'm opening the video send. You can take it or leave it."

Number Eleven pushed up a fader. Elijah looked truly shocked at what he saw on his screen.

"Who the hell are you? I thought I was talking to the base commander."

"I am the base commander, at least by default. The majority of the base personnel are dead. They died as a result of exposure to the artifact. I lead a small handful of survivors. We are all extremely sick and may die ourselves before too long, unless a solution is found to our situation."

"You'll excuse me if I find all this very hard to believe."

"I think there's someone here who might be able to persuade you."

"And who is that?"

"We have your rambo. He's our prisoner."

Elijah had a little difficulty pulling his face back into an impassive mask after he heard that piece of news. "Can you put him on-screen?"

"Willingly."

Number Two beckoned to Booth. The rambo did not move until Number Five nudged him with her laser. It was only then that he stood up and walked across to the communication board.

Elijah eyed him coldly. "Booth?"

"Yes, General."

At the word "General," the survivors started looking at each other questioningly. On the screens, Elijah's expression had moved from cold to contemptuous.

"You appear to have screwed up royally here."

"It hasn't gone well, sir."

"Where are the other two?"

"I don't know."

"So what's going on in that base?"

"It's pretty much as Number Two told it—"

Elijah interrupted him. "Number Two?"

"Things are a little weird here, General. I think I should warn you that these people are also holding a couple of newsmen who wandered in here."

"Newsmen?"

"Lech Hammond and his cameraman."

"Hammond?"

"Yes, General."

"Sweet Jesus."

"Hammond's—"

"I know who Hammond is, damn it."

While that exchange was going on, Number Eleven was signaling urgently to Number Two. "Vostok's going crazy. Lysenko himself is ordering us to respond."

Hammond had been so sucked in by the unfolding drama being played out on the communications link that he had all but forgotten that Number Two would almost certainly test out clinically insane. The look of mad glee in the man's eyes as he answered Number Eleven was a forcible reminder.

"Split screen him with the American and fold them back to each other. Now we're up to our ass in generals, we might as well make it a three-way conversation."

Elijah's image was shifted to the four screens on the right of the bank of monitors while General Lysenko's appeared on the four to the left. The telecam picture of the four aircraft remained on the main screen.

Lysenko was now anything but impassive. He barked angrily at Number Two. "Are you crazy?"

Number Two almost smiled. "I believe so."

"You have told an American general about the artifact. As if that wasn't bad enough, you chose to do it on an open channel."

"I decided that the time for secrecy was past."

"And who are you to decide something like that?"

"I'm one of the ones up here slowly dying."

"Your new desire for openness didn't extend to informing me about the rambo and the newsmen."

"I felt I should hold on to some bargaining chips."

Elijah interrupted the exchange. "I think your man is acting according to what he sees as his own best interests, Sergei."

Lysenko looked like a man finding it hard to maintain his control. "Stay out of this, Saud. This is a matter of Soviet internal politics."

Elijah looked grimly amused. "You think an alien artifact that's been killing your people is a matter of internal Soviet politics?"

"I'm warning you, Saud, stay out of this. The situation is precarious enough already."

Elijah continued to half smile. "I think the situation is so precarious that it's time for us to reach some kind of accord."

Lysenko scowled. There was the faintest hint of petulance in the expression of the squat, bullet-shaped man. "I could simply have my MiGs shoot you out of the air."

Elijah looked disappointed. "That isn't going to achieve anything except maybe start a war. Besides, I think one of my pilots has already warned you that we have the base targeted. I believe his words were 'Let's face it, Ivan, my birds will be away and locked on before yours hit.' ''

Lysenko was shaking his head. ''We shouldn't be discussing this in front of the media and anyone who happens to be tuned to this channel.''

Number Two stepped closer to the screens. ''I think Hammond is a fact of life, gentlemen. He's been present for all of this, and he isn't about to go away.''

Hammond was not sure if he wanted to be a fact of Number Two's life, even though the statement did indicate a degree of acceptance. Both the generals' expressions showed a measure of distaste when Number Two spoke. They clearly did not like the idea of a ragged lunatic being one of the major players in the game.

Lysenko held up an appealing hand. ''At least let's go to code before we take this any further.''

Elijah sighed. ''Redphone would be the obvious one.''

Redphone was the descendant of the twentieth-century hot line. It was a computerized random-shift cipher that was reserved exclusively for direct communications between the superpowers, only at the highest level and only in times of most dire emergency.

Lysenko's face was profoundly troubled. ''We've really come to that?''

Elijah nodded. ''I fear we have. We are standing on the brink, but at least we are both reasonable men.''

''So let's test our brinkmanship and our reason and go to Redphone.''

Number Two's right fist clenched and unclenched. ''Wait just a minute!''

The two generals looked at him bleakly.

''Now what?''

''We don't have Redphone in our computer, and we've had quite enough of being discussed in our absence.''

''There really isn't much you can do about it,'' Lysenko answered.

Number Two took a deep breath. He was swaying slightly. To Hammond, it seemed that he was on his last legs.

''When are you military morons going to start grasping reality? We survivors are the only human beings who have the slightest understanding of the thing down here. If you ever decide what to do with it apart from using it as a piece in the power game, you're going to need us. The catch is that we're only holding on here by our fingernails and nearly fatal doses of narcotics, and if you don't take action soon, we'll be dead. What will you do then? Start from scratch and send in another team? Wait for them to die of the effect, too, before you do anything?''

Number Two was sweating. ''You want threats? Okay, here's a threat. We have reason to believe that the effect is spreading. How does that sit with you? Or do you want a better, more direct threat? We're all nuts, remember? If we get shut out of the conversation, we could become very paranoid and unstable.''

His voice was starting to crack. He fumbled in his pocket and produced a plastic bottle. He shook a half dozen assorted pills into his hand and swallowed them without looking.

''We could blow up the place ourselves.''

Hammond stiffened. Number Two had played the suicide card. Now what?

Elijah reluctantly nodded. ''Don't get excited. We'll net you in and feed the code directly into your computers. Get whoever's running your communication board to open a—'' He glanced to the side as though he were receiving the appropriate information from someone off-screen. ''—a nine eighty in-dump.''

Number Two glanced at Number Eleven, who nodded and started keying in a series of commands. The images of Elijah and Lysenko were replaced by swirling, multicolored moiré patterns. White noise roared from the speakers.

Number Two looked around in anger. ''They screwed us!''

White Marsman on the perimeter of the Soviet installation at Olympus Mons—May 30 CEC—08:04 MST.

They were running alongside the perimeter wire of the base. Worthing was looking in vain for a gap in the defenses that would give them access.

''There's no way we're going to be able to crash through this lot.''

Travis was peering out the side window. Irina and Mouly were hanging on for dear life. The sun was well above the horizon, and its light was being reflected at hundreds of tiny points from the razor edges of the coiled ribbon wire.

"The ground under the fence is likely mined, anyway. How's everyone's air holding up?"

Irina rolled with the bouncing of the truck. "My suit warning light's been on for a couple of minutes already. I'm running on empty."

Travis's news was equally bad. "Mine just came on."

Mouly coughed. "Then you're in better shape than I am."

Worthing cursed himself for not recharging his backtanks when he had had the chance. It had been all too easy to assume that he and Travis had pulled the soft detail: laid back, feet up on the console, away from the action, just watching the feed come in. They had not bothered to take any precautions such as replenishing the air in their suits. What could happen to them?

"We've got to get inside this place pretty damn fast."

"Use the emergency hailing channel again."

Travis did not turn away from the window. "I've had it going out on a loop for ten minutes now. I can't tell if anyone's receiving it."

"The MiG did."

"We don't know that for a fact."

"There's what looks like the main gate coming up."

"Is it open?"

"No."

The main gate was as formidable as any other part of the perimeter. The warning signs were in Russian, but the red lightning bolts and skull and crossbones were universal symbols. The gate carried a lethal charge of electricity. Worthing slowed the truck to a halt.

Travis looked at him in alarm. "What did you stop for?"

"There's no point in running around and around the outside of this place if we can't get in."

"We're fucked if we don't get inside."

"Tell that to whoever's in there."

Worthing was surprised that he was not more afraid. The air in his helmet had already taken on a stale metallic taste. The warning light just below his chin was blinking urgently at him. He alternated between wanting a drink and wondering whether dying of asphyxiation was going to hurt or if he would just drift away.

And then the gates started to open. Worthing quickly jerked the truck into gear.

"Did somebody say something about all ye abandoning hope?"

Control room of the Soviet installation at Olympus Mons—May 30 CEC—08:05 MST.

The moiré patterns on the screens resolved back into the images of Lysenko and Elijah, and the white noise became speech again. Hammond was overwhelmingly relieved. For the last few moments he had been expecting Number Two to keep his word and do something drastically self-destructive.

The first voice was an anonymous com-op, presumably speaking from Vostok. "Please acknowledge, Stargrave. Are you on code?"

Number Two faced the screens and nodded. "We are on code and receiving sound and vision."

His recovery was little short of miraculous. A minute earlier the man had been raving. Hammond had been convinced that Number Two had slipped irredeemably over the edge, well beyond the reach of either sanity or reason, and yet there he was, apparently calm and collected and ready to start dealing with two of the heaviest hitters on the whole planet. Either the new bunch of drugs had kicked in or Number Two had almost superhuman powers of recuperation.

Elijah, who was totally unaware of Number Two's lapse, got straight down to business. "My first proposal is that we ground our aircraft."

Lysenko raised an eyebrow. "You'll land your flight?"

Elijah nodded. "I can't circle forever. Call off your fighter, and I'll set down my flight."

"Where?"

"At a safe distance from your base."

Number Two sniffed. "And how exactly do you intend calculating a safe distance?"

The two generals both ignored him. Lysenko was looking
suspiciously from the screen, obviously directing his attention
to Elijah. "And then?"

"And then we no longer have a standoff, and we talk."

*Flight deck of USMC C30 transport plane on the ground close
to the foot of Olympus Mons—May 30 CEC—08:24 MST.*

The serious negotiations had started, but it was hard to reach
any workable conclusions when there were three often opposing
interests involved and a whole swamp of ingrained mistrust.
One of the major stumbling blocks to any speedy settlement was
that the survivors inside the Stargrave installation still harbored
serious misgivings regarding what might happen to them if they
came out of the base and put themselves in the hands of the
Soviet military. They appeared to share a deep-seated fear that
they would find themselves turned over to the KGB. They were
skittish, always ready to retreat to the only position of safety
that was left to them. No one could hurt them while they were
still in the base, because everyone on the outside was frightened
to go in and risk exposure to the effect. The fact that the base
itself seemed to be slowly killing them only added to the tension
and made them dig their heels in when Lysenko, who had a
tendency to bully, tried to press them.

Saud Elijah took the opposing tack. He bided his time and let
his Soviet counterpart make the running. All through his career
he had honed patience down to a fine art. It was not enough
merely to outthink an opponent or beat his firepower. There
were a lot of times when one also had to outwait him. Lysenko
and the one who insisted on calling himself Number Two were
deadlocked over the nature of the care facility that would be set
up to receive and treat the survivors once they agreed to emerge
from the base. Elijah had secretly signaled to Burroughs to run
a fast data search on Number Two. It turned out that in all
probability he was a lateral theoretician from Leningrad called
Alexander Danko who, according to the admittedly slim file that

the marines had on him, had previously done nothing but concentrate on his work and keep his political head down. The fact that he had turned into the uncompromising and potentially dangerous leader of the survivors did a lot to convince Elijah that the alien effect was real and that the survivors' accounts of the damage it had caused were largely true.

Elijah leaned into the microphone in front of him. "Suppose we were to arrange for a facility that would be adminstered by both the powers involved?"

Number Two thought about that. The man looked exhausted, and Elijah hoped that he would not collapse on them before they had reached a settlement. He did not want to have to start the negotiations all over again with another of those lunatics.

Finally Number Two shook his head. "No."

"No?"

"The only way we'd accept a deal like that is if it was administered by U.S. and Soviet civilian agencies. We need doctors, not guards."

"That could be arranged."

Number Two pushed farther. "We'd also demand independent inspections by a third party. Maybe the British or the Japanese."

That did not sit well with Lysenko. "I'm sorry, I really can't agree to this. Far too many outsiders have become involved in this business already. We can't go on expanding that kind of involvement. This is, after all, first and foremost a Soviet matter."

Number Two looked contemptuously at him. "There is no way you can go on with the charade of keeping this thing a secret."

Elijah decided it was time to side with Number Two. "He's right, you know, Sergei. The best we can hope to do is keep the full ramifications of it confined to this planet, where we at least have some degree of control."

Elijah leaned back in his command chair. Lysenko would come around in the end. He could wait while the Russian twisted in the wind for a while before accepting the inevitable. The amber shades were down on the flight deck's forward windows, and the sunlight streaming through them was tinted a rich gold.

His immediate staff members were around him, watching him deal with Lysenko and the crazies in the base. They trusted him. They knew that his will would not waver. He flexed his arms inside the simple grunt's pressure suit that he always wore when he went on field operations. Elijah prided himself on being a man of the people, the leatherneck general. His only concession to rank was the three small stars on his sleeve. His men did not need gold braid to recognize him. He basked unashamedly in the sense of power.

Lysenko was continuing to bluster, but there were signs that he was starting to waver.

Control room of the Soviet installation at Olympus Mons— May 30 CEC—08:42 MST.

Numbers Nine and Ten brought Travis, Worthing, Irina, and Mouly into the control room. In spite of the armed man and woman in back of him, Worthing halted in the doorway and slowly looked around. Even though the weird had become commonplace lately, the scene that presented itself was bizarre in the extreme. The group clustered around the complex of bulky Soviet communications equipment, staring at the multiple images of a Soviet and an American general—women with crosses burned into their foreheads, men in tattered filthy drag, mad eyes, and compulsive nervous twitches—was like something out of a very disturbed production of *Marat-Sade*. The deep layer of garbage underfoot, the unfathomable jury-rigged constructions that here and there had replaced the regular control center hardware, and the strange, illegible, spray-can Cyrillic graffiti that had been scrawled over the flat surfaces of the walls and most of the ceiling all added up to an unshakable certainty that life inside the base had become an unhinged Mars-happy nightmare.

Hammond and Barstow sat side by side, watched by a pair of less than attentive guards. They were still wearing their outside pressure suits, but their helmets and weapons had been taken from them. The marine rambo, with his misshapen head and steel combat armor, sat alongside them, glaring at the group around the screen. The laser-toting woman guarding him seemed to be paying a good deal more attention to her charge than were those assigned to the two newsmen. Hammond, Barstow, and Booth seemed so settled into the place that they were almost starting to fit in with the other freaks in the room. Worthing decided that he wanted out of the high-tech cuckoo's nest as soon as it was humanly possible. No way was he going to become one with that bunch of moonhowlers.

The air in the control room had a sour, stale vomit and rotting vegetable smell to it, as though the recyclers were well on the way to breaking down and no one had bothered to change the filters. After the last few minutes in the damaged truck and the desperate race for the base air lock, however, he did not care that the air all but made him gag. He was grateful for anything that was even marginally breathable. He had blacked out while the lock was only halfway through its cycle, and Travis had been forced to drag him inside, rip off his helmet, and apply CPR the moment they had reached Earth-normal atmospheric pressure.

Number Nine motioned with his assault rifle to four empty metal chairs next to Barstow.

As Worthing sat down, he grinned at Hammond. "We've got to stop meeting like this."

The tall weirdo in the leather coat, who appeared to be running things, instantly turned and glared at him. "Please don't talk."

Worthing shot Hammond a questioning glance. Hammond resignedly spread his hands in a clear indication that he would try to explain everything if he ever had the chance. Worthing slid down in the chair, realizing that he had no choice but to watch and wait. He had made it from the frying pan to the fire, and now it appeared that he had joined the circus.

Irina, once she was over the surge of initial shock, viewed the situation from a very different angle. For her it was a reprieve. The base might be full of lunatics, but at least it was not the KGB stronghold she had expected. Between the madness of the inmates and the presence of Hammond and his crew, there had to be a way out of both the place and her predicament. There were generals on the com screens and altogether too much high-profile insanity for Melikov to simply make her disappear. It was with a weird resignation that she recognized that it was no longer Melikov she had to worry about. If Lysenko was in on it, and Saud Elijah, too, the whole situation was out of Melikov's league. She was in a bigger game now, no matter how it might come out.

Of all the newcomers, Old Mouly settled into the base with the greatest ease, if the least grace. He immediately started making demands—hot food, recreational drugs, alcohol. "You can't tell me that a bunch of eggheads like you, crazy as you might be, don't have a functioning still around here someplace."

And he had one response to anything that did not please him: "Fuck you, sonny. I'm the original, the first one in. Me and Boogie Boy are the grandfathers of you bastards."

Control room of the Soviet base at Olympus Mons— May 30 CEC—12:52 MST.

The negotiations seemed to go on forever. After four hours, a conclusion was not even on the horizon. The control room was warm, and Hammond, who had not slept in what seemed like a week, found that his eyelids kept drooping. He fought off sleep. Beside him, Dan Worthing was snoring softly. Hammond wished one of the survivors would offer him some of their speed, but so far none had been forthcoming. The triple waltz—the trialogue between Number Two and the generals—was like a slow crawl up a stretch of barbed wire. Each point that was settled seemed to create five more that were even harder to resolve. A small voice somewhere inside his mind started telling Hammond that he was going to spend the rest of his life listening to that crap. It suggested that maybe he should take matters in hand and do something. The small voice did not quite specify exactly what he was supposed to do, but there was a definite implication that a resort to violence might be the answer. Hammond was surprised by the voice. It was not any one of his own inner voices. It was something from elsewhere. What also surprised him was that the presence of a strange voice in his head did not disturb him in the slightest. It was almost as though he had been expecting it.

Despite Hammond's misgivings, there was in fact some progress being made. By 14:30 the matter of the care facility for
those who were suffering from the ravages of the effect was
largely settled. It would be administered by the Soviets and under Soviet jurisdiction, but there would be a permanent U.S.
presence and regular visits by an international inspection team,
the members of which would be selected at some later date. All
efforts would be made to exclude the KGB. Number Two was
not exactly overjoyed by the arrangement, but he seemed willing
to accept it and had not mentioned blowing up the base for at
least two hours. It was possible that a part of Number Two's
new willingness to acquiesce derived from the fact that he was
now green with fatigue. God only knew what voices were talking inside his head.

The new mood of accommodation ebbed considerably when
the discussion moved on to the matter of the fate of the artifact
itself. General Lysenko had a plan that had apparently been put
together by his staff while the other negotiations had been dragging on through the Martian morning.

"I have been advised that we should be reasonably safe, even
though we are not certain of the exact nature of the effect, in
treating it like any more normal source of harmful radiation. I
already have a design team working on a containment jacket for
the artifact. They tell me that if we encase the thing in multiple
layers of lead and concrete and then only allow researchers to
approach it in specially constructed protective suits, we should
be reasonably safe in continuing our studies of the thing."

"Reasonably safe, General?" Number Two's voice was suddenly dangerously low. "What exactly does your team mean by
reasonably safe?"

Lysenko did not appear to notice the change in Number Two's
tone. "That such a procedure would, when coupled with declaring the entire area this side of the mountain a restricted zone,
reduce emissions from the thing to acceptable levels."

"Acceptable levels?"

Lysenko's eyes narrowed. "That's what I said."

"And what exactly does this advisory team of yours mean by
acceptable levels?"

"You'd have to talk to them about that."

Number Two was silent for about ten seconds, and then his expression totally changed. He looked as though he was once again about to reach for the dynamite. "Your advisory team is full of shit, General."

Lysenko seemed to swell up. His face took on a purple tinge. "I beg your pardon."

"I think you heard me, General."

Elijah quickly assumed the role of mediator. "Perhaps you'd like to explain exactly what you think is wrong with the general's plan."

Number Two was making an effort to get a grip on himself. He took a deep breath. "It repeats the very same errors that got us into this mess in the first place. We're making assumptions based on our own very limited knowledge about something that is totally beyond our experience. There is absolutely no reason to believe that jacketing the artifact in high-density material will do anything to mitigate the effect. Our tests have shown no evidence of this, and believe me, General, we have tried. Nothing would have pleased us more than to discover some form of shielding."

Lysenko was still looking as though he were about to explode. "Surely it's better than nothing."

"If you believe a false sense of security is better than nothing."

Elijah stayed in the neutral corner. "So what do you suggest?"

Number Two looked from one general to the other. "I think the only answer is to get the thing off-planet altogether."

Both Lysenko and Elijah looked at him in disbelief. "Blast a thing like that into orbit?"

Number Two shook his head. "Not into orbit. It's far too dangerous to be hanging in planetary orbit for the rest of time. We'd have to go all the way and cut it loose completely. Interstellar deep space is the only place for it where we could feel completely safe."

Lysenko had started vehemently shaking his head. "Are you aware of the burn cost of putting a payload like that into deep space?"

"We have the math in place. It's possible."

"You're crazy."

"We've already discussed that. It doesn't necessarily mean that we're wrong."

Even Elijah looked unconvinced. "It can't be possible. If what you've told us about the thing is correct, it's simply too big."

Number Two spoke with the patience of a teacher talking to less than bright children. "I didn't say that it had to be transported in one piece. Clearly it's too big for that."

"You're saying you'd hack it into sections?"

"One of the few things we do know is that we can cut the material with a concentration of GS lasers."

Elijah frowned. "It seems to me that if, as you say, the ultimate answer is to ship the thing into space—"

"There really isn't any if about it," Number Two brusquely cut in.

For the first time, the marine general ceased to be the picture of equanimity. "Kindly let me finish."

Number Two took the hint and backed off. "I'm sorry."

Elijah nodded and continued. "Even though the ultimate answer may be to get the artifact out into deep space, it seems to me that in the short term we'd still be exposing hundreds more people to the effect—the space crews, the workers who did the cutting and the loading . . . Everyone involved would be contaminated."

Number Two's expression was bleak. "That doesn't seem to have worried anyone up to now."

"That's as may be. From this point on, though, we surely want to cut contamination to a minimum."

Number Two nodded. "We've already done some work on this. The actual cutting would be done by robots. This is normal procedure. Concentrated GS is almost always carried out by robots or mechanical remotes. There's too much chance of lateral flickerflash to use human operators."

Lysenko made his first positive contribution in over an hour. He seemed to be getting over his resentment over the fact that he and his people were losing their first alien artifact. "I suppose it would be possible to use unmanned rockets to launch the material into space. That would eliminate space crew contamination."

Number Two half smiled. "I think we can do better than that."

Lysenko raised an eyebrow. "You can?"

"Number Eleven has been doing some research into the matter. He feels that a mass driver would be considerably more energy-efficient. Perhaps he should tell you himself."

Number Two signaled to Number Eleven. The communications engineer stood up and moved into camera range. He looked extremely nervous.

"I could simply transmit the figures if that would be easier. I have prepared a fairly comprehensive data shot."

Elijah did his best to look reassuring. "That can come later. For the moment, why don't you just give us the broad outlines of your plan?"

Number Eleven hesitated.

Lysenko did not have the patience of his American counterpart. "Come on, man. Do you have a plan or don't you?"

Number Eleven glanced back at Number Two. Number Two nodded, indicating that he should go ahead. Number Eleven squared his shoulders.

"The mountain is the key to it. Its summit is practically in space already. All we would need to do is construct a progressive acceleration rail straight up the side of Olympus Mons, say twenty quarter-mile power-load sections. Each one could be driven by a single cold-fusion unit. It'd not only be cheaper than using rockets but also safer."

Elijah frowned. "Safer? How do you figure that?"

Number Eleven seemed to be getting over his nerves. He was starting to talk to the two generals like a professor delivering an orientation lecture. "If a rocket was to malfunction, it'd either explode or fall and burn up. Either way there'd be atmospheric contamination and fallout. If a section of rail went down, the payload would only slow and slide back. There'd be no loss of integrity."

Lysenko, who had previously been peering from the screens with a decidedly dubious expression, started to look interested.

"Would a rig like that actually accelerate the sections of artifact material to escape velocity?"

Number Eleven shook his head. "No, but it could put them in high orbit."

"I thought you people didn't want them in orbit."

"Once they were in high orbit, it would be very easy to use construction drones to attach simple light sails cannibalized off a regular slowboat. All it would need then to start them out to Jupiter and beyond would be a couple of short-duration thruster packs to overcome inertia."

Elijah thought about that. "Wouldn't it be a hell of a lot simpler just to let it fall into the sun?"

Number Eleven smiled. He had completely warmed to his subject and seemed quite unintimidated by the brass on the screens. It was all too easy to forget that before their exposure to the effect, the survivors in the control room had been the top people in their respective fields. The generals appeared to be starting to remember that at last.

Number Eleven shook his head. "I think that it would be taking an unacceptable risk to introduce this material into the inner areas of the solar system. I mean, suppose it altered course and began moving toward Earth. We would have unleashed a monster."

Elijah was nodding. "Send it out. It's by far the best idea."

Lysenko, however, still was not happy. "The material would be very vulnerable out in deep space. Suppose the Iraqis or the FLA tracked the stuff and got hold of it? Or maybe just some free-lance ice prospector came across it by accident? They'd have a lethal weapon in their hands. There are a lot of weird ships between here and Jupiter."

Number Eleven already had that covered. "I think the only answer to that is first to mount a radio beacon on each segment of the material that constantly broadcasts a here-be-dragons warning on a broad channel and back that up with an automatic gun rig that will lock and fire on any ship that approaches. Of course, nothing can be foolproof. The one aspect that I haven't covered is what happens at some point in the future when this material floats into the space of some other advanced civilization."

Number Eleven had gone too far. Both Lysenko and Elijah were looking at him as though he had slipped over the edge into madness.

Elijah held up a hand to stop his flow. "Thank you, Number Eleven. We're grateful for your suggestions, but I think hypothetical aliens can take care of themselves. Please put Number Two back on."

Number Two stepped into camera range. Lysenko faced him squarely.

"Are Number Eleven's proposals for the disposal of the artifact backed by the rest of you?"

Number Two nodded. "They are."

"You realize that they will cost a great deal of money."

Number Two's lips pursed. "Almost as much as has been spent on this base."

Lysenko's eyes narrowed, but he did not respond. Elijah stepped in.

"I do see one problem. I think Number Eleven is being overly optimistic in thinking that the whole operation can be carried out without the involvement of human beings. I don't believe this. There are going to have to be people involved in both the cutting and loading of the sectioned material and in the construction of the rail gun. The artifact will also have to be guarded while it's still on the ground. Those people are going to have to come from somewhere."

"If you're thinking we'll volunteer, forget it," Number Two said immediately.

Lysenko sighed. "I might have a solution to that."

Elijah raised an eyebrow. "And that is?"

General Lysenko actually looked uncomfortable. "The KGB have left me with a considerable number of political prisoners. If we were to adopt this plan, they might be pressed into service."

TEN

FOR ALL PRACTICAL PURPOSES, A SETTLEMENT HAD BEEN
reached, and evacuation of the survivors would start as soon as
Elijah could arrange transport. A temporary holding facility was
going to be set up out near Marsbad until a more permanent
unit could be constructed. That arrangement would be super-
vised by the marines. At first Lysenko had balked, but Number
Two had insisted on the marine involvement partly as an act of
faith and partly as protection against the Soviet general or any
of his men going back on their promises. It had been Elijah's
turn to balk when Number Two had suggested that the simplest
solution might be for the American general to take them out in
his C30. His excuse had been that they had no way of knowing
if the effect might be contagious, and quarantine facilities could
not be set up aboard the aircraft. Those in the control room
suspected that Saud Elijah just did not want what he thought of
as a bunch of unstable freaks messing up his beautiful command
ship.

The agreement had been reached only after a very tense hour
during which the two generals had gone off the air to discuss
matters between themselves. By the time they had reappeared
on the control room screens, the nail biting among the survivors

295

had reached an all-time peak. Number Two was once again making suicide contingency plans, and Booth appeared to be brooding on some last-ditch mayhem of his own. It had been a considerable relief for Hammond and the other new arrivals when word had come that Elijah and Lysenko once again were willing to resume discussions.

Essentially the two generals had decided that, subject to the analysis of Number Eleven's data, they would go along with his plan as he had outlined it. The Danes and the Canadians would be approached to form the oversight teams to monitor the progress of the survivors. It seemed that of all nations, Denmark and Canada enjoyed the highest instinctive trust profiles. After that, only one problem remained—a single point but a crucial one. After the brushfire and proxy wars of the late twentieth century, the world's military had come to realize that short of all-out global nuclear conflagration, public relations and spin control had become everything. Armies not only had to win battles, they had to be seen to win them. Perception had become the better part of valor. It had to be decided what they were going to tell the world about the recent events at Olympus Mons. The major complication was that Hammond's transmissions had already written a major lead that was uncomfortably close to the truth.

"Please step into camera range, Mr. Hammond."

Hammond stood up. Worried that someone might start asking questions about her, Irina watched him with some trepidation. So far it had simply been assumed that she was merely a fifth wheel in Hammond's party. Before Hammond walked across to the screens, he glanced down at Worthing.

Worthing grinned back at him. "This is all yours, boss. That's why you get the big paychecks."

Lysenko regarded Hammond with a bland smile. "The easy solution to all this, Hammond, would be to have you and your people shot."

"You can't shoot me. I'm too famous, and I'd be missed."

"We are unfortunately all too aware of this."

Elijah was not smiling. "Hammond, you don't have a particularly good reputation for cooperating with authority."

"I do have a fair grasp of reality, however."

"I hope so, Hammond. I really hope so. You see, we have to know, and we have to know right now, just what we can expect from you."

Hammond had known it was coming from the moment they had called him to the screen. "That really depends on what kind of bullshit you intend to feed to the public."

Both generals were nodding.

"You've started off true to type, Hammond."

"I'm also a prisoner here and have to be prepared to listen to any proposal."

"It is imperative that we continue to keep from the general public the positive knowledge that alien life exists."

Hammond was shaking his head. "That's not something you could ever hope to cover up. It's just too big. You're crazy if you think you could."

Number Two stepped up beside him. "I don't think we can go along with that, either. It was this obsession with secrecy that got this mess started in the first place. It was the positive confirmation of the artifact's alien origin that gave the KGB the excuse they needed to run all over us."

Lysenko's face hardened. "This is one area in which there can be no room for compromise. It's nonnegotiable."

Hammond sighed and raised his hands in a gesture of helplessness. "What is it with you people? Okay, so some folks may go into culture shock if they find out they're not alone in the universe. They'll adapt. They'll get over it. Nobody appointed you guardians of humanity's illusions."

"We are, however, the guardians of civilization as we know it. The status quo, if you like."

"What's that supposed to mean?"

"It's not something we can discuss."

"You're going to have to do better than vaguely bleating about planetary security if you want me to keep quiet about this."

Elijah looked as though he were sucking a lemon. "It isn't just a matter of temporary civil disturbance. It cuts deeper than that."

"You're going to have to explain that one, General Elijah. There's no retreating now."

"Back in the mid-twentieth century, during the UFO scares,

a study was conducted; it concluded that the certain knowledge of the existence of spacegoing alien species would have a truly disastrous effect on the whole of mankind. The first result of this was Project Bluebook in the nineteen-fifties.''

"Project Bluebook was back in the dark ages.''

"Other studies since have only served to confirm the original conclusion.''

"But Bluebook only convinced people that there actually might be something out there. Before Bluebook, there were all kinds of theories about the origins of UFOs. A lot of people thought they were a secret weapon being built by renegade Nazis living in Patagonia. It started the world focusing on aliens.''

"It distracted the world, however, from other possibilities.''

Hammond blinked. "You mean you knew what UFOs were?''

Elijah shook his head. "No, we never knew what UFOs were, just that they were a great deal weirder than anyone even imagined.''

"So what does happen to mankind if it finds out that it isn't alone? I mean, we here all have certain knowledge that there are aliens, or at least that there were aliens once upon a time. What's happened to us?''

The rueful voice of Number Two came from behind him. "We went mad.''

"It has always been the opinion of our experts that mankind would go into a full decline once the reality of another advanced species sank in. It would cease to try—we'd just be waiting for the aliens.''

Number Two rather surprisingly agreed. "He does have a point. There are historical precedents. The arrival of just a hand-ful of Spaniards was more than enough to make the Incas fall apart. Even worse happened to the Amerindians.''

Hammond was not convinced. "I'd have thought that this would have been a boon to the military. The biggest threat of all. Think of the budget appropriations you could get on it. It'd make what you guys have spent on Mars look like a day at the races.''

Lysenko actually looked sad. "It might work briefly at first, but very quickly the world would realize the futility of any kind of defense. Our species has the technology to reach the inner planets of its own solar system. Any alien that comes here will have crossed the galaxy. We'd be as far behind them as cavemen were behind us. If they were coming, we'd have no choice but to wait."

Number Two smiled sardonically at the cameras. "So what you're saying, General, is that you're protecting the military from becoming obsolete."

"The same goes for scientists. What point is there in striving when something out there, with a culture that's maybe a million years in advance of ours, has done everything you could imagine doing and will imagine for the next twenty generations?"

Hammond was skeptical. "Even if I accepted that the knowledge of aliens is going to turn us into some kind of cosmic cargo cultists, we're hardly at that point yet."

"The principle still applies."

Hammond shook his head. "You know that this is going to get out, one way or another. It's too big to remain a secret for long."

On the sidelines, Barstow muttered under his breath. "Damn right it is!"

The words were an exclamation before the thought. The moment they had left his mouth, he realized that he himself was in a unique position to do something about what was going on between Hammond and the military. He casually stood up and stretched, then glanced at Number Five, who seemed to be doing most of the guarding.

"Seeing as we seem to have reached a settlement, do you mind if I go and take care of one or two things? I've got a lot of valuable gear in our truck, and I'd like to see how badly it was damaged."

Number Five was surprisingly unsuspicious. "I don't see what harm that can do."

Barstow picked up his helmet and sauntered as casually as he could to the door. Nobody except Dan Worthing was paying any attention to him at all. Then he was through the door and on his way to the air lock. Even though he knew that he was on his way to carry out what might be the most momentous action of his life, he took it slow. The survivors appeared to be glued to the communication screens, but he was sure there were big brother cameras all over the base. It never hurt to be too careful.

He was not sure of the exact route to the main air lock. They had been led through the maze of tunnels that connected the various sections of the base for so long before they had been taken to the control room that he was more than a little confused. He took his direction from a combination of guesswork and dead reckoning until he came across an emergency sign in Russian and Spanish that directed him to the main exit. Seconds after he had passed the sign, he ran into a woman. She was stooped and huddled in a dirty blanket, exhibiting the same mannerisms of being constantly cold as Number Two. She also had the same crazy eyes as the other survivors. Her first silent appearance caused the already nervous cameraman to all but jump out of his skin.

"Where the hell did you spring from?"

"Are we getting out of here?" The woman's voice was cracked and tremulous.

Barstow nodded. "It does seem like it."

"That's good."

She was gone as quickly as she had come, and Barstow was left scratching his head. So the survivors in the control room were not the only ones left alive in the base. He moved on, going directly to the lock.

Main air lock of the Soviet installation at Olympus Mons— May 30 CEC—20:03 MST.

The warning lights flashed in the air lock, and the pumps started to hum. By reflex, Barstow double-checked the seal on his helmet. While walking through the tunnels and corridors, he had formulated a detailed plan. He would get to the truck as quickly as he could and find out how badly the relay gear had been damaged. All he really needed was for either the squirt antenna on the roof or the smaller portable unit to be intact. He could feed all the footage of the artifact from the concealed data storage in his suit directly to the satellite. The quality would not be great, but the word would be out, and the military would no longer be able to keep its stinking secrets. The people of Earth had a right to know.

The air lock completed its cycle, and the warning lights turned amber. Barstow undogged the outer door and pushed it open. The truck was just fifty yards away. It had grown dark outside, but the floodlights were on all over the base, and he had no difficulty seeing. The truck looked more of a mess than it had on the screens in the control room. He marched quickly across the open space between the air lock and the stalled vehicle, wondering how many cameras were watching him. The outer door of the truck's air lock was hanging open, and the vehicle was presumably depressurized.

He swung up into the lock and found that the inner door was also open. Worthing and Travis must really have come out in a hurry. The forward cabin was not in terribly bad shape, but the relay equipment was all in the rear pod, where the truck had been hit. The connecting tube between the two was sealed, and it took him five minutes to open the double doors manually.

As he pushed the second door open, his heart sank. The interior of the rear pod was a mess. There was a gaping hole in the rear bulkhead about a foot across and two feet long. Even objects that had not been directly damaged by the blast had been thrown around by the resulting rush of decompression. The wall panels had been blown out, and cables and power lines hung in forlorn loops. Some surfaces were blackened as though there had been a flash of fire the moment before the atmosphere had been sucked out. He was surprised that the truck had survived at all. He began sorting through the debris, taking special care that an edge of jagged metal did not snag his suit. There was a certain despair and desperation to his search for anything usable. Most of the relay hardware was a mass of fused or shattered parts; bright copper glittered like wounds from stripped cables, and snakes of optic fibers were strewn around like tangles of pasta.

Barstow turned his attention to the dish on the roof. As far as he had been able to tell during his approach, the dish was intact. He had reached the moment of truth. Either the explosion of the missile or the subsequent decompression had blown the cover off the manual calibration unit, but the mechanism inside seemed undamaged. He ran a line from his suit's tuner to the contact points and turned the hand crank. At first the nylon bearings stuck, but then, as he applied pressure, the dish started grudgingly to move.

Control center of the Soviet installation at Olympus Mons—May 30 CEC—20:15 MST.

Booth suddenly exploded. "He's lining up the goddamn dish!"

The rambo was out of his seat and going, amped to the limit. Everyone in the room seemed to be moving very slowly. Number Five was bringing up her laser. Booth's right hand shot out like lightning. There was a crack as her neck snapped. He thumbed the release on the belly gun, and the hidden compartment in the leg of his suit opened. The flat plastic .22 with the miniature banana clip was in his hand. Practically everyone in the room was coming at him, their expressions witless, with no idea what they would do even if they reached him. On the screen, the two generals looked on in amazement. The words "Don't start a massacre" echoed in Booth's head. Instead of going with his first instinct and clearing the room, he fired a burst into the ceiling, and the others all started to scatter. There was a clear way to the door. Then he was through, and it was closing behind him. He was away down a corridor after Barstow, doing the superman power run.

Worthing was the first to realize what was going on. "Jesus Christ! He's going after Barstow!"

He had thought it odd when Barstow had strolled out of the room. Now he realized that the cameraman had gone to send off as much of the story as he could get out. Worthing was filled with admiration for Rat Barstow—except that now Booth was after the cameraman and going like a rocket. Worthing did not hesitate. He was out of his chair and after the rambo without thinking. He, too, was through the door before anyone could stop him.

Hammond had a little trouble catching up with what had just happened. Like everyone else in the room, he had been too occupied with Lysenko and Elijah to notice that Booth had been ignoring the action and watching Barstow's progress through the base and out to the truck on a small big brother monitor on the other side of the room. The first he knew about any of it was when he looked around and saw the rambo hurling Number Five across the room. When the gunfire had started, he had hit the ground along with the rest. Before Hammond could pick himself up, Worthing, too, appeared to go crazy and raced out of the room. Then it dawned on him. Barstow had left the control room to try to send a squirt from the truck. Booth had gone to stop him, and Worthing had gone, too, probably with little or no idea of exactly what he was going to do when he caught up with the rambo.

Hammond looked at the screens. The two generals seemed to have also grasped the situation, and all deals were off. Hammond had at least been going through the motions of compromising with Elijah and Lysenko. He had pretty much decided that he would agree to whatever it took to get himself and the others out of there. What he would do after that was still an open question. He had been telling himself that he would allow a period of soul-searching before he decided whether to blow the story wide open or go along with the brass. Now, if Barstow got through, the question would never arise. He was not sure whether he was pleased or sorry.

Both Lysenko and Elijah were glaring at him.

"You better pray that your man isn't going to get through and that my man isn't going to have to kill him to stop him," Elijah said.

White Marsman immobile outside the Soviet installation at Olympus Mons—May 30 CEC—20:23 MST.

The twin violet pulses on the tuner merged and became one. The dish was lined up with the satellite. Another couple of minutes and he would be done. He unclipped the jump leads and reattached them to the data output that was hidden beneath one of the studs that decorated his pressure suit. Two more operations and he would be ready to downdump all the audiovisual data he had stored in his suit's memory. It would be going out raw and would have to be sorted when it finally got to Earth in about twenty minutes. Professional pride gave him a moment's regret that he did not have a better way to do it, but at least he was getting the story out and stopping the military from wrapping what had to be one of the most important discoveries of all time in a cloak of secrecy. Hammond could cut all the deals he liked, but they were not going to kill this story. Three amber LEDs were alight inside his helmet. The data were loading to squirt. In just a few seconds the data would be ready to send.

There was a sudden vibration all through the truck, as though someone were tearing off one of the air lock doors. Barstow stiffened. They had come after him. He half turned. There was the flash of a stainless steel suit in the forward pod. It was the rambo. The goddamn brass had sent the rambo after him. The supersoldier was coming through the connecting tube. There was a gun in his hand, a little plastic thing. He had probably had it concealed in his suit all along. The three LEDs were still glowing. The rambo was inside the rear pod. Come on, come on, for Christ's sake, finish loading.

"Stand right where you are, Barstow. What you're doing is treason. Don't move so much as a finger."

The three amber LEDs went out and were replaced by a single green one. Ready to send. Barstow had the squirt send patched to a tongue control inside his helmet. He hit it. The panel above the faceplate on the inside of his helmet lit up like a Christmas tree.

Barstow laughed. "You're too late, Booth. I've sent it. The world's going to know all about this place and what's in it, and there's not a damn thing you can do about it."

The rambo halted. The little gun was still pointed at Barstow's head. "There is one thing I can do."

Booth pulled the trigger, and a burst of .22 slugs smashed into Barstow's head and chest, exploding through his chestplate and helmet.

Booth was still standing over the body in the shattered suit a minute and a half later when Worthing climbed into the vehicle.

"What do you think you've done, you insane bastard?"

The rambo whirled around. Worthing found himself looking

down the barrel of a miniature burp gun. Assuming that he would be the next to die, he reflexively raised his hands in front of him. Instead of bullets, a snarl came from the rambo.

"Silence! If you want to stay alive, keep your mouth shut."

Worthing was in shock, but nothing could have made him utter a sound.

Booth nodded. "What we are going to do is walk back to the base. You will not say a word and do exactly what I tell you. If you don't, I will shoot you."

Worthing knew in an instant what Booth intended. He was going to kill everyone in the place. He was hyped on violence and looking for a solution, and his rambo brain, warped by its training and conditioning and now almost certainly given an extra twist by the artifact effect, had fixed on the simple ultimate in cover-ups: Kill the witnesses.

Control center of the Soviet installation at Olympus Mons— May 30 CEC—20:27 MST.

Elijah glared grimly out of the screen like a Zulu emperor ordering his impis to certain death. "You will have to kill him. He's undoubtedly coming back to do the same to you."

Number Two had taken over the role of spokesman again. "How can you be so sure of that?"

Elijah at least had the decency to look a little embarrassed. "He's a rambo. We designed him that way. He's trained to go for the military solution. He's programmed against gratuitous slaughter and unusual cruelty, but I'd tend to think that exposure to the artifact has weakened, if not destroyed, those inhibitions. I'd advise you to take no chances. Kill him before he even reenters the base."

"Will we be able to kill him?"

Elijah nodded. "Lasers will burn him down just like anyone else. He's enhanced, not supernatural."

Hammond was standing behind Number Two. "You don't seem to be particularly bothered by the idea of losing your prize secret weapon."

Elijah looked tired. "Cut the crap, Hammond. After your

buddy's grandstand play, we've got enough trouble without having a possibly crazy rambo running around loose.''

"Expendable, huh?''

Elijah lost patience. His voice was acid. ''Yes, Hammond. You want me to say it? He's expendable. What was your boy? An unfortunate mishap? You want to shut up now so we can get on with stopping him?''

*Outside the Soviet installation at Olympus Mons—
May 30 CEC—20:28 MST.*

Booth and Worthing were out of the truck and walking across the bare floodlit ground toward the air lock. Booth had to keep himself from hurrying. In his heightened state, it seemed to him that Worthing moved painfully slowly, but he forced himself to match steps with the reporter. Those back in the control room were no doubt watching the two of them, and he did not want to give any warning of his intent. Possibly the freaks inside, with their advanced paranoia, already suspected what he was going to do, but he was certain that Elijah would keep them confused. He could count on the old man to cover for him. There was an additional reason for wanting to hurry. He could go for only a few more minutes on full burn before the pain started. The prudent thing would have been to power down, but somehow he could not bring himself to do it. It was as though he were drunk on the sense of power and too far gone to relate to the idea of pain.

Worthing walked as quickly as he could. The rambo seemed to be straining at the leash, eager to get on with the slaughter. Worthing knew that if he just opened his radio and yelled out a warning to the others in the control room, they would have a chance to save themselves. He also knew that he would be dead in an instant. Was he going to sacrifice himself to save a dozen people? The hell he was. It was not even a dilemma. He knew that he would play along with the rambo until the last possible moment and hope for a miracle.

Control room of the Soviet installation at Olympus Mons—
May 30 CEC—20:29 MST.

"He'll be in range of the lasers on the north tower in fifteen seconds."

The generals were reduced to the two top screens of the monitor bank as Number Eleven brought what was left of the automatic weapons system on-line. The other screens were filled with a graphic representation of the target situation. Bisecting lines that showed the remaining watchtowers' fields of fire reached for two tiny walking figures.

Number Two nodded. "Lock in on them and time for first contact."

The bisecting lines were closing on the two figures.

Hammond made a final appeal to Number Two. "You can't just kill Dan Worthing."

"We have to stop the rambo. I don't see how we can do it without also hitting your friend."

"I've lost one man already."

"All the more reason to stop the rambo before he gets here."

"At least let me warn Worthing."

"That would also warn Booth."

Number Eleven interrupted. "They're in range."

Number Two looked away from Hammond. "Fire at optimum."

Hammond lunged forward and opened a mike. "Dan! Hit the dirt!"

A fraction of a second later, Number Eleven twisted the fire-control key.

Outside the main air lock of the Soviet base at Olympus
Mons—May 30 CEC—20:30 MST.

Worthing was diving before his brain had even absorbed what the shout from the radio meant. His body accepted it as the crucial miracle and threw itself flat. Amazingly, Booth, for all his amplified reactions, hesitated. He seemed torn between fulfilling his promise to kill Worthing and seeking cover for himself. The hesitation did not last more than a brief instant, but it sealed his fate. All hell broke loose. The floodlights were gone, and lasers were slicing through the night in huge looping arcs that threatened to cut him in two. Where one touched the ground, showers of sparks fountained up. In the first second, no fewer than three beams glanced off Booth's armor, but he did not go down—in fact, he hardly staggered. The fire was concentrated on Booth, so Worthing quickly rolled away from him.

There was something inhuman about the death of the rambo. He was still standing long after he should have been cut to pieces. A half dozen lasers were going at him full force. Reflections blazed in every direction, and raw light energy flash-danced across the surface of the steel. His screaming reached every open radio receiver for miles around.

Flight deck of USMC C30 transport on the ground near Olympus Mons—May 30 CEC—20:31 MST.

The whole of the flight deck crew clustered around Elijah as the rambo slowly went down. Booth's screams were being relayed by the speakers, and the general made no attempt to have them cut or even turned down. When they finally died into the monotonous hum of static, Saud Elijah sighed.

"I guess that's the end of an era. He was kind of magnificent."

His staff officers were still staring at the screen.

"He was the last one?"

Elijah nodded. "That's right. He was the last one. Everyone thought we had a few of them left, but the truth was that the others all died of retrocancer, or else they killed themselves. We won't see another like that."

Elijah stood up. He was immediately businesslike. He began issuing orders, starting with the com-op.

"Signal to General Lysenko. Tell him I'm not going to wait for the transports. I don't want anything more to happen. I'm taking those people out in this aircraft. Relay the same message to the base. If you get any argument out of anyone, ignore it." He turned to the chief engineer. "Prepare the ship for immediate lift. Short hop to the perimeter of that base.'' Finally he issued general orders to the rest of the crew. ''All ranks will stand to. Deck sergeants will organize landing parties to go in and get those lunatics out of there.''

Control room of the Soviet installation at Olympus Mons—May 30 CEC—20:47 MST.

The whole control room watched in silence as the big C30 came down on its thrusters, every light blazing, just beyond the perimeter of the base. It gently settled on its huge landing legs, and before the dust had even settled, the giant bow doors slid open and a ramp came down. Files of men in full combat armor started to emerge.

Number Two turned and faced his people. ''Any moment we will know whether this is a rescue or an invasion.''

Hammond sighed and looked at Travis. ''It could be that our troubles are just starting.''

''What did Worthing say? That's why we get the big pay-checks.''

ELEVEN

*The departure lounge, Burroughs Interplanetary Spaceport—
July 20 CEC—11:09 MST.*

LECH HAMMOND WAS LEAVING ON THE NOON SHUTTLE. He
and Dan Worthing sat in the small VIP lounge and waited for
the boarding call, drinking in the manner of two men who had
become good friends over the course of a shared project but
faced the reality that now that the project was completed, it was
quite possible they would never see each other again.

"I guess you won't be coming back to Mars for a while."

Hammond shook his head. "Practically everyone has made
it very clear to me that I'm not going to be welcome on this
planet at any time in the foreseeable future. What about you,
though? They can't be making it comfortable for you, either."

Worthing grinned and signaled for another drink. "About the
only people who'll give me the time of day are bartenders. I
think I'm up for the title Forgotten Man of Martian Journalism."

"So why don't you come back to Earth? God knows, you
stand to make enough money on this deal."

Worthing sadly shook his head. "I'm not in shape. I've been
on Mars too long. I could never take the gravity. Besides, Mars
is a small town. People will come around. In the end I'll blame
it all on you, and they'll accept it. Like you say, I'm going to

make enough money off this deal, and that's got to help. People forgive a lot of a rich asshole.''

''What if they don't come around?''

''Then I'll look up Old Mouly and go prospecting for gold.''

''You, him, and Boogie Boy?''

Worthing laughed. ''Just the three of us. Maybe we'll dig up some more aliens.''

The two of them lapsed into silence. They were going their separate ways, and there was really very little to say. Over the last seven weeks, rooming together at the care facility for those who had been exposed to the artifact, they had had every chance to tell each other their entire life stories.

The period in the care facility had in fact been fairly painless. There was very little that could be done for the exposure victims, particularly those like Worthing and Hammond, who had received only a minimal dose of the effect, except to keep them under constant observation and offer unlimited, if rather uncertain, counseling. The bulk of the efforts of the medical and psychiatric staff was directed toward the painful detoxification of the original survivors of the base.

When Elijah's marines had come in to the base to take out the survivors, Hammond had been surprised to discover that there were over a dozen others, living as hermits or weird frightened couples, in addition to the group that had been attempting to run things in the control room. A pair of army officers who seemed to have been existing in some strange homosexual symbiosis had resisted going, and the marines had not hesitated to shoot them. Fortunately for Worthing and Hammond, the best therapy for the effect seemed to be a matter of rest and simple removal from proximity to the artifact. Within a week the gray mist no longer came when they woke, and the nightmares and disturbing daydreams had been considerably reduced. What might happen to them down the road in the long term was, of course, anybody's guess. Only time and regular checkups would tell what delayed nastiness the effect might have triggered in their bodies or minds.

Irina Orlov had also been released early. She had been reinstated in the Vostok militia under Lysenko's reorganization of the settlement, but the last time Hammond had seen her, she had not seemed exactly happy about how things had turned out.

The military might be in charge for the moment, but there was no telling when the KGB might stage a comeback.

With fitting irony, Old Mouly, the first human being known to have suffered exposure to the effect and survived, never entered the facility at all. Somewhere along the way back from Olympus Mons, he had simply vanished in the way that only he could.

Although the survivors from the base would remain in the facility for some months to come—many of them had yet to recover even their names—Hammond, Worthing, and Travis had been discharged as apparently healthy after only six weeks. While they had been in the facility, they had been totally isolated from what was going on in the outside worlds, but when they had emerged from their seclusion, reality had jumped on them hard with both feet. Every journalist was well aware that the public at large had a tendency, when bad tidings were delivered, to blame the unfortunate bearer. Most of the time it was possible to dismiss the problem philosphically, on the grounds that it went with the territory. In this instance, however, the blame came in spades. All across both Mars and Earth, politicians, preachers, defense spokespersons, the man in the street, and even some of their more cheap-shot-prone colleagues in the media took time out to vilify both Hammond and the network for letting the alien cat out of the bag.

Humanity had failed to take the news that it might not be alone in the universe especially well. Shiite Muslims across the Middle East had gone screaming crazy, seeing the existence of the artifact as direct evidence that the hour of the Great Satan was at hand and calling for an immediate jihad against the usual representatives of the forces of darkness. Much the same reaction had come from the two million or so members of the Church of Twice Born Evangelicals in Europe and the United States. Although they had stopped short of rioting and attempting to burn foreign embassies, their hysteria and mass rallies were featured nightly on the global news. So far there had been 127 suicides apparently related to the news of the alien artifact. The Pope had blustered his way into the act by condemning the 22C-Fox network for creating an atmosphere of fear, panic, and doubt about the Almighty. The sales of automatic weapons in California and the midwest had rocketed, apparently indicating that large numbers of middle Americans believed that the aliens would be descending in their saucers at any moment.

The one consolation was that the public outcry had not been able to stop the efforts to get the artifact off Mars and safely out into deep space. The rail gun had been completed well ahead of schedule, and just two days earlier the first payload of artifact material had been fired up the track that had been laid on the mountainside and into orbit.

Finally the announcement came over the departure lounge PA.

"The shuttle *Glen Miller* is now boarding. All passengers should proceed immediately to gate number two."

Hammond downed the last of his drink and stood up. "I guess that's it."

"Feel like you're going back to face the music?"

Hammond smiled ruefully. "Let's hope that by the time I get out of coldsleep, things will have quieted down a bit."

Worthing clasped Hammond's hand. "Good luck, old boy. Don't let the crazy bastards grind you down."

Hammond nodded. "I'll do my best. Take care of yourself."

He picked up his flight bag and headed for the gate.

North Pole trail just south of Marsbad—July 22 CEC—09:17 MST.

An unmarked Chrysler Star Ranger headed south at full speed. The driver's papers claimed that he was an environment systems engineer called Jordan Frost. In fact, his real name was Marvin Kafka, and he was a marine captain who, just the previous day, had been watching the full-stream firing of the artifact material into orbit. In the Chrysler's trunk was a specially constructed lead-lined flight case that contained two four-kilogram chunks of the alien material. He had spirited them away from the base under cover of darkness. With political prisoners running the cutting operation and manning the rail gun and a Red Army penal battalion guarding them and the installation, plus a constant stream of international visitors and observers, security was understandably lax.

At approximately the same time Rosanne Montana, a Cuban clerk in the KGB headquarters in Vostok, thought she heard strange, indistinct whisperings inside her head. What she did not know was that a regular Sanyo S-70 electronic safe in the next office contained a Hefty trash bag full of chips of the artifact material.

With only three days to go before the last package of material would be accelerated off the planet, the race for bits was in full swing.

Deep space beyond the orbit of the planet Mars—
July 28 CEC—15:42 MST.

It was pleased that it had left the Planet of Dry Winds. Even with its inconceivably expanded perception of time, its unending life span, and its capacity to wait almost to infinity, it knew that it had been in that place too long. When the little creatures had come and freed it from the gravity of the dry planet, it had come as a great relief. Its real home was among the stars. The little creatures had amazed it. They were so fast, and their lives were so brief, yet they seemed to spread their works across the surface of the planet in little more than a blink of consciousness. The removal from the planet had been fast and violent, but it was worth it to be back, free to drift in the solar winds. It was unfortunate that it had been necessary for the little creatures to break the corporeal structure in sections to get it into space, but it knew that the parts would reunite over the coming centuries. They were all going in the same direction, powered by the strange sails of the little creatures. In time the corporeal structure would be one again, and the wholeness would once more be able to evolve out of the mineral condition to grow and re-construct itself.

The little fast creatures had done it one other service in addition to placing it back in space. The mind parasites had nearly all left it, seeming to prefer the violent speed of the little creatures. It came as a relief that they were gone. They had been responsible for the weakened state that had prevented it from resisting the pull of the gravity of the Planet of Dry Winds. During the long wait on the planet's surface they had become extremely irritating. The little fast creatures were very welcome to them.

ABOUT THE AUTHOR

MICK FARREN recently moved to Los Angeles where he maintains his sanity by reminding himself that, for every Joan Collins, there is also a Charles Manson.